Book 1

# ROMANCING THE SCROLL

THE GLASS PLANET

NM Reed

Copyright © 2021 Tattered Unicorn Publishing

All rights reserved. No part of this publication may be reproduced, distributed, or transmitted in any form or by any means, including photocopying, recording, or other electronic or mechanical methods, without the prior written permission of the publisher, except in the case of brief quotations embodied in critical reviews and certain other noncommercial uses permitted by copyright law. For permission requests, write to the publisher, addressed "Attention: Book Rights and Permission," at the address below.

Published in the United States of America

ISBN 978-1-953904-70-6 (SC)
ISBN 978-1-953904-71-3 (HC)
ISBN 978-1-955243-61-2 (Ebook)

Tattered Unicorn Publishing
222 West 6th Street
Suite 400, San Pedro, CA, 90731
www.stellarliterary.com

Order Information and Rights Permission:
Quantity sales. Special discounts might be available on quantity purchases by corporations, associations, and others. For details, contact the publisher at the address above.

For Book Rights Adaptation and other Rights Permission. Call us at toll-free 1-888-945-8513 or send us an email at admin@stellarliterary.com.

This is a work of fiction, although the discoveries and translations are adapted from historical facts.

All of the names have been changed, however the fictional characters are based on the lives of the many people involved in the discovery, translations and controversies. The murder/mystery elements are added for fictional interest only

The translations of stories are adapted from the actual translations from the original ancient languages and have been modified for the English reader's ear.

# Contents

**Book 1** .................................................................... 10
- Prologue ................................................................ 11
- 1. Home Life .......................................................... 13
- 2. A Few Years Later ................................................ 16
- 3. A Future ............................................................. 20
- 4. Costa Rica ......................................................... 22
- 5. Archaeology ...................................................... 27

**Book 2** .................................................................... 40
- 1. Secrets .............................................................. 41
- 2. If It's Not in the Bible.... ...................................... 43
- 3. The Next Bridge Game ........................................ 47
- 4. The Rising Sun ................................................... 49
- 5. Antony and Bethany ........................................... 53
- 6. Christmas Time .................................................. 55
- 7. The Market ........................................................ 64
- 8. The Papyrus ....................................................... 70
- 9. Anna's Daughter ................................................. 90
- 10. Gwydion's Apocrypha ..................................... 106

**Book 3** .................................................................. 114
- Prologue .............................................................. 115
- 1. Monastery ........................................................ 117
- 2. Antiqua Shops .................................................. 119

3. Dinner ..................................................................... 124
4. Scroll Divided ........................................................ 129
5. Mary ...................................................................... 133
6. Life of Joseph ........................................................ 136
7. Capture .................................................................. 142
8. Intentions .............................................................. 146
9. Doubts ................................................................... 149
10. Followed ................................................................ 154
11. Classes ................................................................... 158
12. School .................................................................... 161
13. Older than his years ............................................... 166
14. Another bed time story ......................................... 169
15 Phone call .............................................................. 172
16. The Professor ........................................................ 177
17. Fear ....................................................................... 183
18. Confrontation ........................................................ 187
19. Secrets ................................................................... 191
20. The Team .............................................................. 194
21. Adversary .............................................................. 197
22. The Death of Joseph ............................................. 200
23. Anointed ............................................................... 205
24. Phone Call ............................................................ 214
25. The Dying Professor ............................................. 217
26. The Attempt ......................................................... 219
27. Restitution ............................................................ 224
28. Away ..................................................................... 231
29. Epilogue ................................................................ 234

## Book 4 .................................................................... 237

Prologue 4000 Years ago ........................................ 238
1. The Young Man's Mind .................................... 239
2. Story Time ........................................................ 244
3. Going Ashore ................................................... 248
4. Gwydion's Apocrypha ...................................... 251
5. The Hotel ......................................................... 256
6. Central America Lecture ................................. 258
7. Aztecs and Maya .............................................. 262
8. The Reception ................................................. 264
9. More Apocrypha .............................................. 268
10. After the Reception ....................................... 274
11. The Stone Temple ......................................... 279
12. Palenque ........................................................ 281
13. Inside the Temple ......................................... 289
14. Deep Inside ................................................... 293
15. The Chamber ................................................ 296
16. Unconscious .................................................. 302
17. Antony's Lecture Continues ......................... 308
18. Don't Say That To Me .................................. 312
19. Sleep .............................................................. 322
20. Morning ......................................................... 325
21. The Night ...................................................... 334
Epilogue: Gwydion's Apocalypse ........................ 336

## Book 5 .................................................................... 338

Chapter 1. Discovery ........................................... 339

Chapter 2. A New City ............................................................. 347
Chapter 3. Death Feud in al Tarif .............................................. 350
Chapter 4. Voices in His Head .................................................. 353
Chapter 5. A Setup .................................................................. 355
Chapter 6. The House .............................................................. 358
Chapter 7. New Jobs ................................................................ 363
Chapter 8. The Superintendent ................................................. 371
Chapter 9. High School ............................................................ 384
Chapter 10. Stack of Scriptures ................................................ 391
Chapter 11. Oh, Hallowed E'en ................................................. 396
Chapter 12. New Translations for Antony ................................. 401
Chapter 13. Dead Dance .......................................................... 405
Chapter 14. Late Night ............................................................ 415
Chapter 15. Late Nightmares ................................................... 419
Chapter 16. Morning Church ................................................... 424
Chapter 17. Monday Morning .................................................. 429
Chapter 18. A Story ................................................................. 435
Chapter 19. Trip ...................................................................... 438
Chapter 20. A City of Ancient Angels ...................................... 442
Chapter 21. Grande Canale ...................................................... 449
Chapter 22. Damp Stones ........................................................ 454
Chapter 23. Convocations ........................................................ 457
Chapter 23. Listening .............................................................. 461
Chapter 24. Dinner .................................................................. 464
Chapter 25. The Alley .............................................................. 471
Chapter 26. Escape .................................................................. 474
Chapter 27. Guardian Angels ................................................... 490

Chapter 28. Capture ................................................................. 494
Chapter 29. the Island ............................................................... 498
Chapter 30. Rescue.................................................................... 508
Chapter 31. Homeward ............................................................. 513
Chapter 32. Imprisoned............................................................. 517

# Book 6 .................................................................................. 518

Prologue .................................................................................. 519
Chapter 1. Wild Lands ............................................................. 521
Chapter 2. Morning................................................................... 525
Chapter 3. Branding ................................................................. 531
Chapter 4. Wakeful................................................................... 536
Chapter 5. Convicted ................................................................ 540
Chapter 6. My Enemy .............................................................. 543
Chapter 7. Damages ................................................................. 551
Chapter 8. Revelation ............................................................... 555
Chapter 9. Mother on the Couch .............................................. 561
Chapter 10. haunted past........................................................... 565
Chapter 11. Old Stuff ............................................................... 567
Chapter 12. .............................................................................. 572
Chapter 13. .............................................................................. 576
Chapter 14. .............................................................................. 581
Chapter 15. The Couch ............................................................ 583
Chapter 16. .............................................................................. 588
Chapter 17. .............................................................................. 594
Chapter 18 ............................................................................... 602
Chapter 19. Indian Rocks ......................................................... 610

Chapter 20 ................................................................................. 618
Chapter 21 ................................................................................. 622
Chapter 22. Light Beings ........................................................... 626
Chapter 23. ................................................................................ 633
About the Author ....................................................................... 636

Book 1

# THE GLASS PLANET

NM Reed

# Prologue

Antony was running. He felt his legs pumping and his heart racing. He felt the hot breath of the demon, his pursuer, at his back. He could hear its ragged breath brush against his neck. He ran with the knowledge of escaping the unknown, unable to cry out or even wonder at its nature.

Of a sudden he heard a small voice, not much more than a squeak really, over the roaring of the demon's cry.

"Grand Papa!" The small voice said in his mind. "Grand Papa!" it cried again. "Wait for me!"

Antony froze.

Who possibly could this be? He had no children, let alone grandchildren.

He stopped and turned and slowly he faced what was behind him, the thing that was pursuing him in the dim red setting of the desert sun.

Or was it the sun?

He turned and saw boiling red clouds filling the sky, the firmament on fire with rage.

"We need you now," said the small voice.

And then he heard the tiny voice call for his grand papa again. And Antony strained his vision to search for the source of this plaintive sound in the roiling red conflagration.

"I need you, grand papa. Come and find me!"

Against his better conscious judgment Antony began to move toward the sound coming from within the raging torrent, towards this apocalypse of sight and sound.

"Grand Papa! We need you. Keep up or all will be lost!"

Antony tried to call out, but his voice seemed locked in his chest. He strained against a demon gripping a strangle hold on his throat.

Antony woke with a small cry, tangled in sweaty sheets. The normal world came slowly into focus around him. The normal sounds in the street below the window, the comforting clamor of his girlfriend busy in the kitchen.

# 1.
# Home Life

Water rushed into the sink through the clanking pipes beneath, competing for dominant sound over the clank and roar of machines outside in the street far below, and in the air above. An argument ensued, completing the metropolitan din.

"I can't believe you want to study that thing anyway," extorted Antony, in the general direction of his girlfriend.

"It's just part of the master's class program. Relax. I don't *believe* the stuff."

"I *hope* not," he said dripping with sarcasm.

"It's just fascinating what's really in that thing. Do people even really read it?"

Antony looked at her blankly, affirming her suspicion that he hadn't either.

"I mean, did you know that there are actually seventeen commandments given on that mountain?" she said with an incredulous snort.

Antony laughed. "Maybe he dropped the last stone tablet, the gods forgetting how weak mortals are in comparison. Three tablets was just too much for him to carry back down." He chortled again, as Bethany rolled her eyes away, and continued to set the table.

"Seriously, Antony, what's all this ten commandments hooey if there is actually seventeen?

Or nineteen if you count the part about building an altar out of natural raw stone and sacrificing animals on it for him. I had never even heard them talk about *that* part."

"Oh, gimme a break," he said without looking up.

"No! It's there!" she cried.

A bang and slam interrupted their argument. A little tousled girl of seven stomped into the cluttered kitchen. Her parents exchanged glances.

"How was school today, Maggie?" her mother tried.

"OK," the little one said haughtily.

Anton looked at his daughter and smirked. She snarled back.

"OK! Ms Tibbits is a creep."

"Excuse me?" said Bethany.

"They made me stand in the corner for the last half of Cattle schism."

"Why?"

"Because I told them it doesn't make any sense."

A profound exhale came out of Bethany. She looked at Antony, who then walked out the kitchen door into the den, leaving Bethany to fend for herself with the seven year old.

"Well, sometimes us adults don't make any sense but it's for your own good. You have to learn that stuff. It's just required," she said with her hands open imploringly.

"But it's stupid and doesn't make any sense!" the girl cried.

"You shouldn't say that about your superiors. Now go in your room and start your homework. Dinner's in half an hour."

Maggie grabbed her book bag with a grunt and swung back into the entryway heading for her room, with stomps and slams all the way.

Antony re-enters gingerly, shaking his head. "What's that got to do to a kid's head when he has to memorize stuff that doesn't make sense, to believe things that couldn't possibly be true, and act like it's true because he's told too?"

"She needs to learn that stuff to be accepted as a part of this world today."

"So, she's going to learn that what she says must be true as long as she can make people believe her? Isn't that called psychotic lying?"

"Don't be ridiculous. You always over-react to these things. She's just a child. It's not going to hurt her."

"Ya, she'll fit in this world alright, where lies are true as long as everyone believes them. Shall we start persecuting non-believers today, or tomorrow?"

"Jeez, would you just relax. Get the plates out, please. NO no no the big blue ones. We are having Sloppy Joes and salad tonight."

# 2.
# A Few Years Later

Antony attempted to rustle the paper out flat against his lap. Sitting in the lounger made it harder to read the paper. But better than trying to read in the kitchen, where a battle ensued each time he became absorbed in his paper.

Banging and clanging increased in crescendo from the kitchen. His attention was diverted appropriately. He rolled his eyes and looked back down. "So why is Mags coming home?"

"She is having a hard time with her chemistry class."

Under his breath he said, "Who doesn't."

"What was that, dear?"

"I was just saying that chemistry is hard."

"Well, yes dear I think she just needs a break." Bethany answered from deep in the kitchen.

"Well, I didn't get a break and I was holding down two jobs to finish my Anthro degree last year," Antony said half talking to himself.

Bethany poked her head around the corner of the door jam. "Yes, dear, of course. And you walked to school in the snow uphill both ways. I know, I know."

Antony rolled his eyes. "I just don't think kids see how easy they got it. All the cool clothes and fancy gadgets; we were lucky to get new boots once every couple years."

Bethany grunted a little and slipped back into the kitchen, where the banging and clanging resumed.

A few hours later, the front door opened and closed with a bang. A bustling figure hustled into the kitchen and set things down with a clunk.

"You are home early," observed Bethany carefully.

"I just had to get out of there," said Maggie breathlessly.

"Did your class just end?"

"Oh, I walked out. That teacher is such a trog," scowled Maggie.

"A what?"

"A troglodyte? You know, caveman?"

"That's no way to talk about a professor."

"It's the right way to talk about this one!" retorted Maggie.

"Besides," added Antony, "Troglodyte means chimpanzee. It's Latin."

"That works, too," answered Maggie sarcastically.

Her mother returned to cleaning dishes, shaking her head.

She let a few moments pass. "So, when are you going back?"

"I'm not."

Her mother turned around, stunned, hands dripping, standing there, mouth agape; not her usual stance at all.

Her daughter returned the stare with anger, and said "I'm just *not!* What a waste of time. Since gramma died and gave me that money I am going to take a break. Go to Florida or something."

"Florida!?" said Bethany a little too loud.

"What's wrong with Florida?" chirped Maggie.

"Oh, nothing I guess. But you need to finish your education. *Make* something of yourself."

"I *am* something, *someone*, mom."

"Go talk to your father right now!" Her mother turned, pointing over Maggie's head toward the living room, her face reddening.

Maggie stomped into the warm living room, where her father had been surveying the conversation out of firing range.

Maggie exhaled an exasperated sigh, standing in front of her father, with her arms crossed.

He waited for her defense wordlessly, pretending to still be reading the newspaper.

"We're just going for six months."

Not a word.

"Ah, come on, everybody is going to Costa Rica!"

He looked up suddenly. "Costa Rica!? I thought you said Florida."

"We'll we stop in Florida first and I thought I would visit aunt Rice there."

Antony just shook his head and dropped his eyes to continue pretending to read.

"I'll come back to school later, I promise."

"No. You probably won't. You will suddenly be forty and have no education and no place to live and no family to come home to."

"Stop with the family thing. I don't want to get married. Stan and I will never get married." She made an abrupt stop sensing she'd gone too far, a wide-eyed look on her face.

"Is that who you are going with?"

She looked around and fidgeted. "Well, he's going, ya."

Her father grumbled an answer and looked away again.

Maggie whined, "I am not going to argue about him again. I love him. And besides we have gramma's fund money she gave me and we will be fine."

He looked up at her, over his reading glasses. "Have you actually done the math? How long will that really last?"

"Oh, we've thought of that," she answered smiling, feeling like she had won some kind of small victory being able to answer his reasonable question. "When we get down there Stan will get a job and we'll be fine.'"

Her father looked back down to his paper, sighing, shaking his head, knowing he was right but realizing he had lost the battle anyway. "You mean *you* will get a job waiting tables or picking fruit," her father grumbled miserably, staring unseeing at his paper.

"What?" Mag said innocently.

"Nothing."

# 3.
# A Future

"Have you read this?" she exclaimed loudly.

He quietly looked up at his girlfriend soon to be wife, Bethany, over the top of the evening paper.

"The guy was a pimp," she said looking him straight in the eye, with her hands on her hips.

"*Now* who are we talking about?"

"He was supposed to be a prophet. When they would visit a new land, he would offer his wife to the king, saying that she was really just his sister, so go ahead."

"Oh, him. Abram. No, he was trying to show the heathens the fear of God."

"By lying and tricking them? Oh, that's OK as long as your hosts in a strange land are not of your religion?" she said, slapping the book down onto the kitchen table, exasperated.

"He told the Kings that he saw that they were lacking in the fear of God," he answered.

"Not the first time. The first time he said he thought they were going to kill him and steal his fair wife, so he lied to them and pimped her out and told them she was his sister."

"She was his sister. His half-sister, his father's daughter," he continued, explaining.

"Oh, that's great. No, he is not lying, he is just sleeping with his half-sister. That's so much better," sarcasm dripping red.

He just looked at her, and rustled his paper a little, and settled in to read again.

"Either he is pimping out his wife. Or married to your own sister, and pimping her out. And he is lying to his hosts, to save his own ass. Now I see, it really is all written in there. It really is OK to lie and trick people of a different faith."

"Just written between the lines. Talk about nuance," he added without looking up.

"It explains a lot, actually. On the outside, if you don't study the thing, they talk about love and compassion and all that. But their stories, if you can wade thru the fourteenth Century gogglty-gook language, their stories paint a different story."

"Oh, that's just the old book. You haven't gotten to the new part yet. It's really quite different. But the stories aren't as juicy, though." explained Antony.

"Speaking of Lot..." he added looking up at her. "Have you seen the part about Lot and his daughters?"

"Ya. That's just a sweet little bit, ain' it?" she says, shaking her head. "Oh, and of course the daughters thought it all up, because they wanted to be molested by their father. Right'o, cheeri'o". She looked at him reading his paper. "Do you want some dinner?"

"Whadda we got?"

She rustled back into the kitchen to search for food.

# 4.

# Costa Rica

Bright colored birds squawked and called in the jungle that got deeper as you moved from the settlement. They had been here for some time now, and had adjusted to life simply and plainly here in the verdant forests of Central America. It was nothing like she had expected.

And Mags had learned to enjoy it. It had a magic of its own. Stan was not quite so thrilled and he talked of moving back to the States, where things were kept in sealed boxes for you to buy at the store, and the ice came on automatically in the box on the side of the wall. But Mags was here to stay. She had never known such simplicity and loveliness. She thoroughly enjoyed the sounds and the smells of the wild clean jungle. The birds were so colorful and beautiful and only rivaled by the flowers which bloomed in profusion everywhere, and all of the time too, even when it was supposed to be winter. Which was really never, now that she thought about it since they lived right on the equator.

Keeping the child fed and clothed was a challenge and it had been up to Stan to find work and make some money. But they didn't need much. She bartered her own work for rent, and since she and the landlord enjoyed each others company, things were worked out and they often shared meals, he and his old funny wife. They laughed and told stories and occasionally shared a beer when they could afford to make some themselves. Grain was expensive.

But other things could be used. And they were resourceful in using anything that this jungle gave them in gift.

The forest was truly magical. The ocean waters rising up to meet them were so beautiful, and Mags loved to walk there and as the baby Gwydion grew she was soon able to let him walk along with her and chase birds skittering in the sand following the wake of the waves.

How long had she been here anyway? She could not recall exactly except by approximations made by guessing the baby's age. It didn't matter. The flow of life was different here, in the magical jungle. Oh, it was not all sweet dreams and sugar plums. Occasionally a villager would be bitten by a snake and would die a hideous death by blackening of the skin and convulsions. Or a child would wonder off and disappear, believed to be consumed by one of the panther cats that lived and hunted deep in the jungle, but dangerously often on the outskirts of town. These rumors were only to be confirmed when a piece of what appeared to be human would be dragged in by one of the village dogs.

But there was definitely a magic to this place, something she could not quite put her finger on. She felt it in the cooler breezes coming in the evening to wipe away the hot humidity that seemed to breed bugs. It rumbled in the night sounds that thankfully stayed at the boarder of the dark forest. It niggled the mind when ever she saw one of the village elders, dressed up for some kind of ritual, and spent the night in such, and confirmed with the far off sound of drums and chanting deep in the night. All felt aright after a night like that, she felt the next morning. I am just glad I do not have to participate.

But there were some things that were a little disturbing about this enchanted and frightening forest.

Like the way somethings glowed in the night just off the waters edge. How vibrations late at night, or perhaps was it too early in the morning, that seemed to shiver their way into her rooms and give her a tingle up her spine. Or the way that sometimes she would enter Gwydion's little room and find him in his crib, his blankets settling around him, as if he had been floating just above his mattress. These feelings could not be accounted for, but she accepted them as the illusions of this strange land she had adopted as her home.

Back at home, things were growing within the Jacobs household too. Bethany and Antony traded places in school, and Antony became a full-time student of the world of man. And some of the things his wife said stuck in his mind and would not let go. Then several discoveries in ancient anthropology changed the way Antony looked at the world forever. And something niggled in his mind until it grew strong and began to haunt him. He finished his anthropology degree, with a minor in linguistics, and began to pursue his masters and a PhD. And his studies started him on a path that would take him and his family on a journey around the world.

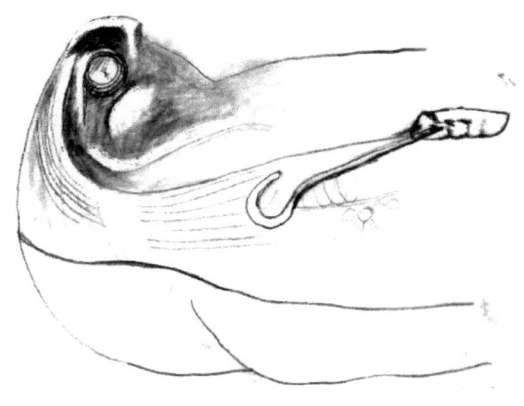

*The Silver Sarcophagus*
*News Release International Associated Press*
*August 9, 1931*
*A Tomb Within a Tomb*

"Another tomb of a great Pharaoh has yet again been discovered. Excavations had begun in the great ancient city of Tanis in 1928 in the multi-tomb burial complex in the time of the pharaohs dating back to before the time of Jesus, in the state of Egypt. The archaeologists were convinced that the ruins were of Pi-Ramsses mentioned in the Book of Exodus. But what they found seemed to create more questions than answers.

Behind the first several tombs they discovered another, but this one stood undisturbed, and there on the floor lay a solid silver coffin carved with a Falcons head. Alongside this lay four solid silver mini coffins that had been used as canopic containers. Where the silver came from can only be guessed at. For even today there are no known silver mines anywhere near in the Middle East.

The mummies were taken to a nearby laboratory for analysis. The first mummy was found to be over 50 years old when he died with a cranial injury that probably precipitated his death from meningitis infection, quite old for persons of that era. The second more deeply buried mummy, which was also held within a solid silver sarcophagus, was found to have died at an even older age. His body riddled with arthritis and disfiguring ossifications. A third mummy was found buried in a sarcophagus deeper yet in this complex of tombs. But details of the scientific inquiry into the mummy itself have yet to be released. Does this indicate that it is a normal mummy? Or does it indicate strangeness beyond explanation, and they hide from us the truth. We wait in anticipation for the answers.

# 5.
# Archaeology

Antony sat in the deep worn armchair of his office. The morning sun glinted and shifted with the spinning mote of dust that rose when he plopped down in it.

Suddenly his office door opened and a young student burst in. He just smiled at the insouciance. "Take a look at this. This just in from the middle east."

Antony reached sullenly toward the sheaf of papers the young researcher held out to him. He pushed up his glasses disconsolately and glanced at the first page.

He read from the top sheet, " 'From Tanis. New finds' . Thank you, Will. I will take a look at these when I am done proof reading these thesis papers."

The young student just stared at him, shocked that there was not a more animated response. New finds were always a thrill. But he held his enthusiasm at bay and nodded his head, and said respectfully, "You're welcome, Professor Jacobs. See you later in Levantine Morphology?"

"As usual." He looked up at his sixth period student. 'Maybe try not to be late today, huh?"

"Yes, sir. I will." said the young Will Smithershins. He left and closed the heavy anthropology office door with a thud. Modern equipment was never this field of study's equipment's strong point.

When the student was gone, Antony quickly set aside the thesis papers and picked up the ones the student had just rushed in with. "New find at Tanis. Tomb with mummy. How fascinating," he mumbled to himself. It suggested a find equal with that found a few decades earlier in a near area, that had soon become famous and was traveling the globe as an exhibit of ancient treasures. Maybe....Just maybe...

He doubted it, though. This find was by a French Archaeologist, and hastily done. Probably professionally approached, but with the World War about to rage, everyone was walking on eggshells and trying not to be in the way of the Fuhrer's next unpredictable move. They would have to move fast. There were unopened rooms. And yet hopefully they would remain professional. These finds opened up such possibilities in the studies of man and his ancient works and societies. It opened such interesting vistas into their minds and lives.

Antony scanned through the next few pages of the hastily arranged article on the new find in the Middle East. It was a necropolis, a city of the buried dead, with dozens of buildings, all partially covered with sand and other old junk, of course the newest junk on top. In fact, the find had started, as often it was, as a lump of dust and dirt that looked like and probably was a midden pile, being dug out for it's fertilizer value. But under that, as often was case, was found a burial chamber of unknown proportions until they simply kept digging.

But shovels were exchanged for finer instruments of digging, like painter's palette knives and tooth brushes. And the farmers looking for fertilizer had to move else where. And digging slowed to a crawl.

Archaeology was difficult in many ways. And probably what was the most infuriating was the amount of painstaking patience

that was needed to dig slowly enough not to destroy what you were digging up, and yet stave off the rending
excitement of finding amazing things in the dirt. Shovels simply were not allowed.

But in this one instance, they had come up against a solid slab of granite, a square, and obviously a carved one. And the king, uh, the live one currently, had arrived and, because of the archaeologists' indecision on how to proceed, ordered it chipped away to get at what lay beyond.

And they had, according to this article, been rewarded. A treasure of ancient artifacts had been found behind this palanque of black granite. Oh, sure there was a gold mask. And sure there was beaded masks and fine flint carvings and intact bowls and vessels. But what was real treasure was the fully intact mummy inside three layers of carved granite sarcophagi and a solid silver one.

"Solid silver?" thought Antony. "There is no silver in the ancient Middle East. Where did they get it?" For there are no known silver mines near, anywhere near at the time of the burial. In fact, contrary to popular belief, gold was less valuable than silver six thousand years ago, before trade with the mines in China and southern Africa came to the fore, and slowly increased the availability and decreased it's value and price.

Gold had it's own intrinsic value in that it does not corrode. Gold had it's own intrinsic value in that it does not corrode. And this inviolability of the yellow metal made it likened to the character of their chosen Gods, fine, resilient and nontarnishable. But up until modern times, silver was simply extremely rare, which made it extremely attractive and expensive.

The next factoid surprised him too. Now, although there was to be found more rooms, with other treasures and artifacts, there was to be found absolutely no furniture.

Always, in every large burial chamber there was always found, to be in the company of the buried king, articles of everyday life. Clothing, food, sandals, and furniture, to accompany him in the next life. This tomb had none. Why would that be? thought Antony.

He continued reading. It came as no surprise to him that within this necropolis was found the swapping of artifacts: bodies in coffins inscribed with another king's name. Jewelry on the wrong mummies. It seemed as though sometimes they re-used the chambers and the artifacts. And this mummy and sarcophagus were no different. Several kings were named on different things.

But no furniture. I shall have to ask Professor Happenstance what he thinks about that. It suggests a departure from normal burial procedure for these people. At least that was what Antony was thinking.

Later in the afternoon, Antony managed to find the old professor in his unbelievably cluttered office. It looked like there could be buried ancient artifacts somewhere at the bottom of *this* office midden pile, Antony thought to himself as he entered. 'And since this man was a professor of Archaeology, there probably were!' Antony chuckled to him self.

He stifled a small giggle as the old wizened professor turned his squeaky wooden chair towards him as he entered the cluttered room.

"Ahhhh. "sighed Professor Happenstance. "Antony. What a pleasure. What have you got there?" asked Aloatious Happenstance, noticing the pile of papers halfway thrust toward him. Antony explained the new finds that he had been handed, and yes, professor Happenstance had glanced at them earlier too.

He said to the younger professor, "Yes. No furniture. Did you see the mask? Quite some work of artisans there I'd say. If I had to gander a guess as to why no furniture, I would say these people had thought about it and decided that the wooden furniture would all disintegrate in the more moist climate of the Tanis area. Where as the other site, in more arid Nile Valley the wooden artifacts would stay intact longer."

Antony nodded his head. This seemed to be such a simple and perfect solution. These people knew what they were doing and there would be different burial procedures for different environments. They exchanged a few pleasantries and Antony said goodbye and returned to his office to get ready for his drive home at the end of this exciting day.

On the drive home, Antony thought distractedly to himself about what Professor Happenstance had said about the reason for no furniture. "How smart of them to know that the wooden artifacts would all disintegrate by the time we got to them, six thousand years later." He hummed with the radio. "Why would they think that? If they truly believed that the furniture would travel with the king to his afterlife, then they would believe that the furniture would not remain in the hole in the ground at all."

Another thought occurred to him that never had before.

"They probably would not ever even want to ever open those tombs again to find out, in fear that they might find all that stuff in there still, proving their idea of the afterlife a total sham, and a waste of perfectly good stuff.

"Now *that* would have been a shock to those believers.

"But I am sure, just like modern times, the priests knew the afterlife to be untrue, but continued the practices as it served them to placate the people who would have really believed and hoped it all true."

He drove in some silence, listening to the sibilant sounds of the cheap radio trying to replicate the rich sound of a full orchestra, and succeeding very poorly.

"But still why no furniture, then? We are not seeing something about why that sarcophagus is in that tomb." He turned at a red light, getting a honk from a driver he had distractedly turned in front of.

"Like he was put there later, in someone else's tomb. That was not a public burial. That was a convenient place to put an important body. But, then, where did he come from?"

*The City of the Falcon*

Antony's lecture today was to be more animated than usual. Things had been coming together rapidly, bits and pieces of his discoveries in books and in the field were fitting up against one another like strangely shaped pieces of some puzzle he did not have a key for. He could not see the whole picture yet.

But he felt compelled to lay it all out for the listeners of this lecture.

And there were a lot of them. The hall was dimly lit, the mood increased somewhat by the somber wood colors of the walls and the bent wood chairs they all sat on. His lectern was far in front, with a screen behind him that could be lit up and used to show pictures of the things he was talking about. He had arranged the slides in the carriage in the room up above behind every one in the hall, and the actuator was a little switch in his hand he could advance or go back one slide at a time.

He hoped he got the slides in the correct order, to match his list in front of him on the sloping lectern surface.

The clock struck the top of the hour quietly, the lights went down gradually, and quiet filled the large hall. A few coughs and the dropping of a pencil filled the hall with an eery echo.

"Thanks for coming today," he started slowly. Public speaking was not his strong point, but archaeology was, and he knew his enthusiasm for the subject would take over and he would stop sweating and his lecture would be just fine.

"We have all heard about the recent discoveries in the ancient burial valley of Tanis and other places in the middle eastern desert. But there are still so many questions yet unanswered." He made a few more mundane comments and thanked various bodies and professors for their invaluable help, and then he plunged into the fun part.

He pushed the slide button. Nothing happened. "Uh, Will,?" speaking to his assistant in the last row, who turned and ran up the carpeted stairs to the projection room. A moment later the light came on in the room and the over-head projector light switched on. Antony tried the switch again and the first slide loaded.

"Here we have the most recently found sarcophagus of an unknown Pharaoh. Its a falcon head and can be seen carved smoothly into the surface of the upper part of the casement. It is exceptional in quality and realism. Historically, the falcon has been represented many times in ancient life. The falcon was occasionally called an eagle, and if you remember another famous book of history, was said to be how Moses and Christ went from the ground to the heaven.."Upon the wings of Eagles." This is a city in Egypt where a bunch of pharaohs are buried, some of which have some weird attributes. And it has come to be called City of the Falcon, Heirokonpolis."

There was a moment of silence as the screen clicked a new image, and students could be heard quietly turneing pages of notes. Professor Jacobs continued. "Heirokonpolis is a Greek word. Or shall we say, its a word designed in Egypt and carried with a culture moving westward away from dwindling resources and increasing environmental degradation and drought, to a more fertile area along the coast, in ancient times part of Greece. Heiracon means hawk in Greek, and was the name of the falcon-headed god of the city whose original name was Nekhen, the original older Egyptian name. The Pharaohs were considered the earthly incarnation of the all-seeing celestial bird, which is also the patron deity of Kingship itself. One in every five inundations of the local Nile was a disastrous flood, known to the Egyptians by the word 'Chaos', the destroyer. Control of the food supply was of vital importance, a key step in the concentration of power into just a few hands, that is Pharaoh rule. How did they have the technology to do that? And why did they fling themselves into chaos so totally during that one era, about 2000 years ago.

They just disappeared again, these leaders, on the wings of Eagles or Falcons." It showed the picture he had projected onto the lecture hall screen. It showed one of their works in gold. "Of course these are representations of feathers." Antony the scientist explained to the students in rapt attention in his audience of hundreds.

## Antony's Questions

When Antony got home, dinner was waiting for him, for once. Maybe he was a little late. Maybe his wife had gotten home from teaching just a bit earlier than usual. He had wanted to head straight into his study to take another look at the papers that had been handed him this morning by the student who had come bursting into his office. But no such luck here. He had to wait until after dinner.

"What is up with you?" Bethany said after they had eaten a while in silence. He was obviously brooding or thinking about something.

"Oh, nothing much," he answered.

"Nothing much, my foot," she answered somewhat sharply.

"Ya, I got some papers today on a new find in the Middle East. A tomb and a mummy. But there are some discrepancies from other finds."

"Why is it that they always have to fit a pattern. Maybe they are a group that just did things their own way," she suggested.

Antony just looked at her over his nose and reading glasses. "Now what fun would there be in *that* for Archaeologists if each time was totally different. As if it were a separate civilization doing its own thing. We are talking about humans here, aren't we?" He asked the rhetorical question as if to shame her for making such a strange suggestion, but half way through he realized, in light of what he had been thinking earlier, she might be making sense.

"You guys are always trying to make it fit with your expectations. Maybe it just doesn't," she said reasonably.

They looked at each other with wide eyes. How did this turn into an argument so fast? Bethany cleared her throat, and tried again, "So what did they find, my dear?"

"A mummy fairly well preserved in triple sarcophagi, with different inscriptions, a gold face mask, and no furniture," he answered plainly.

"No furniture? And that is strange?" she answered surprised. It must be; he mentioned it.

He looked up at her with exhaustion on his face, as if dreading to have to explain the whole story of why furniture was expected. "Well, remember that fancy exhibit that traveled all over the globe? That tomb had furniture. Lots of it. And it is thought to be of help to the important person in his next life."

"Furniture? Like of wood and skins? Wouldn't that just rot in the tomb after so long? Why would they waste the effort?"

"Professor Happenstance said the same thing. As if it explained everything, this idea that they were practical people and just waiting for us to discover this in another 6000 years," Antony explained to his wife.

"So wasting stuff by burying it in the sand shows how important a person is to the future? Is that their plan, do you think?" she asked.

"I think they understood it as ritual salvation by giving them the things they would need in the next level, hoping, I think they were hoping, that they really didn't die but simply moved onto a place where we couldn't be with them anymore. And they thought that stuff would simply travel with them. I don't think they would ever want to reopen a tomb to find out what happened to that stuff. Wouldn't that be disillusioning to find all that stuff still there?" he suggested his new thought to her, trying it out.

"Ya, I guess it would. That came later, during the Golden Age of Disenchantment, otherwise known as the Industrial Revolution," she said with a sharp nod of her tousled head.

"My, aren't you scornful today," he said to her as he picked up a forkful of rebellious spaghetti.

After some time he was able to get away and take a closer look at the papers he had been handed this morning. This other ancient village was really very primitive, and it involved the excavation of dozens of burial sites. Very primitive burial sites. It was found, when these bodies were exhumed, that all of these people had expired between 25 and 35 years of age.

All of them similarly had cuts on the frontal parts of their neck vertebra, very high up on the neck, just under the jaw.

Perhaps this was part of the dismemberment that they seemed to practice before burial, but most of these heads were not hacked off like from a beheading or fight, maybe carefully, surgically removed from the body. But still those cuts on the cervical vertebra were inexplicable. And some of the bodies had had their internal organs removed and then replaced back inside the body after being wrapped in gauze.

Now, thought Antony, that sounds like the beginnings of mummification, forgetting about the strange cuts on their cervical neck vertebra.

Book 2

# The Glass Planet

## The Apocrypha of Gwydion

NM Reed

# 1.

# Secrets

Secrets was all Gwydion had.

If you were different than everyone around you, and everybody knew it, you yourself were a secret.

If you couldn't talk very well, then everything you thought about was a secret.

If your mind worked differently than everyone else's, and no one would understand you if you could talk anyway, your ideas would be secrets.

And if your grand papa was a translator of ancient scrolls, and he read those stories to you for bedtime, then after two thousand years of being buried beneath desert sands, those stories would be re-discovered secrets.

Such was Gwydion's life. He was a nine year old autistic boy with special powers.

Well, he thought he had special powers anyway. And one of his special powers was that he held these secrets deep in his chest like a glowing lamp.

He could feel them there all the time.

When people looked at him like they were afraid of him, he felt his secrets glow inside him and give him strength.

When people yelled at him and called him names, he felt his secrets glow in his

heart like the biggest lightning bug in Kansas, ever. And he kept that big bug deep in his heart, safe from anyone who wanted to squash it.

But sometimes his secrets became heavy and he wished he could let them out so they could fly away, and stop fluttering up his chest.

Sometimes he would tell his secrets in the silent secret way to some animal he would meet. Squirrels usually listened. So did the birds. And cats. Yes, cats listened quietly all the time with wise owl eyes to Gwydion's secrets.

Sometimes he needed to run into his mother's or grand mama's arms and share his secrets with them through his tears. And they would soak them up quietly, and tell him things were going to be just fine.

And sometimes he could listen to his grand papa's stories, of ancient stories hidden in the Egyptian sand. He would listen for hours and he would feel his secrets vibrate and break free and float away on the troubles of other people. People thought to be long lost. Lost but for these secret stories retold in the Apocrypha of Gwydion.

# 2.
# If It's Not in the Bible....

Antony and Bethany found themselves becoming closer as partners. As they entered their 50's, they had not only grown as people themselves, but together they had gotten to know one another very well. And instead of becoming tired of each other, they had grown more curious as to the others ability to survive the crushing blows life gave them.

They had had many discussions; arguments, you might call them. But in their separate explorations and discoveries, they had to come to some sort of accord in their disagreements. Always playing devils advocate for one another through the years, the young years of Mag's rebellious stages, her leaving, and then with the grandchild, they had become grandparents and that had changed the way they saw things. And with Antony's time away at this new and controversial "dig", Bethany had resorted to Bridge. Twice a week she traveled to a different friends house to play bridge. And the discussions were varied. But as usual with social groups, they stayed away from certain verboten subjects.

At least most of the women did. But not Bethany. She had grown tired of the insincerity. She figured on some subjects, they were just content to disagree. Or so she thought.

But for some of the old gals it came as nothing less than infuriating that they could not get Bethany to backtrack, conform and swim with their school of fish.

One such issue was the daily glass of wine. The old gals felt this to be most improper.

"You should not drink wine. It is the decay of the soul," one of them said.

Bethany looked up from her cards and just stared at this long-time friend of hers like she was seeing her afresh.

Another old gal said, "Yup. You start there and who knows where you will end up."

Bethany rolled her eyes.

"That's Satan's way," another whispered. "He starts with simple sweet things to entice you, then slams you hard with Chippendale's abs."

Bethany positively snorted in derision. She just had to answer. "It says in the bible that you should drink wine and eat only certain kinds of meat. "

"Oh, no. Where does it say that?"

"Book of Moses 4 and 5 I believe. Leviticus and Deuteronomy." She always made sure she thought she knew her facts before talking to these doubters, or anyone for that matter. Because, it seemed, everyone was an expert on the bible. 'Read your bible. Read your bible,' they had always taunted her as a child when she tried to discuss it. She figured then that they knew something she didn't. But upon actually having read it and even re-read and studied it at master's classes at the university, she discovered that maybe those people didn't know so much about it as they attested.

One of the old gals spoke up after just a moment's thought about Bethany's facts. "Oh, that's the OLD testament," she said with a pinched look on her face.

Bethany just looked at her stymied. So this old gal wasn't arguing the facts. But this was something new. The old gal was discrediting part of it because it was older than the other part?

Thinking fast Bethany answered, "So the old testament is not the bible anymore?"

The old gals all looked up all together for a moment, then buried their faces in their card game. They could not answer that one.

I wonder where they got that information? thought Bethany. They all seem to agree with one another. Its not really a fact, what they are implying, but a kind of shared prejudice. Sounds like a church-spread non-factoid.

When she got home she eventually relayed this story to Antony.

"So what did you say to them?" he asked without looking up from his paper.

"I was so nonplussed, I did what I always do when I can't think of anything else to say, I start in on facts. So I told them that, yes it says to drink a certain amount of wine each day, only eat certain kinds of meats. And insects. It instructs us to eat certain kinds of insects. Locusts, to be exact. "

He looked up at her for that one. "And what did the ol' gals say to that?"

"They laughed and said 'Nuh uh!' "

Antony shook his head and snickered. "So, I get it, its not in the bible if its in the old testament. That's kind of like when you say you are a vegetarian and people ask you if you eat chicken." He laughed again a little.

"Ya, I like that one too," answered Bethany. "Speaking of chicken..."

"Oh ya. It smells good. Do we have some white wine to go with that? I have something I want to tell you."

Her eyes got a little wide, then she turned and sauntered carefully into the kitchen to look for that bottle of white wine buried somewhere in the cupboard.

"Yes, we are going to Egypt for a new job," he announced at dinner.

# 3.
# The Next Bridge Game

Bethany had been going to bridge for over a year now. She didn't really even think about it anymore, she just went each week whether Anthony was away on a trip or not. It was something to do and it was something to pass the time in a mild state of thought around other people having conversations and engaging and generally being social.

So she felt some consternation when she walked into the room the next day and things felt different. As she entered the room all female sets of eyes looked at her then looked away. She shrugged this off as normal. But as the card game wore on she thought that the voices were more quiet this time than ever before, and each time she looked into the face of one of her comrades in cards they seem to be trying to not look back at her.

In the middle of some chatting, just as the laughter was dying down Diana, the one, who if Bethany was pressed would call the alpha of the group, said without looking up from her cards, "So Bethany, what do you believe in?"

Startled, Bethany looked up from her cards and said, "I'm sorry. What?"

"Well, if you don't believe in the Bible, exactly what do you have faith in?"

She looked down at her cards. Her mind spun for a minute as she thought, wait, I was the one who was quoting parts of the Bible you guys didn't even know. And then she realized she was prevaricating because she really didn't. And it must be obvious to the 'followers'.

So she said agnosticly, "I believe in my family, I think. It seems they are always there for me with support, even when things are really nuts." And this she thought would kick them in the knee about not being supportive.

There were grunts and shiftings around her at the bridge table. "And besides it is very interesting, when you're open to new things." She knew they were attacking her so she thought she would deliver the blow now. "We are going to Egypt on a dig next month."

All around her all heads looked up, then quickly back down. There were more shufflings of feet and cards and someone mumbled, "so what?"

And Bethany looked at their pinched faces and thought to herself, 'Well, "so what?" is that you guys are jealous. And I wont have to sit around anymore getting abused by you all for being different. So that's so what. So choke on it,' she thought to herself silently, with a tiny smile forming on her face, thinking about this new adventure the family was about to set upon.

# 4.

# The Rising Sun

The sun rose with an oblique ray of golden light off the dark side of the pyramid. The day always started all of a sudden here deep in the desert for there were no softening factors at all. Just a hard edge of yellow sand, and the hard edges of ancient artifacts thrusting themselves towards the perfect light blue of the sky.

And Antony was glad that he was heading straight downstairs into the caverns below the archaeological Museum near Luxor. There deep in the ground where no sunlight penetrated, he could adjust the soft overhead lights down to be soothing and allow him to focus on his tedious work in hand.

He had given up dreaming of entering the field again, after the debacle with the aborted South American dig, and he resigned himself to the painstaking after-work and studying categorizing and storing artifacts found in the field by others. But it was not such a bad thing. Anthony was no longer young and the bending over and carefully digging around ancient crumbling artifacts was backbreaking work to say the least.

And the brightened sun during mid-day glinting off stone surfaces was really beginning to hurt his eyes. So the caverns below the museum studying and cataloging was really rather a comfort at this point in his life.

Rarely were there new and exciting finds exposed. And when something new was brought in, the museum would be all a twitter. Sometimes in fact things weren't brought in from the field at all. But were instead found in the bazaars and markets deep within the city.

Many times this was true; artifacts were brought in by nomads and farmers, having found them on their wanderings or digging in fields.

And usually people had no idea what they had, thinking that these things were simple junk antiques, common bobbles to be sold to tourists. Few people had a working knowledge of antiquities.

And tidy profits could be made.

But one would hope the truly valuable antiquities would not find their way into the living rooms of lay collectors. But would eventually find their way into a museum of archaeological history, to those that worked collecting and studying archaeological artifacts. And if they were lucky, maybe they would find their way into the main archaeological Museum near Luxor.

The museum hired scouts to keep their eye on the tables of the markets for anything that might appear to be of greater value than simple collectible antiques. Things that might be antiquities of very ancient quality.

One such find was brought into the museum a very hot summer day very recently since the big war had ended. It immediately caught the attention of Antony. They were an old set of books, of as of yet undetermined age that had been found by farmers digging for fertilizer. In the land where civilization began cities don't get torn down and rebuilt. But rather new cities are built on top of old ones. Or the village moves to a fresh site with less junk and waste and they allow their old town to crumble. And when that old town has crumbled the ground becomes a raised area rich with soil good for fertilizing fields. But in digging these farmers often disturb valuable archaeological sites of old towns.

On a clear summer day some years before this time when Antony was contemplating potsherds deep within the bowels of the museum near Luxor, a couple of itinerant farmers were digging in a midden heap out beyond their fields. They were digging for fertilizer and would fill up their baskets, lay the strap across their foreheads, and carry their new found treasure back to their farm and carefully spread it between their plants. But this one day they found something quite different and unexpected. As their trowels cut through the soft loam, the metal blade made a sharp clanking noise on something hard. They stopped and looked at one another crinkled their brows in consternation and dropped to the dirt and began to to dig around the object they had struck. After a few moments they had uncovered a completely whole and sealed ceramic jar. It was a large jar shaped like a woman's hips and had a large ceramic bowl-like lid on the top surrounded by goop that must have once been paraffin or tar.

Being simple farmer folk, of no education or experience in the larger world, their understanding led them to believe that there was probably an evil genie in the bottle. And they argued amongst themselves and discussed and worried over what to do with this not so valuable old ceramic jar. Finally curiosity won out their superstitious fear and they took the metal bladed shovel and smashed the jar. And out came something much more worrisome and tragic than an evil genie. For the jar contained lost texts from almost 2000 years before, during the life of Christ.

But they could not know this, that their buried treasure was something of value because they had little value for
books. But they thought they might get a few pennies for themselves at the market. So they stuffed their pockets with these valuable manuscripts and headed home with full baskets of fertilizer. And on a day off they took these books to the market.

Fortunately for the museum and Antony and all the students of antiquities, these books eventually ended up in the archaeological Museum near Luxor. And with time and painstaking patience their secrets were teased from between the leather sheets.

# 5.
# Antony and Bethany

The smell of cooking emanated from the kitchen, and Antony smiled as his stomach rumbled. As usual dinnertime was the stage for the satisfaction of appetite for food and companionship.

He looked forward every day to coming home and sharing that with his wife Bethany. Their daughter had long ago left the nest for wilder realms on the Isthmus between the two American continents. So they had each other and they actually reveled in their time alone.

And often their discussions took on a heated tone. For they both were connoisseurs of history and historical philosophy. Times change and people change. And there is little but an ad hoc recorded history of their experiences, which very poorly relay the sensations and the thoughts of the people of that time. And we can only guess at the experience of their unique and possibly incomprehensible situations.

But people read and they study and they try to place themselves in someone else's shoes. And they try to understand what another person was going through in ancient times, and try to fathom what possesses them to commit their experiences to writing. Most often ancient writings are probably an oral history, spoken stories that are then written down. So the stories change with each teller, and with each generation, so the details might change but most likely the lesson or the moral probably remains the same.

"So what did you do today honey?" Antony asked Bethany as she began setting the table for dinner. Antony noticed that there were more than two place settings on the table, and several bottles of wine when usually there was only one.

"Oh, I cleaned house a little then I went shopping with some of the girls. Then I came home and started making dinner. Pretty simple day."

"Ya, that's gotta be nice," he answered safely.

After a pause she added, "Oh. And we got a letter from Mags. She and Stan are coming for a visit."

"What about Gwydion? Is he coming too?"

"Well of course silly. He's only seven," she answered with a shake of her head.

He ignored her reprimand, he was so happy, and he smiled and said, "when are they coming?"

"Actually they should be here any moment," she answered with a straight face.

# 6.
# Christmas Time

With her usual hustle and bustle, Maggie entered the kitchen of her parents' small apartment. There were cries of joy and glee as the family reunited for Christmas time. The apartment was small and cool but was just large enough to hold everyone and just cozy enough to be loving.

"We are so glad you are here, honey," said Bethany to her daughter. Just then a small person burst through the door and began careening around the room making a flubbering sound of a motor car. Sort of. All of them knew what this important sound was that was coming from this child. His favorite thing, riding in a car. And pretending to drive one. Or pretending to BE one.

As they had learned from their expedition to Costa Rica the previous year on, literally, an expedition, of the archaeological kind, they learned that this smart little boy was pretending to be something other than himself. His imagination provided the substance and his wet sounds from his big soft child lips provided the soundtrack.

"Gwydion!" his grand mother exclaimed. "So how is my little motor car?" He continued to flubber around the room in circles, with his small fists out in front of him, turning the imaginary wheel of a motor car. He did not answer her, but she knew that he heard her ask, she could tell by the almost imperceptible change in his smirky face that he was trying actually really hard to ignore her. And by the twisting of his brow further, she knew he was gonna break in a moment.

Finally he got tired of spitting flubbery sounds into the kitchen air, and he stopped his motions and allowed his grandmother to sweep him up in her strong embrace and smother his wet face with kisses.

"You little rascal," she gently admonished him. He squealed with glee but didn't really fight her too hard.

She reluctantly set him down, and he ran into the living room, and she heard her husband exclaim something out loud as this happy intrusion of small mankind, his grandson.

Then Bethany turned to Mags and tried to determine the look on her face. Sullenness maybe, something there a bit inscrutable. As usual with Mags. In all these years, Bethany had never really figured out what was going on inside her daughter's head. So she waited for her to take the lead.

"This Christmas stuff is so dumb," Mags said cryptically after a moment.

"Oh, dear," Bethany mumbled. "Well at least it brings us together. I am glad you are here. Where's Stan?"

"Down carrying up some stuff." Mags pulled some things out of bags and set them on the kitchen table. "I bought a few things at the market on the way through. We will have a nice dinner. I cant believe they have nativity scenes out here. This is Egypt, for Christ's sake." She looked at her mom at her slip of the tongue. "Sorry. I didn't mean to use the lord's name in vein."

"It's alright, dear. I have loosened up a bit, after all that has happened. It seems less important than other things now. Besides I've learned a few things in my master's class that I just didn't expect. There are other things going on underneath all that pomp and circum.."

Just then a big bustling figure banged open the door and rustled into the kitchen, his arms laden with bags of stuff. "Hi, ma," he said. It wasn't said completely in sarcasm as usual. After all the hullabaloo last year at the dig and the political fallout afterward, Stan had actually come to respect his mother and father-in-law. And he in turn had eventually earned their respect by landing a pretty nice job that supported his little family pretty well.

Dinner went well. The family had grown closer during their time in the Isthmus, working to unravel what was happening around them, things far out of their control. But the confusion had pushed them closer together. And had caused them to ask themselves some hard questions. Questions few people really liked to ask themselves. Like what was really going on. Who was really in charge there. And mostly, the big one, what did it mean that there was an ancient astronaut in that tomb. Or, if it was just artwork on a stone slab, how the heck could it look so much like he was sitting at the instrument panel on a fiery machine? These things had grown to worry, and even frighten the 26 year old Mags to no end. Eerie post-modern things found in the place she had run off to, to find solace from all the crazy modernness.

She had for most of her life rejected religion as paranoid silliness of older people. She had rejected the strict teaching of the catechism as silliness or even vaguely as mind control. Because none of it made real sense. The details of the stories seemed like myths or legends, with some false-feeling morality, wrapped in goopy old language to make it sound important. But it never seemed to touch the real aspects of her life.

So she had run away from it all. To the deep rich forests of Ancient Costa Rica with the man she loved.

And they had had a child. And that had brought more questions. What kind of world were they bringing a child into? What would she explain to him about all the things he would inevitably ask, things she had never decided how she actually felt about in the first place. Sometimes all these questions made her feel like a child herself. So what the heck was she doing bringing another child into this over-populated world?

But reconnecting with her parents was answering some of those problems. She was finding that not only did they absolutely love being with Gwydion, but they were able to deftly answer his strange questions and deal with some of his more uncomfortable quirks. Her parents seemed to thrive on this exchange with the little boy. And her little boy badly needed their easily given affection. And Mags needed a break sometimes, that's for sure.

So after dinner, when Stan and her mother were in and out of the kitchen carrying plates and cleaning up, and she was chatting and grunting with her father, which was all sometimes she could get out of him from behind his newspaper or some book or thick sheaf of papers, she broached this subject that had been niggling at her mind, a subject she thought him to be more versed in than any other person she knew. And since he was an actual anthropologist and archaeologist, she felt that maybe he was a bit more objective than other people she might have a conversation with.

"I'm sorry about all that stuff last year, " she started out. There was a silence as her father was not much for expressing emotions. So she went a different tack. "At least you found a job here. How do you like working at the museum, Dad?"

He looked up at her, knowing she was trying to talk to him, but still being somewhat inscrutable at best. "It's good. Lonely. And weird quiet. But maybe that's OK. I'm approaching fifty you know."

"What do you do there?" she asked feigning curiosity and showing naivete'.

"Mostly I catalog old finds. Bits and pieces of things that have been found. No more digging in the dirt for old Antony Jacobs!" and he chuckled a little at his own imprecation.

She chuckled a little to, just to mollify him. "Like what?" She could sense he was warming up to this conversation, despite himself. And there was something she really wanted to ask him, but knew he would never answer if she just blurted it out and asked him outright.

"Pot shards mostly," He looked her right in the eye, almost challengingly.

"What is that?" she asked.

"Mostly what we find in the field," his now using the first person involved in the digging of archaeology, she knew she had him, "are pot shards. Broken pieces of old pottery."

"Sounds dry," she said with a straight face. A few years before she might have laughed at him and dismissed the conversation. But she sensed something deeper now, so she held onto her adult face.

"Oh, no. There is so much we can know by studying these little pieces of the left overs from ancient people's lives. What they ate, their level of technological advancement, so many things. We study them microscopically and place them on a map of where they were found and we can draw out their villages. We can even discover, now with our science machines, just how hot they were fired, which gives us a clue of just how technologically advanced they were."

"All that from little pieces of broken pottery?" her face showed true surprise and interest.

He looked at her young face, this pretty face of his only child, his daughter, and saw true interest there. He smiled in satisfaction at this and said, "Yes. We are a little like forensic detectives, using the smallest of clues to draw the big pictures."

She sat back in the shallow chair, and looked at her father, deep in his recliner, surrounded by the comforts of home, the hand table on the left side with his cup of after-dinner coffee, his lit pipe smoking silently and aromatically in his left hand, a huge stack of books underneath, and the paper in his lap, and she smiled at him. They sat in companionable silence as each enjoyed having discovered something interesting together, as if it was their little secret, and theirs alone.

But of course it was not theirs alone. These and many many other secrets sat deep in the Museum of Archaeology of Egypt, waiting, many of these finds waiting, to be analyzed and cataloged. Maybe some of them would be understood; most are probably not, their true secrets buried deep in the ravages of time, often ripped from their original place and purpose of burial by the unsuspecting people finding them in the daily process of going about their simple lives.

One such recent find weighed at the back of Antony's mind. It was still a secret, for its mysteries had not yet been uncovered.

These scientists of little renown had learned to take their time, wait till more of the artifact's secrets had been divined before exposing the find to the public. Speculation and conjecture always ran rampant with the paucity of information. Antiquities always fostered speculation. So it was still a secret, this little find in the desert. Because of his notoriety, he had been allowed to examine the find. And it was his responsibility to keep it quiet. But as he looked at his eager daughter now sitting before him, and seeing the interest and desire to please him, her father, he thought maybe he could let her get just a peek of the cat in the bag, without actually letting it all the way out.

"There was just something new they found came in a few months ago." Her eyebrows shot up. "We haven't figured it out yet but I think it will be very interesting," he ventured humbly, sitting back in vague conspiracy.

"What is it?" she asked, naked excitement in her voice.

"Just some books," he answered simply.

"Books? What kind of books?"

He nodded his head knowingly. "*Old* books."

She leaned back a little, unconsciously giving away her doubt that this could be anything important, books never had been important to her. "Like what kind of books? How old?" she ventured trying to stay interested.

He saw that her interest was waning a bit, so he poured on the detective mystery juice just a little. "Old biblical texts."

"What?" He knew he had her there. "Which ones?" She had never really read the thing, although people had always told her to. Read your Bible, Read your bible, they always told her when ever she tried to talk about philosophy and religion.

She thought she knew some things about it all, and tried to tell people the things she thought, some things she thought might be important. But no one ever seemed to want to discuss it without going oogie boogie and all 'faith' on her.

"What do you mean which ones?' asked Antony. Then, realizing the general public misunderstanding, he said suddenly, "Oh, no. These are books not in the Bible."

Her eyes grew really wide at this. "Nuh, uh." She showed her doubt and yet was entertained by the possibility. Antony gave a little nod. "What? What do you mean, not in there?"

"I hate to break it to you young lady, but what is in the Bible is not all that what was written during that time. Loads and loads of stuff was written, some texts and Gospels by famous people like James, and Joseph and Mary. The bible you read was selected to include only certain things. Over the years it has changed, been re-translated and rewritten."

"What?" Still her mind could not grasp that this book she had savaged and discredited was not the thing she envisioned. It was not absolute truth and the only written word of God and the teachings of Jesus, as she had been led to believe. How could they do that to us, with this sacred book, leave things out and put other things in? Her mind leaped to the conclusion that young people often do: conspiracy! "How could they mislead us like that?" she almost yelled at her dad sitting there sipping his after dinner coffee.

"Oh, its not quite like that. They had to decide what to leave in and take out. If they hadn't, I assure you, the Bible would be 10 feet thick."

Her mind in a disbelieving sway, Mags said nothing back to

her father, the conversation over for her, with her mind reeling and swaying in this new startling information. Only one thing was possible for her to think now, maybe she really had to sit down and read the thing.

Seeing her confusion, and understanding it somewhat, having seen other people thrown off guard by this information regarding the text they once thought an immutable rock, a sacred plaque of heavenly truth, he instructed her, "You should really read the King James version. It is the oldest version to read and be understandable by most people. It still contains some of the original poetry and yet is still readable. Some of the new ones are really just modern adapted stories like you might see on TV or in the movies. Most of that stuff is not in there, or anywhere else at all, for that matter, but just someone's story telling. Might as well be fiction."

Mags sat and listened to her father educate her on these things that had held a very emotional place in her mind, something that she had filed away as silliness and the torture of the young perpetrated by older people. But now she saw that her father was an adult, an extremely well educated and experienced adult, and he studied this stuff. There was obviously something very serious and fascinating going on here, something deeper and richer, and more meaningful to our lives and history than the mere moralistic teachings of that old Catechism she had once suffered and rebelled against.

Clanging and banging increased in crescendo in the kitchen and the door burst open with Stan and Bethany carrying forth dessert. Ah, dessert. They could settle in for some chocolate cake and coffee. Not exactly usual Christmas fare. But chocolate cake? Oh, ya.

# 7.
# The Market

A small brown boy ran between the tight packed stalls of the foreign market. Birds swooped and called over head, wheeling black against the blinding sun. The noise of the sellers hawking their wares, and the children playing in the streets and the buyers haggling over value and prices made a din that echoed back through mellenia of time. Back to a time not in a far away place but to this one exactly. For this market was old, very old. And the exchange of goods for like value of money or other goods had been taking place here under the scorching sun for a decade of mellenia. At least that long.

But this little brown boy was born in a different land. He skin was maybe not so brown in any other place than these rich places of sun and wind. But here, he became this place. This was the origin of his ancestors, of all our ancestors, and his soul rose to it's call. And he ran in glee of the excitement.

Antony smiled at his grandson's antics. He was just getting to know the child well after a long absence during his early childhood, with just one visit last year. But now they seemed to be here to stay a while. The imprecations of long ago, her vague threats, her running away from family, school and everything seemed to have been lost in the years of separation. And then with that humiliation last year. His mind spun away from these thoughts and he focused on the child.

"Is he usually like this? He is so excited," he asked his daughter.

Maggie answered, "In places where there are a lot of people, ya. He just loves it."

"Aren't you afraid of him getting lost?" he asked her.

"Nope. He stays very close and watches us carefully. But he is sneaky and stays just out of range. He knows exactly where we are. Anyway, he could probably find us in a second if he got too far."

"Hmmm," he said thoughtfully. "Back in America we would worry about him getting taken. You know how it is."

"Ya. But he has this way," she started. Her answer was interrupted by a seller yelling in another language. "Stay away from that, child!" And with that, Gwydion turned and bolted out into the crowd in the street and got himself lost in the tumult there. "What was he looking at?" She wondered out loud, knowing the interesting curiosities this child often found himself.

The family wandered over to the market booth and poked around on the spread out tables. It was various bits and pieces of things old and new, in no arrangement or order on the table surface. The rug the table was laid with was actually rather beautiful, with brightly colored wool threads interwoven in complex and contrasting designs.

But as he stood and stared, Antony's eyes began to focus on the small things displayed in a jumble on top of this brightly colored surface.

"That boy..." began the seller in a rather gruff voice.

Maggie looked him in the face, rather against custom here in this other land. And the dark faced seller looked her frankly in the face, his dark eyes wondering at the challenge. She said, "He is ours. Sorry. But he is just very curious."

"He is strange. He would not even look at me in the eye. I don't trust him." The man looked away and clutched his arms around him, then looked back at Maggie then the older man, the grandfather of the child, Antony. But Antony was studying something on the table and wasn't paying much heed.

"He's fine," said Maggie defensively. With that she turned away to look for her son, now hiding himself in the crowd from this big mean man. She picked him out between the passersby but did not pursue him. She knew he could see her and would stay just out of range, watching every move the adults made.

'"Where are these things from?" Antony asked the man.

"Oh, a bit from here. And a bit from there," he answered evasively, his face changing to show a sellers"smile.

Antony tried not to show interest in the thing that had truly caught his eye. So he pointed to a few broken objects, some of them obviously not so old, but few perhaps ancient. He knew that the dark glaring local was onto what often happened here in the market place. Foreigners often came to buy trinkets, and these foreigners were known to often have a great deal of money. And often paid handsomely for trinkets of little value. But sometimes these foreigners were antiquities dealers or they were from the museum and knew exactly what these antiquities were worth. Some of it was junk. And some of it had value. And more often than not, the sellers had no idea how to tell them apart, the things with value and the things of little worth. But often the buyers did. And the sellers had grown shrewd. And had learned to watch closely the faces of these foreigners for signs of desire, for the flash of something more. The look that they had found something of worth, like in a poker game, a tell that their hand was a good one. For then the price would go up in the seller's mind.

Antony tried not to show his interest in these bits of rare cloth. Or really paper it was, but it was so old there was very little difference between the two things. Yellowed, the fibers coming apart, with inked markings on them in Cyrillic or even older. He would love to get a look at these bits under his scanner microscope, get out his dictionary of letters and written languages and study the scribblings there. Antiquities are old, very old. And the difference between a thousand years old and two is impossible to tell at a glance.

But the machines in the lab would tell. They could date objects, although he could not tell you how it was done. Archival antiquities of manuscript was his specialty. And these pieces and bits looked very interesting to him.

He pointed to the group of broken metal things, and drew his finger around the group of bits there. "This whole group here, how much?"

The seller's eyes lit up despite himself, and Antony tried not to smile at this other man's 'tell'.

"What is sir interested in?" pretending interest in his interest, trying to pry which piece he was actually interested in.

"These shiny bits." Antony said in segue, "these bits might make a nice mobile for my grandson. I'll take all these bits including the paper pieces. How much?"

The light went out of the old man's eyes as he surmised this foreigner had no knowledge or interest in true antiquities and was not mistaking this little basket of junk as anything of value. He stated a price he felt was a little high for this little spread of junk.

Antony tried not to reveal his surprise at such a low price. He forced himself to frown, and shake his head slightly. He did a little math and subtracted about 20% from the man's price and told him he would give no more.

The old man shrugged his shoulders thinking he was really getting a better price than this little pile of junk was worth, but feigning acquiescence, he began to wrap the little pile of junk in a piece of newspaper. Antony got out some change and laid it on the table as the old man handed him the small sack of junk. Antony nodded his head and with a mutual salutation, he turned and stepped away from the seller's booth.

As he entered back into the flow of the foot traffic, he was met mid-stream by his daughter, and in a moment Gwydion was right beside him, having watched the whole thing from deep inside the concealing crowd in the middle of the street. Daughter and father smiled a little at one another. And Gwydion came up behind them and reached out and touched the little bag in Antony's hand. Antony reached out his other hand and placed it on his little tousled head. The boy leaned over quickly and bumped up against his grand papa's hip like a cat.

As they left the crowd and din of the market place, Antony had seemed quiet and distracted, so Maggie hadn't pushed to stop at any of the other stalls, although colors and sounds beckoned. She figured she was here for a while and they could always shop another day.

They walked awhile with the child Gwydion racing in and around behind them, evasive but always staying near.

When they reached a quieter area, Maggie said, "So what did you get?"

"Don't know really," he answered. "Might be nothing."

"But what?" she pressed. Obviously he saw something, because he didn't ask her about it at all. Something serious for his studies most likely. Not a gift or a bauble.

"Ummm... Some paper fragments. Some junk too. But I just didn't want to give the guy ideas." He smiled conspiratorially.

"What is it?"

"I don't know. Just some writing." They walked for a few minutes, before Antony said, "Do you guys want to go to the Museum? Dinner is not for a while."

Maggie looked up into her father's face and smiled. She had begun enjoying her father's occupation, the old secret manuscripts, the dusty files and the weird mysterious objects. And her son was fascinated too. He would stand in front of the old glass cases in the basement of the museum and stare at the old dusty objects inside. He would stick out his tiny index finger and with great care and reverence, gently touch the tip of it to the surface of the glass and watch as the moisture from his skin would make a foggy halo glow on the glass around the tiny object he was pointing to.

# 8.

# The Papyrus

Antony was in the museum long hours that day, after they had found the scraps of writing. The rest of the stuff he had purchased from the seller was pretty much junk, but he was glad to had made off with any of it as long as it included those precious bits of paper.

Maggie was peering over his shoulder as he slipped the fragile bits under the micro scope one by one. He made gasping noises and mumbling grunts assenting himself to one thought or another of his.

"What is it?" she finally asked her father.

"Oh, its papyrus, alright," he answered.

"You mean old paper?"

"Yes. What was used in this Nile delta thousands of years ago."

"I thought they used animal skins."

"Well, yes. That would be vellum. And that was used too, but Papyrus almost became a god, it was that highly revered. The plant was seen to represent the pharaohs themselves, with the stalk looking just like a pyramid when it was severed, and the blade-like leaves representing the rays of the sun shooting up from the roots. And the properties of this paper is fairly astonishing. It is very strong and highly resistant to aging. Very important for important documents. I am not sure they realized when they were making this stuff that it would last for thousands of years," he answered as if he were leading one of his college lectures.

"So, how old is this?" she asked.

"I am guessing by the letters and the few words I recognize right off, like this word "karphos", an unusual Greek word that is found six times in the old Greek Bible. It means small dry twig, and is attributed to one of the sayings of Jesus. This would suggest that these scraps are contemporary with the Gospels."

He turned and looked up into her young expectant face as her eyebrows were about stuck in her hairline.

"Wow. That's a find isn't it?"

"I think it is, yes."

The two took their tiny family and headed home after this eventful day. Not much was said between them and the little boy Gwydion frolicked behind and around, taking joy of everything that was of immediate interest to him. The birds in the acacia made a sound of music in the golden air, punctuating this song of love with the soft beating of their wings. He found scraps of paper in the street and swung them like his own feathers in this dance down the dreary street of one of the most ancient intact cities on the planet.

The rush and tumult and fluttering of birds wings and song ended as they entered the cool dark apartment. These outdoor sounds were replaced by indoor ones, the clanging of pans, and the humming of the mistress of this domain.

She was preparing dinner for her family, one of her most cherished activities. For it brought them all together at the end of the day.

"Mom, we found something today!" Mags called out to her mother down the hall.

All three rushed into the kitchen, little Gwydion running to his grandmother's arms, where she scooped him up with a flourish, her wet sticky hands held out from his sides like sticky newly hatched baby angel wings. His attention satisfied, he jumped down and ran down the hall with a swoosh and then some flubbery motor car sounds, leaving the adults talking in the close confines of the kitchen.

"And what did we find today, my dear?"

"Like, some scraps of paper that are, like, two thousand years old!" exclaimed Maggie.

Bethany smiled but did not acknowledge this outburst from her daughter. She was an adult, but not a learned professor like her husband. And through the years of exciting discovery, and tortuous research there was almost always agonizing let- downs. Things were rarely as important as they first felt like when you found them. So she waited for her husband's explanation. He took a deep breath and sat down at the kitchen table, obviously willing to wait a few minutes for the kettle to settle before striking forward on this subject.

"Didn't we, daddy?" she looked at her father waiting for a response.

"I think actually Gwydion found it. On that old junk dealer's table," he said quietly. "It was a piece of papyrus we found in that junk." He looked at his wife and a conspiratorial grin spread over his face. "But I couldn't let the seller know that!" He smiled and his wife smiled. "So I acted like it was nothing and bought this little pile of junk that he wrapped up for us. Some trifles, really."

"But papyrus means old, doesn't it?" asked Bethany, now interested, and she allowed herself into the intrigue by her husband's now willingness to discuss the possible find.

"Papyrus might mean its old. It looks old. And by the letters and condition, it is old. Some of the words are significant, I think maybe even contemporary with the Gospels."

"It seems weird to me that there aren't any books from his lifetime. Why is that?"

"That's really old Maggie," her mother said, as if that covered it.

"At first stories being written down were just being stored away, like they didn't know these stories would become so controversial and important in a hundred or so years. Remember it didn't become a religion until a few hundred years later. Then, I think a lot was being destroyed, actually. Kinda like destroying the evidence. It was all pretty controversial for hundreds of years, or a thousand or more. Still is," Antony answered knowingly.

"But if they actually found some writings from say between 0 and 60 to 100 AD, now that would be something," quipped Bethany.

Father and daughter looked at their mother, holding a dripping wooden spoon in her hand over the stove, her head turned back toward them, trying to be a part of this conversation.

"And why would that be, honey?" her husband asked her, not really understanding her meaning, but, trying to be indulgent.

"Well, that would mean that the person who wrote it might have probably actually met him or had heard him speak." They continued to start at her. "You know, first hand."

"Who?" said Mags.

"Jesus!" said Bethany.

"Don't curse, mom. I just don't know who you're talking about," cried Mags.

"No! The Christ!" exclaimed her mother, turning around and throwing out her arms, dripping spoon and all.

Daughter and father looked at Bethany blankly for a moment, then slowly their heads turned toward one another and their eyebrows hitched up another notch.

Leave it to her to tell them the significance of these bits of papyrus, and turning something interesting into a possibly very significant find.

For many years after the finding, these fragments were housed in an old glass case with some other bits of archaeological errata, some pieces of mummies that had been hauled in from these same 'antika' shops along the delta, along with two weird fully mummified ibis, the tall reed birds that lived along the water line of that river. Very strange offerings for the dead.

But it wouldn't be till many years later, with the advances of technology, microscopes and what they were to call radio-logical dating, or carbon dating, that they would take another look at these little scraps of papyrus and discover that they were just a little older than what they had at first thought.

About one hundred and fifty years older.

Just about what Bethany had guessed.

At the time of the writing on these bits of papyrus, this age of civilization was not called what we call it now. The years were not ordered as we do now, after the life of the Savior. They stated the year according to what Roman emperor reigned, like the Tenth year of our lord and Emperor Claudius the Third, or whom ever, etc. Some probably still referred to the year as the number of years since their favorite Pharaoh died. But a few hundred years later, after the birth and death of this Christ, the western world began telling the years by how many years after his birth it was. What is known as A.D., ado domini, or also known in the science of archaeology as A.C.E., a later prescription used by scientists and archaeologists, "After Christian Era", but these would be all ad hoc titles.

But with new scientific dating methods, this papyrus found at the junk dealer was dated to around 60 A.D. And the significance of that took a while to sink in.

For if, as Bethany had suggested, these pieces were written near around 60 AD, that would put it's author as a contemporary to the Christ. The writer of these letters on the papyrus was possibly alive and had heard the Man, Jesus, Himself speak.

And this had extraordinary implications.

Quietly the Genie lifted out of the bottle.

## Questions

Gwydion played on the floor of the cool apartment with his stacks of blocks and toys of all sorts. His life was a little different than for most children. He had grown up almost a wild child in the free forests of Costa Rica, where his toys were wild birds, butterflies and plants in such a profusion that is rarely seen in but a very few other places on this planet. He loved the sounds of the rich jungle. His vision showed him a world of swirling prismatic colors and shades. In his world things did not have boundaries, but were just swirls of concentrations of energies that mingled and changed.

His was not a world of divisions and boxes, but of interrelationships and gradations of oneness-es. When people would point to something in the jungle trees swooping by and say that is a so and so bird, he would turn and look at them and wonder how such a complex entity could have just one name, when it came into contact with and depended on and altered so many other things around it in its swirling world. He wondered how they could decide to divide the thing into this separate thing and not be included in the things around it. Gwydion would have problems relating to the world of boxes. The world that everyone else seemed to live in, the world he could not and did not want to ever understand. Because all of these things belonged together, and their rich beauty and his joy in them depended on it.

He began to speak late in his babyhood. Full sentences didn't actually come until he was 8, about the time they moved to the desert to be with his grand mama and grand papa. He was held in the warm cocoon of their love and adulation. And being in a foreign country, it would not matter and would not seem strange to anyone that he did not have a full grasp of the English language. Well, maybe he did have a full grasp of it actually. He thought he did. But he just simply didn't want to speak to anyone very much, it was too difficult to divide his world into those separate parts that they all called words. This thing from *that* thing. When everything was so beautifully fit together in a beautiful kaleidoscope, in his colorful prismatic vision.

But he listened. Boy did he listen. When his grand mama and grand papa sat and talked and raised their voices in the kitchen in the evenings around dinner, he was all eyes and ears.

He took in the things they were saying, the nuances of their arguments. And no one would have ever thought that he was absorbing all of it. All of it. Even the gradations of the differences between their opinions. He may not understand how it all fit in the outside world, but he understood it as shades of the big prism of his reality. And that prism grew and grew each day until one day he started asking really big

questions. He not only knew big sentences but he knew how things fit together, and he knew when things did not fit together.

There was little guile in this family. The hardships and simplicity of living in Costa Rica alone with her mate and their little son had wrung out the rebelliousness from his mother Maggie, and she had become forgiving. Strong but forgiving. His grand mama and grand papa had dropped their guile and their yearning during the difficulties of the closed down dig last year, when his life's work felt to be ripped away from him, his grand papa. When that sort of thing happens, Gwydion saw that people became more bare, and more vulnerable and thus clung to the things that were permanent and strong: the love of a mother, the love of married couples, his father. And in that he could see the shining ray of truth. He could tell when there was honesty and he could tell, especially when he was around others, maybe in the market or in the museum, when there was not-truth, when there was something off, something false about communications between people. He may not have known what it was exactly. But he could always sense it and he would steer away and not allow himself to become caught up in their deceptive web.

But this was Christmas time. He loved Christmas time. The weather got cooler and the palm trees blew hard in the winds sometimes.

Sometimes there was a lot of rain and the great river would flood and wash away some places that people had been living. But always the colored lights. He loved the colored lights. He would pretend that the strings of multi-colored lights that ran up and down the slender palm trees shafts were in a specific order, like the ticking of a clock or the ordered steps of some colorful bug leaving footprints in the sand. He loved those colors and would squint his eyes and watch the orbs of color blossom into small suns, bright with those unnatural and beautiful colors. That must be what stars look like, if he could just get close enough.

Grand mama's glass balls would come out of their boxes of paper stuffing at this time of year. Always after the dinner with the turkey and the round red jellied fruit you put on it. So good.

Always then getting ready for the colored lights after that.

Soon after, a couple weeks, the plastic tree would go up and the lights and the glass balls. Some of the balls had sugar on them that would twinkle when they rotated underneath the lights on the plastic tree. The one ball was his favorite. It had a little cave in it and inside this cave was a tiny little baby. And he was in a little wooden rocker with hay. Baby Jesus, his mother would say. Jesus in a manger, what ever that is.

And Gwydion would watch the glass ball spin and throw off its glinting light in the dark room after he had turned off the lights. Around and around the baby Jesus would go in his safe little cave in the glass ball covered with sugar.

"What is Christmas?" he asked his grand mama who was rolling some flour into balls that she would bake in the oven to make cookies.

"Christmas in the time we celebrate the birth of baby Jesus. They say he was born on December 25. In a manger with his mother Mary and his father Joseph, with donkeys and other barn animals all around. And they knew he was special so he was visited by the wise kings from the east, the Magi. They brought him Frankincense and myrrh. Whatever that is."

Gwydion watched the ball spin round and the baby Jesus spin round safe in his glass cave. "Why?" asked young Gwydion.

"He would become our lord, Jesus Christ," She answered simply.

Gwydion did not answer this but stored it away in his mind for later. He enjoyed the lights and the glass balls and the sensations of Christmas time far too much to be worried about its meaning. That would come much later in his curious life.

Antony rocked slightly in his chair. He was enjoying his reading, but he looked up at Gwydion and his question. "He was a special child, probably kinda like you, Gwydion," he said to his grandson. He allowed him these indulgences because he really loved the boy. And he knew that he was very essentially different from other boys his age. He didn't necessarily need to be protected or indulged, because it probably didn't matter much. The child seemed to have a 6th sense about danger and could stay out of any trap set by any adult. But he was special. He had a special vision, a special way of looking at the world that Antony did not want messed up by some mean person getting inside the child's head and ruining the innocence and wonder he saw there too early in his life by some mean or corrupting act. There would be time enough for that as Gwydion grew older and would begin to take on more of the world.

Hopefully by that time, thought Antony, he would have enough experience to take on any kind of obstacle and be strong enough still to resist the evils that surrounded and tempted us all. So while he was still young and of that innocent, grasping curious mind, Antony would endeavor to foster its growth. Nurture its wild abandon of discovery.

"But you know, Gwydion. What is written in the big black book over there is not all that was written about that special little child. And his life has many secrets."

"Secrets?" said Gwydion, as he suddenly looked around like someone was trying to fool him. "Secrets? What kind of secrets?"

"Well, this special child called Jesus, he was smarter than he was supposed to be. He confounded everyone. He challenged everyone's idea of what was proper and what should be. He knew things he was just not supposed to know." He looked Gwydion in the eye, during the moment that the young skittish child let him and Antony gave him a big wink. Gwydion squealed with glee and shook his whole body with happiness. Antony leaned his head back and laughed, always happy when this amazing child found such joy in such simple things.

And so the seed was planted in young Gwydion's mind that things were not as they seemed in the rigid world of adults. And that secrets lay everywhere around them. And one day he would delve deep into that memory of that pleasure of the great secrets shared with his grand papa on the cold dark wondrous Christmas evening. And he'd crack open the forbidden old and forgotten books of the bible, the ones stacked to the side and lost for 2 thousand years in old jars and catacombs, only to be found when the ravages of the old stifling religions had faded and these old secrets could be found, translated and wondered upon. The ancient lost gospels of the contemporaries of Jesus.

One evening Antony and Gwydion were sitting alone in the living room late by themselves. Gwydion was getting tired, but would not yet give up the ghost and go to sleep. But he came crawling over to Antony on his hands and knees and leaned against his grand papas legs as he sat in his deep comfortable recliner.

Antony set his book aside and reached down and pulled Gwydion into his lap. The little boy with the tousled dark curls curled in a ball and put his thumb in his mouth.

"So what shall we do now, little man?" Asked Antony quietly. Of course he expected no answer for Gwydion, but he got a small wiggle and a tiny coo of assent from deep in the boy's throat.

"I know. Why don't I read you a bedtime story," said Antony with a small spark of an idea. He had uncovered recently hidden deep in the Museum the ancient books found in an old jar, discovered in a field somewhere by some itinerant farm workers. The scrolls had been obtained by buyers and were brought in to the lab and there the scholar's were just beginning to translate them into English from the ancient Hebrew and Semitic. These stories were all ancient and quite controversial. And they had not yet been released to the public yet.

But Antony found them fascinating and kind of beautiful. They seemed to be variations of the stories found in the New Testament of the Bible. But these were better stories; fuller, more realistic and told in more readable story form when translated directly from the old languages.

The scholars at the University had placed all these ancient scrolls in an old locked cabinet, which they then called with humor the "scrollery" rather than the scullery. They would be translating them and as they compiled them, they ordered them by the chronology of happenings, and put them into a book for publication. They would call these stories the "Apocrypha". This is the ancient Latin word from which was derived the more modern word for these biblical stories not found in the Bible, hypocrisy.

"But," reasoned Antony, "what would it hurt to read them to Gwydion? He won't understand them anyway, and there will be no secrets revealed." At least so he thought. And he began to read out loud but quietly, as to not wake the rest of the family, the infancy Gospel of Thomas....

"I cant stand this child. Joseph, come take him away." The old teacher tottered around in an agitated but careful way. "Every time I try to teach him something, he acts like he knows something so much more than I do."

"What are you muttering about, old Zachaeus?" Joseph asked the old man. "He is just a child."

"Oh, more than just a child. some kind of strange being, perhaps born before the first forming of the earth, he seems to know so much. What kind of womb could have produced such an one (sic) as this? He is not of this world, but from somewhere else, most assuredly, your lady Mary even confirms this to be true."

The boy Jesus had been playing in the mud that fine day, and forming small animals with it. He clarified the water around him with one word.

When one of the elders of the old religious leaders saw him making these things on the day of the Sabbath, he ran and told the elders of the church. One of the elders came and admonished the 5 year old Jesus and asked why he profaned the Sabbath, the day when no work or creation can be done. Jesus, seeing that the things he had made good with his hands, the 12 mud sparrows, had angered the older men, he clapped his hands and cried, "be gone!". And the twelve sparrows took flight and flew off. And all were amazed but they ran off and told their leaders what this young Jesus had done.

One of the younger boys that was standing there with Joseph took a willow switch and scattered the water that Jesus had gathered into pools. Jesus became irritated with him and said, "What did those pools of water do to harm you? So now you will wither and never grow leaves or root or bear fruit." And the little boy withered in front of their eyes. The withered child was taken to his mother and father who mourned his lost youth, and asked Joseph, "What kind of a child do you have that does such things?"

Then another child ran up and bumped into Jesus and Jesus was irritated. And he said to the boy, "you will travel no further." And the boy fell down there and died. The people of the village were aghast, and asked Joseph, " where was he born? Everything he says, happens. You can no longer live in this village, unless you teach this boy to bless instead of curse, for he is killing our children."

So Joseph grabbed him by the ear and yanked hard. "Why do you vex these people? Can you not see that they are angry and are persecuting us?"

Jesus answered his father, "It is enough that you seek and do not find. Do you not know that I am yours. Do not grieve me."

Antony looked at Gwydion, who was still awake, but barely, and said, "I guess little boys everywhere are the same."

Gwydion looked up at his grand papa and shook his head. Antony smiled. "Not you? Well, then that's because you are more evolved. A more adapted cross between those aboriginals and the divine."

And Gwydion smiled at that and settled back in Antony's lap. Antony was a little disconcerted. Perhaps he had under estimated how much this little boy was understanding these old stories. But he continued reading out loud these newly translated stories of old.

"This story was when Zachaeus first invited Joseph to lend him this bright child for instruction. "Come let me take him and teach him to read. And through reading he will learn everything. Including how to honor his ancestors and fathers. And to love children his own age." But Jesus questioned his teacher sharply about the first letter alpha, and proceeded in great detail in allegorical explanation of the subtleties of its construction that the teacher was at a complete loss."Though I am an old man, I have been made a complete sham by this child. So I ask you, Joseph, take him back home. I do not know what kind of great thing he is, whether divine being or angel, I do not know."

And the young Jesus laughed and said to the poor teacher, "All right I'll give you a break here. But know that I have come from Above to curse all of you, and enlighten you into knowledge of heart just like the ones who commanded me here." And all those he had cursed were healed and then everybody was afraid of so much power and the cowered before him.

Some days later the children were playing on top of a roof. One of the children fell off the roof and died. When the adults saw this they immediately blamed it on the little boy Jesus, saying it was him who threw him down.

"I certainly did not throw him down," objected the boy. But they began to verbally abuse him for it anyway. So Jesus leaped down from the building, from a height that had killed the other boy, and spoke the dead boy's name, "Zenon! Rise up and tell me, did I throw you off this building?" And Zenon stood up and said, "No you didn't, but you have brought me back to life!" And the parents of the little boy glorified god for this sign he gave and they worshiped the boy Jesus.

On another day, a young man was chopping wood in a secluded spot in the forest. The ax fell wrong and cut his foot nearly in two and he began to lose a lot of blood and die. A crowd began to gather around the dying youth, and Jesus saw the gathering and wormed his way through the crowd. When he lifted the cut foot in his hands it immediately healed and the young man got up and continued his work. Jesus said for him to remember him. The crowd worshiped the child and said, "The spirit of God lives in this one."

His mother remembered when the boy was very young and she had sent him for water with a ceramic jug. Jostling in the crowd caused the jug to be smashed and broken. But the boy took his cloak and filled it with water and carried it home to his mother. She knew of his special-ness and did not speak of his deeds to anyone.

Antony chuckled at that. "Then how do we know that those things happened? What that means is that he did far more than was observed and written down, and his mother kept the secrets."

He continued: "But Joseph often saw the advantages of having such a child. One day when he was building a bed frame, Joseph realized the one piece of timber was shorter than the other. When he mentioned this to young Jesus..."

Antony observed out loud, "he never speaks of him as his own son, how interesting."

"... the boy took the smaller timber by the end and stretched it until it was the same length as the other. He embraced the boy and said, "I am blessed that God has given me this child."

It was getting really late. And Antony had to work the following day. So he stopped reading. And with very little resistance from the little boy, he carried him into his bed room and tucked him in.

A few days passed before Antony and Gwydion were able to start the stories again. More had been translated at the University. And Antony had copied the pages and brought them home and set them at the bottom of the stack for him to read when they got a private moment to do so.

With the little tousled headed boy in his lap again late one night, Antony began where he left off a few days back.

"So Joseph decided to send his son to school again, because he did not want him to go with out knowing how to read. This new teacher took the boy in and was soon vexed by the same questions as poor Zachaeus. Jesus taunted him with the demand, "If you are really a teacher, then tell me the power of Alpha and I will tell you the power of Beta." This aggravated the teacher and he struck Jesus in the head. This hurt the boy and he cursed the man who then fainted and landed on his face. Jesus walked back to Joseph's house and Joseph was smitten with grief and ordered the child's mother to never let him out the door again. "For those who anger him die."

Later, there was another instructor who offered to take the boy and teach him to read. "Perhaps with flattery I can teach him to read."

Joseph said, "Man, if you are that brave, take him then."

The teacher with fear and anxiety took the boy to the school. The boy walked into the schoolhouse full of confidence and grabbed a book lying on a desk. He opened it and instead of reading from it, he opened his mouth and the holy spirit began to speak through him teaching the law to those around him. The beauty and great craft of his words amazed the people there and a crowd began to gather around him. When Joseph heard about this he was afraid and rushed to the school to take his boy home. The teacher amazingly was still alive, and he told Joseph, "This boy has grace and wisdom. But please take him home now."

The boy laughed and said, "You have told the truth, so I will spare the other teacher too." And the other teacher he had cursed was healed, and Joseph took the boy home.

Joseph's natural son James went to gather some wood when a snake bit his hand, and was laying there starting to die. The boy Jesus had followed him, saw his hurt hand and the serpent and he breathed on the bite. The pain and the venom went away and the snake exploded, and James was fine.

Soon after this, an infant in Joseph's neighborhood died and when Jesus heard the wailing of its mother, he went there to see what was happening.

He saw the dead child and he put his finger on its chest and told it to live and come be with his mother. The child then opened it eyes and laughed. The crowd had seen this happen and they said, "This boy is either God or an angel of God and every word he says happens." And the boy Jesus went out to play with the other children.

Antony said to Gwydion, "This boy has very special powers. Do you have powers like that Gwydion?" Gwydion's big liquid eyes rolled up at him and he smiled up at his grand papa.

"I think it is a good thing you don't talk much, little man," said Antony quietly as he lifted the boy off to bed. "And when you do start talking, you will have learned what not to say. You can see what trouble it got the boy Jesus in." When the story continued in a few nights, there wasn't much left, but enough to take them late into the night.

Antony continued quietly:

"This small family made a customary trip to Jerusalem each year in a caravan for the Passover feast. As they turned for home in the caravan, Jesus went back up to the city instead. They traveled for a while but not till later did they realize that the boy was no longer in the caravan. So they went back up to the city and after searching for a while, they found him sitting in the temple surrounded by teachers, both listening and speaking. Although just a child, everyone was amazed that he was questioning his teachers sharply, explaining chief points of the law and the parables of the prophets. But his parents were not amused. "Why have you done this, we were worried." But the boy was irritated with them. "Why are you looking for me? Don't you know I am supposed to be here with the people who belong to my father?"

The scribes and the Pharisees teachers asked if she was his mother, and she answered yes. And they commended her that god had blessed her womb so. The family got up and started home and Mary didn't say a thing to those learned men about what was really going on."

Antony stacked the little papers on his side table and carried the little boy to bed. "I guess I will have to get to work and translate some more for us. For now it is bedtime."

# 9.
# Anna's Daughter

It was after Christmas time and things were beginning to be packed away again for the year.

Gwydion was always sad to see the pretty balls and lights get put away. But he knew they needed to get some sleep so they would be fresh and exciting next year when Christmas time came around again.

When they came to his favorite glass ball with the sugar and the glass cave with the baby in it, Gwydion began to put together who this represented, and who this woman was in there with the baby in a manger. Mary.

"Mary?" Asked Gwydion pointing to the figures in the glass ball.

His grand papa was helping pack up the Christmas decorations.

"Mother of Jesus," Antony said simply in answer. When Gwydion continued to stare at him in question, the answer got longer. "Well she was lots of things. Over the course of history she became the symbol for motherhood and saintly virginity"

"A virgin and a baby?"

"Well, that is a hard one. And I often wondered that myself. But when I started reading those translations, the ones we read at night, I realized how these things that were written in stories long ago were really quite different than what people thought."

Gwydion did not look up from stacking the glass balls in the packing paper. "Immaculate conception," he said to his grand papa. It always surprised Antony when his grandson used these big words, words you wouldn't possible think a ten year old boy would know the meaning of. He wondered if maybe the child was a really just a good mimic. He thought probably so. But maybe not just that. Maybe he understood more about the concepts than one might think.

"Ends up Gwydion, immaculate conception is a misnomer. Really when you read the oldest stories you realize that not only was it an immaculate conception, conceiving a baby without the father's 'donation', but it could also be called an immaculate birth. There was no mess like with usual births. In fact the midwife that examined Mary found her completely clean and there was no blood. And it is even said her hand where she examined the mother burst into flame from the doubting of God and the defamation of the virgin. And the newborn baby Jesus put out the flame."

Young Gwydion wagged his head back and forth in a motion that Antony had come to understand as the settling of new information in the young boys head.

"In fact," said Antony, "one of those stories says the baby Jesus came into this world in a ray of light."

With that Gwydion stood up, danced a small jig in a circle and sat back down with a thump.

"But you know he was not the first one. It is written in the oldest of books on Jesus, written by his half-brother Jacob, like our last name. Or the more modern name, James, His father Joseph's first son, by Joseph's first wife. We don't know her name. But apparently there is a long story as to how Mary came to be Joseph's second wife. This James wrote a book that became well known within 150 years of Jesus death and became popular and inspired many works of pictorial art in the middle ages. Well known, so soon after, very fast. Though not as fast as nowadays, with encyclopedias and stuff."

Antony got up from his chair and picked up a wide flat book from the shelves and sat down next to Gwydion on the floor. He cracked it open for both of them to see and Gwydion would cock his head a little and look at the pages as his grand papa flipped through them and described the art work. Pre-renaissance paintings in the great galleries of the world.

Gwydion poked his finger onto one of the pictures, a pi-eta of Mother and child, the child holding his finger in the air with a wise smile on his tiny face. The mother Máry has a wise look of her own secrets on her quirking mouth.

"The lady have a halo too!" Gwydion said in his high falsetto voice.

"Very good," Said Antony. "You noticed that right off. Its been debated that perhaps the medieval folks had too much worship of the virgin Mary and later the Christian church tried to wipe out those heathen ideas. But in truth, in the oldest of bible stories, those left out of the big black book, Jesus was not the first born of god on earth, no. It was his mother, Mary."

"This one we call "Proto-Gospel of James."

Joachim was a wealthy man who lived in Israel." Antony continued reading to Gwydion late one night the newest stories that had been translated from the recently found scrolls.

"His name can be found in the histories of the twelve tribes if Israel. He was so wealthy that he used to offer double his

portions of his gifts to the lord. But on the great day of their lord, he approached first to give his gifts, he was
stopped by Reuben who said, "You are not allowed to give your gifts first as you have not born any children to Israel."

So Joachim went and looked in the book of the histories of the twelve tribes to see if truly he was the only man in Israel who had not yet born children. And, lo, it was true, he was the only one. He was very sad in his heart. But he remembered the old story of Abraham, who near the end of his life was given by god a son, Isaac. But even then that was no comfort and he did not venture home that day to his wife, but headed out into the wilderness where he pitched his tent. He fasted for 40 days and nights and waited to be fed by a visit from his god.

"His wife Anna mourned twice over, as she was now a widow as well as being childless. She dressed in the clothes of mourning although the great day of the lord approached, and she sat herself in the garden to contemplate her woes. She made a prayer out loud to him, mentioning the blessing of the womb of Sarah late in her life with her son Isaac.

She gazed at the sky and..."

Antony interjected here, "This is really long. For an entire chapter she recites Woe is Me, and her various reasons why for her self pity. Lets skip all that and get on with it." Gwydion moved around a little because he wanted to hear more of his grand papa's story.

" After a good long afternoon of this lamenting and self wallowing, there appeared before her an angel of God.

"Anna, oh Anna. The lord has heard your prayer. And you will conceive a child and give birth, and that child will be spoken of world round."

And gladdened Anna replied, "Whether it be boy or girl, I will give this child to my lord and take care of him all its life."

"At this same moment, up on the hill in the wilderness, another angel appeared before poor Joachim, and said, "Go on down to your wife, because she is now with child." And Joachim rejoiced by bringing a herd of ten sheep, twelve calves, and one hundred goats for the people in celebration of this miracle of life.

When Joachim came down the hill, his wife ran up to him at the gate and hung around his neck with joy. And together they rested on Joachim's first day back at home."

"At seven months, Anna gave birth. She turned to the midwife and asked, "Is it a boy or a girl?" It was a girl and Anna felt her soul rejoice. She cleaned herself, nursed her new baby girl and named her Mary.

The child grew stronger every day. And when at six months of age, Anna set the child on the ground to see if she could walk. The baby Mary took seven steps and came into her mother's arms. But Anna said, " I will not let you walk on this ground until I have taken you up to the temple. " Then she cleaned the bedroom and made it a sanctuary for her child. She invited the other un-defiled daughters of the Hebrews in for a party.

On her first birthday, Joachim held a big feast for all, and the baby Mary was blessed by all there. They called on the most high god to bless this child with an ultimate blessing equal to none. Later in the sanctuary of her bedroom, Anna sung to the baby Mary, a song she devised to thank the lord for removing from her the reproach of her enemies.

She bore a beautiful child and now someone needs to report to the sons of Reuben and tell all of the twelve tribes of Israel that Anna has born a child and is nursing her.

When she turned two, they talked of needing to take her up to the temple, to fulfill the promise we made in thanks for this gift. Otherwise we may incur some harm and this gift deemed unacceptable." But Anna said, "Let us wait until she is three, other wise she may become homesick for her mother and father."

So when baby Mary turned three they took her up to the temple, with the other virgin girls carrying torches on their way up. And the priest there received her and gave her a kiss and said, "Your name will be great for all generations. Through you the lord will reveal his redemption to the sons of Israel for all time." He set her on the third step of the alter and she was blessed and she danced happily, and all of Israel loved her.

And until she was twelve, she was cared for there in the temple, and fed by the hand of an angel. But when she turned twelve they began to wonder what was to become of this young girl, as she would not be able to stay in the house of the lord, because she would soon be starting her womanly courses, and that would be an unclean thing to have in the temple. The chief priest, Zacharias, prayed and asked what to be done with this girl as she could not stay there. He prayed for an answer to this difficult question. And an angel appeared and instructed Zacharias, "Go gather all of the widowers, men without wives, and have them each bring a rod with them, and we will give her as wife to the one who is given a sign." And the heralds went forth and blew their trumpets and everyone came running.

Joseph, a local carpenter, set aside his work, grabbed a fagot of wood, and joined them in their meeting. When Zacharias had taken everyone's rods, he went inside and prayed. When he was done praying, he went back out with all the rods and handed them all back. But there was no sign, until the very last rod was given back to Joseph, and a white dove flew out of the rod and flew into the side of Joseph's head. And Zacharias said to Joseph, "You have been called to take the virgin into your safe keeping. But Joseph was stumped. "I cannot do this thing. I am an old man and I have grown sons, and she is just a young girl. I will be laughed at by all of them." And Zacharias threatened Joseph with the memories of how god opened the earth and swallowed Dathan, Abiram, and Korah for their arguing with him, ..."

Antony said to little Gwydion, "Oh, that's in the old testament, them wandering in the desert." Then he continued with the story...

..."and he should be afraid that he might be treated with the same things at his own house.

"But Joseph was afraid to take on the responsibilities of this young girl, the virgin from the temple. He had work to do and had to leave the house for long periods. But he instructed the young girl to stay there and wait for him to return.

Mary and some of the other virgins from the tribe of David were assigned the spinning of the yarn for the curtains of the temple. Mary took a pitcher to go fetch some water, and when she got outside she heard a voice saying to her, "Greetings, you who are favored. You are blessed among women."

But Mary could not tell where the voice was coming from. She ran back in the house afraid and set the empty pitcher on the floor, and took up her spinning and began to work at easing her anxieties.

As she took up the purple silk to spin, an angel appeared before her and said quietly to her, "Do not fear me, Mary. You are favored by the master of all and will conceive a child by his word." She was wondering to herself if this meant that she would have to do the things men and women do to have a child, and the angel answered her unspoken question, "No, His powers will be over you, and the one born from you will be called holy and you will name him Jesus and he will save these people from their sins."

And Mary told him, "I am the slave of my god. And that it be done as you say."

She took her spinning work into the temple and the priest told her she was blessed. She felt great joy at this and made her way to her relative's house, Elizabeth. When she knocked on the door, Elizabeth came running and asked Mary, "Why does the mother of our lord come visiting today? For see how this child I carry has leaped up and blessed you too."

But Mary in her joy of being so blessed, forgot the mysteries that had been revealed to her by the archangel Gabriel and looked at the sky and asked again, how could she be so blessed.

She stayed with Elizabeth for three days, and her belly grew and grew. But when she went home she went in fear. She hid herself on the way home, she was only sixteen at the time.

When she was in her sixth month, Joseph finally came home from his work away. When he came into the house, he saw immediately she was pregnant. He felt shame and proclaimed, "How can I go into the temple now? I am ashamed, I received this girl to watch over her and I have failed.

Who has preyed upon me and done this thing to me? Who has done this wicked thing in my home and defiled the virgin? This is the whole story of Adam played her on me, when he was away, the serpent led Eve astray."

Then he reproached Mary and asked her why she has done this thing to him.

But Mary wept bitterly and denied that she had done anything with another man.

"Then how have you become pregnant, he asked her. "By my god I do not know how."

Now Joseph was undecided. If he hid her pregnancy, he would be going against the laws. But if he reveals her condition to the sons of Israel, they will by law have to stone her for sins she may not have committed, for he suspected the child might be angelic.

So he decided he would divorce her.

But later that night an angel came to him in a dream. "Do not be afraid of this child," said the angelic vision. "For he comes from the holy spirit and this son you will name Jesus, for he will save your people from their sins." Then he felt favored when morning came round so he watched over this girl.

But the elders were not so easily convinced. Because Joseph had been away a few days from attending daily council, Annas the Scribe came to visit him and asked him why he has stayed away. Joseph gave him a weak an excuse, but when Annas turned and saw Mary, he ran and told the priest, "Joseph the one you vouched for, has done a bad thing. He has defiled the Virgin from this temple and stolen from her her wedding rights. And he has tried to keep it a secret."

The Priest looked at him skeptically. "Joseph has done this?"

"Yes," said Annas the scribe. "Send along some servants to see and you will find the virgin pregnant."

So the servants of the Priest went along and grabbed Mary and took her and Joseph back to the judgment hall, where he questioned Mary first. "Why have you done this great sin? You have gone against the temple where you were raised and fed by hand from an angel, heard the hymns and danced before god?"

And Mary wept bitterly. "I swear I am pure and have not been active that way with any man."

So the Priest turned to Joseph, frustrated with Mary's stubbornness, and asked him, "Why have you done this?"

And Joseph said to the priest, "I swear that I am pure towards her."

"Do not bear false witness, you two. Tell me the truth. You have stolen her wedding rights and not revealed this to the sons of Israel. And you, Joseph, have not bowed beneath the heavy hand that your offspring might be blessed."

And Joseph kept his silence, for he knew of his innocence, and that of Mary too, but he could not say what he knew, that this priest could never believe, suspecting the simplest of sins.

"So," demanded the priest, "Hand over the virgin of the temple. I will have you both drink the Lord's "water of refutation", and it will reveal your sins to your own eyes."

"So the Priest gave the Lord's water of refutation, the wild herb tea, to Joseph and sent him off to the wilderness. But Joseph came back soon healthy and happy. So Mary was given the Lord's water of refutation to drink, the green bitter herb tea, and was sent into the wilderness.

But she too returned safe and happy, with no sins revealed to her by way of becoming sick.

And the priest was bound to agree, "if your sins have not been revealed to you and made you sick with your own guilt, then I cant judge you either." So he sent them home.

And Mary and Joseph went home happy that the God of Israel believed so deeply in that kind of superstition.

But still the mystery remained of this girl's pregnancy. Because Joseph had not been there, and he seriously doubted this girl was interested in doing that kind of thing with a man. So he kept it all to himself and decided simply to care for her and her child, and to care of it as if his own.

"On that note," said Antony, "I think it is bed time."

'"Water of refutation?" said Gwydion.

"It might have just been superstition, that if you aren't honest then this blessed drink will make you sick with guilt. Or maybe they had more knowledge of herbs back then. And many plants have medicinal properties. There might be one that makes people tell the truth. Although I can't tell you which one it is."

Antony tucked Gwydion into bed, hoping that was enough of an explanation.

In a few nights, they were up late again and could begin again the story where they left off.

"As Mary grew large, an order came from the King Augustus that everyone from Bethlehem to Judea was to be registered for a census. And Joseph asked himself, "I shall of course register my sons. But how shall I register this girl child, Mary? As my wife? I would be too ashamed, she is so young. As my daughter? But everyone in Judea knows that she is not my daughter."

He couldn't make up his mind, so he relented to the will of the day to decide what was going to happen, and continued on their journey south, trying to get south to the city of Augustus to register his sons in the census.

So he saddled the donkey and sat Mary, now large with child, upon the beast.

Symeon his son led the donkey along while Joseph walked behind. He looked back at Mary and found her to seem sad. Then a mile later he looked back at Mary again, and found her happy. And he asked her why. "Why do you seem happy one moment and then sad the next?"

And Mary replied, "It is that I see two peoples in this land. One is weeping and mourning. And the other group of peoples is happy and rejoicing.

He knew not what she meant so he said, "What does this mean? Do not say these unnecessary things to me."

And there appeared a beautiful child dressed in shining robes. And he said to Joseph, "Why do you call her words unnecessary? She is perceptive and sees the Jews weeping for having lost God. And then the Gentiles rejoicing at the arrival of their savior."

She became uncomfortable on this donkey, and said to the two men with her, "Take me down from this donkey. This baby is pressing on me to come out."

"But where shall we take you to hide your shame? This is a wilderness area."

They found a cave and Joseph left Mary there with his son in charge, and went out looking for a Hebrew midwife in this region of Bethlehem. For this was not a Hebrew region.

They found a cave for her and made a bed and set her in it, with Mary saying prayers all the time. Then the two men stepped out of the cave to go look for a midwife.

But something strange happened, as was later told by James and Joseph.

Later he would tell his son, "I was walking, but I was not walking, as if I stood still in mid stride." James eyes had grown wide at the telling. "So I looked up into the sky, and it was greatly disturbed with clouds and yet they stood still, with the flying birds standing still in it too, in mid flight. I looked around me and people that were eating were frozen in place too. And everyone was looking up. Then just as suddenly, everything began to resume its normal course of movement again. "

As Joseph continued to walk, looking for a Hebrew midwife, he saw a woman coming down out of the mountains. And she asked him where he was going. He replied that he was looking for a Hebrew midwife. So she asked him if he was from Israel.

And then she asked who was the one who gave birth in a cave. And Joseph just looked at her, amazed at how she could have had known this information. He explained that the girl was not his wife, but his betrothed, that she had been raised in the temple and given to him in trust, but that now this girl was pregnant by the holy spirit.

She said a young man had come to her in a hurry, telling of a maiden who was about to give birth with her first offering, the blood sacrifice of birth. And so she had come with the chair often used in birthing children. The midwife had been amazed at this story, so she followed with Joseph back to the cave to tend Mary.

When they reached the cave, a bright cloud stood over the cave and blinded them with a light. As the light faded they all saw an infant standing there. The child then went over to Mary and began to nurse from her breast. And the midwife said that this was a miracle and salvation has been sent to Israel.

So the midwife went back outside and found her midwife friend, Salomey, and told her of this new wonder. But Salomey was doubtful and said, 'I will need to examine this girl to see if this is true. Because I have never seen anyone give birth without there being a great deal of signs of it."

So Salomey went into the cave and told Mary to brace herself because she needed to do an examination of her private birthing area. And as she put her hand in there to check, she arched back screaming, "See I have doubted this miracle and now my hand is burning and falling away from my body!" She dropped to her knees and began to pray fervently, that she was a loyal servant.

Then a bright light appeared again and the angel of the lord stood before her and said, "Yes we've heard your prayer. Lift up this child and you will find salvation and joy."

Salomey's hand was healed and she was so happy. She ran out of the cave to tell all, but the big booming voice told her not to tell anyone until they were back in Jerusalem safely.

Joseph and this group were ready to go back to Jerusalem, but there was a lot of activity going on. Then a group of Magi appeared, wise men, who asked where the new king of Israel was, because they had seen his star in the east. Joseph told them to be quiet. But they said they had asked the high priests, where is this new king supposed to be born?

In Bethlehem, they were answered, as it is written in old scripture. And yes there will be, the wise men were told, there would be a magnificent star shining among the other stars and overshadowing them with its brightness. And sure enough when the wise men got to the cave, the star they had been following was hanging right over the entrance. They took out gifts from their capes and gave them to the child. "

And here Antony stopped the story, and looked down at the drowsy boy. "This is where the nativity story comes from. You know, your favorite glass ornament with the baby Jesus in a manger." Gwydion's eyes looked up and got wide. "Yup. That's the old story," Antony said as he carried the boy off to bed in the dark quiet of the late night apartment.A few nights later, Antony was able to continue his late night telling of the nativity story to his grandson.

"But as they began to return toward home, toward Judea, the angel appeared again before them and warned them not to go back through there. So they decided to go home by a different route.

King Herod realized that he was being mocked by the wise men, for HE was the king, not some babe. So he ordered that all the infants under two years of age all be killed. When Mary heard they were looking to kill hers, and all other babies, she wrapped her infant in swaddling blankets and hid him in a manger. But when Elizabeth, James wife, heard they were going to come kill her son John, she wrapped him all up and headed into the wilderness. And when she found no place to hide, she prayed fervently for a place to hide them for safety. A light came down and an angel visited and opened the mountain and they were able to hide there safe and sound.

Then Herod's servants came and found her husband, Zacharias, the babe's father, and demanded him tell him where the baby is. And Zacharias said to him, "I am the minister of this Temple. How can I always know where my son and wife are?"

So the servants reported this back to Herod, who became enraged. They warned, "This Son is about to rule Israel."

So Herod sent another servant with murderous intent to talk to Zacharias the Priest again. And the servant told him, "tell us the truth, where is your son? Because you know that I have the right to slay you with my own hand."

And Zacharias replied firmly, "I will be God's witness if you shed my blood. Because then I will visit him directly; because you will shedding innocent blood in the forecourt of the Temple."

And he was murdered then around dawn, and his blood made a pool on the floor of the Temple.

And he wasn't found until later, when the other priests came to visit. And there they mourned and after ward they assigned Symeon the role of priest in the stead of the now murdered and dead Zacharias. Symeon they all knew was the one chosen for this place, as he had been informed years earlier that he would not ever die of old age, until he saw alive the flesh of the Messiah himself.

But I, James, the one writing down this account of my step brother, Jesus, hid in the wilderness, while the fervor of the mystery in the death of the King Herod calmed down and died away. But that is another story."

# 10.
# Gwydion's Apocrypha

The child in his lap had not moved in a while. So Antony thought he was probably asleep and probably had been for some time.

But Antony had kept reading, he always found these old stories to be so engaging, even though they were difficult to read sometimes, with their strange sometimes changing name spellings and seeming incorrect diction. They were part of an old oral history of story telling. And who knows how old they actually were. They might even be older than the birth of the supposed messiah. And had been taken up afresh when some miracles seemed to appear. When the old story line matched to something that was happening. And that's when they started calling the story prophecy. People at the time were probably really ready for some refreshing help from greater powers.

But some of these books were later rejected and cast out of the big black book. And when they were rediscovered thousands of years later, that lent them an even greater sense of power, an even greater sense of intrigue, to have been hidden or lost for so long, then rediscovered.

Antony quietly stacked up the papers of the translations. The little boy stirred in his lap. "What?" he mumbled quietly. "What Grand papa, finished?"

Antony was always amazed at this little quiet child's ability to listen and remember things. Maybe it was just mimicry. But maybe not. Maybe it settled somewhere in there to be processed later. And after all, wasn't that learning? If he remembered everything, and then was able to recall it later in his life, he could synthesize and use it. That was a kind of learning. Wasn't it? Just not the kind that was rewarded in the public schools, where they wanted regurgitation of facts, but not thinking skills. Certainly questions were not rewarded, Antony remembered from his harsh upbringing in the single room school house in Kansas, a million years ago. Where he was smacked on the hand with a ruler for asking a question.

Antony's mind jerked back to the present. Bethany was standing at the door to the kitchen. "Don't you think you should put the little guy to bed?"

Antony looked up sullenly. "We were just reading the Apocrypha."

In his lap the little boy said out loud, "Apocrypha."

Antony smiled and chuckled quietly. Coming from this little boy's mouth it almost sounded like a hiccup. "See. He is listening."

Bethany was not so amused. "It's like midnight." She walked toward them with her arms outstretched. "Come on little man. Let's go to bed." Little Gwydion's arms reached out automatically for his grand mama and she lifted him up with a grunt. "Getting to be a big man, aren't we?" she asked him. He did nothing but cuddle her and find his thumb's way into his mouth. "Let's go," she said as she walked with him out of the living room into the room he shared with his mother and father.

When Bethany came back into the living room, she sat down in the not so soft chair next to Antony's. "What is that stuff you are reading to him, anyway?"

"Some new things I am studying. Those fragments are so old, they have really lit my fire. People writing stories down thousands of years ago, in languages I can actually read a little bit. Greek, Latin. Wow. It really blows my mind."

"What are you talking about, hun? That big black book again?"

"You know as well as I do that it fascinates most people around the world, that crazy book whether true or not. Great stories. But the thing for me is that those in there are not all of them. There are stacks and stacks more of this stuff lying around. It was hidden, various parts of it, at different times in history. They were trying to make the story fit their various agendas, and they simply just threw some of this out. But some of it has been found."

"Let me see this. Apocrypha. Not sure what that means," she said with a yawn.

"OH, heresy, hidden. Something like that. Might be the root word to Hypocrisy."

"What's in it?"

"You should just really read them. Gospels that were thrown out. Mary for instance has a Gospel of her own."

"What? Mary has a gospel? What does she say?"

"Well, she was taught by Jesus himself. There are lots of teachings that actually kinda sound like Eastern mysticism. People like to say they were lovers or were married. But why does that have to be?"

"Ya. Why does the woman always have to take the lover role. And not an equal intellectual student role. So it shows that in there?"

"There's nothing about worldly love in there that I see. Not one tiny bit," said Antony.

After a moment he continued, "You know what is really strange about those passages in that particular apocrypha? Her friend, Elizabeth, the wife of Zacharias? She took the babe up into the wilderness and God opened a mountain for the two of them to hide in. Now why would god do that for just any friend of Mary's? Just because Zacharias is an important priest?"

"I have no idea," said Bethany. "Because, you know, this baby John he protected? Now this particular John, that becomes John the Baptist. "

"Whoa," says Bethany. "I didn't know any of that. "

Antony opened his eyes wide and nodded his head.

"These stories are so intertwined. They were stories told orally over and over again, and when you do that, they become consistent. They begin to reflect what people want, expect, to hear."

"As in the story of Scheherazade, mmm Arabians Nights. 'If you don't catch the people in the few seconds, you've lost them listeners."

"Yes. The story has to immediately hit a chord. And one way to do that is to use the same characters over and over. So these listeners would know just who this John was they were talking about. John the Baptist, and they would be thinking, 'Oh goodie. Here comes the part about John the Baptist as a baby.' But we who have never heard this part of the story because it was taken out of the bible, aren't even wondering yet who this John baby is. We don't know yet, so it slips by us. Yet those people a thousand years ago were ready for it and knew exactly what was going to happen without the story teller being any clearer than just saying his name."

"Fascinating," said Bethany yawning and stretching. "Now can we go to bed?"

"Always thinking of my health, huh, Bethany."

"Yes, dear."

He dropped the book on the table. The book that had now been compiled of the old apocrypha into a manuscript getting ready to be printed and presented to the public.

On one of its pages, a paragraph hung between the 'then' and the 'now', spanning almost two thousand years of history.

"On their Egyptian exile to escape the wrath of Herod's decree to kill all infant boys, the holy family, Jesus and his mother, visited the city of Luxor, already then a monument to extreme antiquities, the ancient past, the writings of the Pharaohs by now being unreadable by the more modern era Nazarenes.

Near the river, the Luxor temple languishes of old. It is the awe-inspiring monument built by Amenophus 3 and others of the eighteenth dynasty to the greater glory of the God Amon. It had become also a monument to the ages of Roman, Christian and Muslim worship with its inscriptions and carvings, some of them of Ankh Anhoten and Nefertiti, the mother and father of Tutankhamen, with their oblong skulls and long jaws.. And as they wondered north, they saw the avenues of sphinxes towards the spectacular Temple of Karnak."

As the family walked along this alleyway of forgotten Kings and Gods, Bethany looked around at these giant figures and said to Antony in bewilderment. "What are all these figures?"

"These are called the idols of the Days. There is one for each of the 365 days of the year. "

"And that little statue of the cat over there? That must be the one quarter day each 4 years."

Antony rolled his eyes at her whit and chuckled. "But really, it is said in one of the Apocrypha, that on their Exile in Egypt, Mary, Joseph and Jesus walked down this very alley. And in some of the stories that were left out of the big book, they said He, the boy Jesus, had strange powers over these statues. One says they all came to life and danced with him. In another, the statues all fell flat on their faces, for they could not face his brilliance, for they knew of his true divinity."

"Sounds metaphoric, for how he changed the way people thought about other gods." She looked around at all the different representations of God in these figures towering over their heads, and said, "So this is true paganism, isn't it?"

"Yes, in the true sense of the word, being of many-Gods. Although some would say it really means 'religion of the earth.' But I think the meaning of God here is different. Although later the church became very protective of its way of understanding that term."

Gwydion squealed and ran over and hugged a big statue of a cat. The basalt rock carving had a collar and huge eyes staring forward. Mags ran and grabbed Gwydion. "Now honey. We are not supposed to touch anything."

Gwydion scowled a little, but took off in another direction squealing the word 'cats' over and over again. "He really likes the cats," said Mags as she walked back over to her family, and Gwydion prowled nearby.

"Well, the Egyptians worshiped the cat above all other personages of God. Images of them are everywhere. They were thought to watch over and protect us and the dead from the underworld."

Bethany gave him a curious look. "That's odd. The Europeans for centuries considered the cat to be evil, to be the work and messenger of the Devil himself."

"Yes. And then they gave us the black plague across Europe." said Antony.

"I don't follow..." said Mags.

"It is widely understood that the plague was spread by fleas, fleas carried in the fur of rats. And what eats Rats? Cats . And when the church decided cats were evil and that they all should be killed, the rats multiplied unchecked in the city streets and in homes. And the plague spread everywhere there were rats."

"Talk about stupid prejudice!" said Mags.

"That prejudice may even have started here, in Egypt, "said Antony.

"Now I don't follow," said Bethany.

"Imagine this old pagan society worshiping cats and other animal deities. And then the new One God religion comes along fighting for its new life, diametrically opposed to this old way. So, logically they will hate cats because they symbolize what was worshiped by this old religion, this ancient culture. Remember, at the time of Jesus birth, this Egyptian culture was thousands of years old. Thousands. Older than Christianity is to us now. Egyptian culture was dying down. But it must have felt like an old threat, maybe even superstitiously so. It was exactly what this new religion had to fight against to gain hold. Oh, and there were other old ancient religions of El, and other gods of the earthly powers. But this Egyptian civilization.

Now that was exactly where these people of the 'One-God ' Religion came from. Remember, the Jews being exiled from Egypt as slaves? They made their own new religion there in the desert, apart from their birthplace, Egypt," Antony said, as they strolled between these old gods carved smooth in huge stone plinths.

"But like I said, I don't think these were gods in the sense we think of Gods now.

These 'idols' represented each day of the season, as they helped them to understand the agricultural seasons which fed these people. Not actual god-people. Because the Egyptians didn't need gods at all. For according to their own religion, the Egyptian Pharaohs were actually the Gods themselves. Or the direct descendants of them anyway."

"What do you mean by that, dad?" said Mags, looking over at his serene face looking up at long dead gods carved in stone maybe ten thousand years ago.

"I don't know. Just that sometimes I think we are still stuck in our prejudices, and still missing the big picture here somehow."

Gwydion continued to prance and dance in this isle of stone god figures, but his mind saw a different thing.

These creatures came alive as he danced before them. They grew fur and began to make their own animal noises, joining him in his little world. The lions stepped off their pedestals and walked beside him. The leopard and its spots trotted regally next to them. Birds flew and hoofed beasts frolicked in joy beside this little god-human that possessed the understanding of all life connected together in one dance.

Book 3

# The Broken Scroll

## A Murder Mystery

NM Reed

# Prologue

The man bled-out quickly, the wound to his neck extensive, the cut going almost all the way through. His last moments of consciousness were spent in utter surprise, as he tried to cry out, but only gargled on his own blood. The small sharp ceremonial knife lay beside him on the bed, half wrapped in a sticky bath towel. His killer finished buttoning his shirt, he flipped over that offensive painting on the wall over the bed, and left the apartment silently, after palming one of the man's keys, so he could lock the bolts on the door from the outside.

That way, he thought, they wouldn't find the body as quickly by accident.

Three days later, the authorities were compelled to publish a news release. The growing rumors and rampant gossip spread quickly throughout the university campus and the foreign scholastic community.

The report was a small entry in the middle of the news papers in several cities associated with his university and church. He was after all an American professor. Ancient languages of the Bible, with an ecclesiastic background.

Needless to say, the communities were shocked.

Most people never saw the press release, but his former associate from the Cairo University read it sitting at a kitchen table in New York.

And the news clip ran as follows:

North Africa. Cairo, Egypt: An American professor at the Cairo university has been found dead in his apartment on September 3, 1964. The details of his death have not been released, but foul play is suspected.

Anyone with information please contact the local authorities. There is no known motive. There are no suspects being held at this time. Names and details will be released when the next of kin have been identified and notified.

# 1.
# Monastery

### May 5, 1962, two years earlier....

The sun was slanting like a golden knife from the west as the monk in the back of the monastery tended the herb garden, as he usually did in the afternoons. His jobs were simple, and he enjoyed the isolation and the simplicity of his life.

On this particular day, as he was bending over weeding the lavender, he heard a loud banging on the back gate. He stood up and dusted his hands off, and listened. The loud banging resumed.

Dafud sauntered over to the solid gate wondering who would be bothering him. He slipped open the wooden peep hole and looked out.. Bedouins.

Bedouins on horses; two of them.

What the heck.

Despite himself, he inched open the big wooden gate and peered out at them. In Arabic he asked, "What do you want?"

Being secretive people of few words for strangers, they rustled in their robes and produced a small bundle which they slowly unwrapped. The coarsely dressed and unshaven Bedouin held out his filthy hand and showed Dafud what they had brought for him.

Curious, Dafud leaned in a little closer and inspected the dirty little pile of stuff the older graying Bedouin proffered.

Old pieces of leather. Crumbling, dirty.

Dafud stepped back and looked them in their dirty faces.

He shook his head no, and stepped back and closed the solid wood gate on them. As he walked back to his gardening, he shook his head in disbelief. What possibly could those old ruffians think I would want with a pile of old leather pieces?

When the solid wooden gate shut in their faces, the two rebuffed Bedouins turned and rode off, promising themselves they would never do business with the Arch Bishop and his monastery again.

And so it took the Archbishop many attempts to get these Bedouins to talk to him again. The simple monk who tends the gardens had simply not gotten the message that they had been expecting these particular Bedouins that day. And that he had intended to buy the things that they had agreed to sell to him.

For they were not just any dirty old pieces of leather. In fact with time these dirty old pieces of decaying leather that the Bedouins had found in some caves in the desert, were the first of what would become known at the Lost Sea Scrolls.

# 2.
# Antiqua Shops

The persistent sun beat down on their heads and shoulders as they walked down the street of Antiqua shops. Most were outside sellers, with canvas covers pulled over onto poles in the early morning to fend off the relentless sun. The sun seemed to be everywhere. It shone down from the sky and was reflected back up from the golden sands to shine under the tables, and back up into the eyes, even when you stood in the shade.

To Mags, there seemed to always be a pervasive humming in the air here in Egypt. This was very different from Kansas where they grew up. Or heavens, New York where they would go to visit relatives on holidays. Now *that* was Mars. Or Costa Rica, where everything was green.

But here in Egypt, besides being an exotic place, it just felt different. The buzzing was always present if the sun was shining. Was it the extreme heat and the total lack of trees? Was the sun resonating in extreme energy forces they could not see? Was it some wild bug in the air or sand? Like back in Kansas, they had the cicada bugs up in the trees that would let off such a loud buzzing clicking noise, sometimes you thought you were hearing things or maybe going to go deaf. Or at least were going to get a big fat head ache.

But here in Egypt it was different from that too. She would often buy a small cup of coffee, what they would snottily call a demi-tass in New York, and sip it slowly, its strong sweet flavor heating her up from the inside and making her sweat. This must be some old Bedouin secret, she thought. Drink this crazy thick hot caffeine drink in the mid day temperatures and it makes you sweat and cools you off.

She finally realized after being here a while that was another of their secrets, wearing all those cotton robes. She had always wondered about that. But she understood it now and always wore a layer of white cotton to completely cover her skin. An uncovered portion of your skin would burn and blister in a matter of hours out here. And you would become dehydrated from exposure. So you wore layers of cotton that absorbed your sweat and kept you cool for hours.

She thought about all those Americans laying in the sun, ruining their skin by sun bathing, and realized how much more experienced these people were with battling the natural elements of wind, sun, and exposure.

But it still didn't explain the buzzing in her ears.

She bought her daily coffee and tried an experiment. She would listen closely and see if the buzzing changed. In a few minutes she realized it felt different. The edge was off, and she felt herself relax into the heat and the buzzing in her ears.

She walked along with Gwydion walking right next to her down the sandy road with sellers on each side and people milling everywhere between. Gwydion was a little more relaxed these days. He had calmed and focused quite a bit of the last few years. But his intensity was still there. He would study things intently with his big brown eyes wide open taking it all in. And people were intimidated by him and seemed to fear him just a little. He learned not to tarry too long at any one stall for fear of getting a swat from the seller and told to leave.

They began to hear a buzzing and rhythmic sound up ahead. She wondered if this was the buzzing noise in her ears?

No. Up ahead was music being played. The strange hypnotic music played here in this part of the world. Gwydion was focused intently on it, almost mesmerized, and they kept walking until they were in front of the booth. Several musicians were playing a strange rhythm and strange sounds. There was one drummer playing a drum with mosaic colors in its surface and what looked like fish skin complete with scales for its drum head. Another played a flanged flute with a nasal sound to it, kinda like a horn. The third man was seated at a flat boxed stringed instrument and thrummed it with several tiny hammers in each hand.

This music never ceased to amaze and move her. These rhythms were totally alien to her western mind. They were not square, and really could not be latched onto. She could not count them. Like you would count a waltz, one two three one two three. Or a Beatles song, one two one two. It was just not there. She would try to count the rhythm, get to eleven and get mixed up, then start again get to nine and then it would change again. She thought maybe she should take some college classes in music. But she doubted this stuff was even there. Had anyone studied this strange ancient music of the desert sands and winds and figured out and written it down? She truly doubted it, and figured she had better just relax and enjoy it. The Turkish coffee buzz was helping her do that, so she focused back on the musicians. The small painted sign propped up on an old jar read, "Nasim Sahara". Desert Wind, that seemed appropriate. And like the thick sweet coffee, this music seemed to mimic the buzzing and held you in it sway.

There was a small lone dancer on a colorful carpet in front of them twisting and swaying to these strange rhythms. Her swaying kept time with the rhythm, although it was very strange. Mags thought this is not anything like what we think of "belly dancers" back in America. There was sensuality; but not that brazen almost stripper quality that there always was back home. This girl was completely covered in layers of beautiful colored silks and shiny bits of mirror and metal and was barefoot. She moved her dusty feet in imperceptible steps to the rhythm and her skirts swayed hypnotically. Her hands were held up and her arms twisted and folded like the bodies of snakes, with her hands, fingers and palms like the neck and head of cobras. Her small veiled head remained still and her eyes wandered and locked onto this or that person. When her kohl lined eyes lit on Gwydion, they grew wide then she looked away.

But his eyes were not on her, and perhaps she thought this strange. No, his eyes were on the santoor, the stringed instrument much like a hammered dulcimer. He watched the player's arms pumping, and the hammers, two in each of the splayed fingers, as he pounded the hundred strings in a rhythm so fast, to Gwydion's eyes it was a syncopatic blur. The sound was a hypnotic blur and it thrilled Gwydion deep inside his bones. The rhythm itself was entrancing by its unpredictable quality. Just when you thought you could follow it, the rhythm would change and take off in a completely different direction. He figured this was something that could not be written down, but had to be learned in your bones from a lifetime of playing.

They threw a couple coins, baksheesh, into the basket and continued walking. Mags felt that the sounds seemed to match the buzzing in her head and seemed to sway with the relaxed feeling of the strong Turkish coffee she had just finished.

The extreme heat and sun, the pervasive buzzing in the air, the strange music and swaying of the lithe dancer, all these things seemed to fit together and form a mosaic that described her experience here. These things seemed to combine deep in her primal psyche, somehow linked through the ages of human civilization.

# 3.

# Dinner

When they arrived home after their fun in the market, Mags and Gwydion found Gwydion's grand mother and grand father in the kitchen making dinner. Well, Bethany was making dinner and Antony was sitting at the kitchen table leafing thru his newspaper. They weren't talking much, it seemed to Mags, but the two of them came in and sat down anyway.

"So how was the market?" asked Bethany trying to start a conversation with her daughter.

"It was fun. We watched some musicians and a dancer. It was pretty hypnotic," answered Mags to her mother. Her father got up and straggled out of the kitchen toward the living room and his favorite slouched leather chair. He seemed mesmerized by his newspaper. The two women just glanced at each other, knowing exactly what the other was thinking.

After a few moments, Mags asked her mother, "Something at the University?"

"Seems like there is something going on, yes. But he wont say. At least not yet," answered Bethany. She was used to her husband taking his time to lighten up and tell her when things were going on in his work day, things that often made him clam up.

Changing the subject, Mags asked, "What are we having?"

"Sloppy Joe's. Yum. Only vegetarian. No meat in the market today. At least none worth affording," answered Bethany cryptically.

"Sloppy Joe's!" cried Gwydion. This must be his favorite meal, thought both the women, and they opened the cupboard and pulled out the large blue plates which were required for this particular favorite meal of Gwydion's.

In a few hours when stomachs and minds were settling in for the night, the family had gathered in the living room for the last few minutes before it was actually bedtime. Antony set down his newspaper and looked around, as if suddenly aware of those around him. Bethany took this as a sign and actually asked him a direct question, although she did not look right at him when she said it.

"So what is happening at work these days, dear?"

He looked over at her, as if just arising from the mists of Loch Ness. He was thinking, "How do I even start?"

He breathed deeply and then blew it out slowly like a small gentle Poseidon, blowing away the monsters of his particular little lake.

"Some new things were discovered in the desert," he said simply.

"Secrets!" said Gwydion, throwing up his arms.

Everyone looked at him and smiled. Antony actually guffawed. "Yes, kiddo, Secrets. Lots of them."

"What do you mean honey?" Beth asked, trying to keep him going on his favorite subject, his work.

"Manuscripts. Lots of them. Old ones. Really old ones," he said.

"New ones?" asked Mags. She remembered the fragments that they had found in the Antiqua dealer a few years back. And how those tiny old fragments of papyrus had startled the world.

A couple tiny old fragments with a few Greek words that hinted that they had been written by a contemporary of Jesus Christ. And the carbon dating of them had verified the fact. And it had shocked the scholarly world.

"A veritable hoard of new scrolls have been found in the desert," he said.

"Where?" asked Bethany.

"They are now at the foundation musee."

"No, where were they found?" she asked again.

"In the desert. By the Dead Sea," he said half numb with the discovery still.

"The Dead Sea? There's nothing there," said Mags. "Rocks and dirt."

"Well, there has been these old ruins that have been just sitting there forever and no one ever bothered to go take a look. Well it turns out there are caves there too and in them, treasures of manuscripts. Some Bedouin found them when he was looking for a lost goat."

"A lost goat!" Gwydion cried to the ceiling. They all laughed again.

"Yes, a lost goat. They guy goes to look for his lost goat and falls into a cave that is housing a bunch of 2000 year old manuscripts."

"No," said Bethany skeptically. "Not actually two thousand years old. Couldn't be so simple. There was that big thing about those little scraps that were dated at around 60 A.D. That caused a stir last year." Bethany thought for a moment then asked, "Have you actually dated them yet?"

"Ya, they have that fancier expensive machine now that dates them really fast. Over 2000 years old. They found one that is the Book of Isaiah. Amazing. Treasure."

Everyone just looked at him for a minute. Gwydion, because he had never seen his grand papa look so spooked. Bethany because she knew what the book of Isaiah meant.

And Mags because she had no idea what that meant but didn't want to show her ignorance.

Finally Bethany said, "The book of Isaiah, that's Old Testament. Lordy. Is that the oldest they have ever found?"

"Yup. The oldest previous to this was 800 year ago translations from Greek that we sitting around some castle, and they used those to make the modern bible. Before that there is no record. We have no copies of any of this stuff before 800 years ago. That means, that when the bible was written, the one we use, that stuff was already 12 hundred years old. No records for 1200 years. Seems impossible. I guess they were just destroying things. Copy them how they wanted it to be remembered. And then destroy them." He looked at his wife with haunted eyes. "They think they have found as many as one hundred separate documents. I think this is going to blow this thing apart."

It was beginning to sink in to Mags now. And she let out a slow low whistle. "Atheists have been waiting for this forever. Some real proof."

"Well, it will either prove it or disprove it," Antony said.

"Oh, I cant wait to hear what it translates," said Mags in youthful enthusiasm.

"I assure you, there are plenty of people who are very happy to make us all wait for these translations," answered Antony.

"The world needs to see those things," said Bethany quietly. "We deserve the truth."

"But they are in certain people's hands," said Antony.

"Those ancient words belong to the world," said Mags emphatically.

"I agree. By the way, I have been chosen to be on the translation team," said Antony quietly.

A little cheer went up from his family. But he did not look that happy. To Bethany, he looked weighted down. Perhaps even a little scared.

When it got quiet, he said, "It is a little heavy. But I will do my best."

# 4.
# Scroll Divided

After two thousand years of Christianity, there had never been found any proof of the oldest origins, any older than about 800 years, those old documents which were the basis of the modern "Old Testament." It was never dreamed there would be found anything older.

Documents just didn't last that long. Especially if they were on papyrus or leather parchment, they would never survive the elements.

No one even thought to look in the small unnoticed area of the desert . No one suspected there it could harbor such secrets. In the crux of the ancient old dead sea, where no one had lived in forever and ages ago these secrets lay waiting to be discovered. The sea was dead and lifeless and hung with a foggy stink almost year round. Life did not grow there as the water there was poisonous, and there was almost no rain. Ever. Less than two inches of rain fell in this dry crackling region of the desert. How could the origins of one of man's great religions grow up in this area of lifelessness? It was never even dreamed of.

But when those old pieces of leather had been found in the dry caves, where they had been ransacked and tossed into the cavern as so much heretical garbage by invading Roman soldiers trying to wipe out these new sects of a new religion that defied the old pagan Roman gods. Yes, Christianity was the heretical new religion at the time.

The caves were accidentally discovered by a shepherd chasing a lost goat, who literally stumbled into it. The startled shepherd broke open the old dusty pot and found rolls of what looked like leather. When he first presented these scraps to some clergy men at the monastery, they were skeptical and there were only a few who believed. This Arch Bishop at that old monastery believed. And he wanted to buy these old manuscripts from the Bedouins. And he wanted them to find more.

And find more they did. After that first accidental discovery in the dry caves at Qumran, the Bedouins went back and looked for more. They broke open the few big earthen jars and found some more intact scrolls. These would fetch a fine fortune for the starving nomads living of the fringes of life here in the acrid desert.

Then the search for ancient documents almost became a chase, and as word started to leak out, there was a flurry of searching and digging. And all told over 400 scrolls were found. And for a while the price for these old scrolls sky rocketed. I mean in the millions for a little pile of dusty rotting leather or papyrus. A million dollars! Unbelievable. The locals were motivated and so were the forgers. And both of these developments made the discovery and verification of authentic ancient Dead Sea documents more difficult for scholars.

Scrolls were sold in the antiqua dealers along the street. Scholars and church men were approached by what seemed to be dirty beggars bearing piles of what might or might not be authentic priceless ancient scrolls. In fact one of the first scrolls was listed among tools and hardware in a news paper in New York. And went almost unnoticed. But as scavengers are, it was discovered and that bit of moldering parchment entered the stream of priceless antiquities.

These piles of scrolls were gathered in the local museum libraries where it was decided by government officials that a team of international experts would be assembled to study and translate these ancient documents. These experts would come from the fields of biblical texts and linguistic anthropology and religious studies.

The translators they chose were ll learned men. And most of them believed they had found what they needed to prove that the Bible was true. But they made one mistake in their selection, and they didn't notice their error until it became irritatingly obvious. The selected one man who, though was decidedly an expert in anthropology and biblical translations, he was not an ecclesiastic. But came from the secular disciplines. He was what they would scornfully call a humanist.

Antony was thrilled to have been selected. The international team was ramped and geared to begin the tedious process of re-piecing together this old half destroy pile of manuscripts that had been found somewhere in the desert. After all of his dedication and study in different fields of ancient linguistics, this one subject excited him. It was certainly a far cry from sorting pot shards.

And it was a far cry from that mix up at the last dig in Central America. He was glad to have survived that controversy with his reputation intact enough to be offered this position on the international team.

This discovery was important. These were the oldest documents ever found that related directly to the elements in the bible. Some of these writings seemed to be the originals of new and old testament stories.

How exciting was that! We could take a fresh and serious look at the bible stories and reflect on their origins and validity. There seemed to be gospels written by the Disciples of Christ himself. Can you imagine the importance of that! Antony thought to himself. The originals! Or darn near to it.

He wondered which portion of this mass of texts he would be allotted. Regardless he vowed he would do hims best to be honest and careful in translating them correctly and skillfully, to the truth of the original documents.

He settled back into his office chair and began reviewing again the material he had just been translating. A story he had never seen before. Something of a bible story but one that had been chosen to not be in the big black book. It was a long version of the story of Joseph's death, as Jesus has related to his disciples later on the Mount. It seemed to point to the difference in the ages of these two men. And it seemed to describe a more transcendental understanding of death, one that Antony found fascinating. And this death of Joseph took a while, and much was revealed about life and death to the prophet and his disciples, and Antony wondered if it would be too much of a story to read to young Gwydion for bedtime.

# 5.
# Mary

Many more scrolls had been obtained by the university and brought to the lab and the scholars were just beginning to translate them into English from the ancient Hebrew, Greek, and Semitic. Some of these stories were quite ancient and controversial. They had not been released to the public yet.

But Antony found them fascinating and kind of beautiful. They seemed to be variations of the stories found in the New Testament of the Bible. But maybe these were better stories; fuller, more realistic and told in a more readable story form than provided in the old King James version he was used to trying to read.

He thought to himself, "What would it hurt to read these to Gwydion at night for bedtimes stories?" He figured it wouldn't hurt a thing. These stories should not be secrets, after all.

In the next few nights, he found himself alone with his grandson in the quiet living room late, just before bedtime. "Would you like to hear a story, Gwydion?"

The boy's head spun around, his eyes wide. Who was he kidding? His favorite thing was to get read stories by his grand papa.

"We have translated another story, this one is a Gospel about Mary, by her step son, James, one of the sons of Joseph by his first marriage, before Mary."

When he mentioned Mary, Gwydion lit up and said, "Immaculate conception!"

Antony laughed a little. The things he remembered. Big words sometimes.

"But, you know, he was not the first one born of immaculate conception and birth. Oh, no. And this story has been left out and forgotten about. You see, James, one of Joseph's sons by his first wife before he got with Mary, wrote this long testament about their lives. He describes how Mary came to be his stepmother. She was given to Joseph by the church when she became too mature to stay there.

"Ends up, Gwydion, that Immaculate conception is really a misnomer. Really when you read the oldest stories you realize that not only was it an immaculate conception, but it was also an immaculate birth. There was no mess like normal births. In fact the midwife that examined Mary after his birth found her completely clean. There was no blood. In fact, strangely, one of the stories said that the baby Jesus came to earth on a ray of light."

Gwydion smiled at that; he liked magic.

"But if you notice in the paintings of mother and child," said Antony. Then he got up and went to the shelf of books. He pulled out a large flat book with color pictures in it. Pre-Renaissance paintings. He opened it to a famous Pieta, mother and child, with the child holding his finger up in the air, and his mother smiling a quirky smile of her own hidden secrets.

Gwydion took one look at it, pointed at Mary and said, "Look. She has halo, too!"

"Very good, Gwydion. You noticed that right off," said Antony to his very observant grand son. "It has been debated by the church that perhaps the medieval folks had too much worship of the virgin Mary and later the church tried to wipe out those heathen ideas. But, in truth, in the oldest of stories we are finding, Jesus was not the first one born of a virgin. No. It was his mother Mary."

And with the wonderment of that, the two of them sat on the floor and leafed through the huge book of religious paintings for about an hour and then retired to sleep. He would have to read on a different night the story of the rich gentleman Joachim and his wife Anna who bore him a girl child, named Mary.

# 6.
# Life of Joseph

Antony and Bethany were seated in the living room doing their quiet individual activities they'd grown to love doing together, in complete silence. It had taken years together for this kind of comfort to grow. Where once the need to fill the uncomfortable space of silence with sibilant structure, now a warm cocoon of quiet study and respect had grown.

Gwydion seemed a part of that too. Or perhaps was it his studied silence that taught them to be more this way? He sat on the rug with a project on the floor before him, but he did not do the normal kid thing, where they build up a structure and crash it down with smashing and crashing noises, like most little boys. When he built something, he would study it for a long while and then quietly, reverently, disassemble it into its component blocks, and then start on another building project.

Bethany was reading a paper Antony had published in the university academic magazine, Antony his sacred newspaper. She looked over at him, and said, "You wrote this?" lifting and shaking gently the thin stack of papers.

He looked over at her and said, "Yup. That's mostly what I am doing these days. But its work. So I read this drivel to relax." He shook his newspaper softly.

"These stories are really fabulous. I wish more people would read them. They just took them out of the big book. I think these stories are better tellings of what happened."

"Probably. But imagine if all that was in one book, how big that book would be. Huge," countered Antony. He seemed to support the idea of the filtering out of many many stories that had happened in the making of the bible as it was today. Many people read into that selection all kinds of conspiracy theories about what the Church was trying to do, to sway people into believing one thing or another. Maybe there was that. Some. But jeez, there were a lot of stories told with a lot of different voices. They had had this discussion before.

"But I get this really strong reflection of Eastern Mysticism here, in this story of the life and death of Joseph, Jesus' father. I got that strong feeling too in the gospel of Mary, although of course that was a later story, after He had died, and come back as a spirit to teach his disciples more. But this sense of the body being the seduction into sin of the spirit. That is so Eastern Zen Buddhism. Just really makes me wonder, if those stories I used to hear were true. That Jesus traveled all over the world to learn other mystic teachings. Druidism, Zen Buddhism." She looked at her husband, who was so intelligent, but also very difficult to get a rise out of him about any of these "theories" of hers, as he liked to call them.

But he surprised her this time and said, "Sometimes I wonder if those people back then, two thousand years ago didn't have a greater understanding of the mysticism of life. We call them barbarians and uneducated rabble. But some of their sentences I read in Greek translate out to something deeper and more reflective than anything I ever see in any of our daily writings here in today's world. Or even anything I see in any books on any shelf except the philosophy section of the university library."

Her eyes widened. "Geez, you are right. I never thought about that. Are we really that vapid? Maybe we are the barbarians? Today, I mean." They both chuckled a little at that, and Gwydion looked over at them for just a moment.

They sat in silence for a few moments, Antony looking down at his paper and pretending to read but really thinking about what she had just said, and some of the translation secrets he had just been going over. He rarely spoke of these things to her. He didn't like to talk about them not so much out of secrecy, although there was that, but more out of wanting to keep his mind free of other peoples ideas and musings. Most of which usually seemed like superstitious nonsense from the guilty teachings of religious practitioners. But his wife sometimes had some really fresh reflections on this stuff, and he had learned to listen, although take it with a grain of salt. But sometimes her ridiculous seeming theories held a refreshing new perspective. And he knew, working with this stuff everyday, his perspective was probably anything but refreshing.

Bethany started again, after she had cleared her mind of their little shared joke. "This is one of the stories of Joseph, his life. Jesus is on the Mount, telling this to his disciples and others. Its pretty normal stuff, until he gets to the death of his mortal father, and he describes the process of death, as Joseph was experiencing it." She shook her head a little, then looked straight at Antony. "I mean, where do we hear this anywhere else? Nowhere. We don't talk about that. Like I said, Eastern Mysticism."

She sat back a little, looking transfixed at a point ahead of her in the darkened living room. "He at first is praying to the Father for his sins, and how his body had drawn him in to sin. That's the Seduction of Mayra from the eastern teachings.

Then as he is leaving the body, he explains the transmutation of material of his body into spirit." She looked at Antony with wide eyes, "Is this like Einstein's change of mass and weight into light and weightless travel?" They just looked at each other as the similarity sunk in.

"Then as he became spirit, he forgot to eat and drink, and his knowledge of his carpentry craft turned to error. This seems to me like the dawning of awareness that his revered craft was just another adjustment of his body to fulfilling its needs, and maybe at the destruction of the world in the process."

"What?" said Antony now intrigued and confused at where she was going with this.

"This Greek word for Carpentry, Fabri Lignarii, to fabricate Lignum, wood. Which must be the root of Lingum, tongue, male member. I can see the connection there in those word, I think those middle letters were switched, as they were hard to pronounce, and probably rarely written and read out loud anyway. The lignum being life. And yet, his occupation was to cut down and reshape the lignum, wood, into other things, thus killing and destroying the tree in the process. Thus killing life in his need to fill his body's needs."

"For the living, us still bound by our needs and desires, that all sounds like death-bed mumbo jumbo. But the way you said it, Bethany, I can totally see it. Maybe you should come work for us?" he said with a smile.

A smile grew on her face too at his suggestion. "Nah. That would just kill it for me. I have no discipline. My mind goes all over the place. You know when I was a child, I was kinda like sweet little Gwydion here. They didn't know if I would ever talk.

It was decided very early on that no way could I ever make it in college. So I just didn't go. Until much later of course, at your prompting."

"You know, Bethany. Sometimes I think you and Gwydion are way ahead of us all. You just choose to not speak because you refuse to learn all the zillion little deceits that surround us and ensnare us into our limited little culture of humanity." He shifted in his chair, his mind working now on all the things she had suggested and been theorizing about. "In fact, I just read a little ditty about that great guy you were just talking about, Einstein."

"I really like the man. He had way more to teach than physics," she said.

"Yup. Almost like an Eastern Mystic," he said.

She smiled. "There you go!"

"People look at pictures of Einstein and they see all that hair and the rumpled clothes. And he was criticized at his time for being funny looking and not caring about his appearance. But he said that we are slaves to a million little useless things. He didn't waste time at the barber, didn't bother with socks, because socks one can go without. Even selecting a tie each morning he said, drew him away from what he really wanted to do most, sit in quiet and work. I told that to someone today, and they just looked at me. I don't think most people can even get an inkling, that inner drive to explore and reflect, and reject all the little social conformities."

"Is that genius?" asked Bethany, truly wanting to figure that out. "I don't know. Maybe it is just a special trait in just a few people. That inner reflection, that clarity. It takes a clear being to do that kind of work. "

They waited a moment, then Bethany said, "We could probably use a little more of that these days."

And they both simultaneously looked down at Gwydion working silently on his inner musings there on the floor with his building blocks. And they both felt a love spark in their chests, and then a tightening, knowing the delicacy of that love and innocence, and feeling the urge to protect that spark.

# 7.

# Capture

The thick white metal door swung closed behind him. He looked back to make sure it wast tightly closed. He looked at the handle, but there was no lock on it. Oh, well.

He switched the light off which just dimmed the cold sterile room, there were several small windows on the one side, facing out into the bright day lit air, this being an upper story bathroom.

Sounds bounced around inside this room like in a tin can. He could hear the other person banging around a little in one of the stalls. He stayed quiet and waited.

The little gray metal door opened and a young person came out of the tiny stall. He was surprised to see his professor standing there in the bathroom looking at him with his arms crossed.

The older person regarded the younger person with a sharp eye. Meant to intimidate. Although that wasn't difficult to do. That was the nature of the student -teacher relationship. It was also a relationship that was not meant to be violated.

"How is it today with you?" asked the older man with a little twist in his voice.

The young man looked up at him then dropped his eyes. From years of obeying a cruel father he had learned to avoid trouble by acting docile. And the older man sensed this and moved in.

Pretending the young man had answered and that he hadn't heard him, he said sharply, "What?"

"Just fine," said the boy in a small voice.

"Look at me when I am talking to you."

The boy looked up using his eyes only, not lifting his head, but peering at the older man from beneath young dark brows. Looking at this older foreign man in the eye terrified this young man. But he did as he was told. He was here by chance and providence, and needed to spare, no worship, his opportunities every where he could and not ruin it with needless pride or anger with his own childish fears or foolish pride.

The professor looked down at the younger man, seeing his large dark eyes, just slightly crossed from a natural strabismus peer at him from darkened brows, with just a curl of his dark hair falling over his face. Perfect. He knew he had trapped his quarry.

The door to the bathroom pushed slightly open, and another student started to come in. The older man slapped his hand on the inside of the door, and said in a loud commanding voice, "Occupied!" and the student backed away and walked off with a quiet, "sorry".

The older man turned again to the young student trapped with himself between him and the only door to leave.

"I will be seeing you later in class, I suppose," said the professor.

"Of, course," he said quietly.

"How many classes are you taking? I don't see you often." The professor suspected, by this boy's shabby clothes and hand made book bag that he was not supported by family or state in his scholastic endeavors.

"I can only afford to take the one, sir," he said, his eyes beseeching, then looking down again. And this affirmed the professor's suspicions, that the boy was here hanging onto an opportunity by his fingernails.

Now for the bait. "What do you want to study?" he asked the kid, lightening his imposing posture just slightly.

"Anthropology and ancient linguistics," answered the boy, knowing that this was the professor's specialty.

A smile lit the professor's face. "Well, then. You will want to take more of my classes them, wont you?"

Seeing a doorway, the boy answered, "Oh, I would love that, indeed sir!. But I cannot afford any more than the one."

"You seem like a smart lad. Come by my office this evening and we will discuss some options we have open to us," said the professor, his voice echoing slightly in the small hard space.

"Yes, sir. I would be grateful."

"It's room 312, Anthro'," said the professor.

"Oh, I know," he said. He was then embarrassed he had admitted knowing exactly where the professor's room was. But he was terrified out of his mind and his hands were shaking and sweating there holding his home made back pack, looking at this imposing foreign professor. But the deal had been made. He had not figured on its form or just who, but he had hoped this would happen. He had been formulating the wish, and had seen his chance the first time he had noticed the hungry look in this foreign professor's eye during class when he looked at the young male faces. He knew that look well.

The professor turned and opened the door for the boy. He stood aside and allowed him to pass into the hallway. Neither said anything to the other, the deal sealed, knowing that their voices would carry down the empty hall to any one that might be lurking there in the semi darkness at the water fountain or at lockers.

The professor allowed the door to close naturally and turned back into the bathroom and looked at himself in the mirror. His aging pallor was now a lively pink. He turned on the water in the sink and washed his hands and splashed a little on his face. Refreshing. Yes very refreshing. He hadn't needed to use the bathroom or wash his hands, but had entered here for this other objective entirely.

He dried his hands slowly, savoring this new development. He took his time straightening his pink bow-tie and the buttons in his jacket, he needed to allow his small quarry time to vacate the hallway. And so to not be seen leaving the bathroom together, before he opened the outer door again, he headed back to class.

# 8.

# Intentions

The lights were kept low in the building, not just for energy conservation, but because it was such a relief from the outside shine. Antony suspected they kept the lights low so they wouldn't notice when the electricity went completely out from the bombing in the districts nearby. He figured they didn't usually bomb educational institutions and museums, did they? He hoped not. Hoped he was perfectly safe in this foreign country.

There was a slight tap at his door, and he called, "Come!" The door opened and a graying scholar poked his head in.

"May I?" asked the researcher.

"Why, of course, Professor Shallot. A pleasure to see you," said Antony enthusiastically, standing up from his chair at his desk.

"I wanted to formally welcome you aboard our team. We are glad to have you here with us."

"It is a pleasure to be here," Antony said, reaching out to shake hands with this other scholar who he had really just met a few weeks ago. "I am honored to have been selected for this team of international minds. I think we can do great things. With this discovery of such great magnitude," said Antony to whom he thought was probably his superior.

"Well yes. It is such a great discovery. We are all pleased to be working on this interesting find. We will be approaching this with the utmost care and caution," said the older man.

Antony heard the word caution and wondered at that. He had to assume he meant of course the fragile condition of the scrolls. "Yes, these ancient documents require the utmost of caution and care. I understand some of the first scrolls that were found were opened up on the roof top because they were of such length. And that some of it blew away in the wind."

Professor Shallot winced a little at this retelling. Then he recovered and selected to say to this foreigner, of a concern more closely at hand. "The scroll material has now been housed in the larger conference room in the basement. Cool air, low lighting. And No breezes." He chuckled a little at his joke, having taken control of his embarrassment at having been party to that first scroll opening debacle a few months back.

"Oh, yes. A good call on your part," Antony said stroking the little man's ego a just a bit, just in case. "I myself will be visiting the scroll room quite often in the future. Thank you again for assigning into my care a portion of these documents to analyze and translate. I will be doing my utmost to be careful and true to them in their treatment."

"Ah, yes," said the older man, with something like a confirmed suspicion on his face. "The Scrollery will be a busy place in the next few years."

Antony wondered at the name they had informally assigned the room full of tables with the zillion bits of scroll laid out. Using a word that was not in the dictionary must be some kind of joke to these linguistic scholars. But he imagined it was a play on the word Scullery, which was a place to keep dry goods in a kitchen for later use. Let them have their little jokes, I suppose, mused Antony.

But he was encouraged by the older man's use of the time frame "a few years" for the assembly and translation of these ancient documents. He was encouraged that they would be working with speed and honesty to transmute and then relay them through publication of these important finds.

"Yes. We would want our findings to be finished and published as soon as we have them. This is an international treasure, and we will need to share it with the world," said Antony to the older man standing in the doorway of his office.

The older man cleared his throat. Then he began slowly, "Well, we will release them as we see fit to do so. Sometimes it may not be prudent for everyone to see certain truths. We will want to proceed with caution and care."

Antony's eyes grew wide, then he checked himself. This man was not actually his boss. He was, they were all, being paid by the foundation, and this man here did not hold the purse strings. Thank goodness for that, he thought. I need to feel like I can be honest with these things. I will translate them in a scholarly way and publish them as soon as I finish them.

# 9.

# Doubts

Antony rang up the phone service and requested the connection.

The call came back in about an hour. There were always wars going on out here and the phone service was intermittent. "Someday," thought Antony to himself, "they will have air wave phone. I don't know what that is yet, but it will be something other than these dumb hard-lines in the ground or the air that can be cut or bombed."

As he picked up the phone, his heart wrenched a little. What was he getting himself into this time?

"Professor Jacobs," he informed the telephone operator.

"Just one moment," said an efficient female voice, and the line clicked and on came another.

"Antony, ol' boy! Is that you?" said a scratchy but jovial old voice.

"Professor Happenstance, good to hear your voice. How are things in Jolly ol' Engl...

"Don't start with that old stuff again. We are perfectly fine, except that we've dropped another fine province there in your neck of the woods."

"Why, yes, I see that," said Antony with sincere sadness in his voice. "Sorry, but looks like that can't be helped. They are saying they want to rule themselves. They say."

"That's what they say. I don't know if they have it in them," said the older professor.

"Well, I for one am heartened they want to try," said Antony, realizing that he comes from the other side of the pond from this other associate, from that rascally group of insurgents that had also broken away from the crown, several centuries ago. Antony saw it as a budding of Democracy and civilization. But he knew the older professor would feel it as deterioration of civilized culture, barbarians in the castle, so to speak. So he tried to steer it away from that, into the direction he needed to go with this discussion.

"Yes, we were a little concerned there for a bit, with the division of the museums, one east of the Sea and one West," added Antony.

"Oh, yes. We were watching that too. And when the insurgents captured the museum, we were convinced all would be lost," said Professor Happenstance. "They considered it spoils of war. "Shiver!", he added.

"Ya, that felt a little dicey," said Antony. "Seems in the short time they held it, those things were not concerning them as it turned out anyway. But then the Six Day War took care of that after all."

"Yes, now it is reunited under one nation," said Happenstance. "And I do believe the correct nation."

"I am in concurrence with you on that," said Antony. "But we will see if the Prime Minister made the right choices. Does not appear like he will be allowing them to study any of them. But will be handing out everything we have here only to our group."

"And you, my dear chap, are lucky to be a part of the team," said the older professor congratulating his younger comrade.

"Yes, I feel honored to be a part of the translation team," said Antony with reserved pride in his voice. "I am hoping to bring them to the world."

Aloeatious heard that reservation in his old friend's voice and said, "But....?"

When there was no immediate answer, he said again, "But, what dear old boy? What is bothering you?"

"I am so hesitant to say. After that debacle in Central America, I'm afraid to say anything."

'What, should we have a secure line with the FBI or something?" said Aloeatious.

"Well, it would be the CIA, and they are involved already. But its nothing like that," said Antony. "It's more... secular versus religious."

"What do you mean ol' chap?" asked Professor Happenstance. Neither of these scholars were religious scholars. Both were from what the church men would call the secular sphere, that of the public interests and perspective. What they were scornfully called by the others as "Humanists".

"Interpretive freedom," said Professor Jacobs. "Non-consensus view?"

"Really? Is there really that kind of controversial information in there?"

"Well, that's just it. It might not seem to be so much so to you and me. But some of these guys get a little, um, sensitive about this material."

"Can you give me an example?" asked Aloeatious.

"Sure. In one of these stories, the boy Jesus kills some people."

"Oh, boy." He understood immediately how insulting that might be to some adherents. "Not kidding. I've been reading the translations to my little grandson at night and we have been discovering such things in these old stories we are translating."

There was silence on the line for a few moments, then the older professor said, "Yes. I could see how that would disturb some hard liners. Heretical actually."

"Yes. And that is really only the beginning of it. This international team they picked. Well," Antony started dubiously. "I'm not sure what I should even say."

"Say nothing," Aloeatious answered, saving Antony from perjuring himself. "I was watching those choices come 'round, and I have my doubts too. They are all from the church, and I don't even know any of them."

"Well, that's just it. None of them have credentials, other than being affiliated with some religious figure or another. None of them are published, as far as I can tell."

"Oh," came the curt reply. Academics relied on publication. It was how careers were made. You researched and studied, and then published papers in the professional magazines for others of your colleagues to read and learn. But also careers were broken in this manner too. Papers too far off the beaten path would be renounced and the authors, reviled. Reputations could be destroyed this way, and often were. New ideas were exciting. But if they were too radical, you could be renounced by the consensus opinion and run out of the field. And really that kinda happened already to Professor Jacobs, back at the dig in Central America. He had stated an opinion, opposed to the growing 'safe' consensus, and he was removed. He wasn't really renounced, fortunately, and he was allowed to continue work elsewhere. Somewhere else deemed safe by academics. But now he wasn't so sure he was safe any longer. His 'outsider' ideas may get the best of him and his career once again.

"Chin up! My good fellow," said Professor Happenstance. "You are making a good contribution to academia and the world at large."

"I would like to think so, that I am doing some sort of good," said Antony.

"Well, of course you are. These are exciting times. Someone needs to be doing the translations of these old stories and scrolls. This is history right there!" he said getting animated.

"Well, there is part of the problem," said Antony. "These people mostly don't want to see it as history at all. That in fact is what scares them."

"Oh, yes," said Aloeatious. "The old conflict of Christ as historical figure or as religious figure."

"That's it exactly," answered Antony with resignation in his voice.

"It is the cusp of understanding for our age," said the older Professor. "You just don't see it because you are deep inside it."

"On good days, I wanna keep working and fighting this inertia," said Antony. "But sometimes I just feel tired and want to curl up with my family."

"Well, you are still young," said Professor Happenstance.

Antony guffawed at that. "I just turned 60, old man," he said.

Aloeatious guffawed back. "That's nothing!" said the octogenarian. "I'm just glad I am not over there traveling with you."

The phone line began crackling like it was about to give it up. "Take care of yourself!" he said quickly.

Antony shouted over the crackle, "I'll keep in touch and let you know what's happening!" But he suspected the line had already gone dead by the end of his sentence.

# 10.

# Followed

Gwydion had grown up very fast and was doing things on his own. Perhaps he felt somewhat invincible because he was small and young. He could move in and out of places where he was largely ignored.

He would slip from his grandfather's office out into the university campus. And he found his way into the anthropology rooms. Where he would sneak in the back and sit and listen to lectures which he found fascinating. And again he was largely ignored. He was a cute boy. Small clear face, with tousled dark brown hair and big brown eyes. But he rarely used those eyes to look into those of others. So he was taken as shy, which always helps to have a person be accepted in social groups.

His family didn't know yet that he had been sneaking into lectures sitting behind the older students taking notes and recording in his hungry mind everything he saw.

And recording not just what the teacher was saying, but the social interactions between the people in the classroom and between them and the teacher.

So it was understandable that he would notice the other boys that followed the professor around. They were quite a bit Gwydion's elders but still quite a bit younger than the professor himself, who had a paunch and was gray.

Sitting in the back room allowed him to leave quickly at the end of the lecture. He could pack his books and papers so quickly and be out the door before hardly anyone.

He would head down the corridor and out the doors before anyone saw him. Or so he thought.

On this day though he thought he'd been followed. He had picked up his pace down the hall and left through the doors slipping through the crack with hardly opening them out into the sunshine and headed towards home.

He defied himself and turned against his will and saw students coming out the door after class. He had had the sensation that as he left the classroom another of the students was hurrying to exit the room just behind him.

Coincidence, he told himself.

He told himself that he had left quickly enough. But as he walked along the street, he sensed a pair of eyes on his back. And hastened his step some more.

He turned a corner and stopped behind the edge of brick, and turned to people around the corner to see if there is anyone there. And of course there were people everywhere there walking down the street, doing business chatting, standing smoking cigarettes, and none of them seem to be any more interested in him than any of the others. So he turned and continued down the street on a different route towards home. But he kept his pace quickened, just in case.

This was a smaller street he was on and there was much less traffic, people or vehicles. And he suddenly thought he heard the cadenced step of someone right behind. He started to step off the curb and looked down the street pretending to look for traffic which he knew was not there but he glanced to see if anyone was following him. And sure enough there was someone back there. A tall youth he wasn't sure if he had seen him before at the school or not.

So he hopped off the curb and trotted across the street trying to hold his book bag firmly against his shoulder. He looked both ways across the street and hopped up the curb on the other side. Here he found an alleyway he was familiar with. There were small window businesses that he had become familiar with in his explorations. And he picked up his pace and trotted down this narrow alleyway barely the size to fit a donkey. He heard the steps behind him in pursuit. His pace picked up to a run.

As he exited the alleyway at its other end, a sunny street of sunlight, people and traffic assaulted his senses. He turned right into the flow of traffic on the sidewalk and continued down the street past businesses he was familiar with. He did not bother to look back because you knew he would not be able to see who it was the following him in the crowd anyway.

He quickly ducked into a small busy café, where he knew the waitresses. He often went there to buy a treat and crack a book and sit and feel the life of other more normal people flow by.

But today he was using it as protection. He wandered toward the back and stood by the counter, where a young woman was taking money and talking with customers. She gave him a glance and a slight nod, acknowledging that they knew each other. And he nodded quickly and stepped aside and stood protected behind the group of people standing there at the counter.

After a few moments he began to feel conspicuous. And he looked at the woman at the register, and she looked back with a questioning gaze, as if asking him if there was anything wrong.

He just looked away. Then he glanced back and she held her hand to the side of her face as if it were a phone and gave him a questioning nod. And Gwydion shook his head slightly in the negative. He would be okay, he didn't want her making trouble for him by calling home.

He watched the doorway without turning his body toward it. And after a few moments he noticed a tall thin college age boy step in through the doorway. He thought he recognized this youth from his class, but he could not be sure. He was tall and thin with dark curly hair a bit like Gwydion's actually, and he had a funny stare. Slightly feral and a little disturbing when Gwydion looked into his face.

The tall thin youth glanced around the coffee shop quickly, apparently didn't see his quarry, and turned on his heel and left with the jangle of the doorbell.

Gwydion felt his heart racing against his eardrums, and he took a deep breath. He was gone. And now he knew who was following him. But he did not know why.

After a safe period of minutes Gwydion decided to head home because the coast seemed clear. He turned and gazed at the girl behind the register, but she was busy talking to handsome young men her age, so he turned and left. As he was walking home he decided not to tell anyone in his family about what happened today. Besides what really *did* happen today? He really didn't think anything had, and that it was probably just his imagination anyway.

What he did not notice in the throngs of people was that the tall thin dark-haired youth had backtracked and stood waiting for him to exit the café, leaning on the building smoking a cigarette. And this kid thus followed Gwydion all the way home, keeping just out of sight.

# 11.

# Classes

Mags and Gwydion decided to head on to the college where Antony was working. It was not customary for family to visit the professors at the university during school. But the Musee always seemed to be hard at work and there were always things going that seemed to keep it open at all times. At least one could find Antony there at almost any time of the day or night. The weather seemed to lend itself to that. Even during the winter, the evenings were so splendid and the days so brutal, that the night was often the best time to get work done and to socialize with family and friends.

So it was just accepted that family would visit whenever they could. And Antony was always glad to see them. The dust of the afternoon in the markets settled off their clothes as they entered the clean rooms of the musee. The lights were low and subdued there. It was understood that bright lights diminished antiquities, quite literally the light waves broke apart atoms. So low light was kept in most places at the musee, except for right where studies were going on, there could be bright lights of course to see. And of course where there were exhibits, there were spot lights to light up displays. But then those were allowed to be on for only so many hours of the day. And only when customers were there looking at them.

"How are you two today?" asked Antony looking up momentarily from his close work on sorting some paper scraps. Gwydion ran over beside his grand papa leaned a little on the back of the chair without actually touching him, and peered closely at the stuff of the study table.

"I want to do that," he said simply.

"What's that, Gwydion?" asked Antony.

"He wants to go to the university and take classes in Anthropology," said Mags, his mother.

"I think you are a bit young for that, aren't you?" Antony said doubtfully.

"Oh, no. They allow gifted kids to go to the classes. And if they can keep up with the writing and exams part of it, they can actually save those units for when they go to college full-time later," continued Mags.

They had Antony's full attention now. Gwydion was only thirteen, but he was so obviously different from other children, any that Antony had ever encountered. He knew the child was gifted; his quiet exterior was misleading. He seemed to absorb so much information, and sometimes when he would speak, which wasn't often, although he probably trusted Antony better than anyone else to open up and talk, Antony could tell he had really absorbed the information, and was really starting to make sense of some things. Some things that were astounding to Antony. The child seemed to have a gift with logic and finding new ideas and truths inside old traditional ideas. Not that people usually liked that kind of thing. But Antony felt there was always room for another Gnostic philosopher in the world. Although he knew that the family would have to surround him and keep him protected forever. People did not like people who reflected too clearly on the world. And people did not like other people knowing and revealing their hidden truths.

But these days of seemingly dwindling truths, Antony thought that would be something to get behind and support. Especially since it was his little grandson who seemed to be so reflective on this big strange world. A good mind, the kid had. And Antony wasn't about to let anyone cut him off from growing and learning anyway he wanted.

"OK, but lets take it slow. You know Mags he has always been a bit protected with us. He's never really gone to public school, even," said Antony protectively.

"I know. But at a University, it will be different. He is pretty safe you know. And it will be so interesting for those college students to see a bright little kid going there. "

# 12.

# School

"So do you think its a good idea?" Mags asked her mother as they were putting together a dinner for the family that night.

"I think its up to Gwydion," she answered without much commitment to the subject.

"No, really, mom. What do you think? I mean, he went through that stuff at the regular school, with those kids doing those things. Do you think it will be OK for him?"

"Actually I think it will be way better. Honestly I do," she answered strongly to her daughter, looking her straight in the eye. "Its different over here, and he seems to slip right thru the cracks as far as that kind of treatment he received over there."

Mags busied herself with dressing some lettuce into fork sized pieces from these huge green heads they had bought at the market earlier. She was thinking about what had happened that last year in the States, those few months that they had come back to live with the grandparents and Gwydion had gone to public school for a while. He had been wholly unaccepted. By anyone. The children had brutalized him and the teachers had blamed it on him. She remembered one particularly bad day, when she had gone in to pick him up from school early because of the problems he was causing. His last day.

"You need to just take him home now. It will be for his own good," the school secretary had informed Mags the moment she walked in the door. Mags had not answered, but had walked right back to the nurses' bay where she knew he would be sitting on the little gray couch.

When she found him sitting there, he was looking off at a photograph on the wall, one with fields of flowers and dogs romping through it. He did not look up at her when she walked in.

She walked over to him and put a hand on his shoulder. He looked mostly unhurt; a little dirty and tousled, with a fresh scratch on his arm. He rarely responded in any obvious signs of affection. Not just to her, but anyone really. But she really didn't know this to be unusual or not. He was her first and only child, and she loved him anyway and was never rebuffed by his cool reaction to affection. She regarded him with the love from inside her regardless of the offish way he seemed to regard her, or any of the people in this world for that matter. She knelt down in front of the bench and looked up at him and said quietly, "Come on little man. Let's go home." And he reached his arms out and let himself be picked up.

Just then the nurse walked in from the back room with a band aid for the scratch on his arm. "There you are. I am glad you came to take him home. He is causing such problems. The kids just don't like him," she said as she attached the tiny strip of rubber to his arm over the fresh scratch that had stopped bleeding.

Mags looked at the nurse with her pinched face turned slightly away from her gaze. "But that's not really his fault is it?" The nurse did not look up, just pinched her lips a little more, as if to seal in a remark that she wanted to keep to herself because she knew it might sound rude. "He's just who he is, and they don't like him so they pick on him. Where are you, doing anything about that?"

Finally the nurse spoke up to defend herself. "Well, I cant make that kind of decision. I am not judge and jury," she said defiantly.

"So you are gonna let third graders make the decisions?" said Mags a little too loud. This must have carried to the next room, because another woman entered the nurses' bay and stood by the small group. She was slightly younger than the nurse and had a more official air about her. The principal, thought Mags. Now I've done it.

Just then a boy burst into the front door of the office. He started yelling, "He's just a freak. A total freak!"

"Tommy, now calm down," said the Secretary sitting there in her chair at her desk just inside the front door to the office.

"He was just standing there," continued the boy yelling so he could be heard in the back. He was obviously older than third grade. "Just standing there at the back fence looking at those.... animals! I tried to stop him. But that noise! He's a freak, a total freak!" He stopped screaming and saw the terrified look on the secretary's face and turned and bolted out the door.

But Mags face had turned bright red as she watched the loud boy run back out of the office and disappear somewhere in the playground.

Gwydion was being squeezed tightly by his mother, and he squirmed in her arms. He remembered in a flash just what happened. He had been watching a family of squirrels beyond the playground fence. The other boy had come up and yelled in his face, calling him a freak. The bully had looked over and noticed the squirrels staring at him. So he'd shoved Gwydion to the ground, making Gwydion cry out. The squirrels then had begun shrieking and the biggest squirrel had dashed and thrown itself onto the fence at the boys. The older boy had fled. Then Gwydion had found himself in the nurse's office.

But now the nurse and the principal seemed to be ignoring the older boy's outburst. The principal was calm and looked at them all one at a time. She looked away and moved around the little group to command them all three. She seemed to be slowly judging her words and decided to say, "We need calm and quiet here in the school."

Mags stared at her in disbelief. She looked over at the front door just closing as if a violent wind had just blown through the office.

But the principal continued as if nothing else was going on. "And the introduction of your little boy has caused quite a stir." She smiled a little and glanced down at Gwydion with something like pity and fear masked as affection. "You must admit he is very different. And special." She added that last with a nod of her perfectly groomed head to make it sound like a good thing, even though it was obvious she was judging.

Mags was confused. So much so she was at a loss for words to connect what just happened with the weird denial of the principal's attitude. She was a little intimidated by this advanced game of denial. And she became afraid of becoming more of a problem to these people. She knew she was a rebellious sort, and she was ready to defend Gwydion and afraid she might say something that might really get her in trouble.

So she kept quiet as the principal went on with her official decision making. "We do not have the special facilities to deal with special children here. We are a small school and cannot take on such responsibilities.

Maybe we can find a special...place for him." She smiled that smile again looking from Gwydion to Mags. Mags knew the word 'place' had been substituted for the word institution and her face began to redden again.

"I don't have money for that kind of thing!" she almost shouted. "He is just a kid and he has the right to go to school!"

The principal took a deep breath and did not move a muscle. "Well, lets get him home and see what the new day will bring," she said soothingly. They were being dismissed. They all knew that once the boy went home with his mother after this kind of a day, he probably would never come back. And who would? The humiliation would be too much. And maybe it even was dangerous for the little boy.

Mags was getting the feeling she really didn't understand what was going on here. And in her mind she decided that she wouldn't say another word. Maybe she wouldn't want him to continue in this place where her little guy was being bullied and no one was going to do anything about it. They were turning a blind eye to the bullying going on by bigger older students of the little new guy who wasn't really doing anything wrong. She could tell there was no advocacy going on here for some certain students.

And by the time she had swifted Gwydion out of that office and into the car to drive back to grand mama's and grand papa's she was pretty darn decided that he was never going back there.

# 13.
# Older than his years

It was now a few years after the confrontation Mags had with the nurse and the principal of the school back in America. But she still burned with the injustice of it. How dare they treat her sweet little boy like that.

In light of Gwydion attending college classes here in Egypt at the foreign compound and museum, she asked her mother about it one night in the kitchen.

"Mom, do you remember that last day at that school in Kansas, when Gwydion got in a fight and I had to go get him and take him home?"

"Oh, sure. How could I forget that day," her mother said.

Mags remembered when she had gotten home that day, she had been full of heat. She had stomped into the house and her mother gave her a grave look of grave concern. She had waited before asking questions till Gwydion went back for a nap. After she had spirited Gwydion away to the big room with some toys and picture books, Mags had told her mother the story from the day.

After she listened to this story with wide eyes, Betha had said to her, "Well, they could maybe educate those little children and help them learn that not every body is exactly the same. How simple would that be?"

"I don't know. Maybe too simple. Maybe they just need someone to bully. And he's the new kid so why bother with patience, I guess," Mags said sarcastically. It was better to joke about it than get caught up in the seriousness of it.

They talked about that day for a few more minutes. Then they both quietly got up and continued working on getting dinner ready. After a while, Mags asked her mom, "Do you think Gwydion was harmed by that day?"

"Did he seem to be?"

"He didn't seem like anything. Its like the stuff just goes through him," said Mags with a frown.

"Ya, I've noticed that too. He's so different. Maybe this stuff just goes by him. He doesn't really get the human stuff at all I think. He likes his animals and the music. But he doesn't really even look at people. Or even respond to their questions and stuff. He kinda just functions and figures it out without interacting with people. Maybe he's smarter than all of us."

Mags smiled big at that. "Sometimes I get that feeling too. He functions really well and nothing seems to flap him."

"Maybe he's not absorbing any of those command phrases people are trying to teach him," said Beth. "Wouldn't that be great."

"Command phrases? Oh, you mean like, you have to do this, or look like that, kinda thing? Huh. Maybe that's not such a bad thing," said Mags.

"They want him to be hurt by their bullying and he doesn't react at all. I bet that makes them even madder."

"And it makes those women really mad that they cant humiliate him, I see the hostility in their eyes. They cant train him, and he doesn't respond by being hurt by anything anybody does. That must really make them mad." The two women looked at each other for a moment, the Mags added, "Then they resort to violence to get the effect they want."

"Get rid of him so their source of frustration goes away," said Beth. Then she added quietly, "But I hate that they win."

"Ya. I don't like being run off. Then they think I am afraid of them. But I'm afraid of the physical thing. Maybe I don't want him there. Around those primitive aboriginals." And Beth looked at her daughter and that rude comment about those children and the staff.

And they both had another good laugh together.

"He's growing up. He'll be fine," said Beth finally, over slicing the cucumbers for the salad.

"You know, dad lets him run all over that place anyway. I guess he has snuck into classes a bunch of times. The teachers have told him about it, but they don't mind, so they just let the little genius participate in the lectures. Well, you know, sit in and listen anyway. I guess he takes notes and all. He never talks, though."

Beth just glanced at her daughter. She had learned a long time ago that pretty soon a parent had to just let go. Even when they thought it was dangerous for her baby. Oh, no. They are not babies for long. And Gwydion was fourteen now and probably older than his years.

# 14.
# Another bed time story

Antony often read to Gwydion late at night before they went off to bed, when the house was quiet. He had translated so many old stories from the old findings in the desert. Some of them were old bible tales. Some of them seemed to be part of the same group of stories, but maybe these had just been left out. Antony thought they were the living stories of the life the Jesus, before they had a chance to be rewritten and changed by the makers of the Bible itself. Perhaps they even came from before, when stories weren't written down at all, but were spoken to a group of people by story tellers.

These stories they were piecing together and translating were older, written in Hebrew, Aramaic, or Greek, they had an old flavor that Antony really liked, and he thought it would be good for the boy to hear these old stories told in this way. It even occurred to Antony that these stories even seemed to reflect his little grandson, and the way he related to the world, and the world related back to him. He saw himself drawing a parallel between the two children and was a little embarrassed at himself. But he allowed himself this one small indulgence.

"Would you like to hear another old story, Gwydion?" asked Antony from his big over stuffed chair. Gwydion was sitting on the couch, surrounded by big books. He set them down with a vigorous nod of his head. This was a treat for him, special alone time with his grand papa. He scooted over to that end of the couch which was closest to his grand papa and cuddled in to listen.

"I'll start here, one of several absent infancy Gospels," said Antony. "Here we go.

"I cant stand this child. Joseph, come take him away." The old teacher tottered around in an agitated but careful way. "Every time I try to teach him something, he acts like he knows everything so much more than I do."

"What are you muttering about, old Zachaeus?" Joseph asked the old man. "He is just a child."

"Oh, more than just a child. Some kind of strange being, perhaps born before the first forming of the earth, he seems to know so much. What kind of womb could have produced such an one as this? He is not of this world, but from somewhere else, most definitely, your wife Mary even confirms this to be so."

The boy Jesus had been playing in the mud that fine day, and forming small animals with it. He clarified the water around him with one word. When one of the elders of the old religious leaders saw him making these things on the day of the Sabbath, he ran and told the elders of the church. One of the elders came and admonished the five year old Jesus and asked why he profaned the Sabbath, the day when no work or creation can be done. Jesus, seeing that the things he had made good with his hands, the 12 mud sparrows, had angered the older men, he clapped his hands and cried, "be gone!". And the twelve sparrows took flight and flew off. And all were amazed but they ran off and told their leaders what this young Jesus had done.

One of the younger boys that was standing there with Joseph took a willow switch and scattered the water that Jesus had gathered into pools. Jesus became irritated with him and said, "What did those pools of water do to harm you?

So now you will wither and never grow leaves or root or bear fruit." And the little boy withered in front of their eyes. The withered child was taken to his mother and father who mourned his lost youth, and asked Joseph, "What kind of a child do you have that does such things?"

Then another child ran up and bumped into Jesus and Jesus was irritated. And he said to the boy, "you will travel no further." And the boy fell down there and died. The people of the village were aghast, and asked Joseph, " where was he born? Everything he says, happens. You can no longer live in this village, unless you teach this boy to bless instead of curse, for he is killing our children."

So Joseph grabbed him by the ear and yanked hard. "Why do you vex these people? Can't you see that they are angry and are persecuting us?"

Jesus answered his father elliptically, "It is enough that you seek and do not find. Do you not know that I am yours. Do not grieve me."

"Pretty smart little guy, I'd say," said Antony.

"He had special powers," said Gwydion.

"That's what the story indicates. And people didn't like that he was different. I think we all feel that way sometimes, don't you think, Gwydion?"

The boy looked over at his grand papa and gave him a half smile, maybe because he was tired. Or maybe because he knew more than his grand father ever would.

# 15

# Phone call

Antony sat at his elevated chair in the darkened room. His eyes were getting dim from the close-up reading of these microscopic bits of paper with old writing on them. He had been at it for hours.

And so it was actually with some relief that the door to his musee study cracked open, letting a little bit of the ambient light from the corridor outside.

"Dr. Jacobs," said the young intern. "There is a call for you."

"Yes, thank you, David," Antony told the younger man. He turned in his seat and began to walk to the door, his knees cracking with the movement of standing up and walking after sitting on the stool for so many hours.

He closed the door behind him as he and the intern strode down the hall toward the main office. He saw the black phone head set laying on the receptionist desk and he picked it up and held it to his ear.

"Yes?" he inquired.

The old familiar voice began to rattle in his ear. "Antony ol' chap? How have you been?"

"Ah, professor H.!", he cried. "So good to hear from you. Why not ring in my office?"

"The line doesn't seem to be working for me," he said with slight irritation in his voice.

"Well I cant imagine why", said Antony to his friend. "What's up in your neck of the wood?"

After a few minutes of the requisite small talk, Aloeatious blurted out his question. Usually quite circuitous in his conversations, this seemed a little odd to Antony. "So when is your translation of those scrolls coming out?"

Antony heard the question, and looked around himself in the open room. There were other people there and he could be heard by anyone. This was not an easy question to answer. "Well,..." he started.

He had been assigned some particular scrolls to translate, and had done a fairly swift job of it, considering the slow progress apparently of his colleagues on their assignations of ancient scrolls. In fact he had been the only one who had finished the translations for all of the soft scrolls he had been assigned. Now lay ahead the final translations of the scrolls that had become known as the copper scrolls. And some unusual things he had found there indeed.

But he didn't exactly want to tell it to his colleague on the telephone. So he tried to steer the conversation into safer waters, and wait for a more private time to divulge his suspicion.

"Oh, you mean the copper scrolls. Yes, coming along just fine. Taking some time though." He could not divulge that he had actually finished and was being held up from publishing by some of the members of the team.

"Very good then, we await your results. There were two of them, were there not?" Professor Aloeatious Happenstance asked his younger friend and colleague.

"Well, actually we found that they were one scroll broken in two."

"And what did you find on them?" asked the old professor, across the continent in London.

"There are some interesting things on them. More of the same you know," he said evasively. Whether the older professor was getting this or not, Antony decided he had to get off the line. So he said, probably too dismissively, "Well I have to run. The lines are crowded today and the phone is ringing off the hook. I will call you back soon." He pretended to wait for the older man's comment then hung up the phone and smiled at those around him. The feeling in the office had grown from tense to tenser in the last few months, with the sense that he was a total outsider growing.

As he hung up, one of his professor friends strode into the main office there. He looked over at Antony and gave him a funny look. Antony wondered why there were clouds brooding over his associate's brow.

"What's happening, Mechel?" he asked lightly of his friend.

"Nothing," he answered and lowered his gaze.

"Ah, well then, I must get back to work." And with that Antony turned and removed himself from this busy body office.

As he smiled and strode back to his dark office, he wondered if his dismissive tone would come across to Aloeatious in the right way, tipping him off as to the sensitive nature of the matter.

"Make sure and check that phone coupling under the desk, Susan," said the other professor to the receptionist. "I noticed that it came unhooked sometimes when you shift your chair. " She gave him a doubtful look, then scooted her chair back, bent down still seated, and looked at the phone coupling just under her desk.

"Oh, my," she said quietly. "Look at that. It is unplugged." After struggling to get it back in the receptacle, she sat back upright . As she scooted her chair in, she looked around the office. But the professor had disappeared.

He waited a few days to call his friend back. Finally the line seemed to be open. He had been checking every once in a while and they had been impossibly unserviceable, as if the line were not working at all.

"Sorry about that the other day, my old friend," he said to Professor Happenstance when he finally got him at the overseas university. "Too many people around and I just couldn't talk."

"What was that all about?" he asked Antony. "You seemed tense so I didn't press it."

"Things are not what they seem here. Its gotten worse. Of course I get handed the scrolls that end up making the most waves."

"What? How do you know?" asked the old professor.

"I've completed translation of them."

"Oh, fantastic! When will we be reading them?"

"I have the book for the public written, but they are sitting on their hands as to publication date. And they won't publish their professional version."

"Why?" asked Aloeatious.

There was a pause, as Antony tried to figure out just what to say.

"I guess I have been rather naive in figuring they would even want them to be published."

"What is in them? Reports of Ufo's or something?" Aloeatious, the Englishman quipped.

"Might as well be," answered Antony cryptically. "But they wont allow it to be published. Not by me or anyone. "

"Oh, nuts," groaned the older Professor. "Why don't you just publish it any way. It is your responsibility; they gave you that responsibility."

"Well, there have been hints of dire consequences if I do," Antony added quietly to his old friend.

"Threats?" the older man whispered into the phone. "How silly. What are they protecting?"

"I just cant really tell you right now," said Antony. "But I will let you know as soon as possible what is going on."

As they signed off on the phone, Antony was thinking about his translations of the broken copper scroll. The formal statement prepared by the group would be released in a few days, and it would read that they scroll was translated to find very old stories of lost treasure belonging to an older Judaic sect in the Dead Sea area.

But Antony knew how skewed that was. He sat down and read his most recently translated part: 1200 bottles of gold and 745 amphorea of silver.... a list of treasure of unimaginable size.

# 16.
# The Professor

Gwydion clunked along the darkened hall of the university. He had been attending classes for some time now and except for the one episode of being followed, which he had now mostly forgotten about, he had been thoroughly enjoying himself. He passed by one of the classrooms just as the class had let out. There were a lot of students in the halls coming through quickly, all of them a great deal older than young Gwydion. 5 years was a great deal to him. He was only fourteen. And many of these students were in their twenties. This was not a university in the states after all. But in south west Asia, where not everybody had the same opportunities, or expectation to go to college right out of high school. Many of these people had families to take care of and a job to attend during the day to help them pay for those families on top of their schooling.

But Gwydion had learned to overlook all of that. Or really he just never felt any separation from these people just because they were older. He just assumed that they were more like him than they probably actually were.

But they had all seemed to accept him and let him move from class to class without too much interference.

He was about to pass buy the door of the room in anonymity, when he noticed in the stronger light by the doorway, the teacher standing holding the door open. Gwydion tried to look away and pass by, but the teacher caught his eye somehow, and he was propelled toward the door, and this teacher.

"Well, young man," said the bigger man in the doorway. "I would like to see you for a moment. "

For the life of him Gwydion couldn't imagine what this man could possibly want. From him, little ol' Gwydion.

But he was the teacher and maybe he had forgotten something in the room, or he wanted to help Gwydion with a project or something. So he quietly obliged and walked into the doorway and stepped around the teacher, who then gave a cursory glance around the entryway, closed the door and locked it quietly. Neither of them had noticed the other student, one a bit older than Gwydion, standing on the opposite side of the hall in the shadows glaring at the two of them with just slightly crossed dark eyes.

As Gwydion took a seat in one of the wood chairs with a desk attached, the teacher asked, "So young man, what have you been doing these days?"

On the board was written some things, notes from the last class. And the teacher's name, which Gwydion had not remember till he saw it written right then. He felt the pressure come across his chest whenever anyone cornered him in a situation. He was alone in the classroom and yet, his ears were buzzing with voices of no one there. He looked down at the desk top he had quietly sat at and said nothing.

"Well, its nice to see that young people have so much going for them at such a young age and at such a reputable university," said the teacher a little too loudly, as if he were lecturing to a classroom full of students.

Gwydion heard mostly the ringing in his ears. And said nothing. But he sensed that his teacher's voice was tinged just slightly with sarcasm.

And to Gwydion this meant that this man was trying to get something from him or hurt him. He often knew what people meant by the way their voices sounded, but he knew it was not the proper thing to know, and felt guilt and fear at knowing such things.

The teacher took three steps from the front of the room toward the desk where Gwydion sat. Professor Hartig was his name. Now he remembered after seeing it written in chalk up high on the chalk board.

"Your grand father is the professor of linguistics at the Musee, isn't he?"

"Anthropology," said Gwydion matter of factly.

"Oh, now it speaks. Anthropology. Big word for a little man," said the professor glaring at Gwydion.

Gwydion thought to himself, what is this man's problem. At first Gwydion had been intimidated, but now he was beginning to feel angry. How dare he talk like that about my grand father. Then he chided himself for being angry at this leader of the university, when really what had the man said, anyway? Nothing, really.

The Professor took another couple steps toward Gwydion's desk, and he stopped right beside him.

"And what really have you done to deserve to be in my classroom? These other students have earned it. They work hard and have earned their own way most of them. While you just sweep in here on your grand father's coat tails and take advantage."

The professor leaned his body right up to Gwydion's face, his crotch just barely inches away from him.

He leaned in and Gwydion was trapped by the metal arm that was holding the desk top to the chair. If he could climb under and escape he would have. So he sat, his face turning red, his ears burning.

But the old professor perhaps mistook his growing red face for being intimidated, and thought he was gaining the upper hand.

But he did not know Gwydion too well. This jack rabbit was just waiting for the right moment.

The Professor stepped one step back and started to lean down toward Gwydion breathing his fetid breath into his young face, when Gwydion, a master of escape, slithered under the man;'s torso and walked briskly back to the door to the hall.

The professor called to him, startled by the boy's sudden nimble movement, "Where are you going young man?"

Gwydion tried the door and realized that it was locked. From the inside to keep students from intruding upon the professor's little game. Gwydion grabbed the mechanism and easily turned the nib in the door handle, unlocked the door and ran from the room and down the hall.

As the door was skimming shut behind him, he could hear the professor's last retort, " I am going to report you for insubordination for this!"

And Gwydion was gone. A taller dark headed figure turned out of the shadows in the hall and followed discreetly behind him, down the hall and out into the busy street.

Gwydion was determined to get home fast. The rest of his classes were not going to see him again that day. Or perhaps any other day for that matter.

But the boy with the slight strabismus knew which building the pretty young Gwydion lived in from the last time he followed him home. And he easily followed him home all the way, just out of sight until he turned and took a short cut to cut him off.

Gwydion never saw him when he looked back sensing someone behind him a couple of times.

But as he got near home, Gwydion saw him just as he was crossing the street in front of his apartment building. He was waiting for him in front of the building. He recognized the boy standing right by the door, smoking a cigarette. Gwydion froze, but he knew he could not retreat, so he kept walking straight at him. He would walk right by him and get in the building, if he just ducked his head.

Just as he was going to walk by, the boy moved right in front of Gwydion and physically blocked his way into the building. Gwydion stopped and waited for the boy to decide what he was going to do. He figured he could always scream, but that would seem cowardly and make him feel shame. So he just stood his ground and did not look at the boy.

"Where are you going, boy?" the older kid said with a snarl, the way boys do to make a smaller boy feel stupid.

Gwydion said nothing.

"What's your name, stupid boy?" he asked, although Gwydion was pretty sure he actually did know exactly what his name was.

"Leave me alone," he managed to squeak out.

"What, punk?"

"I said leave me alone," this time louder and more confidant.

"Why don't *you* leave *me* alone, punk. Stay away. You don''t know what you are doing," the older boy said drawing on the cigarette and blowing smoke into Gwydion's face. Gwydion looked up at him. He had absolutely no idea what this kid was talking about. His face changed to disgust and looked up at the older boy like there were bugs crawling out of his ears.

The older boy saw Gwydion's unafraid look and said, "You are a freak. You deserve to die. I'm going to slit your throat." Gwydion just stared him in the face and shoved his face even closer.

The older boy drew the last of his cigarette down, turned to toss it away. And with that slight movement, the smaller boy ducked around him and darted in the glass doors of his family's apartment building.

"I'll get you for insubordination. Stay away, punk," the older boy shouted as the door swung closed behind Gwydion.

# 17.

# Fear

For a few weeks Gwydion managed to evade his mom and grandparents, so they did not find out that he was no longer going to the university classes. He would leave at the usual time and then spend the day somewhere else entirely.

Until one evening, Antony mentioned it. "Professor Hartig says that you haven't been coming to his class anymore." Gwydion grew red in the face.

Antony knew Gwydion pretty well, or perhaps he just cut the kid a lot of slack because of his affection for him. So he took the reddening in the face as something other than embarrassment at having been caught cutting class.

"What?" asked Mags, standing in the kitchen doorway. "What is that, Dad?"

"What happened, Gwydion?" He knew something must have happened. He was an associate of the Professor and was not all that fond of the man. He figured maybe Gwydion had had some sort of run in with the man, too.

Gwydion just tilted his head and fiddled with his books. Mags walked into the room. She had seen plenty of how the boy got treated back in the states. And really hadn't been waiting for it to happen here. But now she suspected that's probably what was going on.

"What happened, Gwydion?" she asked him.

When he didn't even look up or answer, she knew it was something scary, something that he did not want to talk about. He had trouble even knowing what happened sometimes. He just didn't see things the way other people did, but he would just get scared and even more silent.

Bethany wiped her hands on the towel, set it on the edge of the sink, and walked over to the little group in the living room. She looked silently from her husband's face to her daughter's, then to Gwydion as he rose and walked to his room. She held up her hand when they started to speak again in protest. She simply nodded and started to follow Gwydion to his room.

"Mom, he will never say a word to you," said Mags.

Bethany just looked at her and shrugged her shoulders, and slowly walked back to the back bedroom, where Gwydion now slept alone.

When she entered his messy little room, Bethany saw that Gwydion was curled up in bed facing away from the door, straight into the wall. She walked over and sat on the edge of the bed. She didn't expect him to say anything, but she wasn't using that as an excuse to let him go away in silence either. Something was really bothering him, she could tell. And whether he would say anything or not didn't really matter. He just needed someone there right now, and not someone who would be interrogating him for explanations.

She picked up a little book off the bedside table, and began to read a sweet little story of the travels of an elf and a troll. One of Gwydion's favorites when he was a child. She felt that maybe he felt like he was still a child tonight and needed some comforting.

"So, as the Elf and her protector, the Troll, traveled on their journey toward the Kingdom of the North, they carried a message for the great king, from the Queen, his neighbor to the south," she began, picking up where they left off some time ago. Gwydion rustled in the covers and turned a little to listen better, and maybe even snatch a glance at the small thin book his grand mama was reading. He was coming out of his shell just a little at a time, and this comforted Bethany to no end.

"And the elf found a new friend and traveling companion, Francine, the giant messenger Eagle. They soared down from the craggy peaks with their friends and prepared themselves for a meeting with the King."

Gwydion nodded his head and said, "the King."

"The King, the good King from the North," said Bethany adding to the story.

"Not such a good King," said Gwydion. Bethany just looked at him, with raised eyebrows. "Professor," said Gwydion. Bethany hoped he was onto something here, so she kept quiet for a moment more to see if he would continue.

He looked up at her for just a second and said, "Hartig." Bethany just looked at him then opened the book again and continued with the sweet story of Elf and Troll traveling to unite the Kingdoms of the North and South.

Gwydion settled into the bed deeper in the covers, put his thumb in his mouth, and slid slowly off to sleep.

Bethany supposed he had divulged what he had needed to get off his chest, and ventured to remember the name he had told her so she could maybe figure out this little mystery.

The next day she and Mags found themselves in the kitchen alone.

"Do you know a Professor Hartig?" she asked Mags.

"I think it is one of the professors at the university," she told her mother. "Although I couldn't tell you which one."

"That was all he said that night when I was reading him a story. That was all he said, just Professor Hartig. Then he slipped off to sleep really fast like he was relieved to tell me," she told Mags who stood wide-eyed looking at her mother.

"I have no idea what that means. Maybe that professor knows what happened to little Gwydion, what ever was bothering him so much. Maybe I should go to the office and see if I can ask him about what happened. Maybe something with another student or something. Wouldn't be the first time."

"Ya, but don't tell your father," said Bethany. "I think they know each other. I might be upsetting to him."

And that was that for the two women, until Mags could find the time to head into the university and try to locate this professor and try to find out what was going on with Gwydion and maybe figure out why he wasn't going to the classes any more.

# 18.

# Confrontation

In a few days Mags found some spare time to head down to the college and talk with this professor Gwydion had named. She had no idea what was going on. But she thought if it was that traumatic for Gwydion, maybe the teacher would know something about it and point her in the right direction.

She found the school directory in the main building and looked up this Professor Hartig's room number. It was in a different building. There were a lot of buildings. She hiked around a while in the heat and finally found the right building. It was the same building where her father worked. Maybe that made sense; the anthropologist types all housed in one building, even thought they did not necessarily teach in that same place.

She entered the front door and encountered the receptionist's desk as usual.

"May I help you?" the older woman said.

"Hi. Yes," said Mags. "I guess I'm looking for a Professor Hartig. He's one of the professors' ."

Susan colored just slightly, then looked down, recovered and said to Mags, "Yes. His office is over that way and down the hall." She pointed around inside there toward a darkened hall.

"Thanks," said Mags, and Susan looked down at her typewriter and resumed tapping its keys.

Mags walked down the hall, walked passed her father's door with his Prof. Jacobs stenciled on the door, and kept looking from side to side at each door and the names stenciled there in block letters. After a few doors on each side she came to the office lettered Dr. M. Hartig, and figured this was the place.

She rapped slightly on the door and heard a loud, "Come!" from within. A commanding voice, she thought to herself.

She turned the knob and the old heavy door opened with a groan.

"Yes? May I help you?" said the voice. There sat an older man, of rather imposing stature, even sitting. As he looked at her, his face changed slightly, perhaps of recognition, but not really enough for Mags to notice.

He knew who this woman was. So he held his face in check with great care. Things were never as they seemed around here.

"Hi, professor Hartig. I am Gwydion's mother," she said tentatively.

His face did not change, although he knew this already, but was glad she volunteered this information.

He didn't respond to her statement so Mags continued forward. "I understand Gwydion has not been attending your classes in a while. "

He nodded non committally, but said nothing.

When he didn't answer in anyway but a little nod of his head, Mags continued. "Do you know why?"

He tilted his head a little, and said, "Well, he is awful young to be going to college classes." Then he gave her an overly friendly smirk, which irritated Mags for some reasons she didn't quit understand.

"I mean, he seemed upset, and I was wondering if maybe you might know why," she persevered.

"Just what are you suggesting?" he answered, his fake smile having disappeared.

Mags was a little embarrassed that he had assumed that she was saying maybe he did something. "Oh, nothing at all. I just thought you might know."

"Know of what?" He said a little loudly.

"Well, I don't know. Maybe something that happened to him in one of your classes."

He stood up suddenly. "How dare you come in here and accuse me of something?" His face was growing a little red and he had stepped back and folded his arms across his chest.

Mags took a step back. "Accused? What are you talking about?" This was not at all what she had expected. She tried to explain further, but probably was getting in deeper than she really wanted to go. "I thought maybe one of the students said something to him. Or maybe you were, you know, got irritated with his, you know, strange behavior."

"You might want to come in here with proof before you start slinging around accusations like that," he said, pointing his finger at her face. "We can sue for that kind of thing, you know," he said in a menacingly low voice.

Mags took another two steps back toward his door. She didn't know why, but this did not make any sense and she wanted to beat as hasty a retreat as possible, and figured at this point anymore discussion, or her attempts to try to clear the air was not only going to not work but would probably make matters worse.

"Oh, jeez, I'm sorry. I guess I caught you at a bad time," she said in cheap segue. "Don't worry about Gwydion," she said comfortingly.

"He wont be coming back to the university classes anytime soon." She wondered if she was burning this bridge? Of if it really mattered. Maybe it was better this way. She turned and as quietly as possible exited the doorway and
pulled it closed, leaving the red faced man fuming behind his desk.

Her mind was a swirl as she walked back down the hall, past the receptionist desk and out the door so fast, the receptionist barely had time to look up from her typing. But when Mags was gone, Susan gloated for a moment, "Well, I guess that little romance is over," of course completely misunderstanding.

# 19.

# Secrets

Mags was obviously brooding that evening at dinner time. Antony hardly noticed. But her mother had wide eyes and was more quiet than usual. She held her silence until Antony and Gwydion retired to the living room after the meal was finished.

"Do you want to talk about it?" she asked her daughter as they began clearing and cleaning dishes.

Mags back was turned, but Bethany knew that no answer was a kind of answer, so waited out her daughter.

After a minute or so of waiting, Mags finally made sound like an animal growl Bethany heard over the clink of dishes and the running water in the sink.

"I can't even sort it out. It doesn't even make sense. I don't know if I can even explain it." After her visit to the university and that person's office, she had felt tremendous guilt and panic and other feelings all mixed together. She had just wanted to find out if anything had happened to Gwydion and that maybe this Dr. might have witnessed something.

"What?" said Bethany. "What are you even talking about?"

I big sigh from Mags. "I went to the university today to ask that professor about Gwydion. You know, the one who he mentioned?" She couldn't even say his name out loud now.

"Oh, good. And what did he say?" asked Bethany.

"I'm not sure. I think he attacked me."

"Huh? Attacked you? He hit you?"

"No. I mean he yelled at me about stuff, I don't even get it. He accused me....he said I accused him..." Mags stammered. "I don't know what he was so mad about."

Bethany just sat there for a minute. Then she said, "He was protecting something."

"What?" asked Mags, turning around now and looking at her mother.

"Well, when people get defensive like that, they are protecting something. And they don't even realize that they are sounding defensive and revealing that they are guilty about something," said Bethany with wisdom of years.

"That's pretty smart. How do you know that?"

"We went through this on that last dig. They wanted us to go away to keep us from revealing their secrets. The things that we found in that dig. There were things upsetting to the powers that be."

"But maybe those things need to be uncovered. What could it be?" said Mags in the heat of her youthful rebellion. "Expose the fraud!"

"Sometimes secrets are so scary for people, that they will go to any lengths to cover them up. And sometimes they are willing to protect themselves with violence. I think sometimes it is not worth it. Its best to just back away.'

"That's what I did. I just backed out, apologized for bothering him, and walked away."

"Hmmm," said her mother.

"What?" said Mags.

"NO, that's good," said Bethany. "I think sometimes people might do more than just get mad." She looked directly at her daughter. "You know, that's not the worst thing that can happen to you."

"What do you mean?"

"I think there are great lengths people will go to cover something up. I mean if you've already committed on crime, then one more to cover up the first one is no big deal, is it?"

"You think so?" not sure what her mother was onto.

"I do," she said cryptically. "I think sometimes that's why people murder."

# 20.

# The Team

For months now things had been growing tense in the offices of the specialists studying the manuscripts that had been found in the recent year. Antony was trying to ignore these stresses and strains. Trying to pretend they did not exist. He was tired of this stuff that happened between people. People that were supposed to be professionals and supposedly working towards a common goal of translation of this ancient texts. They were working towards the goal of introducing this new information to the public, the world wide public, as these documents belonged to everybody.

But apparently some of these gentlemen did not quite see it the way he did. And he was beginning to feel that they did not appreciate his working on these particular manuscripts, and they did not particularly appreciate that he had translated them so fast and was already prepared to publish his results.

They had on numerous occasions told him to slow down, told him that the public was not ready for the dissemination of this information

Not that this new information was startling, they would never admit that. But, they tried to say, it was really not that important.

"Not Important!?" Antony had objected. "This stuff is very important! In fact I think it may even turn this particular religion on its head, when these things are revealed." And some of his colleagues had bristled at that. And Antony had thought them foolish.

So they had arrived at an impasse. Each side knowing the other would not budge, so the subject was no longer talked about. But still there was a rock wall between these two camps. Antony on one side. And everybody else on the other. His singularity was beginning to wear on him.

As if to make matters worse, his friend, or who he once thought was his friend, this Mechel, seemed to take umbrage to his mere presence in the halls of this institution, now. Lately when they passed each other in the hall, Mechel would grumble something under his breath. And Antony's phone never seemed to work when this Dr. was in his office. He recalled finding him behind the receptionist desk, on his knees, and not always when the receptionist was present. Was he trying to block his private phone calls? And why did Susan always blush when this Doctor walked by. Who cares? You know, Antony figured, it was none of his business. But getting anything done was getting more difficult. As he walked by the other professor's office, Antony winced and resisted the impulse to walk in and announce he didn't care and was going to publish his books very soon, despite the delays of the rest of the group. Despite their veiled threats. And in the case of this Dr, the not – so – veiled threats.

Besides they had already had that conversation before. Although he was hard-pressed to call it a conversation; a yelling match, is what it really was. He had tried to argue the importance of publishing all of these document translations. How important it was for all people for these things to be known.

But the other Dr. had argued that releasing the information translated from the copper scrolls would most likely trigger a cascade of digging and looting, before real scientists had a chance to take a look and find and carefully document any new findings.

Antony had thought in actuality this colleague was probably afraid it would trigger a land slide explosion in prices for such treasures, and a boom in forgery, which always made things more difficult.

"And there was no way," argued the other doctor, "you can in good conscience publish the facts about the hoarded treasure of the Essene. It would trigger a flood of gold diggers and fortune hunters like never before."

Antony had argued that this was nothing new. And that publishing the truth was worth taking these kind of chances.

Besides, Antony thought to himself, but did not say to this gold-addled associate, what was most important to a religious group anyway? Not gold and silver. But their written wisdom. Knowledge. Now *that* was what the references to gold and silver really were, he figured. The hidden placements of more ancient biblical Gnostic documents. Worth more than their weight in gold to these religious people.

But the professor had started raving about finding the lost treasure of Solomon's Temple, or some such.

Antony had grown very tired of these arguments. Arguments based in fear, dogma, and greed. So he looked away as he walked from the basement door, down the hall past the door marked Dr. M. Hartig, and continued on down to his own.

Repeatedly he tried to put it all out of his mind. And get some more work done. Polishing this translation was first on his mind. He was pretty sure he was going to go ahead and publish this if the other translators in the group continued to drag their feet over their own projects. That was their own problem.

# 21.

# Adversary

The young man leaned against the building smoking a cigarette. He had been standing there for quite some time. And he could safely remain standing there for quite some time. He did not stand out in this crowd. Besides his long hair, he fit in well with his countrymen that moved around him in their everyday pursuit of life. His average clothes, his lanky stature, he leery look of hunger. His long hair he got away with for his young looks, and was often mistaken for the intellectual he fancied himself to be. So many of these people came from very disadvantaged beginnings, cunning was a skill set accepted and excused by his fellows here.

But things were better for this young man since he had ventured into the university. There were opportunities there, he had known that. He had predicted that. Perhaps he was used to having opportunities, although he wasn't sure exactly why. Not the kind of opportunities that most people wished for of course. But when your existence was as meager as his had been as a child, well, you took what came your way.

And that professor had taken to him very enthusiastically. The boy's cute looks, with a bit of pitiable disadvantaged scruff, and a slight strabismus giving him a docile simple look, and the door opened. University classes, a bed to sleep in occasionally and food in an electric refrigerator. Riches beyond the imagination of most of the boys where he grew up. A far cry from a beating, no dinner, and sleeping with the goats out in the rocks.

A shiver ran up his spine. Don't think about that part, he told himself. Thinking about that always resulted in something bad. So, don't think about it. Think about something else. This building across the street. He refocused his attention.

He leaned back and touched the back of his head to the cold bricks of this old building. The cigarette dragged deeply into his young lungs, sending a thrill to the membranes of his tongue and the tips of his fingers. Almost better than food.

Thinking about this building and who lived there gave him a thrill too. But of a different kind. There was a debt to pay. How dare he come in and disrupt things. The little upstart. Who did he think he was. He was just a boy, all his dark curls and downcast eyes. Was he a little magician, to catch his professor's eye like that? So fast. Punk.

I'll show him, he thought. Him thinking he was going to move in on his territory just like that. I'll show him. Going into the room alone with the professor the other day. I watched it from the hall, and did nothing. That's not happening again. And the time before that, when he came into the classroom and interrupted the two of them, private time. Who did he think he was! Just come in and sit down and act like nothing was going on. Like he owned the place.

Well, I'll show him, the little punk.

That thought gave him a little thrill too. Almost better than food. What he would do when he got him alone. All of the little things he would do. To get even for what the man did to him, when they were alone. The things he had to let him do to him. Humiliations to pay his debt of gratitude.

If that's what it was. Survival anyway.

He dragged on his cigarette till the cherry burned down almost to his fingertips. Then he tossed it to the ground and twisted his heel over it once and pushed off the brick wall.

Not today though, he thought. He's not coming out I guess. I have other things to do anyway. And its date night tonight. Dinner and a bed to sleep in. Then paybacks.

# 22.
# The Death of Joseph

After a late day of shopping in the antigua shops downtown, Antony found himself alone with Gwydion in the living room. The soft sounds of mother and daughter talking wafted from the kitchen, accompanied by the percussion of dinner ware being cleaned.

"Would you like to hear a story?" Antony asked quietly. Gwydion looked at him wide-eyed quickly and looked away, nodding his head as if to an inner tune.

"Alright. I have a new one for you. Come sit over hear and let's begin." Gwydion crawled over to Antony's chair like a young person would. But he had been growing like a weed and was no longer just a little boy. And he no longer fit in his grand papa's lap. So he hunkered down on the floor in front of the recliner and rested his back next to his grand papa's legs.

"This is a new one I just translated. It is one of Jesus teachings while on the mount. It is about the death of his mortal father, Joseph. You remember Joseph, Gwydion?"

"Yes, grand papa. Jesus father," answered Gwydion in a strong clear voice, Antony noticed. Since the boy had been going to the college, actually attending college classes, auditing they called it, he had changed. He was still quiet and reserved, especially around strangers. But with his family, he had adopted a new, more vocal way of responding. It may have been out of respect for his family, as if he knew they would rather him say things out loud, to let them know he was listening. They had practiced never ignoring him just because he was very quiet. He was always inside there, listening, they knew. Always.

But this more normal way of acting, this vocal response, was a kind of relief for the family, although eye contact was still a stranger to the boy. Someday, Antony thought. He will grow into himself and be OK with living on this planet. "My sweet little alien boy," thought Antony to himself.

"So, Jesus is speaking to his disciples on the mount, and anyone else that is listening there. He is teaching people. That's what he did, after all. He began speaking about his father's life, his mortal father, Joseph. Joseph had had a wife before Mary, Jesus' mother. Her name, his first wife, is not here, but I know that I know it from another story. We'll look it up later. Joseph was forty when he first married, then stayed married and had some children with his wife, and she lived another 45 years, until she died. That makes him…"

"Eighty-five," said Gwydion without looking up. He was keeping track.

"Very good, you're listening well," said Antony with a smile.

He continued, "Then he lived alone for a year before the priests gave him Mary to take care of. She lived in his house for three years, and when she was fifteen, she bore me, (this is Jesus talking), on the ground in a strange and mysterious manner, one that none but myself, my holy father and the holy spirit understand completely. Joseph lived to be one hundred and eleve.So, Gwydion, how old was Jesus when his mortal father died?"

Gwydion tilted his head, and said, "Thirty-two."

"Yup. That's what they say. Well, that's what they say was his age when they put him on the cross. But we will see what this story says, won't we?"

Gwydion tilted his head back and forth with the fun of the discovery of this story.

Antony continued. "And on the day of his death, Joseph knew that it was his time to go. And thus began the exchange of this earthly life, the exchange of the body that is considered the gold of life, and the exchange of the silver of life which is that that is contained in the gold body, the mind and wisdom. And on that day of transformation, eating and drinking and his worldly craft of wood working became unimportant and seemed to be all wrong to him.. And Joseph began to speak, and spoke at length of his regret at having lived this empty life on earth, and lived the empty seductions of corporeal life. He lamented his life in the earthly body, that had seduced him into sin and had taken him far away from the knowledge and love of his real father in the heavens. Just as he remembered his father Jacob having done when he lay also on his death bed.

So Jesus went to Joseph as he lay on his bed, much troubled by the things he was feeling in his time of death. And Jesus spoke to him and tried to comfort his father in his time of fearing his passage to death.

And Joseph was comforted by his son's words. And he told his son of his love and respect for him. That this son of his, come to him in mysterious ways, was brighter, wiser and the fulfillment of his dreams more that he could ever have imagined. And Joseph there confessed his greatest of sins to his beautiful wise son, when he felt most vulnerable and aware of his silly earthly toils, of his doubting the blessed virgin and her babe, and how he had vowed to himself to deny her and cast her aside secretly. "And had not an angel appeared to me," said the dying Joseph, "I would never have believed. And your mysterious birth, of a sealed virgin, if it had not been foretold, then I would never have believed."

At this point in the narrative, Antony put down the thin stack of papers and looked at the top of Gwydion's head, nestled against the old leather chair below him on the floor of the quiet dark living room.

"Did you know, Gwydion, that there is one of the documents that we are translating that prophecies about a savior that will be born of a virgin and be sacrificed on a cross? " He asked his grand son rhetorically. "Now in order for this to be prophecy, it would have to occur before the actual birth of Christ right? Well, we dated the papyrus, and it is true, it appears to have been written before his birth."

Gwydion just made a humphing noise in his throat, Antony figured it was a sort of agreement or at least an "I'm listening..."

"So can you imagine these supposed professionals at ancient manuscripts, half of these guys say it is proof that the story of Christ is true and was a real prophecy. And the other half?" he asked Gwydion. "Say that it means it is NOT true. That it proves it is only a story and that people were waiting for something to happen similar to happen to say it is fulfilled."

"Humph," said Gwydion again.

"And do you know which group is the devout Christians?"

He waited a beat, then said, "The devout ones deny that it is that old, they deny the dating! They don't want this to be a true old story! They don't want it to be prophecy. Because we cant believe in prophecy anymore. They want their story of the Christ to be the original one. The only one. So the devout ones don't even believe in prophecy anymore. Wow. And the ones who believe there is an older story are called Alien Theorists"

Gwydion said nothing when the older man laughed, but just looked up at his grand papa with wide dark eyes. Antony thought maybe this kid didn't understand any of it. Then he thought, "I better just watch myself. This kid knows more than I think! I think he remembers every word."

Then he said aloud to Gwydion, "I think the church was the first real expert propagandists. They know exactly what and how much the people will swallow. Used to be, you would think, they would want to pursue this prophecy stuff, say it proves it because it prophesied it. But now they know that people just don't fall for that prophecy stuff any more so they go with the opposite, cover up the documents that show the concept and the story existed before his birth, before all the hoopla caught on."

"Hoopla?" asked Gwydion.

"Fandango? Uh, Big Deal. Much Ado About Nothing!" said Antony.

"Anyway, they want this, their later story, to be the only one, the original story."

# 23.

# Anointed

Evening came too fast. But the boy knew where he had to go. It was his duty.

No, that was too strong a word. That word made him feel like he had to do this for someone else.

But he knew he did this for no one but himself.

Not that he enjoyed the actual acts. But that he knew that it kept open this one small door of opportunity, one otherwise firmly closed to him due to his social and economic lack of birthrights. Which were almost nil.

He walked along the darkening street, passing street vendors closing their carts and stalls. He passed beggars closing up their coats and rags, getting ready for the passage of another night of ravaged lost time. Some would make it; some would not. But the young man was fairly certain he would be among the living when the light of the morning came, relentlessly, once again.

He pulled hard on the cigarette, taking it down almost to the fingertips of his slender hand, then he tossed it to the cracked sidewalk.. A sidewalk of half cement and half dirt, pitted and rocked, with the potholes partially filled with bits of the detritus of lost lives.

But as he entered the front doors of the apartment building of where he was expected on this night, his night of opportunity, the air changed. The clangor quieted, and the air itself seemed to soften. The colors were muted and so did the voices. There was no loud music playing, or loud voices calling out here in this padded building. It was the place where those from out of the country came to live and be insulated from the exotic world they came across the sea to visit.

He started up the padded carpeted stairs, he ducked his head in his coat collar when he got near the older man in a uniform standing at the door. He knew who this college boy was. No doubt informed and tipped by the very man who invited him up. Such things happened all the time and were best ignored.

This was not the first time he had visited this professor. No. Not the first. But only a few times.

It was a game of predator and prey, he sensed. Who was which was often blurred. And he knew he would always have to stay alert, without letting it show. He would need to watch his mouth and his actions, to never let on how he really felt about these rendezvous. About this man he would be visiting. About the reasons they did what they did when he visited.

The door was locked and he tapped the secret code out onto the solid wood surface when he reached the landing of the apartment. He could hear noises going on inside the apartment. Then feet walking toward the door. His heart raced as always, when these moments approached. Why was that, he often asked himself? He wanted to do this. Although he loathed the actions that took place in this apartment. Yet he wanted their outcome. He wanted what he got paid by allowing himself to be the prey of this older man. He swallowed his fear and pride, and tried to empty his mind of the fear that one day he would tell this man exactly just what it was that twisted his rage into a knot after every single time he visited...

The door clicked and clunked as the locks were thrown and slowly it opened before him.

His mind emptied as his companion stood smiling at him from with the cool comfortable apartment smelling of all the things he had come to expect from visiting here. Incense, tea, old furniture, the European musky smell of this older man's perfume. A perfume the young local boy figured must cost him a bundle.

And each time, sentences would start racing thought the young man's head, as he adjusted the volume to his thoughts, and began to edit which lines to say and which to not say in the presence of this man. Sometimes his reactions came out a little slow. But the foreign man seemed to not notice. Sometimes his answers came a little haltingly. But perhaps this foreign professor just thought it was the young man's inability to understand the language very well, and figured he was taking his time to translate back and forth.

Just as well. It was working, however sweaty the boy's hands were. How ever shaky his movements seemed to be to himself. Perhaps the old man just thought that the boy was in love with him. He hoped he was giving that impression. That would make things easier.

The older man smiled as his friend stood framed by his gilt doorway to his apartment. He felt lavish in being able to give this unfortunate young man some things he had probably never had before in his life. The young man always seemed so astonished at the smallest things. A glass of wine, a steaming plate of food. The poor young thing seemed even sometimes to tremble at the slightest touch. These were all small things for the elder man to give. And he treasured the small trembling responses he received from his friend.

His student. His confidant. Their actions here were highly objectionable in this society, well, probably in all societies. In fact in this one, it was punishable by death. And yet all societies seemed to have this brotherhood, regardless of how underground it was kept. In fact, it seemed the more taboo it was in the society, the more prevalent it seemed to be in the underground. But they had to be very careful about the things they said and did when they were in the open. Even the slightest look or word could covey something that could land the both of them in a great deal of trouble.

But these meetings here were secret. There was no surveillance in this building. And the doorman was easy enough. The lack of foreign funds in this country made green paper very desirable.

The tall thin boy strode slowly into the apartment, glancing behind himself as the older man shut the door, and began locking its several metal bolts.

"Well, then. I see you made it thru the streets of Egypt alive once again, today," said the older man with a warm but commanding air. He outstretched his arm and motioned for him to sit on the large overstuffed couch. The boy did as he was bid, and the older man kept the conversation going comfortably as he strolled into the kitchen. He came back, still chatting quietly, with a glass of red wine in each hand.

"Well, here's to the University," he said as he handed the paper thin crystal goblet to the younger man seated on the couch. "A fine place to meet friends and increase with the world," he said grandiosely.

A heart beat and a quick translation, and the dark haired boy answered smoothly, "Of, course." He took the proffered wine and raised the thin edge of the goblet to his lips. He took in its warm aroma but did not drink. He looked up at the older man over the edge of the fine crystal and said, "We are lucky, yes."

This brought a smile to the older man's face. "Lucky, yes."

They both ceremoniously drank a small sip from their wine goblets at the same instant holding eye contact over the edge of their crystal. As was custom, the older partner spoke first. "Shall we have some music before dinner?"

The young man just hinted at a smile with his lips, then took another small sip of the red wine. It was good. Not like the new green wine they used to have sometimes, to add to the water to flavor the smells from it. But rich and full bodied. It must be an old wine, stored somewhere and bought for a good price, he thought, wondering at how much it must have been, and his mind wandered to dollar signs and he began doing math in his head, perhaps to distract himself from what what really going on here. His hands were sweating just slightly and his fingertips made faint foggy impressions on the fine crystal he held. He carefully reached down and set the tall thin delicate cup on the knee-high table in front of him.

The professor adjusted some machinery on a cabinet shelf and some music floated into the air, something the young man was only familiar with because of his time spent here. This strange music with strange instruments that was nothing like the passionate music of his own country.

But the professor had said it was "real music". Music from the highest types from his own country, played by large groups called something he could not remember.

"Nothing like your own wild unstructured music you hear here in the filthy streets of Cairo. This is sophisticated music with a history of the finest composers from Europe," he had been instructed by the professor. Always instructing, like he was some stupid child that this man was electing to bestow this great gift of knowledge on him, some poor street urchin. He looked away as he thought these things, afraid he would betray his scorn toward this man who could not see his old world sensitivities.

Slowly the professor walked over to the couch and placed his glass on the table next to the other one. He sat down beside the young man, then turned and smiled wanly at him. Always this dance. Each time. Slowly he would approach, like a jackal would approach a kill. To make sure maybe it wouldn't react suddenly and bite him. And he always felt fear in the pit of his stomach and his body would beak out in a cold sweat.

But he always held his ground. He remained focused on his goals, and tried not to think of the actual presence of this other, much older man.

This older man casually put his hand on the boy's thigh, and kept on chatting about things, most of which the kid did not hear. This did not seem to be noticed by the professor who continued amiably chatting, as if they were great friends having a nice time together.

He looked him in the face, and then looked away. He made a decision; he would take charge at this point. He hated this waiting. He stood up just enough to bring his bottom off the couch, and turned his body and knelt in front of the couch, he looked at the professor in the eye and settled on the floor right in front of the other man's legs.

The professor seemed a little surprised at his boldness. And had a slightly shocked smile on his face. The boy smiled back and slid his hands up the mans thighs while he looked him in the eye. He bent over just a little and touched the older man's leg with the side of his face, a surprisingly intimate gesture for the older man, and it sent a thrill through out his body.

"We could do this now, if you like?" he said tentatively to the anxious boy. "I have some dinner. Just some salad, it has been so..."

"Yes, I would like that," answered the boy breathlessly. Waiting was making him feel things he could not stand. Best to get it done.

"Usually we should wait and break bread together. It is how it is written to be done." The boy just looked at him when he said this. "But I suppose the wine is a good enough start. It is part of the process you know."

He stood up and pulled at the younger man's hand and they walked into the bedroom. He lit a match and lit the four candles at the corners of the room, one of them with a small stand and a small pot of something on it standing just over it. A small stick of incense in a round burner was lit and the room came alive with shadows and smells behind an ancient veil.

"First we begin with this little bit of oil," said the older man, as he sat the young man on the bed. And he walked over to the small brazier and pointed to the oil in the small metal pot. "For anointing," he said.

He then walked to the head of the bed, and as the boy began to disrobe, he grasped the edge of the European style painting and flipped it over by its frame. "That's better."

The older man slipped his robe off, revealing his pale pudgy body in the nude. The younger boy looked away. "I should make you shower. When was the last time you cleansed yourself?" he asked the boy.

"I showered at the gym at the university right before I came here."

"Oh, that will be just fine." He dipped his finger tips in the warming oil and grasped the boys toes and began his ritual anointing. It cover eventually his entire body, preparing him for the love ritual.

Its entirely took about an hour. And afterward both were exhausted. The boy had never been treated like this before. Always at home this had been his duty for his uncles and others that visited his fathers compound. It had disgusted him. But this was something different. He looked the older man in the eyes and wondered what he saw there. If he saw something different, something new and encouraging. The feeling in his chest was about to burst out. So he said, "That was very different, um,..." he stumbled on a name. He didn't dare to speak the older man's name out loud. That didn't seem safe.

"You may call me Master, if it suits you."

That somehow seemed the right term, for the boy here in this segregated society. "Master," he tested the feeling of its use. Yes, it was right.

"Very good. That was a very satisfying ritual, my young friend. I hope we can do this again soon. Maybe next time we will make it to dinner first."

The boy felt sadness that he was being dismissed. But he knew he had to go.

He looked again into the older man's eyes, looking for something more, something he was feeling and could share and take away with him. "I too, look forward to the next time."

The older man smiled and looked into the boy's eyes. He said dismissively, "Oh, do not think this is love, young man. This is but an ancient ritual in all societies of men. And you are but the vessel. Its written in the old Gospels that were removed from your great texts and mine." He reached for and wrapped and tied his robe back around his ample middle and looked down and said, "Oh, yes. Almost forgot." He reached out to the young man's private area and dipped his fingers into the mess that was laying under the towel there. Then he reached up to his forehead and swiped across it and up and down. "Anointed," he said with command. He stood back up, said "I am starving," and turned from the room to rummage in the kitchen for some food.

The young man drew back. His face felt hot and his ears began to burn. How could he have dared think this was different, he was such a fool. He hated this man for fooling him. For taking advantage of his youth and naivete, and using him for this sick ritual of his. The candles, the incense and this swiping of their filth across his face. Inside his chest, hate replaced the gentle feeling that had been there just moments before. He turned to find he clothes and retreat from this dark den of sin.

As he stood up to button his shirt, he noticed a picture over the head of the bed and was horrified to see an amateurish painting of their western savior on the cross. Only in this painting he was looking out, smiling, completely naked and fully engorged.

# 24.
# Phone Call

The line came with a crackle. "Hello?" came the voice suddenly.

"Hello?" was his quick reply.

"Is that you professor "H"?"

"Why yes, hello, Antony." The old man's voice was getting weaker each time Antony called him on the phone. "How are things out there?"

Antony scooted a little closer to his desk as if this would protect his call from listeners. "Things are getting worse," he said cryptically to his elder and respected gentleman scholar.

"How so?" he said. "I thought you said it couldn't get any worse."

"I will be the first to admit I was wrong."

There was a moment of silence, then the elder Englishman spoke, "And that is a darn shame, that one must come to terms with such embarrassment."

"No, I mean it," said Antony quietly but emphatically. "Its worse. And each thing we uncover just seems even worse. Or maybe it is just that I am seeing their sensitivities more now than before."

"Alright, I'll bite, but this time only. No more surprises!" joked the elder professor through the scratchy telephone line overseas. He had read the article in the newspaper where the scholars had renounced his friend's publishing of the paper disclosing the translation of the ancient manuscript. But both he and Antony were playing the game of not mentioning it in order to be polite.

"Tell me what it is exactly they are not saying that it is exactly why they are mad at what you said."

"There is actually no doubt now that there was another prophet before this one. One of the Essenes and they called him "Teacher of Righteousness." He waited a second, but the other man did not interject, so he continued. "And it is so upsetting to these guys that they are ignoring it and calling it unimportant. And denouncing me, but not saying exactly why."

"Antony my friend, I think you are paranoid," said Happenstance soothingly. "Take a deep breath and stop and think a moment." He let there be a moment of quiet space on the line, then added, "OK. You know there have always been prophets standing on street corners preaching this or that, hell fire and brimstone. But You, and it seems only you, seem to think that this "Teacher of Righteousness" was something different. Something of equal or greater significance to the Christ. Now was this guy before or after the Christ?"

"What? Huh? Oh," stammered Antony. He thought he heard steps going by his door, and felt them pause at his threshold. The door was locked, he thought. He was locking it these days when he was working here alone late. "No. Before. 88 years before. Well that's when he was crucified."

"Crucified? He was crucified? Before the Christ?" he asked incredulously.

"Yes, before. 88 years before. By the priest – King Heiro Jeneaous, for defying his rule."

"Well of course defying his rule. They were all defying the rulers, by speaking out at all. There was no division of church and state, as you state-siders so blissfully enjoy.

So much we can say for our little island on this other side of the pond..." the old man's thin voice trailed off with that thought.

"Heiro-Jannaous had him crucified. In front of his family. And then his family was murdered in front of him as he died." Antony's voice was stone cold.

"Well, now that was not nice at all. You are sure crucified?" asked the old professor.

"That's what it says. But if I remember correctly, crucifixion was not as common as it might be thought. It came from the old Persian kings and spread like wild fire as these new religions sprung up and defied the old ways, both Hebrew and Roman gods. Looks like this was the event actually that turned it into the sport of kings. And the punishment for religious heretics or political rebels in need of suppression."

"Whoa. Wait. Janneous was Jewish. And he was crucifying his own Jewish subjects?"

"That's what it reads." Antony waited a beat. "Now you see."

Aloaetious did see. This was really a serious deviation from expected history.

But still, to be so afraid of these facts as to make threats? Ostracize your associates? Block publishing? For translations of old texts?

He had known that these findings of these ancient scrolls would bring to light new things. But he didn't realize one of those things it would bring to light would be the paleolithic closed mindedness of these so-called scholars. This was supposed to be scientific research. But the more that came to light, the deeper into its hard shell the old turtle retracted its dense bony head.

# 25.
# The Dying Professor

Another phone call to Aloaetious, and Antony's world was again turned upside down, just in another totally unexpected way. I suppose we all think that we are immortal.

And Antony felt very mortal right now. He had found things he had not suspected, not ever dreamed of in his wildest nightmares. And these scholar colleagues of his were amping up the threats. And Antony needed someone to talk to. Someone on his side.

"More? I think more will always be found," said the older professor with resignation.

"What I have read, from another colleague actually, are some things I do not want to say over the phone. Totally unsuspected. Sex rites," he said simply.

Al answered "I thought so, always suspected that. Something they will really want to cover up."

"But it is sick!" said Antony.

"Oh, come now. All religions have been like that. Don't you see? Masons, OTO, Thelema, those are the fringe types that show it. The other biggies have packaged that old stuff up as pagan. But really they just shoved it underground."

"How can you say that, H, my old friend?" said Antony with a whine in his voice. As with all westerners who consider themselves atheists, when religion shows its ugly under belly, they show their sensitivity to heresy. "Its always been suspected. It had never been actually shown to me in text before.

Original text," he said quietly. "Do you have the copies of it ?" he said even more quietly.

"Yes, I do," said Antony. "I have the infra red plates of the things given to me to study. I have them. I will be leaving soon."

"I suspected that too." Aloaetious paused a beat. "But there is something else I have to tell you."

Antony waited. He also most didn't want to know, but now had to. "What now?"

"The old rat bastard is coming to get me, Antony. It is time for Old Aloaetious to cash it in."

"What do you mean? NO, you're a spring chicken yet," he said loudly.

"No, an old bird perhaps. But the old doc says its inevitable. The old ticker is going and its just a mater of time."

"How long?"

"Could be any day. But I want you to come out. You must come back. You will need to witness the will."

Antony said nothing. This was unapproachable sad news to him. Happenstance gave him the name and the address of his London solicitor, and the two old friends signed off.

# 26.
# The Attempt

Antony often went downstairs deep in the bowels of this huge museum. The old scrolls were housed there, in the cool protecting dark. Usually tho, he retreated to the solitude and relative safety of his den office upstairs along the rows of the rest of the professors' offices. They were allowed to take infra red photographs of the parchments so they could study them at their leisure, without breathing on or touching or shining lights on the ancient crumbling artifacts themselves.

But Antony found himself once again deep in the dark caverns surrounded by the spirits of all of these documents written by mortal men, all now long dead. Many of whom died the horrible deaths of martyrs for the things they believed in and dared to put to paper. He was uncovering things he never imagined. He knew there were secrets there. He always knew he would be uncovering some things that the church would be very uncomfortable with. But he never imagined he would uncover some things that even he would not want to read. Old things, old ideas of healing that he never thought he would find here. Here in these old documents that were contemporaries of Jesus. Documents of this old religious society, some called it a sect or even a cult, that just predated the birth of Christ. Essenes, they were called. They had been written about by Greek scholars of old, Pliny the Elder for one, but what exactly these Essenes were all about was not really known, only guessed about. Until these latest scrolls had been surreptitiously found in the desert by an old Bedouin searching for his lost goat and had fallen in a forgotten cave.

Healers, they had called themselves. And they had retreated into the desert to be alone, to study and to write about the ways to heal they had learned from the ancient Greeks, and some new things they were dabbling in and finding effective against the physical ails of mankind. And some of these practices were shocking. Many of them smacked of Eastern Mystical or Tantric sexual healing practices. No wonder, thought Antony, the church had tried to burn all these documents.

He heard a clicking over by the illuminated door. He saw the crack of light slide closed and wondered who could be down here at this late hour.

He waited in silence to see if that person was going to come over here or not. Had they seen him come down here? Had they followed him?

Get a hold of yourself, old man, Antony told himself. There are lots of professors and teacher's aides running around here. And you are not the only one who stays up late to get some more studying done.

He heard the slow rhythm of someone walking slowly around the stacks of files and desks, not quite toward him, but sort of around him. He waited until they were at his perpendicular and then he slowly began to walk toward the door.

The other steps stopped. "Antony?" whispered a voice.

He waited. "Antony? I know you are down here." A man's voice, older, but with the whisper he couldn't quite tell who it was. "Who is that? Isn't it late for you to be down here studying?" Antony said trying to sound a little bit commanding, just in case it was a student.

There was no response for a moment but the soft stepping resumed, this time coming slightly toward him. Then stopped. From around a corner just to his right, he heard someone shuffle just out of view in the dark.

"Look, you are just going to have to drop this. I know where this is going. And the others are becoming, well, very very upset with your research."

"I am just doing the job I was hired to do. Why cant you just leave me alone and do your own job." He knew who it was now, just by the attitude in the voice. The same professor who had threatened him before. He was speaking out of eye sight, just around the metal file cabinets that were stacked 10 feet tall, and probably weighed a ton.

"Come on. This stuff has been secret for so long. For two thousand years. Just leave it alone. You know some people were just not meant to know this whole truth," pleaded the older researcher. Antony knew this man to be ecclesiastic. But he never really realized how afraid they could be about this stuff. But he never had realized either what kind of shocking passages could be hidden in those gospels. They shocked even him, and he thought he had kinda seen it all.

"What is wrong with you people? Why cant you just let go and let the truth be known? What exactly are you protecting? The Church?"

"No. Not the Church. Something much more important. Something...something you just cant know. You aren't a part of it."

"Have you lost your mind? What possibly could there be?" said Antony incredulously.

"You stupid little pip squeak. You just don't get it do you? You want to bring down 2 thousand years of tradition. More . This is far older than that. This is what mankind is." He said the last word twisted and emphasized. "People wont be able to handle this. Not at all. It will take it all down at once and there will be chaos. Total chaos, we will have Armageddon, if this comes out!" His voice raised into a fever pitch. He was becoming crazed by the things he was saying trying to emphasize them to Antony, this non believer.

"Its just stupid religion, a stupid myth. Maybe we would be better with out it all. I will publish it. Actually I have published it. My publisher has put it to print as we are speaking. And there is nothing you can do about it. All of you are just going to have to face the facts," Antony said.

A in-human sound came from behind the stacked files like a roar or a growl. "NOOO!" and then there were scooting, grunting, and shoving sounds and Antony began to back away wondering what was happening. He started backing for the door just as the cabinets started to tilt and move. He let out an expletive and turned and ran toward the door. He heard a huge crash behind him as things began to topple. He could hear screaming of rage as the door swung closed behind him.

He ran up the stairs and directly to his office. He had had enough of this abuse. This was pure insanity, that these so called scholars could be put into such a homicidal rage over some old documents. His mind couldn't even fathom it. But he knew he was in danger and he'd had enough.

He picked up the phone, and sure enough it wasn't working. Someone had unplugged the lines again, he knew who it was.

He had asked the secretary and she had shown him how sometimes the line came unplugged under her desk, just where he had seen his college rummaging around that day. So he slammed the phone receiver onto the phone, and it bounced to settle side ways in its cradle.

He slammed his brief case on the desk and began shoving papers into it. He thought better of that, and threw the papers to the side, and a bunch slid onto the floor. He went to his metal file cabinet and took out the infra red photographs of the scrolls he had been assigned to work with, the new ones. The controversial ones this madman below had tried to kill him for.

He grabbed those and set them in his briefcase. Stuffed his brief case full of them and closed it. It barely shut. He pushed and got the small sliders to lock closed. He picked up his few belongings he cared about and left, locking the door behind him. I'm taking the key," he said to himself. "Let them make another key after I'm gone."

He left the building as quickly as he could without appearing suspicious. He hailed a taxi, when he usually walked.

And when he walked in the door of his apartment, he picked up his home phone and dialed the airport.

When he was finished with that, Bethany was standing behind him. When he replaced the receiver, she asked, "What's going on?"

He turned to her and said one word, "Pack."

Her eyes got wide and she went back into her room and began making noise.

Then he dialed Professor Happenstance, who picked up out of a deep sleep.

# 27.
# Restitution

He had his plans, when he had accepted to come over another time.

He swore he would never go back to that madman's place. He could not endure any more of his humiliations, forget the school, forget his education.

But then another emotion had taken over, and he formulated a new plan. It would take all of his acting skills to pull it off. The feelings of hate inside his breast were so strong, when he thought about that old man groping him, his rage swelled like a tide. Stronger than when his father had beaten him. Stronger than when his uncles and older cousins had defiled him. He was a man now and he would rectify his humiliation. And he swore all his humiliations would be resolved tonight.

But after a while of chit chat with the professor in his apartment this time, he couldn't do it. He felt sick all over.

A couple sips of wine, and he felt himself relax. His hands were shaking a little and his eyes must be blood shot from the hatred that had been coursing through his body. But how could he have thought those things? He was just a man, not his uncles or his drunk father beating him. This man was probably the first kind person to pay him any mind. His resolution for vengeance dissolved.

He felt shame and embarrassment at even being in this man's apartment. He stood up and went to the door putting his coat back on. When he got to the door, he had to stop and unlock the metal mechanisms that had been secured behind him when he had come in.

The professor heard him from the kitchen and peeked his head out. "Where are you going?" he asked with honest concern.

Terror froze the boy in place. He wanted to run. Oh he wanted so badly to run, but he hadn't even finished unlocking the door mechanisms yet. He couldn't hurriedly do that and just leave. The man was talking to him. His teacher. His master. His training as an obedient younger son kicked in with a vengeance and he could not simply leave.

He stood with one hand on the dead bolt, and his mind raced, but he didn't move a muscle. Every muscle in his body screamed flee. But he couldn't . He was trapped. Trapped with this madman. His superior. His teacher. The man who gave him this education. The man who gave him meals and attention, attention like he had never had before. Attention almost like the man liked the boy. He had never thought it possible that anyone could actually like him, his father had told him he was despicable, ugly, with his crossed eyes, his skinny legs. His pretty wavy hair like a girl.

He could smell the sweet aroma of cooking coming from the kitchen. "I thought we could have some real food, then relax and see how the evening went after that."

The boy shifted so he could see the man standing in the doorway across the living room, with the kitchen behind him flickering, lit with candles.

"You don't want me to leave?" he asked quietly. He felt like he was asking if he liked him. If there was a remote possibility that he actually cared for him, this skinny stupid boy no one paid any attention to, ever, maybe he could stay.

"Please," the elder man beseeching. "Please don't leave just yet. We have so much to talk about." And his face pulled up into an angelic smile that nearly melted the boy's heart. He nodded his head slightly and turned to walk back in the room. The older man took a few steps into the living room and came close to the boy, still a boy although he was almost as tall as the older man, but certainly did not have the size or weight of the older foreigner. He reached up and touched the younger boys face lightly with the back of his hand. The boy flinched just slightly and dropped his gaze.

"Oh, there now. Are you afraid of me? Have I hurt you?"

"No, of course not," said the boy a little stronger now. He could not be hurt, he knew that. Blood was flowing back to his brain after the fear and terror had torn his mind from his control for a few minutes. He looked at this older man and decided he was just a man after all and not some beast he had imagined at the end of the last session.

"Let me feed you and we will talk. I have whipped up some hot food you will enjoy. Now sit at the table, and I will pour you some more wine."

He looked a moment at the younger boy and wondered at his delicate beauty of a young person. His dark curly hair, clear skin, the dark luminous eyes, if just a little crossed. He found that exotic. No wonder the ancients worshiped in this manner. My goodness.

He turned on his heel as to not allow the boy to see the flush coming to his face and to his lower portion of his robe.

The dark haired boy sat his tall lanky frame at the small dining table and looked at the deep red in his wine goblet.

The crystal was so fine that you could not see how it held the opaque magenta liquid up in the air like that. The glass was impossibly fragile, and he dared himself to lift it by the round globe of it. He could almost feel it give slightly way, as if he could simply squeeze and have it crush beneath his strength. The older man came and filled it to within spilling distance of the top edge. "Oops. Almost too much" he said. The young man bent down and sipped from it, the very full wine goblet, while keeping his gaze locked on the older man's blue eyes.

The dinner was a rich combination of the local exotic fare that the older foreign man had been experimenting with and some western additions that seemed exotic by comparison to the younger local man. Especially with the addition of beef.

The younger man cut it carefully with the silver that was displayed on either side of the china plate. He had watched he older man eat, in fact he had been dined at an expensive foreign restaurant with him some time back, and he had studied the techniques these people used to eat. They didn't sit on the floor and most certainly did not use their hands, both things very strange to this young local boy who was used to fighting his way through a large plate of food against his brothers and male relatives sitting in a circle over a small knee high table. It was strange but he was, by necessity, a mimic and a fast learner.

"They say beef enhances a man's virility," said the older chap to the boy.

"I have heard that too. But it is so expensive. Where did you get it?"

The older foreigner avoided answering and merely tilted his head. And smiled.

The people at the university had their ways of getting what they needed. And others had even better ways of getting the exotic yet expensive things they wanted.

For a while the boy's mind was befuddled with drink and heavy food, and he allowed the older man to lead him back to the couch for some new touching. But as the late evening wore on, the young man began to be aware of a new sensation he felt toward the older man. There was a growing sense of being objectified and being used as an experimental object. Sacrificial lamb perhaps, like the ones they used to butcher in the old compound. Fed and pampered until they were tame, fat and defenseless. And then they slit its throat. Before it even knew what was happening. Before it could even protest.

"So what was that you were talking about last time?" he asked his teacher.

"Hmmm.?" they looked at one another from just inches away from each other on the couch. A smile crept up on the man's face and the boy tried to emulate it, but felt like a wolf's snarl was showing instead. He calmed himself.

"Oh, that. The ritual." He smiled knowingly and looked down at his wine goblet, mostly empty with just a tiny crimson pool staining the bottom of the clear crystal goblet. "We have found them. Oh they have been talked about in all circles of men for so long. In private of course. Others cannot be allowed to know these tings. Just those of us." He emphasized the word us, and the boy got the impression he meant the two of them, and other like them, what ever that meant exactly. A club maybe.

"They really are there, the instructions for the love ritual between two men", said the older man. He looked down wistfully and said, "I have read them with my own eyes."

He looked back up at the boy. "Naked man to naked man. It says it." He lifted his goblet to his mouth, tilted it and realized it was empty. Suddenly thirsty with the nerves at having said this to the young man seated next to him on the couch, he stood to retrieve more wine from the kitchen.

The young boy sat still, looking around the room like he had just arrived. What what this old man talking about now? Why couldn't he just do what he needed and get it over with? Why did he have to make him have these sensual feelings and then dash it back down with this crude talk about rituals and scripture? Didn't this old man know how wrong that was? That it went completely against God's Word? If they were going to do this then lets just get it over with.

He stood up from the chair and walked to the bed room. The ghastly picture had been turned back and the plain oil painting was now visible again. Thank Allah! Did he not ever see such a horrification of a sanctified image as that one? Bad enough their image of the man crucified on a cross? But to change it in that way, make it personal and carnal too?

"Where did you go?" he called as he came out of the kitchen bearing more wine.

"I am in the bed room, Master," he said remembering the word the older man wanted him to use.

The professor, the master came into the room smiling and found the boy already naked on the bed. "I see you are ready. I like your enthusiasm." He walked over and set the glasses of wine on the side table. "I have something in mind. Do you want to try?" The boy said, against the deepening sense of dread he felt weigh down on his chest. " I think we should bind one another. I have these soft bands we can use."

The boy was not going to allow himself to be bound. That had been done before to him and it had not been fun, it had been thoroughly humiliating. And he never ever again would that be allowed to happen to him.

He tried desperately not to let this show on his face, and fought to think for a moment. He had a better idea.

"I would like to be on top this time," he said dispassionately to his master.

His old face lit with an inner glow. "Did I say I enjoy your enthusiasm? Yes, I did. But twice wouldn't be enough, I am sure." He set the soft bands of nylon down on the bed and disrobed. He allowed himself to be tied feet together at the base and each hand to each of the top bed posts. He began to recite liturgy that he had memorized from the scripts he had been translating, while the boy worked over his body. At his moment of climax, the boy reached over to the bedside table, picked up the small sharpened knife with a thick towel and quickly pushed it across the older mans throat.

As he backed out of the room he noticed that during their gyrations the painting had flipped over in their gyrations and now the sickly smiling priapic figure was grinning back at him.

# 28.
# Away

Within 36 hours of arriving home after the attempted assault in the basement of the museum, the Jacobs family were flying over the Mediterranean towards England. They had packed quickly, whatever they could grab. They could have the rest of their stuff sent to them later. They would stop off and visit the ailing Aloaetious in London. Then they would take another flight to New York. They would figure out where to go from there.

Three days later the police were forced to report the murder. Rumors were circulating anyway and some of the wildest things were being suspected. Ritual killing; terrorists, CIA. So they had to say something.

It read as follows:

North Africa. Cairo, Egypt: An American professor at the Cairo university has been found dead in his apartment on September 3. The details of his death have not been released, but foul play is suspected. Anyone with information please contact the local authorities. There is no known motive. There are no suspects being held at this time. Names and details will be released when the next of kin have been identified and notified.

The officials knew a few things they might tell the public eventually, but not yet. The professor had been found en delicto in his apartment, his throat simply slit all the way across and he had ex-sanguanated in a few moments, his bedroom awash in red. There had been little struggle; it was obviously an intimate encounter. With an unknown stranger. And the murderer had escaped completely unnoticed.

Well, almost unnoticed. The officials would not know that the doorman's children would have new shoes that winter. And there was not much of more importance to this elderly man with 5 children than keeping them in shoes when the winter came.

What they could never tell the public was the strange circumstances of the elderly man's limbs being tied to the bed with old nylons, the candles, warmed oil and incense and other ritual objects found in the darkened bedroom. What they never noticed in their haste, something on the back of that boring old painting above the bed stead. Turned back to face the wall was a very different painting indeed.

Antony had seen the article in the news paper. His coffee sat on the kitchen table getting cold, while he stared at the article and the picture of the professor. He did not hear Gwydion come up behind him until he spoke quietly.

"It was the boy," he said simply.

Antony turned to his grandson and said, "What did you say, Gwydion?"

The boy poked his finger at the newspaper and the picture of the professor he knew too well, and said again, "It was the boy."

"What boy?"

Now Gwydion was a little afraid. He was afraid of what he had known but had not told any body. About being followed. About being confronted by the cross-eyed boy. And about how the teacher made him feel when he came up to him that day when he was alone in the classroom. He was afraid of the things he felt and could not put into words.

Antony turned and put his arms around his grandson.

"Don't be afraid. This sounds like a story I want to hear. Please tell it to me, Gwydion."

And so Gwydion told his first story, and his trusted and much loved Grand Papa was the first to hear it.

# 29.

# Epilogue

The waves lapped gently against the hull of the yacht. A few seagulls wheeled overhead. Antony sat in his cabin writing furiously. He had so much to do.

And now he wouldn't have any freaks bothering him. They had betrayed him in so many ways. They had betrayed the world with their delays and their subterfuge. The world deserved to know. The world had to know. The rest of the human populace owned those secrets. Those secrets were the life blood of all of us, of all of our generations and all of our past religion and dreams. He didn't care how shocking or how unrighteous these words were. They were our hidden history; our hidden birthright. We all had the right to know. So he toiled on.

He would study those infrared pictures of those old scrolls and continue to work. He would be true to science and record them meticulously. Letters and many words were missing or obscured by the two thousand years of exposure to the desert and mice. He would do his best to choose the right letters and words. And he would record carefully what the choices were that he made as far as the translations.

But one thing was certain, if one went far enough back with these ancient scrolls, back to the time just before the birth of the Christ, one would find that these religions, these sects or cults as the scholars liked to call them, needed to call them to put distance, they were, what they feared the worst of them to be. They were all life worshiping religions.

And no wonder those scholars had denied the connection between the Old Essenic sect living in the north west coast of the Dead Sea and the birth and death of Jesus and the resulting explosion of a world religion.

The Essenes might have had their own Savior and they might have prophesied the end of the world. With the coming of the event during which their savior would be crucified, as of yet an unknown method of torture murder of Jew against Jew. They became the last sect of this type in the west to be swept away in the tide of Christianity.

It was becoming obvious to Antony that they were not a modern religion, but one from the old times, when life was worshiped, when the acts of conception were sacred. When times were so difficult, that they needed to study and worship human reproduction. And so their sect had been dedicated to the study and recording of the ritual acts that promoted this fact of life.

He felt the boat shift and sway in the tide. They were out in the middle of the Pacific, far away from the western world and its growing crazy electronic influence. Professor Happenstance had left them this fortune, this yacht he had saved for himself but had never used. And the Jacobs were using it now for their work.

Antony was making a modest living off of the work he had surreptitiously published without the permission of the other 7 scholars working with the ancient manuscripts. And he had been banned and he had literally lost his reputation doing these things. He was ostracized. But he didn't care. He had his infra red plates of the manuscripts he still intended to translate and release, someday, to the world.

He looked back down at the ancient scribbling, and it began to feel like a portal to another time, another world. He was beginning actually to understand the onslaught of the new religion two thousand years ago. They were trying to go to a more spiritual way of looking at life. It seemed strange to him really. It almost felt like there was an outside influence trying to push us nutty humans into a more spiritual way of looking at the world, instead of all this fornicating and sex. To help move them away from the physical, sexual way of looking at everyday experience, which had been the old paradigm forever. It seemed now to him that the old testament and the old Hebraic laws were mankind's first attempt to be spiritual and lawful to one another. Almost as if a god were trying to lift us out of our cave, out of the narrow physical understanding of life . To bring a new awareness of our inner life. He wasn't sure how successful the new big religion had been in that goal.

But he was pretty sure that the covering up of facts, of history, and the lying and subterfuge would only drive us back ward further. And after what Gwydion had told him, about a strange angry boy with a personal vendetta, he wasn't sure if this murder of his colleague had anything to do with any of it.

Book 4

# Stone Temple Nightmare

NM Reed

# Prologue
# 4000 Years ago

Deep in this cold cairn, a tall feathered headdress towered over the sweating priest. His naked skin shining, the feathers shaking in the torchlight. The priest cried a while, then let loose with a blood curdling scream as he raised his arms over his head. He bared a shining sharpened dagger and chanted the magic words asking for release from the terror of the wars in the heavens above them. The sharpened ritual dagger pointed down towards the bare chest of the sacrificial victim. But this victim was not just anyone. No, the rolling bloodshot eyes shining from the ricktus of fear was on the face of his son, the one chosen for the highest honor of sacrifice, an ancient ritual preformed over the slab of the Sleeper of Eternity.

In this society, every generation gave one such sacrificial victim. And within this cairn deep within the Stone Temple, and beneath the slab of the Sleeper of Eternity, would lay forever the still-beating heart of the sacrificial victim. For once exposed to the breath of this Cairn of the Sleeper, the heart of this victim would forever remain awake bleeding and beating in the darkness forever.

# 1.
# The Young Man's Mind

The young man continued to go to his classes at the university. He thought he'd better keep going until the end of the term.

It would look suspicious otherwise. And besides, he reasoned, he deserved to be here.

No one knew him. No one paid him any attention. But now that his master was gone, he thought maybe he needed to work on some new connections.

Otherwise I go back in the gutter, he thought to himself, standing outside a small cafe' smoking a cigarette

He usually sat in the back of the class, and used his careful calm to give the impression that he knew nothing about anything.

That first day back in class, someone had come in and announced that the Professor would not be in class that day. All the students stood up and seemed to be happy about getting a day off. He tried to react in no way at all, and stood up with the other students and walked back out of the room and went about what he hoped would seem like a normal day to everybody around him.

Anything but normal for him. His hands were sweating and his heart was racing. And he wasn't sure where to go now. There would be less structure to his days now without his master to guide his thoughts and actions. But he would have to do it. Otherwise drop out. And he saw no future in doing that. There was no future for him outside the university. He would have to figure something out.

He really did want to keep going with his education. He had so few other choices. His family was so old fashioned and he was expected to stay at home and take care of goats, like his father and grandfather, and brothers. That was nowhere for him.

In fact he hated it at home. He loathed it. No, there was no word that completely described how he felt. When he thought about it his mind would begin to change and he would slowly fill with rage and disgust. He remembered the things they did to him, the humiliating things his brothers and cousins did to him when they would play together. He was younger and smaller than any of them and they would taunt him and make him feel foolish. Humiliate him to shame.

One time they coaxed him over to their group, saying that he couldn't be in the club if he didn't come over right now and hang with them. When he didn't want to get too close, two of them rushed him and grabbed his arms so he couldn't get away. They tied him up and hoisted him up into a tree, up against the trunk. He remembered keenly the humiliation he felt. The fear that gripped his guts. And the wrenching sensations when his bowels gave way and he soiled himself.

Then they had really taunted him. They switched him with little branches until he couldn't cry anymore. And he hung there quietly soiled and stinking and humiliated beyond anything he could have ever imagined. Until someone came after he'd hung there alone for quite some time and braved his stink and cut him down out of the tree.

But that wasn't the end of his humiliation that day. No. His parents were so disgusted with his stench and his having ruined his clothes, that they beat him and yelled at him.

His brothers and cousins you see had told lies about him before he even got home. They pretended to not know where he was, so when he got home they were furious with him for having skipped out on chores. They did not believe his explanation because he was the youngest so of course he was lying.

So they beat him and yelled at him, made him hand wash his clothes in the dirt. And then to teach him that he needed to learn the lesson not to soil his clothes, they made him wear a big baby swaddling underwear for the next week, a diaper to prove that he needed to learn how to be toilet trained.

Standing there at the university quad the young man felt the heat pressing against his face, singeing his eyes and lips. His rage burned deep in his skinny chest as he remembered these things.

"Don't think about those things," he told himself for the millionth time. "Something always bad happens when you do. Don't think about it. Think of something else."

He remembered the last time he used that litany to change his mind, to turn it away from those memories that still burned within his mind and body, Memories from fifteen years ago that burned in his breast like they were fresh flames of yesterday.

He remembered the last time he thought those things. And no good did happen that time too. That boy. That boy he wanted to ruin. His cute little face and pretty hair. And his big wet downcast eyes. Like some kind of docile animal. He wanted to slaughter that little lamb. Take him to the meat market and ruin him for good. Forever.

But he never go the chance. He was gone. Other things came around that he had to take care of. Things he took care of on his own. No one needed to know just how he took care of those things.

But he had managed on his own.

And for a time after that, the burning in his heart and soul had cooled. He had felt fresh and alive again, safe and comfortable. His visions of burning flesh had staved and cooled for a while.

But it had been a while now. And he was feeling that hatred come back now and again. More frequently in fact. And it made him afraid. He did not want to go through that again.

Not that again. He felt exhausted. Really exhausted at the effort to stop his mind from thinking of those things. He wanted this to stop. He wanted this to go away forever.

But he knew he could not make it go away just like that. He needed it to be burned out of him. Sliced out of him. That last time had felt so delicious. To cut and see the life flow out of his most hated enemy.

Maybe his enemy, He wasn't always so sure when he thought about it now and he would become very confused. Was that man his enemy? He remembered a moment when he felt differently. Had he felt love?

No, he felt hate, he assured himself that. Not love. Never that.

He glanced up at his surroundings. The quad of the university rolled out before him. People walked across it with intent. Some lounged on the grass and read books. One young man passed closely by and looked the young man in the face. He was smiling but when he saw what was reflected there in the disturbed young man's feral eyes, the student quickly turned away and hurried on.

"That, for instance," the young man asked himself. "What was he thinking about just walking along and smiling? What business does he have to smile at me?"

He pulled hard on his cigarette and threw the short butt onto the ground.

He pushed off the tree he was leaning against and sauntered after the student. He watched the back
of his head for a while, and then gave up trying to follow him. It was random. He had no reason.

Maybe he would go into the offices of the teachers and try to find the replacement teacher for his anthropology class.

What was his name? Shallot? Something like that. Maybe he could get to know him.

# 2.
# Story Time

Gwydion was now 15 and had suffered some bumps in the road. But he and his grand papa still enjoyed their evenings together reading and sharing ideas.

On this evening, Mags had lingered in the pilot room of the boat. Spaces were actually not all that much smaller than their apartment in Cairo. Perhaps it was that the blue see surrounded them and made their space seem almost infinite.

"I've been doing some more study on the local history and stories here. Seems there are stories of mystery in these lands as well," Antony said to his daughter and grand son.

"What, you mean Central America?" asked Mags.

"Ya. It seems a primitive place now. But thousands of years ago it may have had more people than it does now. But now it is growing fast again. You saw that when you were in Costa Rica, huh Mags?"

"Ya, the locals were saying lots of people had come in and started to change things, especially since the Panama went in 40 years ago."

"That changed a lot of things for a lot of people. When the canal opened up, they no longer had to go around the horn, which is really dangerous, with the weather around the cape and through the Magellan straits, near Antarctica," added Antony. "Even San Francisco on the far west coast of the North American continent saw a boom when that canal went in.

But I bet in the late period of this century we will see a huge growth in population and civilization in this wild southern continent, Its beautiful, wild and green. There will be lots of fighting and then it will settle down as civilization settles in soon."

"How do you know this?" asked Mags, with Gwydion looking at them with wide eyes.

"You watch and see trends. World population is growing and is about to double in 50 years. That will make a huge difference."

"What is the name of the cape below South America. I know the one around the south of Africa is the Cape of Good Hope," asked Mags.

"I don't remember. We will have to look it up."

"I've always wondered at that when I looked at a globe that those two continent are so similar. With the similar shape and the cape to the south, and the water between and Antarctica. And both have their the southern continent and the northern continent mostly separated by sea with only a small spit of land connecting them."

"That's where the Latin name comes for that body of water, north of Africa, the medi-, meaning between, and Terran, meaning land." Both of his listeners just blinked at him.

"It may have something to do with the forces caused by the spin of the earth. You know the weather swirls in opposite directions around the equator, North versus South; its called the Coriolis. The air parts and swirls there across the equator like the sides of a mans mustache, And I wonder maybe that causes forces in the tectonic plates too, causing the land masses to part right there near the equator.

Who knows. Science may prove that one day."

"It looks like the African continent and the South American continent fit together," said Gwydion.

"They once did. They called it Gondwanaland, and they were joined, western shore of Africa, to eastern shore of south America. The animals were the same at that time, millions of years ago, the fossil record shows this. And then when the land mass broke right there, the evolutionary lines separated and the animals species became distinctly different between the two continents which were once connected. Isolation of animal groups causes this over a million years or so," said Antony to his children. "And I think we might go see some of that while we are here, over at the Galapagos Islands."

Gwydion eyes lit up. He had heard of that place and he wanted to go there. He really liked giant turtles.

Mags wasn't that wild about giant deformed turtles but she wondered more about the human history here. "Ya, but civilization formed in the crux between the two continents over there, where we were just living. That's where it all started," asserted Mags.

"That's what they say. But I am not so sure anymore. That may be the assertion of the western thinkers. But I think here in Central America, this verdant slice of heaven, there were other things going on. Things still secret to our western minds. Things secret, and still buried here in this wild jungle."

"Take for instance that it is possible that everyone indigenous here in the western hemisphere might actually be Asian. Some say that California was actually of Mexican Indian origin a few hundred years ago.

But maybe all of America is actually of Asian origin. Perhaps they can show this with DNA one day."

"No way. Far too complex. They will never know exactly," said Mags.

# 3.
# Going Ashore

"Well, it looks like we will be going ashore soon," Antony said to the family gathered at the small table in the galley.

"Why? What's going on?" asked Mags.

"There will be an equinox gathering of minds. A convention for anthropologists . I think I need to go. Quite a few of my colleagues will be there. Even some from the Temple dig in Central America we were at a couple years ago."

"Do you really want to see all those people again?" asked Bethany of her husband.

"Its been some years. The hard feelings have got to have worn off by now. I don't feel so bad about it anyway anymore."

"Hmmm..." she shrugged.

"It is also going to be some of the people from Egypt, where we just were a year ago."

Gwydion's eye shot wide open, and he made a groaning sound in his chest. Bethany looked at him and wondered what that was about.

"Besides, I kinda have to go. It is for my field of study. And there will be people I am friends with. And it will give us a chance to set out legs on land for a while and get in some sightseeing."

"Where is it going to be?" Asked Mags.

"Honduras University. Its a small place, but its new and there is enough lodgings for everyone apparently. Supposed to be really nice."

"I don't wanna go," said Gwydion..

"Yes of course you do. We'll all go. I've even been asked to give a class."

"What about?" asked Beth.

"Local archaeological history. There's some fun new stuff that has come out about the ancient times here."

Antony got out his old papers later in the evening when all was quiet, and the boat rocked a gentle lullaby for those sleeping. He was not so lucky, and was still a little troubled, despite his words of bravado to his family, about seeing some of those people from the dig some years ago. In the stacks of papers, he came upon one of the more disquieting reviews that had appeared in the news paper. He read it slowly under the small lamp.

**Palenque** -The Temple of Writings - Cryo Chamber of an Ancient Space Traveler?

The Archaeologist's team members carefully examined the stone slab, as though seeing it for the first time. But, of course, this was not the first time this team had been to this site, nor was it the first time that travelers from around the World had come here to see this strange place. But it was the first time anyone, in known history, had come here to uncover a mystery...The intricately carved stone slab had been a subject of curiosity for many years. The depiction of a man in a seated position, possibly working controls inside some space craft was one possible interpretation. Various other ideas had been put forth. But some had postulated at theories that had caused a stir in the world of archaeology. As well as the world of sciences involving cryogenic suspension...And when an examination of the slab by extremely sensitive instrumentation had turned up an, up to this point in

history, undiscovered seam along its base, the scientific community had come unglued with a new rash of ideas. Because, along with the detection of the nearly invisible seam, detectors had registered unusual chemical traces along the seam's edge. The chemical combinations had been broken down and studied by computers for many months. The results were unbelievable. There were some chemical combinations involved that were not identifiable. But Beleroform was present in minute quantities, indicating a connection to the science of Beleroform. The only course of action now was clear. Someone had to move the multi-ton slab up and off, exposing what ever was secured below it, regardless of its implications...."
International API 1953 by W. L. Preston

Antony slowly set the old newspaper clipping down and stared into the dark space of the dimly lit ship's cabin. That was the last anyone had pursued the matter publicly. It had been hushed up and the Jacobs family, along with the other anthropologists from the universities from around the world, had all been sent home.

With no little trepidation, Antony wondered what this next week of meetings and classes would bring. And he wondered how he was going to feel if, and even if he could even bring himself to revisit the Stone Temple of Palenque.

# 4.
# Gwydion's Apocrypha

Antony was still translating some of the old stories that he had acquired in Egypt, from those old scrolls that had been found in the desert. They were old bible stories about the holy family and their lives. Much of this old stuff had been left out of the bible. Not so much because it was illicit so much as the sheer volume of material off all these stories would have made the bible a ten volume set. At least that is what Antony had been saying. But Gwydion wasn't so sure anymore. As he was growing up he was starting to think about what was in these stories and thought they they didn't really fit with what he had been told about the lives of the holy family.

He picked up the stack of papers that his grand papa had been sorting through after he had translated them, and he began to read some of it.

This one was the last of the story of Joseph's death, which Antony had started reading to Gwydion last year, when they had been in Egypt studying the lost Sea scroll set of documents. His grand pap had been upset at the other professors for some reason or other, and Gwydion was just now beginning to see why. He was proud of his grand papa for translating these old things from Greek and other complicated old languages that Gwydion was only just beginning to be able to decipher. But his grand papa was the only one of these scholars that had published much of anything. He had a stack of stuff and a whole book on it. And the other scholars had almost nothing to show.

Gwydion was glad he had t his stack of papers that represented so much work to understand all those old falling apart pieces of leather, parchments so fragile that no one would even let him touch them,. He wasn't even supposed to be down there to even look at them, down in the basement of the Cairo university. But Antony had let him a couple times. And he had felt subversive, privileged, and a little scared.

But now they were in the pacific ocean, near what his grand papa called the sandwich islands, maybe they never went with out food. He wondered why it was called such a fun name. But anyway all this time on the ocean and anchored at various harbors gave them all some time to rest and enjoy the ocean breezes.

They were not under way yet to go to the Panama and Mexico city. So he had some time to read this last latest translations before they got under sail. For when they got underway and the breeze and the sun slicked by them at a good happy clip, there was nothing to be done except sit on the deck and love it all. So now was the time to read this, tonight while everyone else was sleeping.

This was the last part of Joseph's death, and it kinda fascinated Gwydion that anyone would talk about it this way. He had never had a death in the family he could remember. Except for that old professor friend of his father's and then the other professor at the Cairo university, but neither of those he really understood. One dies of old age and the other, well, they weren't allowed to talk about that. Lots of Taboos, Gwydion thought, about talking about death. And he totally did not understand why it had to be that way.

So he was glad to see this story sitting on the table having been left there by his grandfather.

Joseph's son, Jesus is narrating this story, and tells of how Joseph is lying there breathing his last breath.

Jesus looked to the south, the direction of innocence, an open gate, and before he saw Death, he saw the instruments of death, in fact the Devil himself and his warriors beside him. They breathed out from their mouths smoke and sulfur, their bodies draped in fire. Joseph saw them and became terrified of their wrath for him. These demons came for all souls of humans eventually, and held wrath and rage for them all, especially the sinners, who these demons found reflection of their own character there. Joseph's soul separated from his body with a loud groan, and hid there in his heart, looking for a way to be saved. Then Jesus heard the groan and saw the terror in his father's face, for the good old man had never seen these evil ministers before. Jesus berated the Devil and his evil minions for disgracing this good old man. And the evil ones departed in shame leaving a boiling rage and clash in the air behind them as they left.

Jesus looked at the faces of the others sitting around Joseph and himself, and he noted that they saw none of what he had just witnessed. Not even his divine mother, Mary, had seen these terrible specters that come to consume the souls of all humans. But the one called Death stood there waiting, watching the evil minions, including the Devil, leave the room, because he is not governed by them, but he felt fear at Jesus for wielding such power over them.

And then Jesus came to the side of Joseph, he called a prayer to his Father in the heavens, to hear him, his beloved son, and for the sake of this fine work of His hands, Jesus' own father. And he asked that they be sent a choir of Angels to assist Joseph across the seven eons of Darkness between this place on earth, and the silent tranquility of heaven. Send us

The Angel Micheal, the steward of goodness, and Gabriel, the Bringer of Light, to guide the soul of my mortal father so he will not have to walk the tight path of fear, the path that is bordered by the river of fire that is so fearful to gaze upon. And may Joseph's soul ascend quietly up into your graceful hands, because this is the time of Mercy's greatest need.

Then Jesus turned to his disciples and his family and told them that they all need mercy during this time of passing the fearful path, and the fearful tribunal to make his last defense of his lifetime. Any who has lived his life by using their eyes, whom is all of us, he is acquainted with good and evil, and because of that needs this mercy of the Father above.

And when he said Amen, and turned back to his father, his mother Mary began to speak in the language of the Angels themselves, And there Micheal and Gabriel both appeared with their angelic choir and stood by the body of Joseph, who rattled and wheezed with his affliction of his impending death. And yet Death would not enter his body for his fear of Jesus sitting right there next to the man's struggling body and soul, and because of the power he wielded over the minions of Satan. So when Jesus realized this, he stood up and went outside where he found death standing outside the compound gates.

He said to Death, "go now and have my father's soul quickly. But be gentle, as he suffered with me as a child, as we fled from King Herod's plot." Abbaton, the name of Death, went inside and took the soul of Joseph, who had lived one hundred and eleven years.

The Angels Gabriel and Micheal had a silken container for the soul of Joseph and they wrapped the soul in it. Jesus bade them to sing continuously in front of the soul while they bore it up into the heavens.

The others in the family there next to Joseph did not know he had died, until Jesus informed them of its finality. And then they wept piteously.

Gwydion closed the pile of papers and stared into the darkness of the room. All the souls of his family were safe and sleeping in their beds. And he wondered at the truth of the story. And he wondered if he would see these flaming demons on the day he died. He hoped not. He was scared enough already.

# 5.

# The Hotel

The Jacobs family disembarked onto Terra ferma in the southern edge of the isthmus of Panama. Or rather quite west of there, nearer to the jungle of the Yucatan.

They had last been in this area when they had come to retrieve Gwydion and his mother Mags from their stay in Costa Rica when the boy was about seven.

And stepping from the boat into the forest, they all were reminded with poignancy of its beauty and complexity.

Their legs wobbled a bit upon stepping to firm ground, as happens to travelers aboard vessels of the sea after they have become fully accustomed to the almost constant swell and say of a ship's deck. When they finally encounter the solidness of the ground, their bodies anticipate the swells of sea, and they feel the firmness come in waves.

They walked ashore and took in the simple sights. There was not much here. Nothing like the big city harbor where they picked her up. But they looked around and lingered before loosing sight of her, as their want when they left their new yacht in some strange harbor. They hoped it was secure and left the few deck hands they had hired to stay with the ship for the next week or so as they ventured inland towards their destination of higher learning. The university.

But first they would take in this beautiful area they had left some years ago.

Gwydion had been born here. He knew this place instinctively and ran off to hug some trees.

Yes, trees. They had those here. And Mags thought to herself that perhaps her swaying on this ground my be her reaction to these green beings swaying so high over head, after some years of only having sky and an occasional cloud there. She looked up and heard birds. She didn't see many. But she could hear them and she knew they lived high in the trees, up in the green layered canopy overhead.

# 6.
# Central America Lecture

Antony had decided to give a more general lecture about the history of the central area between continents. Today, and this week, there would be more people than just the elder scientists from around the world. This would be a general audience of students from all over. Some had traveled great distances, even around the world to hear his lectures and those of other scientists. He would be giving a more scientific lecture to his fellows later that week. But today was going to be more like an advanced College class. So he would start generally to include everyone.

He arrived early at the hall and was happy to see that it was furnished comfortably. It was a new installment at the university at Honduras on the Peninsula.

The rooms were dark and cool when he first entered, and he took his slide boxes up to the projection room. There he found his aid from years ago tending to the machinery and lighting.

"Will!" called out Antony when he saw the younger man. "You are here! Oh, thank goodness. I wouldn't want any one else."

"Professor Jacobs," answered Will. "A pleasure after all these years. I am glad to see you pounding away at this stuff still."

"Someone has to do it, the teaching job never ends."

"That''s about right," answered Will. He reached out his hand, "So what do you have for me today? Let's set this stuff up," he said as he took the box of things from his old Professor's hands.

They chatted as he assembled the production. "So sorry about ol' Aloaetious. He was a fine man," said Will carefully. He knew these two professors had been friends.

"Very sad, but we all have to go eventually. He was a fine man, and a scholar," said Antony trying to act casual. "And a good friend too I might add."

"Just doesn't feel the same with out him," said Will, bending over and inserting the box of slides into the projector slots. "But we go on with the work, we do."

"Yes, its up to us now, isn't it, Smythershins, my boy."

Will looked up into Antony's face and wondered that this man had said that just like ol' professor Aloaetious Happenstance used to say it to him. But somehow now it didn't seem to rankle quite as bad. I'm getting old too I guess, he thought to himself.

"That's it I think. Go down there and test it," he said to his older professor.

Antony strolled back down the mountain of stairs to the podium. He touched the mic and it didn't respond. Then it came on with a squeal. "Well that works," he said into the mic. And the several early bird students lounging in the comfortably carpeted chairs giggled.

"Now how about this thing?" He picked up the switch for the slides and clicked it a couple times. Nothing. "Will? the slides?"

The light on the big screen came on and the house lights dimmed.

Antony tried the switch again and his introduction picture came on. "Ah, good. Looks like we're set to go." He flicked the switch again and the picture went off, and the light on the screen went off.

"Will?" he said into the microphone. "I'm going to get some coffee. Back in a few."

He saw the younger man wave in the tiny window way in the back of the room high on the wall.

He walked out into the hall and down a ways until he came to the reception room, where there was coffee and refreshments waiting. Just one doughnut, he thought. There goes my waistline, but I never get to have these.

He poured himself a Styrofoam cup of coffee from the tall silver urn sitting on the white clothed table. And began to look around. There were people beginning to mill around. And he wondered it he was going to recognize anyone, when he was tapped on the shoulder from behind. He turned trying not to spill his very hot coffee, and looked right into the face of Professor Shallot.

"Well, hello there, my friend," said Shallot kindly.

"Well, nice to see you again, Professor Shallot." Antony felt gratitude that the man had seemed to have forgotten about the hardness that had developed during that last few meetings in Cairo, when things were getting a little tense, with the rogue translations and all. Hopefully lets let bygones be bygones, he thought to himself.

"You all ready for today's lecture?" asked the older professor of his colleague.

"I surely think so. I aim to inform and entertain," answered Antony.

"Well, that's good about the informing part. But entertain, well, I guess we each have our styles," he said a bit skeptically.

"Oh, nothing too wild. Its just not everybody can handle all of the truths, you know," quipped Antony. Then chided himself. Why did he say that? This man had told him the exact same thing a few years back when they were discussing the release of the sensitive translations of the dead scrolls. And Antony had bristled then.

He was just about to explain to Shallot that this was after all a college class, not dissertation to colleagues, when some more people showed up and they both turned to look. Antony quickly looked at his watch. Ten minutes to go. He chose this moment to serendipitously slip out of the reception room and back to the privacy of the lecture hall stage.

Some privacy. But certainly better isolated up on the stage where they cant get you, than the mosh pit of the reception room for tigers.

# 7.
# Aztecs and Maya

"Good afternoon, ladies and gentlemen. Good to have you here." Antony started his lecture from the front of the large lecture hall in Honduras University.

"Welcome to Oaxaca Peninsula. Yes, yes I know it is the Isthmus of Panama. And I am sure most of you have or will visit the amazing wonder of the new Panama Canal. But in terms of this land, man's time here has been just a blink. And our modern time with our cars and canals that go from ocean to ocean, is even less of an insignificant blink."

People shuffled into their chairs as they became quiet and comfortable listening to the professor's voice. As they quieted, Antony settled into the lecture he had written so many years ago, and had given to numerous classes at various universities around the world. He was not an expert on MesoAmerican ancient history. There actually weren't many of those. And he could do passably well, as one of the aspects of this land's history was one of his favorite subjects.

"Human kind's history here is a fascinating study, in this land of jungles and exotic animals and mystery. It is a land full of mystery, of a people of ritual and magic. And their time and history here spans a thousand mellenia. *A thousand mellenia.* But one of its great mysteries lay in where these people of south America came from. It is conjectured they either walked down the coastline from what is now known as Alaska, where they had come over the land bridge from Russia and Siberia.

And some perhaps sailed over from the islands thousands of miles west of here. "

He walked to the side of the Podium to emphasize this part here, "But what we do know for sure is that the peoples of both North and south American continents came from somewhere else. Because no where, *nowhere*, are there fossil remains of early man in the western hemisphere. Not one piece. And so this remains a mystery to this day, here in the green peninsula joining the two continents."

"But this ladies and gentlemen is not the only great mystery to be found here in this land. For not only did these people move here and live. But they *thrived.* In fact they thrived and prospered unexpectedly in a harsh environment, with out the help of beasts of burden, small domesticated food animals, nor large crop growing areas. And here lay the greatest mystery of all here in this western continent. Why did these people thrive so, and live to develop one of the most advanced civilizations this planet has ever seen. So advanced that they built what has been become some of the greatest ancient architecture on the planet. " He let that settle in with his audience. But there was complete silence as he had grabbed and held their attention for his introduction. It was a good start.

"I am Professor Antony Jacobs. And I welcome you today to share in discovery, the mysteries of Central America. Lights!" he called out and waved his hand over his head, orchestrating the magic that was controlled in the little room by his friend and student Will Smithershins.

And as the lights dimmed the screen lit up with a bright broad picture of one of the great stone temples of the Mayans.

# 8.
# The Reception

There was a reception that evening for the several speakers that had presented lectures that day for everyone including the attendees. And attendance was high and the room was packed and loud when Antony finally made his way down to it.

The congratulations and handshakes started right away as he entered the room. He may have been somewhat ostracized and reviled after all that stuff in Egypt the precious year, but it seemed people moved on . Or maybe he had notoriety now and people loved dirt. And they wanted to be around people who had endured hardship. Perhaps because they were glad it had not been them that had gone through it.

Or perhaps, Antony chided himself, maybe they really liked my lecture. Lets just try to stick with that, old fella, he said to himself.

He was found by some of the fellows from the Cairo university, although only several. They were of a different ilk and were not so interested in Central American ancient issues as with their ecclesiastic linguistics back in the holy land. Such as well, he thought to himself. This is more peaceful and scholarly than all that conflict about beliefs and faith. Lets try to study things and not veer off into fantasy land or hopeful playground like some of them had been. For many there, the blinders had been firmly attached, And violently defended. And Antony enjoyed working and studying and presenting ideas without that fear of being persecuted and threatened because you stepped on some bodies belief-toes.

"Ah, Professor Jacobs," he heard a voice say, and turned to see his friend from Cairo, Professor Shallot. "I see you survived the convocations. Very nice lecture I hear. Sorry I could not attend. I had other duties. But I understand it was standing room only anyway."

"Well, thank you, James, I enjoyed it a great deal. and I thank all here for their openness to my lectures." Antony said graciously.

"Yes, of course, of course," answered his colleague. He looked around himself for a moment, and then addressed Antony again, "I was looking for some of our people from Egypt. We were able to get some funding for students and interns to come along and have this experience of a large professional conference. But honestly I don't see many of them. They have just arrived and I imagine are holed up getting some shut eye after their trip."

Antony nodded and smiled. Shallot continued, " I will introduce you to some of them when I get a chance. I bet you even recognize some of the faces."

"Ah, very good, very good," he said casually. "I understand there are some activities afield during the week. Some excursions to sites of interest. Is this sponsored by the university, do you know?" he asked his friend.

"Well, if it is not on the schedule than it is probably arranged by the front desk or one or other of the local teachers. Otherwise I really wouldn't know. I am rather involved with the organization of this event and am having a hard time keeping track as it is. You'll have to ask around. Just remember to stay out of the jungle and stick to the worn paths."

Antony nodded and just looked at the man, as he continued, "There are animals and ..." he cleared his throat here, "other things out there. Be careful"

Antony wondered what that meant. But didn't say anything. Was this man superstitious of the hocus -pocus that was said to go on in the jungles by the aboriginals? Voodoo and things like that? He didn't really follow hocus -pocus stories as it really wasn't his area of expertise. He imagined there might be scholars of such things, myth and ritual, followers of Dr Jung and all. But he paid it little mind. He was a scientist after all.

But Shallot had seen the doubt pass over Antony's brow and said, "Oh lighten up dear boy. Nothing out there I'm sure. Its just after that what happened at the end of your tenure in Cairo...." He let that hang for a moment, and Antony gave him a knowing look. The scandal had settled down, as it went completely unsolved. There were simply no leads. No one came forward with information and nothing no forensic evidence was found.

"Yes, that was a shocker," said Antony to his friend. "We were in the states already, and we read about it. But there was no warning of any kind." He hoped that his casual stance didn't give away how close it had all been to him. The threats, the attempt on his life, the fights with that man. But Antony always figured if that man was so hard to get along with, that he finally crossed the wrong person. By the facts it even appeared to have been done in an intimate setting. So a woman killed Hartig? Antony thought we would never know.

Unless someone came forward and confessed or pointed the finger at someone. And even that just seems so unlikely. The murder of professor Hartig had largely gone uncontested and it lay like a festering corpse at the back of everyone's mind.

In a few moments, Antony spied his family and Will standing at the edge of the door. They were waiting for him as he had promised to have dinner with them at the downstairs restaurant. He waved and Mags and Bethany came in to him. "Where's Gwydion?" he asked them.

"He would not come. Something about the people. I don't know. He ordered a sandwich from room service and is watching movies."

"Oh, well," said Mags. "Kinda an adult thing here anyway. All these important people."

And with that they headed out the door, with Will falling into step right behind the family sans Gwydion and they headed off toward the restaurant, amid greetings and handshakes all the way.

# 9.
# More Apocrypha

Everyone was out of his room and there was a party raging down the hall somewhere, he could hear it through the walls and thru the door as the party kids ran back and forth from room to room.

His family were down at the reception and then at dinner. Gwydion was kinda glad to be rid of them. All these people were simply too much. He wanted no more of the lectures for a while. And the dinner and reception held no interest for him. In fact thinking of all those people gave him the cold sweats. And thinking that the other boy might be there, well that about stopped his heart cold.

When they had packed up from New York he had taken very little else but his books. All his toys he left behind either in Egypt when they hurried out. Or a few he left in New York; he just left them there with some family, and when asked, he had said give them to someone.

So he dad several satchel of books and he wanted to spend his quiet time reading with everyone gone.

Then he remembered something. He wondered if they would have been brought with them from the boat. Of course. His grand papa wouldn't leave his work behind on the ship.

Gwydion couldn't help himself. He had to see if there was any more of that gruesome story he had been reading before they had come ashore.

He found his grandfather's brief case and opened it quietly. He leafed through the papers there. This looked like it.

He pulled out the folder of papers and opened it. It was the same group of papers. Now, leaf through he thought, and find where he had left off that night on the boat.

He found the page of transcriptions that he had started before they had come ashore. It was right there.

He picked it up out of the case and carried it over to the couch, transfixed with what might be in there at the end of the story.

He flipped through quickly through the death of Joseph and saw where he had stopped.

The important men from town had come out and taken the body of Joseph back with them to be buried. They noticed the shroud he was wrapped in was not like a normal one; it seems fixed tightly to his body, as if it had been molded around him tightly. And when they moved it, they could not see the seem or the edge of it as if it had no hole in it at all. Jesus traveled with them, and when he looked at his dead father, he recalled all the times they had spent together when he was a child, and all of the pains that the older man had suffered because of him. So Jesus bent over his dead father's shrouded body and wept with grief for quite some time.

And he took this time to explain the subject of death to his followers there on the Mount, explaining that Death only does the command of God. Death cannot make decisions of casting the sinner into the fire or receiving the other up into heaven. Death comes only once to a person, and then only when commanded by God. And Death hears the verdict straight from heaven. And why, asks Jesus, do I not ask my Father in the heaven to come down and deliver Joseph to heaven in a golden chariot, to spare him the fiery roads in death, to live instead with the Angels incorporeal?

Because, Jesus explains, of Adam. Adam disobeyed the Father and obeyed his wife instead and caused all of mankind to have to face death. Even I wear, he said, the troubling flesh of life and must feel death at the end of it to know this death so that I may feel mercy for all of human kind. He explained this was his mission.

Then the Apostles on the Mount with Jesus, hearing this story of the death of his mortal father Joseph asked him why he didn't grant him immortality, like he did Enoch and Elijah. Why did he not grant his father there at his birth in Bethlehem eternal life and immortality?

He explained it this way: Death cannot be annulled now after Adam's transgression. When the Father decides a person will be righteous, that person becomes a chosen one and will leave this plain soon. But when a person loves his work here as the idle hands of the evil workings and takes pleasure of his own will and sins, then God allows him to live a very long life so he will eventually see his bad ways. I know the Elijah and Enoch think of their impending death in a desirous way, so they can escape the endless bounds of this plane, the toil of life. And they know they will die in screams and torment and fear when the devil comes to take them to his home on the last day when all mankind dies and is judged.

Gwydion set the pile of papers down for a moment. He stared off into space until his mind cleared a bit. He had never heard such things. Never. These mechanics of life and death wielded by god and handed down to a naive mankind.

He picked up the papers and walked over to the case to put them back in at the bottom again, in hopes that Antony, his grand papa, would not know he looked at them. As he lifted the pile to put it at the bottom, he saw another stack of papers that looked different. He lifted one pile for the other and glanced into the pages. And what he read there astounded him.

"And there was a place in hell prepared for each sinner unrepentant. For Blasphemers, they will have their tongues tied with rope and hung by them over a pit of unending fire. And the Angels of punishment torment them over this fire for all eternity." His eyes grew wide and is heart beat against his breast bone at this strange tale of torture.

He heard noises in the hall and quickly stuffed the sheaf of papers back into his grand father's brief case and ran to the adjoining room of his and his mother's and jumped in bed and covered his head with the covers. He was sure either he would never sleep again. He knew he would have nightmares all night long. When he finally stopped worrying about not sleeping and having nightmares, he fell off to sleep and had nightmares all night long.

A few doors down the party raged on through the night. The students were from all around the world. But they all spoke the same language of Party, regardless of from where they came.

They were going from room to room, some of them. And some of them were camped out in just one room or another. Every sort of thing was going on, by the sound of it. But all of the hotel personnel were down at the reception, and they really didn't care anyway, just as long as nothing really got broken.

Some one had commandeered a couple bottles of something from the bar below. "How did you get those?" some one else exclaimed.

"I just sneaked in a grabbed them when the bar keep wasn't looking."

"You are such a liar! But give me some or I am telling on you," he said as he grabbed the large bottle of amber brown liquid.

Another couple were on the bed doing things that did not require the bottle. A couple of the boys were watching avidly. A third walked up to them and whispered, "Hey, look what I got!" he proffered a magazine from his waist band of his trousers. It was a pin-up girlie magazine, the other boy could tell. "Where did you get that?" he said as he snatched at it.

"I bought it downtown. They didn't even look at me to see if I was old enough."

"Let me have it!" yelled the other young man.

"No. That will cost you some of that!" He pointed to one of the bottles the other held.

"Alright then, here," He poured him a glass full and reached for the colorful magazine, then retreated with his own bottle and the magazine into the bathroom.

A young man with strange eyes took this all in and decided he needed to find another room to sleep in. He had many friends here as was his congenial nature and he would find somewhere quiet to sleep tonight. He had no use for the scotch or the girlie magazine. He shook his head in disgust and made for the door.

"Where are you going, Enrique?" asked one of his friends from deep inside the room, where a group was watching sports in front of the Television.

"You Americans disgust me," he answered. "I need to get some air and peace and quiet," he spat back a big grin on his face.

There was a cat call and some hissing, but all good natured.

They all wanted to keep this exotic young man partying with them. He was different, he was from Brazil and new and exotic to the mostly Americans and the British students.

# 10.
# After the Reception

The Jacobs had a nice dinner, and after coffee they made their way back out of the dining room on the way to the elevators. Where they ran into Dr. Shallot. The gentlemen shook hands, and the older man ignored the two women at Will's and Antony's side. So they gladly excused themselves and headed to the ladies' room.

"Ya, I wanted to talk to you about that bit just before you left. You know, Dr. Hartig?" Antony stood and looked at him with wide eyes.

"You know, you left so suddenly, I didn't know what to think." said the foreign doctor from the Cairo university.

"What are you trying to say?" said Dr. Jacobs, looking at his associate with wide eyes. It was late and he was full of a good meal and it had been a long day. He felt totally unprepared to deal with a confrontation right now. But he stuck it out. Always better to just be quiet and wait for a small squall to pass. Will stood up straighter, put his hands in his pockets, but said nothing.

"All I'm saying is that his murder is not solved, and you sure left in a hurry." Doctor Shallot's face had grown a better shade of red than the carpet. Will shuffled his feet and looked straight into the drunk man's face.

Antony did not want to talk about it. He never told anyone about the attempt on his life in the basement of the university. He had not seen his assailant.

But the sound of the voice and attitude had said it was Hartig. He never doubted that. The man had been threatening him continuously since they had started on those old texts. He just figured the scholar had finally gotten what was coming to him. He was angry enough that he had finally met someone who did him in. And Antony had decided he wasn't going to take it anymore. He never anticipated the murder would happen the night he and his family left Cairo. He only read about it then a few days later in the newspaper.

"Well. Its just suspicious, that's all," said Dr. Shallot.

"There's nothing to that. We don't know anything. No one ever came forward with any information." Antony said calmly to the old man. And at that instant he realized his young son had told him some story about a boy. But he had figured at the time that it was a child's tall tale. He never would go to the authorities with that kind of a story told by a 14 year old boy.

"You were the one who had something to hide," said his colleague. "you and your translations." He spat that last word out with scorn.

Antony's eyes got wide again. Where was this coming from?

Will stepped forward, but Antony waved him off. "It's alright, Will. I'm used to this."

He had really hoped back at the reception when things seemed blown over, that this man had let it go. Or had at least kept an objective outlook. He was seeing a side to the man he had not ever seen. Perhaps now that Hartig was gone, you know, a void cries to be filled.

"Really, scientific inquiry is so important..." started Antony holding his hand out calmly.

"Scientific inquiry! You people can only think of your science and research. I aughtta..." and he was cut short by the women coming out of the bathroom. They saw the three men still talking and stopped in mid step. Antony offered, "Why don't you ladies go on up and I will be with you soon. Professor Shallot and I have some matters to discuss." The ladies turned and headed for the elevators. Antony thought he saw relief on their faces.

Then he turned back to the other professor. He realized this man was red in the face and obviously had a couple with dinner. So maybe he had been saving this stuff up to say to him when he got the nerve.

So he and Will stood and stuck it a while longer, with patience, not arguing. He figured arguing would just inflame the man.

"Now look here, Professor Shallot. We are all in on that project together. And we were expected to turn out papers on the material. Which you did not do. I on the other hand have published my papers and my book and I still have more work to do."

"More work? Are you publishing more? You need to know your boundaries, young man." He said this as he stuck his finger into Antony's chest. Will held out his hand and the older man removed his finger, stepped back and continued his barrage, pointing at him. "This is OUR religion and you cant just go off flapping your mouth about anything you want. This is OUR religion and I am in charge. I mean, we are in charge. And if you want to flap your mouth about some religion than you better get one, you apostate American Atheist." the man was positively foaming at the mouth now. And Antony would have been entertained if this man wasn't totally serious.

Trying to stay calm, Antony said, " We are trying to be objective, and study this like scholars and scientists. It is our job to be objective and report our findings to the world. It doesn't matter if it a religion or not. These are ancient..."

"It matters everything, its a religion. You Americans with your division of church and state, with your freedom of speech. Why I think we should sue you for Heresy, that's what I think!"

Antony got red in the face. "Heresy? You are nuts!" He threw his hands up in the air in disgust and turned on his heel and headed for the bank of elevators leaving Will to glare at Professor Shallot and then retreat with him..

"I will run you out, so help me God!" said the slightly older man to Antony's back, as the two of them slipped down the hall and into an open elevator, leaving the British scholar fuming in his gin fumes.

Standing in the elevator, he said, "Sue for Heresy?" He laughed and Will laughed too.

"What ancient idea is that?" said Will. "Sue for heresy? Can they even do that these days?"

"Sheesh, don't bring back the inquisition, please!" Pleaded Antony. "Well, professor Shallot," he said quietly, "You can go back to England or Cairo for that matter, and have fun. But when my family returns we will be going home. To the states, thank you!"

Will shook his head and smiled. "You should have been there in Cairo. There were some things I didn't even tell ol' Aloeatious, ol buddy."

"Maybe later," said Will. "Why don't you and your family go get some shut eye."

"Thanks, Will," said Antony. "That is a capitol idea. And," he stammered," thanks for standing there with me."

And Will just winked a little and stepped out of the open elevator door towards his room.

# 11.
# The Stone Temple

It was a day trip over the weekend to the stone temple of inscriptions. A very famous monument in Honduras it had become ever since it's discovery quote unquote by Western observers in the early years of the century. As World War II had grown to a close money had loosened and interest grown and is the archaeological dig it Antony and his family would then become involved with had been started. And it had closed unceremoniously in mystery and intrigue when one group or another one custody of the historical site, and the secrets that lay their.

And lay there still they did. And the Jacobs family knew these grounds intimately. And against perhaps their better judgment they decided they wanted to visit it again. They were after all and bus ride away. And there were busloads going each day, especially now on the weekends when some of the seminars were out and there were no classes at the University, there was time and energy to go on an excursion.

So Mags, Bethany, Anthony, and Gwydion loaded onto the excursion bus early in the morning and headed off down the dirt road into the countryside towards Palenque. With some trepidation Anthony and his family loaded onto the bus carrying their small day packs with water and food approaching the site of the past hopes and dreams and nightmares.

When they stepped up the steep steps of the bus they noticed all of the seats in the back of the car were taken by the boisterous younger dudes heading off for the same day excursion. So the Jacobs family sat in the front row seats. The view was better and Antony could chat with the bus driver in Spanish on the long trip out of the city into the jungle.

They bumped and ground down the dirt Rocky Road, along the steep verdant hillsides, and seemed to hang over precipitous cliffs dropping into hazy blue depths. They hung onto their seats and one another and chunked along toward their day, hopefully to be full of interest. and renewed experience.

# 12.

# Palenque

The Plaza at the Palenque dig had changed. It was no longer an Archaeological dig as the Jacobs family remembered it. But was now a tourist attraction. With all of the media attention, although most of it negative, the place had gained some notoriety and infamy.

So they had cleaned it up for the curious tourists. And the Jacobs family found it very different indeed.

No, it wasn't quite Disney Land. Because you still had to hike 7 miles to get into it. They just couldn't make bus roads for the buses to make it up that last part with out destroying the rock mountain itself, and possibly take down the whole thing, ancient man-made structures included.

So it was the early afternoon by the time everyone got there after the bus ride and the hike, and they came over the ride and saw the pyramid standing in a grassy plaza, cleared of it jungle vegetation.

When they had been here for the dig, some years ago, it had been over grown. That was why no one noticed or bothered with the place for thousands of years.

Almost all of this crowd that disembarked was from the lecture series and conference back at the university and they all sort of gathered together except for a few young people that scampered off to find adventure on their own. There was no guided tour today, just Professor Jacobs and a bunch of students and his family, and they milled around together in wonder at the this pyramid spectacle that unfolded as they topped the curve of the ride into the plaza.

Someone spoke up and asked Antony, Professor Jacobs a question. "how Old is this?"

"Well," Antony started before the next question came out starting the flood.

"How many more are there like this?"

"What did they use all those steps for?"

"How could they ever build something so huge out of such huge boulders?"

Antony held his palms out to stem the tide. "Ok, wait. Let me just start and I'll try to answer all your questions."

"The Maya and the Olmec lived simultaneously in these parts, along with other distinct groups, all very similar, but each having its own distinct flavor of life. It could be said that the Maya were the first, the oldest, say around 2000 BC, before the birth of the western Christ savior. But they did not flourish until about 1400 years later, say 600 B.C. And by this time the Olmec had come and gone. But they left a lasting legacy of culture that extends through subsequent cultures here, through to the present. Such things as these pyramids you see here. But this was not the first built, nor the largest. But it has some attributes that have drawn attention to itself, in the media and around the world."

A small crowd had gathered around him in the grassy plaza. This had not been intended to be a formal lecture. But anyone who had ever gone out with Professor Antony Jacobs knew it would become an exciting educational experience. He seemed to know more about stuff, all kinds of stuff, than anyone. And he loved to talk about it and explain.

And no question was too dumb or ignorant for him to answer. He never reprimanded new ideas or even misguided myths. He would explain as best he could. Or he would truthfully say he just did not know the answer to this question. Antony believed if he said that, then the person would be more likely to want to go explore and find the answers on his own. He had seen too many stingy professors become angry and defensive at a question or hypothesis that he did not have the answer for.

"Some other less savory things also followed through these local cultures, some things the authorities have not been so happy about discovering and even less happy about releasing to the public."

Voices around him said, "Like What?" A little alarmed.

"We've all heard about the human sacrifice aspects and the blood letting. They had a sport that involved two teams who smacked and kicked a ball around the field and tried to get it into the ramp at the top of the rock wall. A lot of us cannot accept however that the losing team captain was ritually beheaded on the field fin front of everyone, and then his head kicked into the goal by the winning team. That part is a little hard for us to accept. But it seems to be true."

There was a silence for about a minute as this soaked into the people around him, and someone said, "There's no way. That can't be true." Abject denial.

"How can they know that?" another woman asked.

"Well, we have recently uncovered what you could call a Rosetta stone, that has helped us translate a lot of these ancient inscriptions.; I am no expert in this language, but many things have come to light. I think there is more they are taking their time to tell us about actually."

"So they are lying," said a young man.

"I wouldn't call it lying exactly. I think these things are pretty darn disturbing. I mean, you guys are scientists, young ones anyway, and you all were just disgusted with what I was saying. So John Q public is going to have even a harder time accepting these shocking things. So they release this stuff slowly and see how people react before they release some more."

"Ya? Like what else?" said some one young and male from the back.

"Well lets see. How about the calendar. Have any of you heard about the calendar?" he asked the group at large to see where they were as far as the latest Mayan discoveries.

"Oh, Ya. Isn't it supposed to end in a while?" someone offered.

"Yes. There is a calendar based on the stars and the writing ends on the date December 23, 2012, about 50 years from now. What do you think that means?"

"That the world comes to an end?"

"I says in the inscriptions on the edges of the calendar that all civilizations will end every 5200 years, at the end of 13 Baktuns, or 400 years cycles. The most recent cycle began early in the 30th century before Christ and will end in 2012. This was their idea of recycle and renewal. Or perhaps they felt that humans needed to be cleansed and then renewed again for some reason, that is not explained. Or it could be based on their most recent experiences somehow."

"Or maybe its just the end of the written calendar," Bethany said under her breath next to Antony, and smiled up at him, remembering one of their heated arguments they had once had about this subject.

"Yes, it may just be that it is the end of the calendar that they had written. And then later people reinterpreted it to mean a great deal more than it was ever intended. We have to ask our selves how much do we believe in astrology. Because that is how this date was determined."

The were some exclamations at that. "Astrology? Or Astronomy?" some one said.

"You didn't know that? Oh, yes. They watched the stars very closely. And we were surprised when we found out how closely their calendar matched the turning of the wheel of stars in the sky. Funny though, these places are so old, that the constellations have changed, and wheeled a little further in the sky than they were at the time these stones were set to align with them. Yes, those constellations move in the sky relative to each other. Just over thousands of years."

There were some murmurings and rustlings as people began to move away to go check things out.

"But you want shocking? There is one more thing that has just come to light," said Antony. He was getting into dangerous territory here. Where he had strayed years ago at this dig when it first started. But he did not intend to go all the way there with these students. He and his family had barely talked about what had gone on years ago at this magical place, Palenque. But there was one part of it he could talk about. His crowd sensed his excitement and mystery and stopped their retreat and turned to give him their attention once again.

"These temples are the sites where the rituals took place. Now, ancient cultures preformed rituals to try to align themselves with the stories they believe, so as to become in tune with their god or what they thought to be the order of the universe, And every culture seems to develop ritual to help them through their lives. Even our modern churches are based on the ritual." He heard some people grumble and he knew that some people could not view their religion objectively enough to see that it was "ritual". In fact some people became superstitious simply at the usage of the word ritual.

"And these rituals involved Human sacrifice, which I think is the most difficult of all things for our western minds to accept. And there was one ritual that was particularly gruesome. It beats even the beheading of the team captain at the gladiatorial Mayan games. "

He let that set a minute. And every one stopped moving. Or even breathing. Waiting for him to continue.

"You will see inside the Temple, if you dare go in there. It is dark and damp and a little strange. The steps echo harmoniously, which is why it is sometimes called the Temple of Singing. It has inscriptions on the walls and a large stone carving deep in the bowels of the thing, which is why it is sometimes called the Temple of Inscriptions or Writings. The carving on the huge slab appears to be a man in some kind of mechanical weapon or craft, which why he is sometimes called the Stone Temple Pilot. But down in the crypt you will see something carved in stone that you will not understand until I explain it to you. And even then, your mind may not allow you to accept it. "

He waited for some people to exhale.

"It is a figure of a human holding a bowl, and it is called a Chocmool. And the bowl is used to hold the freshly dissected still-beating human heart on display." There were gasped and a couple "Yuck"'s from the crowd.

Professor Jacob smiled that his story hit home again. Each time he told it, even sometimes the same old people had heard the story before, responded with the same human revulsion at the story. "Yuck." Disbelief. Disgust. Doubt. Denial.

"The story is that the Priests inside this temple, at least for these people here at this site, practiced ritual dissection of the human heart. Now, you have to understand, anatomically the heart is buried deep in the body beneath layers of muscle and bone. It is in the hard bone capsule of the rib cage and chest. And it takes a great deal of effort to dig it out. And this was done ritually with stone knives while the man was still alive. They maybe had copper knife which may or may not stand up to a grown man's chest bones. Even today, when a cadaver is dissected, it takes a bone saw of steel to get through. Well, these guys hacked thru it with knives and stones." A woman stepped away and retched in the grass.

"And the resulting mess was placed on the ritual chocmool and worshiped. "But Antony noticed that the woman who had been sick came back to listen some more. Fascinating stuff!

"The myth is that they had a way to preserve it somehow so that it continued to beat forever. If they has selected the correct individual as king, for his eventual sacrifice at the temple and his still beating heart was placed in the Chocmool. There is still another story of the heart then being placed inside the Cairn of eternal life, underneath the slab of the Stone Temple Pilot, where the still-beating heart remains forever to protect the people forever, creating a kind of eternal music with it beating.

But we can see of course that this was just a myth, as these people have been gone for a thousand years."

That was it for Antony, he may have said too much as pertained to the secrets that had been buried those few years ago at the closed down dig, where he had been fired as Anthropologist, and he and his family had left in disgrace.

He knew it wasn't disgrace, but the authorities' fear of the truth lay beneath the massive carved stone slab. And he also felt comforted that, like water on a stone, the persistence of human curiosity would chip away at the stone lid of the secret, and as in all things of secret nature, time passes and eventually people will know. He hoped so any way.

# 13.

# Inside the Temple

People wandered off and explored. Bethany and Mags had packed a really great picnic lunch for the family and they opened up the blanket and spread out the lunch for them on the grass.

Antony and Will sat down on the blanket with a thunk. He looked at Bethany and said, "Oh, sorry about that. Always seems to become a lecture."

Bethany said to her husband, "No worries. Its what you do. Educate people."

He patted her knee, and said, "Thanks, hun. My best fan."

Mags laughed, and said, "No, dad. That was great! You even made a lady puke!"

Antony shook his head. "It happens sometimes. Especially that really gory part. I'm kinda used to it and I forget." He looked at his daughter with a sly smile and added, "And sometimes it happens in the auditorium and we have to take a puke break." They all laughed at that and settled down for some late lunch.

But they looked around each other and realized something was missing.

"Where's Gwydion?" asked his grand father.

"I don't know. He was right here," said Bethany.

"No. I think he left at the beginning of the talk you were giving. He's probably heard it a bunch of times." said Will.

"Yup. Probably," said Antony.

But just then, he must have smelled the lunch being busted out, came running Gwydion, red in the face.

They all looked at him. "Where have you been, young man?" asked his grand father.

"In the temple," he added quite out of breath.

"Already?" asked Bethany, unbelieving.

He looked at his grandfather momentarily with hunted eyes and nodded his tousled head vigorously . "There's someone in there!" He obviously had run up the steps and back down in no time just to do it. There is little open area in the temple, just a couple sets of stone steps leading down to several ritual crypts. So it is quite a climb up and back.

"I thought it was closed off?" said Antony.

"And where is the new coat I bought you?" asked his mother.

Gwydion just grimaced and sat down and tucked into a sandwich. And as he proudly surveyed the tall steep temple where he had just come back from his adventure, he noticed a dark figure climb the steps and slip inside the temple.

It was getting dark, he could tell by the waning light coming down the cave stairwell.

I have been sitting down here waiting for you for a very long time, he thought. It's been all day seems like.

He had been watching the boy all day. For days actually, staying just around the corner and out of sight. Or he hoped anyway.

And when he saw the boy in his ugly yellow jacket go up the stairs earlier in the day when everyone was listening to that vapid professor, he started to hatch a plan. Meet him in this cave in the temple. But shortly after he saw the boy come back down the stairs but he was no longer wearing his coat. He must have gotten hot and left it in the cave in the temple, and he knew he would go back in to get it. I'd get a beating from my father if I left a new coat like that behind somewhere.

He'd hiked up just after that. But he'd been sitting here in the dark waiting all day. Why didn't he come back? They would all miss the bus when it headed back to the university.

He just wanted to talk to the boy. Be reasonable, find out what he knew. Explain what happened and maybe be friendly and get him to agree. Wouldn't that be better than this wondering what he was thinking and wondering what he was saying to people? Let's just talk about it and get it in the open, then we can go home and have it done with.

But sitting here in the dirt in the cold dark stone cave was getting on his nerves. Didn't the kid know he had to come back for his coat? I guess I could'a talked to him at the hotel. But with all those people around being suspicious, that would not have been good at all. We don't need anyone listening to our little conversation now do we?

He rustled around and tried to get comfortable. His butt cheeks were getting numb so he stood up and paced around a little.

And what was with this block of stone in the middle of the small room here for? He got up near it and looked at its surface closely. It was carved, he noticed.

He walked around it to see if he could tell what it was. He got to an angle and recognized maybe a face. A strange face, not like people he was used to seeing. But all the shapes around him did not make any sense to him at all.

"Stupid Archaeology!' he said out loud to himself in the small space, and he kicked the stone pedestal.

But he instantly regretted doing it and his foot started to throb. And throb. In fact it wouldn't stop throbbing. And he could feel it all through his body now throbbing to the rhythm of his heart beat, which seemed heavy to him right now. The walls of this small space felt like they were closing in as the sun set outside.

Throbbing and throbbing his foot carried on. So he sat down and untied his boot and pulled it off to rub his foot. It seemed to have swelled a little and the boot was difficult to get off.

He set his boot aside and sat against the stone wall and waited for his heart to calm down. He could still hear it or feel it, which ever, in his ears, behind his eyes, in his stupid foot.

He must have fallen asleep again as he awoke with a start when he heard some scuffling up above on the now rather dark stone stair passageway to the top. He hastily slipped on his shoe but forgot to retie the strings.

# 14.

# Deep Inside

After they finished eating lunch, the family packed up and did some exploring. They had been here years before, but now it looked so different. They had formed a conservation group in charge of cleaning and maintaining the site and making it available for tourists. All part of some conservation committee or something. They had cleared the plaza of jungle and in the course of doing that, there had been discovered some more monuments and artifacts.

Few people wanted to climb up the very steep steps of the Stone Temple. They were really actually quite dangerous. No one has really theorized about the purpose of this type of structure. Indeed in Egypt, most of those pyramids have no writing inside them. There are few rooms, as if it was never intended for many people to live there. They seem to be for housing ritual objects for ceremonial purposes with just a few people present. And those steep stone steps, Antony thought that maybe this was, judging by some of the ancient paintings he had seen, these steep steps were for displaying the remains of the sacrificial victims. The priest would stand at the top and roll the remains down the steps. And the parts would roll down partway, for sure. These steps were that steep. In fact, Antony was surprised they allowed people to go up there at all.

Inside this Temple of Inscriptions there was one long hallway that descended deep into the temple, he remembered from the digs years ago, when they first excavated inside the temple and pulled out the rubble and dirt that had collected over the eons. And they had discovered that incredible carved plaque at the bottom, on top of what looked like a pedestal or dais. But the stone surface was deeply carved with a complicated image and Antony couldn't imagine that it had been used as a sacrificial surface, it would have marred the image there. And it was not marred at all but smooth like it had just been carved. And when they had wiped off all the collected dust and dirt from ages of sitting there deep in the man-made cavern, it looked like it had never aged.

And Antony had wondered then what its real use was. Why carve that incredible art work and never have anyone but a few select, probably just priests, see it? Why was it on a pedestal but not used as a sacrificial dais? And what was the image? What did it mean? How could they have thought of the idea of a man sitting inside a machine spewing fire out of both ends. With hands and feet on what looked like levers or controls of some machine? How anachronistic; modern.

At the time of the dig, the rumors had flared and gone viral. And the powers that be had shut down the whole thing and covered it up politically and with the media, saying it was nothing. But Professor Jacobs had suspected there was something under the slab, something that was very sacred and important to this ancient culture, denoting some strange experience they had had that had inspired them to make this temple, and carve that huge slab of rock and hide it deep inside. Something inside that cairn, something beneath that slab.

But he would never know. When the threats started he backed away and took his family home to safety. Forget them he had thought. Nothing is worth that kind of assault. He faced a similar kind of assault in Egypt when he got too close to some sacred truths with those old texts. And look what had happened. Some one on the team had died. Murdered. Antony felt he had gotten his family out of there just in time.

But now this site had been sanitized and made safe for people to come visit. There was little awareness of anything ever having gone on here, ten years before. Few people knew about the carved slab of the stone temple pilot. It was if a miasma of fear and guilt hung around it that people could feel and they simply stayed away from asking that fearful question: what is the stone temple pilot? What does it mean? And how does it relate to the practice of the ritual human sacrifice of the Still-Beating Heart?

# 15.
# The Chamber

Gwydion ran around for a while, enjoying the sunshine and the jungle he had grown up in. He walked with his family for a while, ooh-ing and ahh-ing over birds and calls from the edge of the deep verdant forest. But eventually everyone grew tired, and settled into a stupor of too much interest in things and they all began to gather near where the buses would be taking them back to the university in about an hour.

The hour was wearing on and the sun was beginning to set behind the temple. The shadow grew long and the deep steps began to be bathed in a dark layer of ink. He seen a person go up and go in hours before, right after he had come down, and now his curiosity got the better of him.

Earlier when he had gone up, it had been bright and mid day sun was shining directly on the steps. The surface was hot and he had to trot up if he was to get out of the glare and heat. He had gone deep inside and down the steep steps to the cairn of the slab dais. It fascinated him. It was dark and he had taken a tiny pen light with him from the university. It worked only so well in the deep dark ink deep inside the stone edifice.

But now it was getting really dark and he was not sure how well this little light was going to help down in there.

But he had to see who that was. And maybe he should go get his coat. So he climbed up after him. No one could see him go up, the sun was slanting through the plaza and would blind anyone who looked over at the temple.

When he got to the top, he stopped and listened. He could strangely hear everything people said down in the plaza. It amplified their voices and he heard a jumble of conversation. He imagined the opposite might be true: his voice from the top of the temple would probably amplify down into the plaza. He could imagine the priests with their high feathered headdresses way up high holding their arms out and calling to the gods to bless them all. He imagined the priests throwing the offerings down the sides of the temple and watching as the pieces of the former King rolling splat plop down each step in a juicy bloody mess. The thought horrified and fascinated Gwydion. How could they ever do that? Wouldn't it be a terrible bloody mess? On everything? He wondered how this could signify any kind of worship or please a god in any way. How could those people believe that. And he had his first real inkling of how far a religion could get out of hand with too much worship time and desperation.

He stepped towards the opening that would lead down into the crypt, and listened.

Nothing. No sounds. No steps, no breathing.

He flipped on his little flashlight and probed its beam around the doorway and then down the top of the steps.

He listened again, thinking anyone down there would call out, seeing the sliver of light from his torch.

He flashed it on the first steps and slowly began to descend. One step at a time.

A slight turn to the left, then a few more steps. He stopped and listened. He thought he heard some scuffling.

He felt his throat tighten up.

He was not too prone to speech anyway and it completely betrayed him now. Not a sound came out of his throat as he tried to ask if anyone was there. So he continued.

A slight turn to the right then a few more steps and he was almost to the bottom. He stopped and listened again. And he heard what he had heard earlier today when he was here. A beating.

He stopped and held his breath. Yes, definitely a beating, like a small deep drum. He took a deep breath a silently as he could. He shined his light on the next step and began slowly downward again. His foot missed and he slipped and stumbled a little. He heard something down at the bottom. He took four more steps and was almost to the slab and dais of the pilot slab. He shined his light around and almost lost his heart.

"I knew you would come," said a voice out of his nightmares. "You just had to follow me. Like a cat," the voice said with deep derision.

Gwydion just gulped and sucked for air. The beating was heavy against his ears and throat, and his hands seemed to be swelling. He shined the light at the face that had haunted his nightmares ever since they were in Egypt. His breathing quickened like a winded animal escaping a predator.

"What is wrong with you, boy? Cat got your tongue?" taunted the older boy as he laughed. "What do you think you are doing anyway? I have been waiting for you for hours."

"What are you talking about?" said Gwydion quietly.

"Your stupid coat!" he said as he flung the ugly yellow coat at the boy. "What took you so long?."

"I would not have come if I knew you were down here!" he spat out trying to put his arms in the sleeves of his too large coat.

"Why? Are you afraid of me, boy?" he asked with thick derision. "If you had just shut up everything would have been fine. But you had to talk, didn't you? I was just going to let it go. But you are such a liar!"

Gwydion wasn't really sure what he was talking about so he just shut his mouth. But it had something to do with being in Egypt, when this boy had bullied him before. Things he didn't care to remember, but things that were vivid sometimes when he closed his eyes at night. There was never anything he could do. He tried to talk about it. But that seemed to make it even worse. He had tried to tell himself it was just a bad dream. But it would come back just the same a few nights later.

And here it was, in living color. How did he follow him? How did he know he would be here?

Gwydion had thought he saw this cross-eyed boy a couple times at the convention this last week. He was never sure though and had put it out of his head for being suspicious. He thought he had seen him at the back of the bus earlier in the day but he had turned away quickly thinking it was a hallucination. Hoping it was.

But here he was ; the boy from his nightmares. In the bottom of the crypt. With no light.

He swung his tiny light around again and caught the older boy in the face. "Stop that! You punk! I'm going to get you for that. And all those lies you told everyone about me. You've been ganging up on me with those stupid kids at the seminar. Oh, they taunt me and make fun of me behind my back. But I know what they all say. The cross-eyed freak. But *you* are the freak! You are not even a student here!" In his rage, the older boy was starting to come forward toward Gwydion in the dark. His arms reaching out like specters in the gloom, and he loomed before Gwydion in almost total darkness. The pen light flitted and amplified the moving shadows into huge shapes across the stone and mud walls.

"Nooo!" Gwydion cried at the older boy lunged at him. He spun away and the pen light flicked away. He heard it hit a stone surface and the light went out. Gwydion did the only thing possible: he ran toward the stairs and followed the very weak rectangle of light leading out.

He was a very agile boy and he could run up stairs very quickly. He had a slight advantage over the larger taller, slightly older boy. But he felt hands snatch at this clothes several times, but he managed to scrabble away, and pull his clothes free. But his coat was starting to come off his shoulders. It was too big, his mother had bought it for him for this trip, leaving room for him to grow some more.

But the running boy behind him caught the hem and held on. Gwydion twisted and grunted with effort and the coat started to slide down his arms. The older boy stumbled on his loose shoes strings, fell and caught himself partly using Gwydion's coat for balance. But Gwydion wiggled and twisted and the new coat snapped free of his wrists and hands, and the coat and the larger boy fell backward down the stairs. Gwydion heard a cry and some thumping taper off down into the gloom of the stone stairs back into the depths of the crypt. And he kept going upward.

He got to the top of the staircase and took a moment to look around for his eyes to adjust to the little bit of light still left in the evening air, and for his panicking lungs to catch air and for his rapidly beating heart to catch up. Then he looked down and involuntarily let out a small cry and could see people waiting near the road for the bus to take everyone back to the university. When all their heads turned towards him.

He jumped down the steps outside of the temple as quickly as he could, and met Will Smithershins at the bottom. Will held out his arms and said something. But it did not register in Gwydion's mind as he raced by towards the group of people waiting for the bus. He ran toward the group of people, as they were just beginning to board the bus. His family was standing at the edge of the crowd scanning for him. Time was running short and they had been prepared to make the bus wait for him. They were very relieved when he came running up out of breath, with Will jogging right behind him.

"Where have you been?" reprimanded Antony with some concern in his voice.

Gwydion avoided his gaze, bent over and tried to catch his breath.

"And where is your new coat?" asked his mother, Mags incredulously. "I thought you went back to get it?"

She looked at Will, who just shrugged his shoulders, and she said, "Well, we're not going back to look for it now. It's too late." She lurched her arm around Gwydion's head, and turned with frustration towards the bus. And they all waited in line to get on the bus to take them the three hour trip back to civilization.

# 16.

# Unconscious

The young man lay unconscious at the bottom of the stairwell made of stone deep inside the stone temple. He lay there for a long time flitting between life and death, with his bleeding head against the pedestal of raw stone, next to the ornately carved altar of the sleeper. The contusions on his forehead in his arms and ankles oozed blood onto the naked cold stone beneath him, his quarry having escaped quickly as he fell to the depths of his cairn.

And as he slept he dreamed. He dreamed in black and white and red, the dreams of the magic of this land, in this green jungle of Honduras.

He dreamed of a war in the sky above them, the native Indians of these plains and mountains. He dreamed of two hero twins that arrived from the stars to fight one another for prescience over this primitive land of magic. They fought a battle of fire and brimstone intending to knock one another out of the sky. While the native peoples stood and stared upward watching the spectacle by night and day.

The bits of fire and brimstone rained down upon the earth and filled these native naked people with terror and fear of God's far greater than ever before imagined. The head priests of this nature cult devised elaborate rituals and sacrifice to wish peace of the warring gods raining fire and wrath upon their heads.

Deep in this cold cairn, a priest with a tall feathered headdress towering above him feathered and shaking in the torchlight, naked but for paint on his skin. He cried a while, then a real cry and raised his arms over his head bearing a shining sharpened dagger and said the magic words asking for release from the terror of the wars above them. The sharpened ritual dagger pointed down towards the bare chest of the sacrificial victim. But this victim was not just anyone. No, the rolling bloodshot white eyes in the ricktus of fear was on the face of his son, the one chosen for the highest honor of sacrifice, over the slab of the sleeper of eternity.

For every generation gave one such sacrificial victim. And within this cairn and beneath the slab of the sleeper of eternity, would lay forever the still beating heart of the sacrificial victim. For once exposed to the breath of this Cairn of the Sleeper, the heart of this victim would forever remain awake bleeding and beating in the darkness of eternity.

The young man remained unconscious and asleep on the floor of this cairn for quite some time. For the cycle of the day and a night, he slept in crooked repose, his body slowly mending those bloody rents in his skin. Because the secret remained buried under the slab of the Sleeper of Eternity that has repeatedly been covered and returned to the secret world. The secret being the rejuvenation powers of what lay hidden underneath the slab. Where the sleeper's heart beats until eternity. And so with his near-death fall to the rock floor, some seeping gas from deep within the rock touched this young man just a bit, and gave him a slight advantage of rejuvenation that none others would have. And when he awoke the day after, his body was mostly mended although his clothing still bore the rents and tears and smears of blood from his fall.

Late into the night Gwydion got out the sheaf of papers he had taken from his grand father's brief case and began reading from where he left off. The word on the outside of the stack read "Apocrophon".

He wasn't sure what that meant exactly and why this particular sheaf of papers was called that, but somehow he knew this was different from the others. Very different from all the other stories and he was fascinated to no end. It dug deep into his young psyche and stirred things that had been awakened by these dark violent events here recently, and back in Egypt with this strange evil boy.

He read on. "Men and women will come to places after they die that have been prepared for them by God and his angels. There are Angels at God's side who prepare for the souls that have followed the right path. And there are other Angels unnamed who have prepared the places for the souls that have sinned.

"And this place is prepared that the blasphemers will go. And there they shall hang by their tongues for the blaspheming they have spoken. And beneath them as they hang, shall be an unending fire that will burn forever as they hang in it's fuming wake.

"There is another pit prepared for those who reject righteousness, those that choose to be bad and make excuses for their behavior. And there, the Angels who have prepared it, will have a fire burning forever for all those who deserve to be burned and punished in this torment of fire.

"And see here as two women who braided their hair, not to be beautiful, but to seduce men into fornication.

And these two women will be hung by their necks and by their hair and are cast into the pit of forever burning fire.

"And behold the men that laid with them in fornication shall be hung by their male genitals in the pit of fire. And these men will cry out, "We did not know we would have punishment forever for what we did." But the time for asking for mercy had already passed.

"And then come murderers and their accomplices. And they shall be thrown into the pit with all kinds of venomous beasts. And they will be tormented by these ravenous beasts without respite, but never consumed. The worms that eat at their bodies shall be thick in number, crawling in and on them.

And the Angel of Wrath Ezrael will then bring the souls of those who were slain by these murderers, for them to see them be tormented for what they had done to these innocent souls. And the souls of the slain will see how God's judgment is righteous. And they will say to each other that they had heard of such judgment, but had never believed that it could actually be true."

Gwydion's eyes were blurry. He turned off the tiny flashlight and looked around the darkened room. He could see just a faint light coming in the window from a partial moon.

It was deep into the night and he could hear no other noises. He was very tired but felt jangled and very awake. He thought he would never sleep. The terror of the day continued to tear down from his heart to his fingertips and back.

But he must have fallen asleep because he woke with a start, slumped over in his blankets and pillows.

He found the pile of papers rumpled and wrapped in the blankets with him and he switched on the flashlight again.

He started with the next paragraph. "In this hell, this area of fire, is a very deep pit. Into it flows all kinds of awful stuff from above, foulness, excrement, and pain. This pit is for women who have fornicated and had children born when God did not ask for them to be, so the women killed their children, or the children died because of the neglect they suffered from their not being wanted. These sinners are swallowed up to their necks and they soak in the excrement with tremendous pain. And beside them are living children and watching what is happening to these women who have wronged them. And lightening shoots out of their eyes and strikes the eyes and blinds these people who have caused, by their need to fornicate, the destruction of these children, these innocent souls.

The parents of these destroyed children have their souls bared for all to see their sins, and they stand before their children this way. And the children understand, and they cry out to God, "These sinners have cried out against your righteousness and have broken your rules, and sent us, their children, to their deaths. They cursed your angels that made us live and thus they denied us the light you have granted all living creatures." And light flickered through their softly beating wings.

And God found a way to give them their due. The mother's milk in them dried up and congealed, then flesh devouring beasts came and ate them slowly, forever, with their husbands. These are the sinning parents of babies who were cared not for their unwanted birth, which was simply an accident of fornication. The slain children will be allowed to wait here in this suspended time until it comes that their parents die, and then they will be confronted for their sins by these angels they have created themselves by neglect."

And with these visions of tortures and punishments, Young Gwydion slid into a ball of blankets on the floor and off to a deep sleep.

# 17.

# Antony's Lecture Continues

The next day Professor Jacobs was scheduled to continue his lecture on the ancient history of the Mayan and Aztec cultures.

He got dressed and started to head out for his lecture early that morning. He turned to Gwydion who was sitting against the wall in the corner. "Are you coming, son?" Gwydion did not even look up.

Antony walked over to him and stood over him. And still he did not look up . He had something clutched in this lap and he was trying to cover it up with a pillow. Antony reached down and pulled the pillow up a little and noticed that it was a stack of some of his works he had been translating.

"Just make sure you put that back in my case, alright Gwydion?"

The answer was a vigorous nod of the tousled brown head.

Antony thought a second, then reached down again and uncovered the stack to see the title. "The Apocryphon". That is not light stuff, my dear boy. I'll tell you what, we will read some of this together tonight, and there is something I will pick up from the library on my way back here after my lecture, OK?"

Gwydion looked up and his dark eyes met his grandfather's for just a second, and Antony wondered at the raw tears that held themselves against his dark lashes. Antony bent down and kissed the boy on the cheek. "I'll be back in a while. You stay put and rest."

As Antony left the room to head downstairs to the lecture hall, he wondered what was going on with Gwydion.

He seemed spooked after yesterday's trip to the temple. He had lost his coat when he came back so late, like he was running from something, all out of breath and looking haunted. Then it looked like he had stayed up all night reading that gory Apocrophon, the one that was also called the Apocalypse of Peter. He would have to explain some of this stuff to the young man if he had some time this evening.

Antony got out his little paper pad and pencil and wrote himself a note to pick up a certain book on his way back from the University library.

Anthony came into the lecture hall for the continuance of his lecture from today's previous. He started in again on the history of the Aztec and the Mayan myths of this green isthmus of Panama.

"I'd like to introduce you today to two of the most famous characters in MesoAmerican myth. There are many many myths in this land of wonder and one of them is of the birth of the hero twins. Their father and uncle of our future hero twins have one continuing passion on this planet, that of the ballgame. The ballgame was a match played between 2 teams on a field of grass and sloping stone surfaces. It was played by many MesoAmerican cultures including one called the Olmec.

It was of such importance, not just source of entertainment. It became a symbolic reenactment of the gods conflict in the heavens. The captain of the defeated team is forced to kneel on the ground and his head is severed and all seem to enjoy the streams of blood pushing out from his neck over the green field." Antony flipped his slide projector and a nice picture of a green field surrounded by sloping stone slabs came into focus.

"And in a macabre manner it is played with a ball. Now this was no ordinary ball. But a ball of leather with a human skull stuffed into its center."

"Gwydion," said Antony as he came in the room after dinner. The boy had opted again to stay in the room while the rest of them went out to dinner.

"I have something I want to show you." He pulled out of his pocket a small red book with gold lettering on the front and back binding.

"This is "The Inferno" written by Dante degli Alighieri in the 14$^{th}$ century. It is the first section of a larger book of poems called La Comedia, or The Divine Comedy. This poem has at one time been considered the most influential work of all time and Dante is often considered the father of the Italian language for the standards set down by this epic poem.

"The ideas about heaven and hell were highly popular for a thousand years after Christ was born. But the original documents it was based on were not found again until 1800's, when a crypt of a monk was opened in France, and found wrapped in with his skeleton. So it is assumed Dante himself had some older copies of this Gnostic gospel known as the Apocryphon, or the Apocalypse of Peter, with him.

But now here we have found more of this story even older in the old libraries dug up in Egypt. Very lucky indeed.

He came and sat near Gwydion on the floor. "Those scrolls that I have been translating, it was very old, over 1500 years old. And Dante must have had some sort of copy too, and during his political exile he turned it into a book that became very famous and was very widely read by the population after his death. It is said that the originals were very widely read in the early christian years and it was even considered to be new testament. But eventually it was taken out of the bible. I think it is probably the source for how we view heaven and hell to this day."

He cracked open the old book and together they began to read passages very similar to what Gwydion had been reading alone to himself from his grand father's sheaf of translations.

# 18.

# Don't Say That To Me

The boy quietly knocked on the professors door. All was quiet in the halls as he chose the middle of the night to come back in. It took him a day to come back around, he was pretty banged up and not thinking all that clearly. Plus he had to come back by local transportation because the tour bus had left already. And besides he couldn't be seen by those people in this state of dishevelment.

But he had a pretty good story worked out and he hoped the professor would believe it.

He had his own room, but it was packed with other students, and like those creeps were going to help him out. More likely he figured they would taunt him, make fun of him and maybe even beat him up some more.

So he hoped, he figured this nice old professor would feel sorry for him and let him in and help him get cleaned up. That was the impression he had given the boy when it back in Cairo. He had told him that Hartig had given him a good review, called him one of his most promising students, although the boy was pretty sure that was not at all what the older man had been thinking about, scholarship, no.

But anyway this professor Shallot had believed him and had taken him under his wing, so to speak, although in not quite so endearing a way as the other one had. But enough that the boy felt protected or at least a little favored. Enough so that the professor had found a small scholarship and a stipend to get him to this conference on the other side of the sea. And a plan a hope had formulated in the young man's brain that he could find where he suspected his nemesis could be found and this mess straightened out.

But he had botched that today. He had waited and waited. He knew he would show up again for his coat. Then he was sure he had the boy cornered, in that dark stone temple, away from everyone. That boy was always going out alone, he should be so easy to catch. So easy.

But he always managed to slip away. Always. That dam coat and his own dam shoe laces.

His temper was starting to rise as he thought about these things and he quickly put the kibosh on it to cool it off. Don't think about him now. I need to get cleaned up and figure out this mess. What a mess. And he was a mess too. Beat up, bleeding, his clothing torn.

But hopefully this professor would help him out and help clean him up. Maybe even go over and get his clothes and stuff so he wouldn't have to face those other mean foreign students.

He heard rustling inside the room and stepped back a little from the door as to not scare the professor when he opened it. It was the middle of the night after all. Step back and lean on the opposite wall. Well, don't touch it, I don't want to leave a smear.

When professor Shallot opened the door he gave a little start. "Oh, my. What happened to you?"

It was deep into the night, just the beginning of the morning hours when Professor James Shallot was awakened by something. He was sleeping on his very comfortable bed in his very comfortable room at the hotel, in the convention complex

that had grown up around the discoveries of ancient cities and the building of the massive canal project, the
Panama Canal. The College of antiquities had decided to hold their conference here, in this wild jungle of mysteries.

He heard the quiet knocking on his outer door again. And why anyone would be knocking on his door in the middle of the night was definitely a mystery to him.

He tied the complimentary cotton robe around his pajamas, slipped on the old leather slippers he always wore, and moved to the door. He had no fear of vandals; this was inside the huge hotel, up about 4 floors, after all. Who could this be? A sick student maybe? A professor with some crazy new idea?

He looked out the peep hole, but saw no one.

He slid of the chain and unbolted the door and cracked it slightly.

"Yes?" he whispered into the dead quiet white hallway of the fancy hotel.

And there to the side stood a slight figure in dirty clothes, one he recognized as one of his students that had traveled with the group.

"Oh, my! What happened to you?" he said as he stood taller and stepped back opening the door for the student to come in.

"I was with the tour group, and I fell and knocked my head. When I came too, it was dark and everyone had left." The student seemed genuinely distraught. Looks like he had been beat up too. His clothes were torn and there was blood on his pants. And several contusions on his dirty face.

"Come on in and clean up." he felt genuinely sorry for the young man.

Away from his home, in a strange country without any real friends. He should at least take a bath and I should take a look at those cuts. He may even need a real doctor.

"Why don't you take a bath and let me take a look at those cuts. You may actually need a doctor to sew you up. Here, look at that," he reached out to touch the young man's arm where a dark bruise was forming around a cut. The young man jerked back from the touch. "I'm not going to hurt you, young man," laughed the professor. "I am after all, a doctor," he smiles, "Just maybe not that kind of doctor. But I've seen my share of bad injuries on digs in my time I assure you. Tell me why aren't you in your own room?"

"Those kids really aren't very nice to me. If I wake them up now they will hate me forever. Cant I just stay here until the morning?"

It seemed like a natural request from a young man who needed some help from an older more experienced person.

The young man sensed that it was safe to enter the room. This man seemed genuinely concerned. How many times had he felt that before in his life? He felt he was in the lap of luxury here. Given a key, which he had lost last night, to a nice room in a fancy hotel. Flown over here courtesy of the university outreach program for under-privileged students. And now this older foreigner reaching out to him to help him after a really hard day of finding his way back and a night of sleeping in the jungle.

He came in through the door and stood inside the small vestibule that every room had. "Would you like to take a bath? I need to look at those cuts on your arms and face. Do you think you need a doctor?"

He swore off the doctor idea really fast. No officials. "Maybe just something to eat and drink." It had been over 24 hours since he had anything but some water he had found on the way. He had been terrified after the confrontation and the fall. He did not trust himself to be around people in this strange place when he didn't even speak the language. He knew he just needed to get back to the hotel where a few people knew his face.

"How about a nice hot bath, and you can get out of those torn bloody clothes," said the professor looking gravely concerned.

"My clothes are in my room, where everybody is asleep."

"I have extra stuff here you can sleep in the extra bed, and I will go get your change of clothes tomorrow. If those kids are as bad as you say, you don't need to go back over there. A room of 5 people sleeping on the floor? How unacceptable."

The boy nodded wide eyed assent.

"Well, you are not sleeping in the bed so dirty as that. I'LL go in and start a bath for you," said the older man. He left the boy standing there in his dirty torn clothes. He was just starting to shake, after his ordeal and now the warm hotel room, the total lack of food, and his injuries were starting to catch up with him. He looked around the vestibule, with its little counter and shelf and towels and a couple drinking glasses. Nothing to eat or drink there at all. He walked into the bathroom where the professor was starting the tub full of steaming water. He grabbed one of the glasses from the counter and ran some water in it from the bathroom sink. He drank it in an instant. Poured and drank another, and another. He was thirsty and depleted.

"Well, that aught to do it for you. Bath, soap, shampoo, already here."

"I am so grateful to you for your generosity," said the boy.

The old man straightened up and looked him in the face, pleased with this boy's awareness of a generosity done toward him. "You are so welcome young man. We are so pleased at the university to have young men come into our midst that are considerate and hardworking students."

"But, yes, you are doing this for me. and it means so much more to me."

Professor Shallot smiled at the torn up young man and felt pity. He knew he had come from a very disadvantaged place, there in Egypt, or Pakistan or wherever, he really wasn't sure. "Professor Hartig had recommended you personally. He said you were one of his more promising students."

At the mention of his master's name, something moved in the boy's stomach.

"God rest his soul, that is. What a sad thing to lose such an important man as that. It may never be understood what happened. But such things cannot be predicted, can they?" he smiled at the boy that was just standing there staring at him with something like sadness or shock on his face.

"There, now," said the professor. "Why don't you have a nice bath and you'll feel better."

"Professor Hartig was more than just a professor. He was more than that." The boy said incomprehensibly. Shallot just stared at him. "And I was hoping you could be like him to me too. More than just that."

The older man just looked at the boy and was beginning to feel a bit uncomfortable, not really knowing where he was going with this. "Well, I think it is good to have a good mentor for all students at the university. I am not sure I am up to that but I can try."

"I thought maybe you felt more for me too." he was trying to express something he had never expressed before. Perhaps it was the shock in his tortured body, lack of sleep and food, to push himself this far in trying to discuss this with the older professor. But he felt a pressure to do it. "I thought maybe we shared something like that." He took a step forward toward the older man and held out his hand and set it on his shoulder.

The older man's eyes flew wide, and he stammered and took a step back. "Really?" he said with disdainful laugh. "Is that what you thought?" he said with disgust rising in his voice. "Do you think I would want to be buggered by a young man? is that what you had going on in your Persian head? "

The boy felt the thing in his gut boil up and over, and he pushed the older man. His feet went out from under him on the bathroom towel on the floor and he fell into the tub, and banged the back of his head hard.

The boy looked with shock and rage as the older man lay half in the tub, rolling himself over to try to push himself out, and moaning, and trying to find purchase with his hands on the edge of the tub. "Don't you ever call me that word again. You are not my father and never will be. He was a man of respect and knew his place with men." The young man reached down and grasped the sparse hair on the back of the older man's head. "You! You do not! You're only a foreigner who cant speak the language of a true believer, anyway!"

He was now ranting in a language that the man in tub would not have understood, even if he was fully conscious.

He pushed his head down into the water. "You will never call me that again, will you?" He pushed his head further under water. "Will you!" he said as he held him underwater. "Answer me, white pig." He held the struggling man face- first into the hot bath water, until after a minute or two, the struggling stopped. The boy stood up and looked at the disheveled man half in the tub. He wiped down the front of his own pants with disgust, then he spit on him, then turned to leave the room.

He found the man's wallet in his suitcase there on the floor, grasped it with a towel and took out some bills. Not all of them, but he had to eat. He did nothing more. He simply left, taking the glass of water with him.

He stood in the hall for a moment while the door slowly closed with a small woosh. What next? where could he possibly go? He was still a mess. He would have to brave his roommates. His things were all in there anyway. Maybe he could sneak in and they wouldn't care. Be too tired to notice him? Only one choice. He could not make it out in the streets. he would have to act cool.

He walked down the hall and went down a floor to where the student rooms were. He went to his room number 324, and quietly knocked on the door. It was almost immediately answered. They were all wide awake. They were having some kind of party. Who would have thought that, in the middle of the night.

The young person who opened the door simply grunted, turned and walked back in the room leaving the door hanging open.

The young man didn't say a thing when he entered. He became his chameleon self and just pretended to be wall paper. There were people passed out on the floor and several drinking on the bed. the primitive TV was on, but just flickering lights.

The boy grabbed his bag, and turned into the bathroom, thankfully vacant, and closed and locked the door. He would clean up on his own, lay down and go to sleep on the floor, and no one there would even notice. He would tell everyone he was there at the party the whole time, and they would probably not even know the difference. Late that night, Gwydion woke up amid flailing dreams with a start. His grand father had taken the book away and he had fallen asleep wrapped in the blankets and pillows on the floor just to the side of his grand father's bed. His grand mother and mother were also asleep there in the other two beds, snoring just slightly.

He didn't want to wake anyone but he had had a terrible nightmare. What to expect from reading such things before you go to sleep. But he had lost his ability to reason by this point. Lack of sleep, these stories he was obsessed with, and these visions he seemed to be having.

He walked over to his mother's bed and watched her breathe softly in the night air. He reached out and touched her shoulder. She stirred. He touched her shoulder again and she turned and saw his dark silhouette standing above her bed.

"Gwydion? What are you doing?" she said in a hoarse sleepy voice.

He knelt on the edge of the bed and pushed her over a little. "No, you cant sleep in here. The bed's too small."

He hung his head and whined a little. "Wrap up and sleep right there. What is wrong with you?"

He wrapped up in his blanket and pillow and sat down right there next to her. He rustled around for a minute and she turned in the covers and faced him in the dark. "What?" she whispered.

He struggled to say something, but it just wouldn't come out.

"What?" she asked again.

He looked right into her eyes, the moon light just reflecting enough that they could see each other's faces.

"He did it again," he whispered quietly.

"What? Who did what again?" she asked again in a whisper.

Gwydion groaned a little, as if saying it caused him pain.

She reached out and put a hand around his head and stroked him a little. "Let's go to sleep now, OK?" They settled in a little into the covers and he slid into a ball below the edge of her bed. "Sleep good, Gwydion. Everything will be just fine."

And with these simple assurances of his mother, the young man finally slid off to a quiet sleep.

# 19.
# Sleep

As he took off his torn and bloody clothes he looked at his body in the mirror . Long lanky muscles just under the surface of white skin that rarely saw the sun. But his cuts and bruises seemed to be healing quickly, almost too quickly for normal. But he thought nothing of it. He had put the confrontation in the stone temple out of his mind; he had tried to anyway. Flashes of the dark dream came back to him off and on and he would start to shake all over again. The sound of the dismembered beating hearts in the cold stone chamber. The echoing of haunting voices from long ago. The chant of strange isolated words and then the sharp "thwack" of the ceremonial knife against flesh and bone, the screaming of the victim. He shivered and closed his eyes again at those thoughts. And told himself never to think of those things again. It's just a dream. Something so horrible could *not be real*.

    He saw on the bathroom sink counter and on the back of the toilet seat the leftover paraphernalia of the party still raging outside the bathroom door in his hotel room. He'd never seen anything like the way these students could party on. And on. He did not understand this. This was not the way they lived in Afghanistan when he was a child. This was all new to him.

    There was a dark bottle of beer sitting amongst the other detritus of party, and when he picked it up he realized it was more than half-full. Then he closed one eye and with the other looked in the bottle to make sure it hadn't become an ashtray for cigarettes or some other such flotsam. Then he sniffed the mouth of the bottle and it seemed okay so he took a swig. The still-bubbly beer burned around his tongue and down his throat. But it felt good after 36 hours not eating and hardly drinking anything. So he took another long pull off a bottle of beer, set it down with a click and said audibly, "Ahhh."

He reached over and turned on the shower water and waited for it to warm up a bit. It was the middle of the night so no one else was showering and the water quickly got hot, steaming hot. He stepped out of his ruined pants, shoes and socks and holding onto the handle stepped into the shower, closed the plastic shower curtain, and stood luxuriating under the hot needles of water. What a relief.

The dried blood from his wounds softened and ran free, leaving his skin once again clean. He soaked and scrubbed and washed his hair and began to feel alive again.

He stepped free of the shower after turning it off, grabbed a big soft hotel towel and scrubbed his body dry. He rubbed his hair with the towel and got as much water out of it as he could, then rummaged in his sack for a comb and some conditioner. He put a dab of it in the palm of his hand and rubbed it briskly to make it foam, fingered it through his hair and then was he able to apply the comb effectively through his curly knots. He smiled and winced as he worked his way through that thick mop of dark hair of his he despised so much. He did not look fully at his own face. But he examined the scratches in the oncoming dark shadow of a beard, but never did he step back and regard his own looks. He could not stand to look into his slightly crooked eyes and allow himself to venture any thoughts of a personal nature, his self loathing was so deep.

He put his old clothes in the garbage can and tucked the plastic bag around it so no one would notice. He put on some new clothes, put his shoes and closed his bag and opened the bathroom door, exchanging shower steam for party noise.

"Bless Allah," he thought. "How am I ever can sleep in this?" No one paid him any mind. They were used to him being there. He reached down and grabbed the pile of blankets that had slid off at the foot of one of the beds, where several people were sucking on the last dregs of this party continuing into the wee hours of the morn, drinking and doing disgusting things to one another half clothed, and he lay down on the floor in the darkest corner, wrapped himself in the blanket, put his head on his satchel and fell asleep within five seconds.

# 20.

# Morning

Gwydion groaned as the morning sun caught him in the face. He heard the sounds of his family puttering around the room, making some coffee, taking showers.

"We are getting ready to go down to breakfast, Gwydion," said his mom.

He started making sounds of protest, when she said, "No, you are coming. You need to get out of this room and get a good meal."

He made a mewling sound and flopped down in the pile of covers and pillows he had been living in for the last 36 hours.

His grandma Bethany came over and sat by him on the bed. "We'll get up and take a shower when your grandfather gets out, OK?" She rubbed his wild head of hair. "And then we'll go get pancakes at the restaurant. And orange juice, your favorites."

He looked up at her, and she would swear there were tears in his eyes, and that kid smile, like he had just woken up to Christmas.

"I thought you'd like the idea," she said to him, getting up as the bathroom door opened with a gush of steam and the grandfather's toweled wet person. "Your turn!" he said to Gwydion, who stood up grumbling and stumbled into the bathroom to wash off the grime of 2 days in hot water.

The older boy woke to loud noises, yelling and calling from the hall. Some of the other young bodies in the room stirred, but it didn't elicit much of a reaction. But he heard it and wondered at it's urgency.

He tilted his head off his bed on the floor and watched people come and go and heard just snatches of conversation, "the professor", "Shallot", "police", but he didn't make much of it.

Stars circled and swam before his eyes on a field of black, and he decided he was not ready to face the day. What exactly had happened last night, he wasn't that sure. His recollection was foggy and disjointed. Then something about a flash of a knife and hearts beating on a cold slab and a strange chanted language.... He stopped those thoughts and tuned out the recollection of the night and day previous. He mentally would never, ever, go there again if he could help it.

There was more banging and door shutting and stomping and calling out to friends around him in the room and the smell of old alcohol. And finally he decided he would have to wake up. His approach to this he decided would have to be gradual, on his elbow for a moment, then leaning against the bed a little with his shoulder, and sitting his upper body upright against the bed with his face in his hands trying to breathe and stop the spinning. He was moderately successful after about 10 minutes, then his first real cohesive thought was of that he was very hungry. Starving. A super nice breakfast down in the restaurant of the hotel would be fabulous. And he could get away from all this noise and stink.

He dug around his clothes bag for his old beat up shoes. Fortunately he had clean socks in his bag which is always a luxury. He got those on his feet, he straightened his pant legs and his shirt.

As he stood up and covered his book and clothes bags in the corner with the blanket, he pushed it firmly against the wall so no one would step on it. They would be there one more day, and the room would be cleaned as soon as the rest of the vagabonds cleared out for the morning. They all would either go to breakfast or attend classes which were taking place at the convention. They were all expected to attend classes. They were all there on some sort of scholarship from one university or another. It had been gifted them and they needed to respect that and do some coursework. They had been promised to get some college credits for their efforts. But he thought ironically, their responsibility didn't seem to stop them from partying all night.

He got himself up off the floor and ambled through the room and out the door which had been propped open with a used room service tray. He stepped over the tray and peered into the hall. Down a ways was a crowd of people milling around and talking in subdued tones. Some kids his age walked by and he said, "What is going on?"

They shrugged and walked on down the hall toward the commotion. He wandered down toward them slowly, wondering what it could be all about. When he got to the edge of the crowd of people he could see over most of the heads into what appeared to be a hotel room blocked off by several security guards.

"What's happening?" "What's going on?" These questions bounced back and forth among the students and other people standing outside the hotel room. With everyone staring anxiously at the doorway and back at one another. The young man casually looked over the crowd of young people he knew by acquaintance here at the conference.

He noticed one other young man on the other side of the crowd staring at him, and he quickly dropped his eyes. Does he know? How could he know?

He gathered some nerve and looked back over at the young man staring at him. And he realized that it was not a look of suspicion on his face, but of something else entirely. He summed up the young man looking at him for more than just one second, and he noticed he was tall and thin, maybe a few years older than himself, gold brown hair and brown eyes. No, not brown. Gold eyes. More like a tiger's. He felt his face began to flush pink, and he dropped his eyes. He took a deep breath and then turned his body more forward with the crowd. But he felt the other boy's eyes on him penetrating in some new way he wasn't sure he felt comfortable with.

One of the professors came out of the room and ducked underneath the yellow police tape hastily wrapped around the room door. He had a grave look on his face and his red-rimmed eyes started from side to side as he surveyed the crowd gathering just outside the room. He closed his eyes and shook his head. He put his hands deep in his pockets and pushed to make his way through the crowd away from the room. One of his colleagues was among the crowd and he said quietly to him, "Professor Shallot. I guess hit his head on the tub and drowned." He shook his head again shrugged his shoulders and walked off, his colleague turning and following with him down the hall.

The news passed quickly between the students and others in the crowd. And one by one they began to turn and leave to head off to somewhere else, And the boy followed behind the group. He was caught up in the sad sentiment. He needed to get out of there and stay with the group, and to act normal.

He thought, take the stairs down alone, but now he thought stay with the group. He looked carefully to side to side, to see if anyone was watching him. He felt a cold clammy grip of guilt deep in his veins, although he wasn't exactly sure why. The last 48 hours was pretty much a scary blur and he preferred not to review his memories ever again. But he felt danger and he needed to get away from that room right now.

He joined his teammates in the elevator as they made their way downstairs. Just as the doors were closing, he looked up and saw the doors of the elevator on the other side of the foyer open. And he glimpsed for just a second the other dark haired boy, the younger one, and their eyes locked for just an instant. Then the doors clicked shut.

He closed his eyes for a minute and the world flashed by him again and a clammy shiver sailed up his spine. He blew out a breath and opened his eyes, and noticed the boy with gold eyes watching him from the back of the elevator. Maybe he had noticed his heavy breathing and his face grow red and had misinterpreted its meaning. Oh well, such was his luck. He returned the stare with a slight smile and down cast eyes.

As the elevator car landed and the doors slid open, some of the students broke off to classes and seminars. But a few headed where he wanted to go, the hotel restaurant for breakfast and some light conversation.

As they headed towards the restaurant, a voice came from just behind him, "Ah, breakfast," the young male voice said. So he slowed, turned to see who said that. The boy with gold eyes. So they walked together towards a table in the corner where some other students were.

"I could use some breakfast after all that excitement," the other boy said not looking over at him. He flashed a look at the golden eyed face in profile and wondered at his ease.

His own ease did not grow as breakfast progressed, although it was divine to eat real food finally after two days. He sat holding himself quietly, watching the other students enjoying themselves and chattering, all the while sneaking looks at his new found companion. He was not sure whether to stare at his eyes or his long slender fingered hands, tanned, with pink nails clean white moons at the top. Or watch his mouth. And those lips! He had to tear himself away from the staring at those lips. Like pillows, waiting, just the right color of plums and coffee. He felt himself heating up for some reason and kept his gaze on his plate and cup of coffee for quite some time. Until he felt the other young man's stare boring into him like a laser beam, then he felt his neck flush, and was sure that his fluster was obvious to all. Which only served to increase his personal tension. But he held still.

"Where are you from?" He mustered enough to ask this new stranger after a while, allowing his thick middle eastern accent to cover the shaking in his voice.

"I'm from Brazil," came the answer from those pillow lips. "And I came up specifically for this convention. And yourself?"

"I, uh, am from Egypt," was all he could manage, as he held those tiger eyes.

"Ah, another dark exotic state." He winked at him and melted the insides of the younger boy.

He looked down then back up and just stared at the slightly older boy and did not know what to say.

But there grew slowly upon the corners of his mouth the slightest of grins. He tilted his head and shyly looked down when he noticed the other young man's smile grow to meet his own.

Breakfast continued for them with this ardent undertone for quite some time. The other students finished, picked up and left to their own schedules. The other boy would say a few words in Spanish or was it Portuguese to the other students standing up and leaving, Few of them paid heed to the younger boy and with very little guile would simply nod their heads in his direction as they stood up and left the table.

"So, where do you go after this?"

"I was thinking of attending the class at noon," he said.

The elder boy smiled, and replied, "no, I mean, when the seminars are over, where do you travel to?"

The younger boy, in his secret way of pretending to translate, he waited, and he always tried to use the thickest of his accents possible so as to not appear to be fully understanding the conversation, took a moment to answer the older boy's question. He had just assumed he would go home, back to the Middle East, perhaps back to Afghanistan and his family now that his plans were so totally derailed and shattered.

But he didn't seem to be in any trouble for what had just occurred. Otherwise he would be in suspicion already. It seemed to be no officials asking questions at all. Perhaps it was just assumed that the older man hit his head and drowned, for that is what happened isn't it?

So maybe, he prevaricated, he hadn't actually done anything wrong. And with all of his dreams at the stone Temple the night before and the day's travel through the jungle and then all of the craziness and partying in the hotel room who knows what had been real and what had been a dream. He knew it would only hurt his mind to think about it too much and to try to figure it out. It best be left alone.

Where *was* he going to go after the seminars were over? They only had two more days and he would have to decide . His mentor was now dead. Well, now both of them, actually. So he figured that conduit of privilege was now closed to him.

So where to go? His foggy mind cleared a little from the food and coffee and from this new companionship found as he looked over at the slightly older boy with the gold Tiger eyes. And he wondered what new thing he had found here. There was a strange tickling in his breast as he watched the slightly older boy sip his coffee with those lips, the other's eyes still on him boring into him like a secret beam. What was this, this something new that kindled in his breast? He was unsure, but he began to consider that Brazil might be a nice place to visit.

Gwydion slammed to the back of the elevator. His family looked at him in astonishment. As the elevator doors finished opening, he bolted out and down the hall. When his family caught up to him, he was walking in circles around in front of the hotel room door. They unlocked the door and he bolted inside the room.

He ran and plunked down next to the bed and covered his head with blankets. They stood around him worried. "What is wrong with you, Gwydion?" his mother shouted.

The humming and rocking continued. Bethany sat down next to him on the floor and put her arms around this bundle of blankets. She started humming one of the lullabies she sometimes did for him when he couldn't sleep. The other two walked away and sat down on their beds for a rest.

After about 10 minutes of this, Gwydion's motions seemed to settle, and Bethany eased off her grip and her humming. She found the edge of the blanket and peeled back just a corner and found Gwydion's face.

"What is it with you? Ever since the day at the temple. What's going on, huh, sweetie?" she whispered really quietly to him. He just looked at her with red-rimmed eyes. In fact he stared at her for a long time.

And finally he said in a very quiet voice, "He did it again, Grand mama. He did it again."

She was used to him speaking elliptically, but she had no idea what he was talking about. But she committed to memory what he had just said, and she would ask Antony if he knew what he was talking about later, when Gwydion was not around. Maybe after they left this strange place in the jungle.

# 21.
# The Night

That night was a small wonder to the young man. He had had intimate contact with men before, but not like this. This felt real. He hoped it was real. This young man with the tiger's eyes seemed to actually like him. Maybe even worship him. He hoped he was a good person enough to deserve such cherished treatment.

The night was spent in and out of wakefulness, sharing intimacy that he had never had in this way before. The softness and the caring, it was more than he could have ever hoped for. Especially after the last few days. He needed soothing hands and a kind word to heal the harshness he had suffered in the cold cave and on the streets trying to find his way back to the university. And the reception by that cruel professor was certainly not deserved.

So he relished in the kindness that this new young man gave to him. He was kind and gentle in return. And he learned a great deal from this only slightly older teacher. Things he did not know could be so pleasurable and satisfying to him, to the both of them.

He was glad Enrique had his own room to himself. Something about his parents being deceased and having entrusted him so that his life would be easier than theirs ever was. What caring parents they must have been. Such a contrast to his own family... No. Don't think of that. He admonished himself to never think of that awfulness again. Never again. He had something new here, something wonderful to cherish in this new person that brought him to states of ecstasy and back again.

They spoke then in the morning of going back to Enrique's home in Brazil, just the two of them.

But he could not tell the others could he.? He would just leave with him. And not tell a soul. No one had asked him anything. Surprising after his disappearance of a day, and then the death of the old professor. He hadn't even seen that little boy, who's coat he discarded in the city that day after. It was torn and had blood all over it where he had fallen, and it was too obviously colored that garish yellow. No worries, no one had asked him a thing. Maybe that boy would keep his mouth shut after all. There was nothing he could do anyway. They were going away to the States and he to Brazil in just a few days time.

Time to start a new life afresh.

# Epilogue:
# Gwydion's Apocalypse.

A small article appeared in one of the larger newspapers in the city of Brazil. It was missed by most because it was a small obituary of someone few people knew. He was not known even to have any local family.

Antony Jacobs didn't see the article. He had no reason to. He had no need to scan Spanish and Portuguese newspapers. He would not have noticed any connection if he had. Accept maybe the strange circumstances involved in the murder.

The article ran as follows:

Jan 14, 1965; in Sou Poulo today was found the body of a young man slain by the hands of an unknown killer. No motives or connections have been found. No one has been detained for questioning. Enrique Rodriguez Gutierrez, 29, was found in his apartment, his throat apparently cut while engaged in unlawful acts of intimacy.

Please contact the local authorities with any information regarding the identity or the whereabouts of his assailant. His roommate has also gone missing; age:24; dark complexion, dark eyes. Name, origin unknown.

The Jacobs family sailed north. They landed in San Francisco and decided to make a go of it there. Several universities had asked Antony to grace their faculty. And he was honored to have his choice of schools. Professor Will Smithershins was also hired and served as his full-time assistant.

Gwydion entered high school, and quickly found a group to belong to.

He was astonished to find that they liked his brooding silence, his elliptic comments and his spooky dark eyes, and those stories that he told when everyone needed a good fright. And thus he entered his adolescence with a suitcase full of haunting visions that would light afire and scramble with his hormones into a volatile mix.

# Book 5

# DARK ANGEL

Hell hath no government
than that fatal law
which punishes perversity and corrects error,
for the false Gods only exist
in the false faiths of their adorers.

Book of Solomon the King
and in the end,
god is our hope
that there can be a better world.
And hell is our punishment
for when we fail to try.

# NM Reed

# Chapter 1.
# Discovery
## Present

The sun was just cracking through the dense layer of fog, and lifted Gwydion's mood as he stepped off the boat. He wouldn't call it a fun trip. Interesting certainly. But his young mind was not fully able to make out what happened nor take in much of its meaning really.

All he could really remember was the cold stone crypt, the black press of damp dark stones, and the sound of hurried footsteps following him relentlessly up those stairs. And the close call as angry arms reached for him from behind in the dark echoing crypt.

But that was behind him now. And he was here is San Francisco to start again. A new school in America with American kids, just like him, he thought naively. His grandfather had work with the Historical Language Institute and his younger professor friend, Will Smithershins, too. And even his weirdo mother, Mags, had been asked to work there. His grandmother Bethany was proud of her little group of erstwhile explorers. And they were all happy to get off that boat, after their long sail up from Panama.

And Gwydion was relieved to step onto firm ground and to have arrived at what he would call home for hopefully some years now. If only he could get rid of the dreams. Those dreams that haunted him just before he woke up, bubbled up in his mind sometimes during the day. Golden eyes glaring at him, a voice in an unfamiliar language taunting him, ringing in his ears just before he would wake from it with a chill.

## Nile Delta, year: 367 A. D.

Sestnost found himself jogging through the streets, his robes beating about his legs, almost tripping him more than twice.

"Slow down," he admonished himself. "It's very unseemly for a friar to be seen running."

"But, I have to hurry," another voice spoke into his head. "We have to hurry or it will all be destroyed! We will all be destroyed!"

And his short legs sped up along the cobble stones with new vigor.

His master needed to know. He needed to hear what Sestnost had just over heard from the Bishop of Pachomia. He had presented the paper from Hippolytus of Rome, that the Gnostic writings would be reviewed, and all heretics and their heresies would be destroyed. He had even called them liars. He had said the members of Sestnost's brotherhood had falsely attributed their writings to an earlier time by falsifying their dates, thus falsifying their validity.

But this just wasn't true! How could the Bishop say that about his honest brethren and their studies? Some of these documents were actually ancient. They were written by some important brothers in the distant past. One of them they had called the Teacher of Light. And he had given his life for the struggle to enlighten all of them.

Some even called him a Savior. But this new Bishop and his followers had their own, newer savior, and they distrusted anyone else. So of course they believed this story of an older savior had to be a falsification, because this newer one was the one and only.

His exhausted legs beat the stones until his strength gave way. He landed on the hard road with a thump and fell into darkness. And in this darkness rose a shadow, its dark wings beating about its legs like the robes of some mad priest, like the wings of some dark Angel. He peered into Sestnost's eyes with amber flames. "Getup, you fool!" it screeched into his frail human ears like a demon wind. "Get up and carry your message. These scriptures of wisdom, bury them now or all will be destroyed!" The demon's yellow eyes and hot breath held over Sestnost's face. "Get up." As it turned into a blinding ray of light, it screeched incomprehensibly into poor old Sestnost's ears, "Get moving!"

Sestnost then found himself peering into the blinding light of the setting sun glancing down the dirty street. The scent of flowers hung in the air and soothed him, he thought, half dreaming. He rose wearily, dusted himself off and began to make his way again toward the monastery, the memory of the dream of the dark angel running it's cold fingers up his sweating back.

Sestnost finally reached the courtyard of his monastery running.

"Quickly," he breathed, "the Monseigneur," as he worked to gain his breath.

And when the man arrived, hurried reluctantly along by two of Sestnost's brothers, the Monseigneur looked down at Sestnost and cried, "What is this hurry?"

"Father," hissed Sestnost, "They must all be destroyed. Quickly!

"What?" cried the older man.

"The Books! They must all be destroyed! Or we will be destroyed with them!"

In a few days, cooler minds had prevailed and their ancient written words of knowledge and wisdom were decided to not be destroyed, but rather hidden. They placed the treasured books in large earthen jars, said an impassioned incantation for angelic protection, and closed them each with a ceramic lid, and plastered that closed with mud. And into these jars they sealed their fear and hatred these dedicated monks felt for their task, against these tyrants of wisdom.

Into a cleft between huge boulders just at the high-waters' reach of the Nile, the greatest river that fed these people, these old books were buried deep in the sand and mud in these giant ceramic jars, so they could be found again by these monks when the inevitable happened once again and these despots of wisdom and tyranny were over-thrown by saner men.

But history that flowed in that river had her own plans. These despots of wisdom and their savior did not fall so easily. In fact their sect grew and flourished and began to systematically stamp out all thought that challenged her. And the great river seemed to be in compliance with this flow of history and she made other plans. She flowed deep and heavy the next year, depositing great amounts of silt and black earth onto the cache of ancient books in the sealed jars. If those monks had survived and even wanted to find those old texts in those jars they had so carefully sealed and hidden, they would not have been able.

So, destroyed, no. But, hidden, most definitely, yes. But so hidden as to be lost. Lost for almost two thousand years. And when the course of the river changed just slightly over the course of the 2000years, and the minds of men were ready to be opened, and when a people had been ravaged enough by drought and starvation that they needed to dig into the black earth for sustenance, these jars were inadvertently uncovered.

And when these jars were broken open by the curious discoverers, these men unwittingly unleashed the powers imprisoned there. Where this fear and hatred sealed in those jars for two thousand years with those ancient books of wisdom had swirled and coalesced into a cold wind of vengeance.

## 1930's

The River Nile flows, in some quirk of geologic fate, from south to north, and empties into a great sea. And along it's way it carries a very important load within it's waters. People, fish, and nutrients are carried with it, along with a deep history embedded into the soul of this ancient birthplace of humanity. This rich river valley, the fertile Nile Delta, provides northern Africa with life-blood Each year the monsoon season floods the delta with rich green waters, and deposits a layer of black silt higher into the red earth country, bringing rich nutrients for growing food high into the red lands of Egypt.

And the Egyptian Copts of the Red-Lands harvest this black soil and take it back to their homes to fertilize their farms.

One such falladin brother, Mahmud, was gathering black

soil next to his hobbled camel, when he unearthed a large ceramic jar, sealed at the top with a bowl. He and his younger brother, Hasyin, discussed what to do with this old jar.

The older brother argued for the possibility of riches.

The younger brother prudently warned of an evil Jinn imprisoned within the jar, and argued of only bad things that would happened if they set him free.

But the thirst for treasure won out, and Mahmud raised his heavy maddock and struck the ceramic jar, crashing it into bits.

And into the air around them flew a cloud of golden dust, thus confirming both the older and the younger brothers' wisdom. But the golden cloud of dust swirled for but a moment, then disappeared with a crackling sound off into the bright blue sky above the cliffs of Jubal al-Tarif.

"What was that, brother?" said younger brother, Hasyin.

"I don't know, but I am glad it flew away!" cried the elder brother, Mahmud.

And they both turned and regarded the jar that had just crumbled to bits on the black earth. They tipped over the broken jar, and out fell... books.

Old crumbling books.

Two tired dark faces fell in disappointment.

"Well, it's something," said the prudent younger brother, Hasyin.

"Not much," said the greedy older brother, Mahmud. "But at least it's big enough to share." And with that, he grasped the large stack of bound folio pages in his strong hands.

And his prudent younger brother watched with half disinterest, while his older brother pulled with his strong gnarled hands and tore the thick stack of dirty old papers bound like a book in half. He stared at his brother with the other half of his disinterest as Mahmud handed him one half of the old crumbling book.

He held out his own dark gnarled hands in the air, and said to his older brother, "Thanks, but no thanks, Mahmud. I think it is time we headed for home."

Not wanting to waste even this worthless old book, Mahmud took off his turban fabric, wrapped the pieces of the old book and some other junk they'd found in it, and packed it away on his camel, and they headed home.

By the time they had ridden their worthy steeds all the way back home, it was getting dark and very cold with the approaching night time, and Mahmud had forgotten about the worthless old book he had torn in half and wrapped in his saddle bags, so he emptied his turban into the midden pile out with the animals in the yard.

A cold wind began to blow in from the south, and soon the ancient book laying there with the goats froze. A page fluttered in the wind, and an old goat grabbed the page and began to chew it. But he found the ancient pages too tough and tasteless for even him, and he spit it back out. The wife of the prudent younger brother tried in her frugality to use a couple of the old pages to start the fire. But the pages were reluctant to burn and gave off such a foul smell, that she gave up and threw it back outside with the goats. Where it froze and blew in the cold north wind.

A few days later the elder brother, Mahmud, with his capitalist nature, decided to make a trip into Luxor to make some trades. Just as he was leaving the courtyard, he spied the old torn book, amongst the gourd rinds and the goat nuggets, pages blowing in the breeze and he decided to take it with him to see if he could make a trade of some kind.

Maybe he could get a piastres or two for it in the old antiqua dealers. And in this he was moderately successful, and he unloaded the dirty old thing for the price of an American watch for his father.

# Chapter 2.
# A New City

## Present

The Jacobs family landed in San Francisco on a foggy wet autumn afternoon. The big ship, The Happenstance Three, landed against the black wooden pier with a lurch as the ship's motors grew quiet. Her passengers were ready to disembark in no time as they were looking forward to solid land after some weeks at sea. Their journey north from the Isthmus of Panama was uneventful for the most part, which they were grateful for. But soon the fatigue of laying at sea began to set in. So the flashing lights and the clangor of the city was a strange and welcomed change.

They had been informed by radio of their destination, and their preparedness for their arrival. The secretary of the Happenstance Foundation assured them of a safe place to stay once they arrived in San Francisco. They had never seen the foundation's new home base, now that Aloaetious was no longer a man living. But they'd heard tales of the city of San Francisco and were excited to explore.

When they stepped off the ship Gwydion 's eyes were wide with wonder. He looked around himself at the bustling Pacific ocean port town of San Francisco and saw more than was there. He saw tall rigging ships swaying in the tide, but this must have been a trick of his imagination. Sailing ships were long gone except for several historical relics that were being maintained and used as tourist attractions. But once this place thronged with the sailing ships come round the southern tip of South America first with Magellan, and then with Cortez, who purportedly landed here and establish this, a port for the Queen of Spain. But then for some years this isolated peninsula of San Francisco languished, surrounded by natives who did not care for imports. But when the Panama Canal was built some 50 years before Gwydion's time, this port and the city swelled and flourished as the trading and delivery business flourished for the onslaught of the gold rush days of the 1850s.

But since then the city had modernized and become a fashion trendsetter and center of commerce on the West Coast of America. History Gwydion saw, what was once life here, 100 years ago. The history was deep, and Gwydion could feel it seeping into his bones along with the cold from the fog. When he looked around at the cars driving on pavement streets, he instead saw tall black narrow cabriolet with tall spoke wheels pulled by snorting horses wearing blinkers tossing leather harness. But the cars of today could wheel circles around the horse-drawn carts of yesteryear. And Gwydion saw it all at once as a clangor of information in his mind's eye.

In his teenage mind this layered complexity put him on a plane different from everyone else. It set him apart and gave him an appearance of dreaminess to others. It was often misunderstood to be aloofness or snobbery. But it was nothing of the sort. In fact usually he just felt confused and at a disadvantage to these other people he could tell did not doubt their reality, as he did. "Ah, yes, this will be the way," Will Smithershins said loudly as he made his way towards a long black car parked against the curb. "They've sent a car round for us, as I knew they would." They all the small group began to make their way towards the shiny black car.

And Antony Jacobs looked over at Will Smithershins, with a wry glance, thinking to himself, "that guy seems to know too much sometimes." Will always seemed to Antony to be where he needed just when he needed to be. It almost seemed to him to be a prater-natural ability to predict what was going to happen. This had frightened Anthony at first when he'd encountered his old friend the former associate to Aloaetious Happenstance at the Foundation, when they met again this last summer at the anthropology gathering in southern Mexico. He seems to be just where Antony would've expected him to be if he just thought about it. And there he was at his side just when he needed him. And then again when Gwydion had gotten lost at the Temple site. And then here now, will seem to know just where to go.

Will glanced over at Anthony looking at him, and seemed to anticipate what the older man was thinking. And he said, "I have been here before remember. In fact I helped ol' Aloaetious set it all up for you."

Antony just stared at the younger man, then said, "Set what up?"

# Chapter 3.
# Death Feud in al Tarif

## Egypt 1930's

Mahmud's father was a loyal working man. Each night he served as night watchman for the small town of al-Qasr.

One night a cold evil wind blew through the small town, when Mahmud's father was on watch, and with it the wind brought an intruder with malintent from the near-by village of Hamradum, the village at the foot of the cliffs where the ancient jar was found, where the evil force had been released when they had broken the ceramic jar. And this breath of wind, this power of hatred and fear, had lodged itself in the breast of a young man who wandered into Mahmud's small town of al-Qasr late that night.

And when this intruder crept into the town streets late in the middle of the cold black night, Mahmud's father was faced with the dilemma of being loyal to his god and church and never taking another man's life, or of following orders and protecting the town and kill the intruder.

His need to keep his job to feed his family won out, so he shot the man and killed the intruder. But his loyalty was repaid quickly, and he was shot in the head a few nights later. It was vengeance of someone from the family of the man from the other village who he, Mahmud;s father, had shot and killed. And such was unleashed a feud of vengeance that it made the pages of history.

And Mahmud's mother, now widowed of her husband of forty years, told the brothers to keep their maddocks sharpened to a bright edge, for someday they would have the opportunity to avenge the murder of their father, her beloved husband.

And about six months later, Mahmud was to recall, six months after finding the jar near the cliffs of Jubal al-Tarif, near the small rival town of Humradum, that opportunity presented itself. The two brothers found the sleeping murderer of their father alongside the road late one evening. And with little hesitation, then and there, they wielded their heavy sharpened maddocks, and slew the young man to bits. But revenge was not nearly enough for them, for fear and hatred had ripened in their hearts with time; they wanted complete humiliation. So they tore the young man's heart from his chest and shared it between them, consuming it then and there on the spot, with the cold wind blowing in their bloody beards.

And thus was unleashed a blood feud that passed with that dark cold wind between the two small towns on the banks of the Nile. Mahmud recalled much later both these events, that they were forever connected in his mind, the finding of the book in the old ceramic jar, and the revenge he was able to exact on his father's murderer.

But Mahmud in his passion for avenging family did not once connect the breaking of the jar, and the golden apparition he had released into the bright blue sky that day.

For what Jinn had he released? A Jinn, is there such a thing? An ancient idea of spirits captured in a bottle, then released inadvertently by some curious treasure seeker? Is such a thing possible?

Or is it just an old tale of ancient warning, of evil spirits that travel from man to man, possessing them with blinding powers of fear, hatred, and revenge.

Or was the Jinn something very different, something Mahmud would never know of in his short life. Mahmud would not live much longer, not long enough to know that that old crumbling book that he sold for a few piastres held a Jinn far more powerful than just a man's hatred and fear shared between one another. For that old book was the first of what was to be found there at the base of the cliffs of Jubal al-Tarif in the black blood of the Nile. That crumbling old book would set off a wildfire of hunting for more jars and more manuscripts at the base of those cliffs. Because what the treasure hunters and anthropologists were to find there in the following years of hunting and digging would unleash powers of greed, hatred and fear, not for vengeance, but for the ownership of wisdom and beliefs.

For that old crumbling book would be the first to be found of what would soon be called the Treasure of the Nile, ancient Gnostic writings and scripture never before seen in 2000 years, the Nag Hammadi Library.

# Chapter 4.
# Voices in His Head

## Present

Far to the south another young man stared in disbelief around himself. He had headed south in a fog. 'Get away, get far from here', a voice had ranted in his head. So he had boarded a bus. And it had brought him here to a new country.

The city thronged with life. But around him voices spoke but he did not understand. He knew he had suffered a shock. But he was afraid more probably he simply did not speak the language. Maybe he was safe from what he had just done. But how was he going to get along not being able to speak the language.

He walked for a while and looked at his shoes striking the pavement. Litter and an occasional animal body part littered the sidewalk. What strange world had he just landed on?

He had traveled such a long way from home, with a group of students and professors, all to come to this other continent to study and learn from one another.

Ah, but the things he had learned were not in the syllabus. No this was his classroom of survival. Again. He thought to himself, I have to do this again. Survive where I was never meant to be.

He walked along and found a newspaper stand. He looked at the headlines. All indecipherable.

He looked up at the stand keeper. It was an older woman. She stared him straight in the face. And then a smile broke over dirty cracked teeth. She tilted her head and said something in their indecipherable language. He just shrugged his shoulders and gave her a pitiful look . He decided to give it a try. And he asked her if she spoke English, in his halting strange accent.

Her body wagged back and forth as she said, "Si, si. I speaka good Englesh. Si!"

And he smiled and laughed because he did actually understand her .

On a whim he asked her, "Where is the University?"

"Ah, yes. Student." And she shook her hand free from her robes and pointed down the street and mumbled some directions about turning right and left, and he wasn't sure, but thought he could give it a try. So he thanked the gal and turned to head down the street and she stopped him with, "Wait!"

When he turned back she was holding a map of the city. He lifted his hands up, for he had no money. But she shook the map at him and smiled. A beguiling smile if he didn't know better. Even from this old woman. And he remembered, that even in his most disheveled state, he often had this effect on women. On men too actually. So he smiled at her daftness of not knowing what lay inside his heart, and grasped the paper map and sai, "Gracias." She gave him a quizzical look at him using her native language, but none the less nodded and watched him as his tall form strode off down the street.

# Chapter 5.
# A Setup

"This was set up for us?" Asked Anthony.

And Will answered cautiously," Well, yes. The old man knew he was dying and he did not have children, not that he knew of anyway," Will said with a wink, "so his foundation had to go somewhere." Will turned towards the car and opened the back door for the Jacobs family. And as he helped Anthony in last he said under his breath "I think you'll like it here. There is much more here than meets the eye. He will find the happenstance historical foundation quite accommodating to you and your family."

Will gently shut the door, stepped forward a couple steps and opened the passenger door in the front and slipped inside next to the uniformed driver. It seemed a strange formality to Antony, who had never known opulence or luxury in his life. This car and driver seemed almost a parody of something he would never have expected, except perhaps in an old movie. But he settled back in the seat and placed his warm hand on his wife's cold one, and looked at her as she looked back at him with mild surprise. The children, Mags and Gwydion were enthralled with the city passing them by as the car drove through town.

After a few moments, the window between the driver's compartment in the passenger area slid open with a snap. And Will Smithershins craned his head around and said into the back compartment, "are we going to dinner?" The two children cried out in unison, "yeah!" The two adults in the back however groaned a little and said, "are we?"

"Well, why not," asked will rhetorically. "It's on the foundation anyway. So in San Francisco, I suggest seafood. Martin?" Said Will looking at the driver, "how about Pier 45."

"Yes, sir," said Martin the driver in a flat voice. In the small group drove for a few more minutes and parked along the edge of the bay at one of the dark wooden piers jutting out into the dark water.

Lights were strung along the boardwalk between the piers bustling with people about their evening in the settling darkness. Visibility was hampered by the increasing strength of the famous San Francisco fog, and on occasion a fog horn could be heard, often from various directions. The clanging of belled buoys rocking unseen somewhere in the shrouded waters mingled with the cries of seagulls wheeling overhead. The smell of the ocean mingled with and complemented the smells emanating from kitchens cooking their evening fair. Ah, seafood being prepared in a bay-side restaurant. Not that they hadn't had any on their trip north in the yacht. But somehow seafood eaten while on solid land seem different.

They selected a small restaurant with bright lights small tables and steam clouding the corners of the windows. They chose a small table in the corner for the five of them, Martin was waiting in the car. And sat down to a basket of steaming sourdough French bread wrapped in white linen set before them.

They ordered and tucked into their food before any of them said much of anything. As fatigue began to dissolve with warm food some white wine and a cup of coffee, they began to chat wondering of their adventures to come.

The children wanted to know where they were going, where they would be staying.

And Will assured them that they would enjoy the lodging the foundation was providing for them. Antony had understood he would be working for the foundation, but had not been given specific information as to what they would be researching. In affiliation with a local university, Will assured them there was a teaching position available for him, and Mags too if she wished. There was a local high school that Gwydion would be attending, and he groaned and rolled his eyes at the thought.

"Now I know Gwydion, that you have some difficulties in your last school. But I assure you San Francisco be different for you. You'll see," Will assured him.

Gwydion just looked at him then looked down at his food without saying a thing.

# Chapter 6.
# The House

Will Smithershins paid the bill with the company card and the small family ventured out of the restaurant and down the boardwalk back toward the car. The black night had deepened and seemed to fade into gray in the distance as if the night had vanquished the fog and only where the lights of the city penetrated was space.

They embarked into the black sedan and headed on their way towards parts unknown. Only Will was privy to that knowledge, and there was no way for him to prepare the family for what they would find when they arrived on Beacon Hill. Only when they got there and began to sum up what their new life had in store for them would this tension inside Will subside. Perhaps that was so, he chided himself, perhaps not. This tension for this project might never subside. And even if he were allowed to divulge that information just yet, honestly he probably wouldn't know where to start. He would not have known where to start on this long tale, even if he were the teller of the story, and not me.

But that information, the reader cannot know yet. And I, the narrator of the story in the far future, will remain a secret fathomable only by those infinitely capable of dissecting a mystery before it's time.

But all in due time, as in all happenstance history, shalt mystery be revealed. Through the city they wound in their comfy quiet ride, surrounded by lights and tumult of the city that rarely slept.

The city was not as sleepless as the one they had come to know on the other side of the continent. But close.

This city seemed to have a greater mystique. Mystery hanging in the fog between streetlights. In the street that beckon the soul to wonder at new depths never before imagined. The mystery that beckoned to the soul of young Gwydion, his mind just emerging from the slumber of childhood into the tumultuous hormonal years of teenage. And as they drove through town he pressed his nose against the cold glass, occasionally wiping away the steam from his breath so that he could look out across the street into the windows where other people dwelt. Strangers he could only in the lights of their home guess about their evening activities. He wondered if they contemplated what life was like outside the glass of their windows, the solidity of their walls. He saw them comfortably enclosed and wondered if they knew the un-moorings he knew, of travel, of the change of space, of something of the confusion he felt at the actions of others. He assumed they felt as he did, similarly confused and disoriented at all of the mystery. It would not be until many years later he would come to understand just how different from theirs his perceptions were.

They drove through winding streets some lined with old Victorian buildings and some lined with new skyscrapers disappearing up into the fog. They crossed market Street and to the right was a tall thin building shaped like a tall slice of cake with Windows like different layers of frosting. As they drove people flashed by his window and stared back at him with ghoulish smeared faces in the fog, and Gwydion wondered if he was seeing things.

Things past or future that haunted these busy streets where past, present and future seemed to meld and coexist.

"Oh look at that," his mother kept saying. "Oh, look at that Gwydion," she would say every few minutes. And he would look and see nothing but the normal people or cars. He wondered that she did not see what he did, the fog and the lights played tricks with their faces, the horses snorting and the narrow spoke wheel of the Cabriolets spinning in the fog. A horn blared and he was jolted back to the present as the black sedan swerved to miss a yellow taxi running a red light.

"Are we almost there?" He said plaintively.

"That's a nickel," said his grandfather. Gwydion groaned. Such a dumb game. He never had any money anyway. But he tried to staunch his automatic tendency to ask if they were there yet. It was something he knew he had to grow out of now that he was a teenager and going to high school. Things are going to be different. He could feel it in his stretching bones. He shook his forelock over his eyes, shrugged his shoulders, and blew a puff of air from between his lips. Will turned and looked at him and said, "Yes actually. Almost there".

The streets took turns and the family knew they'd need a map to go anywhere the next day. Food and exhaustion had softened their memories. And no way on these convoluted streets would they ever find their way to anywhere without a map.

They turned onto a small street going crosswise on the hill above town. Gwydion noticed a street sign, "Alexandra," it said. And he thought how interestingly Egyptian that was.

The long black sedan pulled to the curb and stopped. And Will couldn't help himself but point out the drivers window and say, "and there it is. Your new home in San Francisco."

Everybody turned and looked out the side window across the street to a huge Victorian pile.

"Wow. What a beaut," said Antony.

"Oh my. That's lovely," said Bethany. "That will do just fine," she said as she took in the many high narrow Windows framed with lace curtains, the shingled sides reaching up to a third floor and several pointed gabled roofs. Mags let out a squeal of glee and reached across Gwydion and popped open the car door, and gently hurried him out, without waiting for the driver to open the door for them.

They stood in the street and looked up at the mansion the windows lit brightly in the dark of night. "Wow," said Mags.

"Let's get our stuff mom," said Gwydion impatiently.

Martin popped the trunk and the family gathered around to pull out their travel belongings.

They carried everything across the street and waited for Will to unlock the front door. Inside was a vestibule lined with rock slabs. Several well tended plants grew in china pots on the floor and stone shelves. And a steep set of stone stairs lead up to what would be the first floor. They waited at the top for Will to squeeze by and unlock that door too. He opened it and the family stepped into their new home.

"Oh, look. There's upstairs, too!" Cried mags excitedly.

"The upstairs is closed off." Said Will. She looked at him with disappointment. "I know. But sorry. It's just full of junk and dust. And we haven't had time to clean it out. So it's off-limits for now."

"But I still get dibs on the bedrooms!" cried Mags as the thumped down the hall.

"Actually I think we do," said Bethany about her and her husband. And she glanced at Antony who winked. There were many rooms in this rather unoccupied old Victorian. "so many rooms, " said Bethany quietly.

"This place has been largely unoccupied for many a year," said Will. "Aloaetious got it for a steal. Seems there were some rumors of haunting or something. I've never seen anything amiss myself. But then again I'm not much a superstitious kind of guy. Ghosts and such ." He turned and shrugged his shoulders at Antony and Bethany. And Antony chortled. Bethany was too busy looking at the rooms to notice what he had said. She chose the largest, the one with the biggest bed and the huge windows facing the city to the north, which beamed with bright glow through the fog and the night. She plunked down her bags and turned to Will and her husband. "This is really something," she said to them in a hushed voice, almost reverently. "What a change from Egypt. that was like a cookie box in comparison."

Will just smiled and said, "Glad you like it; Aloaetious would be happy. Rest his soul in peace," he added in a quiet voice.

Antony just smiled and beamed at his wife, perhaps hoping to pick up some of the credit for this advancement in their quality of life. And he accepted gratefully her tight hug and kiss on the cheek. Couldn't be better.

## Chapter 7.
## New Jobs

In the morning they all met in the kitchen. After years of living in the cramped apartment in Cairo, they had learned to synchronize their sleep and wake patterns. And the family always seemed to wake up at the same time to start their day. Will was cooking breakfast, making eggs and toast for everyone. "We have a long day ahead of us today." he said to the small group around the table.

"What are we doing? I thought we would be sleeping in. taking in some sights." said Mags.

Outside the fog was just beginning to burn off. The light of day was bright but still you couldn't see much past the street outside. But you could tell it was clearing and would be a clear day.

"We are going to the university to start things with the foundation. School starts in 2 weeks and we need to get a head start."

Gwydion yawned and stretched and said in his sleepy morning voice, "It would have been better if you guys hadn't been running down the hall all night."

Everyone just looked at him with wide eyes. He realized his mistake and said quickly "Just kidding." Then he put his head down and started in on some eggs.

"Well I don't know about yo all, but I slept like a rock," said Bethany to the group.

"Ya, me too," said Antony as he picked up his steaming coffee cup and then slurped down some of the dark brew.

"i didn't hear anything last night, Gwydion," jabbed his mother. "More of your dreams I suppose."

"They're not dreams," he shouted at them., them looked back down at his plate.

Mags just groaned and rolled her eyes. She had heard all kinds of weird stories from Gwydion through the years. And she'd learned to take them all with a grain of salt.

"There's no one else in this house, Gwydion. But its old. You must have just heard the floor boards creaking, that's all." said Will knowledgeably.

"Ya, sure. whatever. I didn't hear anything." Gwydion was getting surly in his teenage years and he didn't care so much what they thought anymore. Or he tried to think that anyway. He was trying to learn to say what they expected him to say so they wouldn't bug him about stuff. But he never knew which stuff they would believe and which they wouldn't, although it all seemed real to him, so it was still hit or miss .

"We are going to go drive out to the university and get things rolling," he said to his captive audience. Gwydion rolled his eyes and flipped his hair to the side. Will looked at him for a moment and said, "You, Gwydion, start high school next Monday. Are you ready?"

Gwydion did not have any idea what he was talking about so he shrugged his shoulders and looked at his fork. "We'll drive by there today and have a look so you know where it is. There's a bus that will take you straight there."

"A school bus?" asked Antony.

"No. A city bus. Lots of mass transit around here. Bus or rail line right by the high school. Pretty cool."

Gwydion shrugged again and acted like he didn't really care. But inside he was excited that he was going to have the freedom to move around and do things on his own. And in an

American city, where everybody looked like him and spoke like him. What a change from Egypt that would be. Or Mexico where he had not spoken any of the language at all.

They piled dishes in the sink and got packed to head out. Will cleaned up the food and dishes while they went and got ready. Gwydion closed his door and changed his clothes again for the third time that morning. he was more nervous than anyone realized. He had awoken several times in the night to noises or what he thought where noises upstairs in the old house. Maybe it was creaking of the floor boards. But in his sleepy mind last night it had been much more. Not that he would tell any of them though.

As they got back in the car, the fog had begun to really clear and they could see that this house was high up on the side of the hill. There were other Victorian houses surrounding this one. But this one was larger and more ornate than the others. And it was purple, something they couldn't see in the gloom of the night before when they had arrived. And as they headed down the hill, they could see the city sweeping out before them, with patches of water and the bay peeping in between hills.

They drove through town in the long black sedan and Gwydion rolled down the window and breathed in the fresh air. It wasn't as salty flavored here as it had been the night before when they had dinner. But that was right on the wharf. Here it wasn't so strong.

But as they drove, it began to get salty tasting again. They were getting nearer to the ocean again on this drive. And after a few moments, they came over a rise, and there it was. The dark blue Pacific stretched out before them again. After months on the sea, and one night on land, Gwydion had not missed the presence of the sea and it seemed now a stranger to him. He closed his eyes and breathed deeply and heard the call of some seagulls overhead.

They wound down the coast a ways and then turned abruptly inland to the left. Up they drove into a cleft in the steep hills and found the university nestled there in tall dark green trees. Martin parked the long sedan and Will leaned over and said something to him, and Martin answered, "Yes, sir." quietly. Antony saw the subtlety of this and wondered if there was more to the simple seeming relationship of driver and boss. How much does one know about the nature of one's bosses business? Sometimes maybe it's a fine thing to not know too much. Even simple anthropology has its secrets. And Antony had been involved in enough controversy for anyone's one lifetime. He envied Martin's simple imperatives; Park here, wait such and such, simple things.

The Institute was small but beautiful. The red brick buildings were not old, yet the copper roofing had earned its classic verdigris drippings within its short life time. There was, Antony noticed, a wrought iron fence that surrounded the entire institution which had pointed finials all along the top. Perhaps decoration, perhaps protection. But in all Antony gathered that this was probably more privately funded than not. And he wondered how much exactly was provided by the Happenstance Historical Foundation.

The group was taken into the front room and introduced to Prudence the secretary and principal Mr. Hillard that presided in a side office that adjoined. Anthony was impressed by their cordiality and their seeming happiness that they had arrived safe and sound from their journey. Will then led them down along a carpeted hall into the rooms towards the back. One of the rooms had lettering already installed on the pebbled glass window that said Dr. Antony Jacobs. And Will grasped the brass doorknob, turned it and opened the door for them to enter.

What a nice room, thought Antony right away. Mags skipped into the room and flopped herself down onto the thickly padded dark leather armchair. There were dark wooden bookcases on the shelves holding all manner of anthropological texts and scientific journals. Gwydion strode in and sat down on the other padded armchair, while Antony walked around in awe to the heavy wood desk with a black leather rolling office chair behind it, and sat down with a squeak. His wife Bethany stood opposite him and beamed.

"New chair," he said casually. But inside he was thrilled to have such nice digs. He looked across the room and saw a stack of old boxes and crates that he recognized. Will watched his gaze and said, "oh yes. This just came in from Egypt. All your stuff you left behind in a hurry. All here and accounted for."

"Well, thank you, Will did you arrange all that?" Said Antony. "I suspect you did. I figured it was lost to time when we left in such a hurry." He thought about his former colleague that had died while they were in Cairo at the university there.

Under mysterious circumstances, it had actually been deemed a murder, although the details had remained largely undisclosed. He had whisked his family away quickly when things had gotten intense, and hadn't learned of the murder until after they had reached New York, after their stop in England to attend the service of the just-passed Aloaetious Happenstance, Antony's colleague and mentor. That was a tough period for the Jacobs family. And the memory of it occasionally surfaced violently and unexpectedly on Antony. Like now, seeing those simple beat -up boxes of his old office stuff. He wondered at the old manuscripts he had been translating back in Egypt. He wondered how much of that was still hidden in those boxes. He had taken the most important infrared photographs of the ancient documents with him when he fled. But he knew when he opened those boxes ghosts of memories would come flooding back to him.

"I think I'll wait a little while to get to those boxes, Will. They could wait another day."

"Yes, they can. In fact today we have a conference call scheduled. In about an hour," said Will. "So let's take a tour," he addressed everyone in the room.

They went back outside the room and down the hall and out the back into an open courtyard of red brick surrounded by landscaped plants. The air is fresh and bracing so near the coast here and Antony knew he would enjoy working here has a fresh change from the harsh climate of Egypt. He hoped he'd be here for quite a while.

Will led them across the courtyard and pointed off to the right and said, "That there Gwydion is the library."

And Gwydion's eyes lit up, he gave a small quirk of his mouth and walked in that general direction and pushed through the solid wood doors to the sound of Will saying, "we'll come get you when were done." Gwydion didn't even glance back.

Mags chuckled; she understood her sons love of libraries and books and the solitude they entitled. "What about me?" She asked out loud.

"How about the children's room?" Said Will.

"There's a kindergarten?" Mags asked with wonder.

"Yep. All the young children of the teachers and staff attend here instead of public school, if they wish. Most do. It was Aloeatious' wish that all children be treated to a rich education afforded usually only to wealthy children. He found they responded well, unexpectedly well."

Mags looked at him with almost tears in her eyes. But she didn't say a thing. Will looked at her for a moment, then turned and they walked in the other direction toward the sound of children's voices. He opened the door to the children's room and all heads turned towards them. "Mrs. Fredrickson," he directed towards the teacher at the head of the room. "I'd like to introduce to you the Jacobs family. And Margaret here, would love to help with the children."

Mrs. Fredrick beamed and said, "I've heard so much about you. Glad you came."

"Oh, call me Mags, please."

"Mags, nice to have you aboard . Have a seat, we are reading the Iliad." And with that she turned back towards the class of children and began reading from the thick book she held in her hands again.

The three adults turned and exited from the room. They headed across the causeway again to another room which when they entered it became apparent was the cafeteria. "Let us sit a moment then I'll explain some things to you," said Will.

# Chapter 8.
# The Superintendent

The three of them selected a table in the mostly empty room. As in most cafeterias, the sounds echoed off clean hard walls. The scuff of a chair could be heard clearly across the room. But in this one there was a difference. The colors were warm and there was art on the walls. Made it a little more homey, to Antony's eyes anyway.

"Would you like something to eat or drink?" Asked Will of his two guests.

"I think I'm too excited to eat anything," said Bethany.

"Why don't I get you some coffee honey," said Antony to his wife.

"Maybe some decaffeinated tea, with honey and milk, perhaps might settle my stomach," she answered. She grasped her hands in her lap and shrugged her shoulders and smiled it Will. "This is also beautiful and exciting," she said.

"I'm glad you're happy with it. Some of this was prepared for you," said Will.

"Yeah, I could tell by the lettering on the door. That was very welcoming," said Antony.

"We are all glad to have you here." He walked over to the coffee bar and poured himself some coffee and Antony made himself and his wife each a big mug of Earl Grey tea with honey and milk. "That ought to do it," said Antony to will, and they turned and walked back to the table and joined Bethany again.

After a few moments of silence while they enjoyed their hot beverages they both looked up at Will with expectation in their faces.

"Ya, this is a lot isn't it?" said Will. "We set this up pretty fast, Aloeatious and I, and a few others. It was always his dream to have this kind of an educational facility. And I don't think his mortality ever set in even to the last minute, when he was dying."

"Ya, he went too fast for my comfort," said Antony.

"Actually, he knew he was dying for a really long time. He just didn't tell anybody. So although the Happenstance Historical Foundation might be only a few years old, this brick-and-mortar institution is about 10 years old. They have been working on this for a while."

"They?" Antony has caught that word use.

"Yes, there are a few of us involved in this project. One of them you can meet in a few moments. By phone anyway. She's one of Aloeatious' more …." and here Will hesitated just briefly, Antony noticed, "reclusive Associates. I've only met her a couple times. She is a little different. The positively brilliant. A real guiding light for this institution."

"That sounds fascinating," said Bethany over steaming mug of tea.

"She thinks it's important that you be there too, Bethany," said Will. "So important to history. Husbands and wives. Families"

"Well, thank you. I feel honored to be a part of this project," she shrugged her shoulders and giggled. "Whatever it is." She felt the importance of this undertaking although she didn't quite know why. But she wanted to respect the seriousness of it and felt that something astounding was about to be revealed to them. So she just looked at Will, the slightly younger man, about the age of her daughter Mags actually, and wondered about the importance he seemed to serve.

"Does this 'she' have a name?" Asked Anthony.

"We call her Azra."

They finished their drinks, stood up and headed back to Antony's plush office. Will picked up the phone, punched the button and spoke quietly into the receiver. He replaced the receiver in the cradle and looked at his guests. Who were no longer guests really. This was now Antony's office, and technically, Will was now the guest. That made him smile. He felt satisfied that having brought his quarry here successfully. Now for the strange part.

In a few moments the phone rang. Will picked it up listened and then spoke quietly. He punched a button on the front of the phone and set the receiver back in the cradle. And a voice came over the speaker.

"Hello? Is Antony and Bethany there?" Said a soft but succinct voice that sounded neither male nor female.

"Yes, this is Antony."

"I'm here too, this is Bethany."

"A pleasure to meet you, Anthony and Bethany. You can call me Azra. I have other names but that's the easiest. I'm glad you're here; I've heard a great deal about you. "

"We are glad to be here, too," said Antony into the air above the phone, hoping his voice was carrying. The speakerphone was a new gadget to him. He'd never used one before. They had no such thing in Egypt.

But modern marvels were all the rage. If not confusing. It made him feel like an old man, but he was trying.

"Yes, thank you for having us," said Bethany. "We would like to be involved in whatever we can do for you."

"For me, no," said the voice. "For us, this is a project for all. Aloeatious Happenstance has given me discharge to develop new ways to enrich human life. We saw in his last days a frailty and he wanted to ensure that there was a continuance of effort. I accepted the challenge and would like for you to join me on this journey." There was a brief silence. And then the voice continued.

"Is your son there?" she asked.

"Gwydion?" Bethany asked stupidly.

"Is he with you there now?"

"No, he's in the library. His favorite place," answered Antony.

"Well, we are glad to have him aboard too," said the voice on the speaker phone.

"Well, he'll be going to high school at the local public school," said Bethany informatively.

"Yes, that's fine. That's great. It will be a normalizing experience for him."

"He's had problems before in public schools. He's... different, you know," informing the person behind this voice as if she would not know this about her son.

"Different, but special," said Azra on the speaker phone. But Bethany didn't take umbrage to it this time, she took this to be a comfort, not pitying condescension like she usually got from school administrators about her grand son.

And as if sensing Bethany's train of thought, Azra said, "Yes, we think he's very special. He has unusual talents others don't."

"Talents?" asked Antony. He'd never heard anyone say that before. Although he had often thought it himself.

"Yes. Talents. A special insight. He learns really quickly doesn't he?" she asked his grandparents.

"Yes, he learns scary fast sometimes. But he's not great with communicating with words." Said his grandfather.

"We are not unfamiliar with this type of learning. But it seems to be special or unusual with humans, uh, people for the most part. You see, we've come to believe that children are born open to more levels of reality and consciousness then were previously thought, uh, understood. And as they grow into young people a part of their brain that receives information from what is sometimes called the collective consciousness, that part of the brain begins to shut down as the child assimilates into the strictures of society. But with some children this doesn't happen. A rare few maintain the "open doors", as we call them, to the messages from the greater planetary good, as we like to call it. But sometimes this makes them appear strange, maladjusted, social outcasts, even."

Picking up on her distanced word usage, Antony asked somewhat defensively, "Is he going to be a part of some study of yours?"

"No. Nothing is specific as that. It's just, these traits, talents, fall among family lines."

"We don't believe in that spiritual mumbo-jumbo," said Bethany skeptically.

"I'm a scientist, and I rely on hard fact," said Antony.

"Oh," said Azra. "Of course you do." She waited a beat for them to feel that she was considering what they had just said. Then she continued.

"But how can these, as you call "spiritual", aspects of human experience become facts if we don't study them?"

She left it hanging at that for a moment for these people who she knew were intelligent, but who were also defensive, having just been brought into this completely new situation and whose outcast grandson they were talking about. Then continued, "And we are very happy to have your family with the Happenstance Historical Foundation. Very happy, welcome, Jacobs family."

Antony and Bethany looked at each other and then looked at Will's blank face and raised their eyebrows. Will just shrugged nonchalance.

"And that brings us to our next project. Now, Antony, I know you and your family have traveled the world to many different locations, and you've encountered various obstacles and controversy in your studies. But we think you're strength in dealing with adversary makes you the perfect person to direct our hyper human studies." There was a break in her narration as she let these ideas settle on her small audience . Then she continued, "Next summer there is a conference in Italy we will be attending. It will be on the anthropological archaeological findings in the Nile Delta. We think that within these ancient scriptures is evidence for the transmutation of the human soul into energy. It's a new study of the human mind, and it encompasses the human spirit, religion, alchemy... All of the things we've been studying up to now, with the new ideas of space travel and teleportation, and demonology thrown in for good measure. "

This was almost too much for Antony. He was old-school anthropologist, and sometimes wondered how he had even gotten into the field of the translating of ancient scriptures. He was told it was because he was unusually adept at translating languages, and was not an expert in any one field, which usually hindered scholars when they entered the area of biblical translations.

But this talk of demonology and space travel. This kind of talk usually turned him into an ice cube. He wasn't sure any of this stuff was real. They were beginning to call this "supernatural phenomena". And most didn't even consider it a science.

But then again he wasn't ready to poo-poo this stuff yet either.

"So, how does this involve me? I'm just an anthropologist."

"Actually it involves the translations that have recently been uncovered, some of which you have been working on already. I understand you still have some of them in your possession, from your time in Egypt."

Antony wondered if that was vaguely a threat. Like maybe she thought he had stolen them. Or left the country illegally with the ancient transcriptions in his possession. But he had never been contacted by anyone in that regard. And it didn't seem like she was accusing him now. Maybe she regarded his possession of those certain transcripts as an advantage over other institutions that were trying to get an edge on publishing translations of important ancient scriptures.

And maybe that was partly why he was here. This Azra saw him as an asset to her institution.

But he still didn't think there was any of that sort of information in any of those stories he had possession of in his file or briefcase. He didn't know how it related to her fields at all.

"But still, that all sounds like spiritualism, or supernatural studies," he said. "They are calling it "Supernatural Phenomena" I think. That is an unrelated field of study."

"You wont think so after ….but, well, I get ahead of myself. There are some artifacts that have not been released to the public yet. And Aloeatious was very excited to start publishing. But anyway. It stands to be quite fascinating, as I'm sure you understand. The five of you will attend the nine day progress of this convention next June, after the high school year for your son Gwydion ends."

Antony and Bethany sat looking at each other. Despite his arguments, they realized they were being given a new anthropology linguistics project. Which meant full time work and housing.

And another travel journey. Which meant more travel. And they weren't sure how they felt about that, after their recent return, umm, flight, from Egypt.

"You will think about this among yourselves. But I am sure minds like yours will find the idea enticing." There was a shuffling sound over the intercom and they became aware that their conference call was coming to a close. They hadn't given their acceptance of the project yet. But all parties could see that it was something that they simply could not refuse.

"We will be expecting papers published by the both of you, Doctors, either together or separately. And Bethany, you are encouraged to contribute as well. In fact, your grandson

Gwydion shall be encouraged to begin his paper writing career also."

Now Antony and Bethany really blinked at each other, as Will sat and watched their surprise. They were not used to this sort of language from anybody really. Educators usually had their way of speaking eloquently about their dreams for enriching mankind. And no one had ever flattered them, surprised them, with talk of Gwydion contributing.

But no, something about this voice was more than the usual enthusiastic administrator. Richer and less strident. Concerned but less strained. They felt soothed and carried by this voice and were speechless, incapable of adding any thing coherent to the discussion. And they were grateful to have a new direction, to be wanted on an interesting new project.

So they just said thank you.

"With time, more of the professor Happenstance program will be revealed. But for now this is probably enough. I'm sure you are tired from your journeys. Thank you."

With that, the line clicked and a dial tone sounded a solid buzz. Will reached forward and punched off the intercom button. Antony and Bethany just looked at him. He smiled a wan smile and shrugged his shoulders slightly. "Like I said, enigmatic, reclusive."

"No, that was great." said Antony. "I like looking forward to another trip abroad."

"We just got here," said Bethany quietly.

"Look, it's September. That's not till late June next year. We'll get settled and have a good school year. And that will be our vacation next summer. Imagine, Italy," said Will.

Antony and Bethany just nodded. But inside they were just beginning to bubble with the excitement of their new lives.

After the three of them had refreshed themselves and grabbed a quick drink in the cafeteria, they walked over to the library to retrieve Gwydion. They found him sitting on the stairs leading to the reading loft of the library, the sun streaming in through the indoor ficus trees that reached up against the windows. He looked up from some thick old book and saw his grandparents approaching, and wondered at the glowing looks on their faces.

"Come, Gwydion. Let's fetch your mother and will be on our way home."

Gwydion looked at his grandfather and smiled, and knew his grandfather would not forget that they needed to stop by his new high school, so he didn't mention it.

They walked back outside and across the courtyard and entered into the children's day room. Again all eyes turned towards them as they opened the door, and Dr. Fredrickson laid her thick book down and smiled at them.

"I suppose you've come to reclaim your daughter now. She has been wonderful; thank you for lending her to me for a time. I hope she can return on a more permanent basis, professor Jacobs. Bethany."

Mags beamed like a child herself. "Oh, I'd love to come back. Can I come back and help?" She asked enthusiastically.

"In fact, I think something might be able to be arranged with principal Hillard, if we ask nice," answered Dr. Fredrickson.

Mags just beamed and followed her family out the door. She put her hand on Gwydion's head gently tousled his hair.

He bent away from her touch, he was getting too old for that stuff, but couldn't help himself from giggling.

The black sedan gradually turned inland and made its way back towards the city. The way was unknown to them the city being new to them and all, and only noticed that they were stopping somewhere new when they pulled alongside the curb and saw the brick institution that would be Gwydion's new high school. His eyes grew wide as he saw the teenagers his age carrying book bags and coffee cups, and chatting together in pairs or clusters in the school quad. He felt fluttering in his chest that was part mingled fear and apprehension, and excitement at what this place held for him. Nobody said anything for a few minutes as the car quietly hummed and they sat and watched the high school campus life.

Then Will said, "you'll start school on Monday. I'll show you the bus route when I get back to the Institute house."

Another young man had found himself in a new school too. Only this one far far south of where Gwydion was. And he realized when he found it and walked up its great steps that perhaps from American standards, this was as much a school as a church. The stained glass windows told the story. He recognized the angels and the Christ, with his halo and white robes. He recognized the lines of benches and the black books and the small shelves on the back of each wood bench.

The young man walked up to the front of the church, just before the steps and the alter that he knew were the area of the priest. This was not so different, he thought, than his place of worship back home .

He had been told that the white devils practiced witchcraft and bloodletting and that he would never go into one of their damned churches.

But here now he didn't see any of that. In fact it really looked quite the same as from what he remembered from as a boy the few times he went to a mosque back home. And in Egypt too when he was studying there, he had visited a church with his patron there and had felt relieved that it was not all that different from what he was used to. Not that he went to church mosque very often when he was young. But his mother had taught him the importance of piety, of careful living and speech. And to read the Koran. Here they called it the Bible. But when he had read some way thru it, it seemed really quite similar, except that there were strange language affectations in the western book.

He bowed his head and mumbled a prayer for thanks that he had arrived here safely, when he heard steps next to him. The priest must have realized that he was not a regular student. He was here alone at an odd time of the evening, when no one else was around.

The priest said something to him in their unfamiliar tongue, and tears sprang to the boys eyes. He was so tired and so fatigued that he wasn't sure if he could even explain what he was doing here. And the priest's kind words, even if he couldn't understand what he was saying, brought forth the strangest passion of relief in the boy's chest, that he wept with silent wet sobs.

The priest reached forward and touched this child on the shoulder, and said something again in his soothing voice.

The young boy sniffed and said in crackling voice, "English."

"Oh, my," said the priest quietly. "May I help you, young man?" said the priest as he stood behind the praying boy. "Are you lost?"

"Bless me father for I have sinned," he said instinctively.

"Oh, no, young man. You are not in confessional. Although we can do that if you like. I can have someone..." And the young man turned toward the priest. He stood up and faced the older man, who gasped and took a step back.

"I'm sorry. I didn't mean to intrude," said the young man. He thought quickly with a story. "I am traveling and was trying to find the university. I want to study but my parents reject your faith..."

The priest was mute for a moment. Then collected his thoughts and said, "Oh. Do I know you from somewhere?" he asked as he looked stridently into the young man's face.

# Chapter 9.
# High School

Gwydion found himself in the cafeteria. It was lunch time and he had just sat himself down at a long white table with a bunch of other kids. He didn't know anyone. But it was clear that some of these kids knew each other. They sat yelling and gesturing at each other. The noise was terrible. But in this Gwydion found solace; he had anonymity. In fact no one was even looking at him.

He saw kids of all shapes and sizes and different ethnic background. He felt comfortable in the tumult that was freshman high school group mentality. He had never had that before. No one was paying him any attention.

He looked around the area where he sat and realized that someone was looking at him. And suddenly he felt the cold grip of fear. Someone was watching him. A girl over on the other side of the table. She was pretending to eat out of her tray of food, but she was facing right at him and he could feel her eyes on him as he ate. Or tried to eat ; his stomach was turning into a knot of fear.

What could she want with him? Who was she? Did he know her from somewhere else?

He kept his eyes down and tried to finish his lasagna. But his eyes darted to her between bites. She had dark hair and dark eyes. And she was wearing a purple dress and had a black hat on her head. And her face. Her face was dark, like there were dark circles around her eyes.

Like she was sick. And her mouth was red. He thought maybe she painted that color with lipstick like his grandmother wore.

He looked back down to find he had eaten everything. He hadn't noticed he'd done that. He slammed down the last of the tepid, stinking milk, set the empty carton down on his tray and began to stand up to return it to the lunch counter. But he found his lags weren't working so well. He was terribly conscious of the movement his legs made. Each step felt like his legs were turning inside out and his feet weren't hitting the floor right. What was wrong with him?

He walked stiffly to the counter, set his tray down and turned to walk out. Then he noticed the purple girl was staring at him. Oh, god, what now? he thought to himself. Just keep walking in a straight line, and out the door.

When he reached the door frame and stepped out into the sun, his legs began to function correctly and he walked down the side walk. He stopped and pulled out the worn piece of paper that was his schedule and the campus map and studied where his next class was. Down the steps to the right then into the building and the first door on the left. Got it.

He strode forward and ignored the people around him. They seemed to be ignoring him too. such quiet. Kids in their own tumult were so much quieter than adults always trying to peer into your soul, always wanting to know what was going on inside your head. The peace and quiet of peers; he had never known that. At the university in Cairo, he had been mostly with students that were quite a bit older than himself. Mostly college students and some of them quite a bit older than him.

At first then he hadn't noticed them, but soon he had begun to feel a pressure growing inside his head, with these more adult students always looking at him and always studying his movements. This was a relief to be surrounded by kids his own age. Kids who looked like him, Americans he guessed, although there were all kinds of kids here. They all seemed happy. And no one seemed to be following him, No one seemed to be mad at him. It had seemed constant back in Egypt. there was that one kid who had followed him. And Gwydion had never known why. And it had gotten worse.

Gwydion reached the door to the room and stopped thinking about that. It was something he thought about at night when he was alone. In fact he still had nightmares about that boy, the boy with the crossed eyes. Nightmares, banging noises, clutching at his coat, running, slipping, falling, and he would always wake up. Sweating.

But here the art room opened up before him. The smell of paint assaulted his nose and the noise from outside subsided. There was a murmur of soft voices and the tip tap sound of tools being used in an art room. He chose a stool at the back of the room and waited for the teacher to lecture. But that never materialized. The teacher walked over to him, and for a moment he thought he was in trouble, and his heart began to pound. But the teacher asked him his name and then explained the assignment. Draw or paint on the easel a scene from summer vacation. That was it.

He looked at the easel dumbfounded. What was he supposed to do? He looked around at the other students in the room and became aware that they were all pretty busy doing their projects. So he set his backpack under the stool and sat looking at the paper on the easel.

Just then the door behind him opened and in walked, guess who, the girl in the purple dress. He looked abruptly away and studied his paper and picked up a paintbrush. She walked past him and chose an easel to the side and slapped her backpack underneath the stool and began to move tools around. She seemed to know what she was doing, as Gwydion watched her furtively. Then all of a sudden she turned right toward him and gave a tiny smile. And he quickly looked away. Maybe she didn't notice he had been looking right at her. He felt a burning in his chest and a tingling in his fingers. What was with her? he thought to himself and he fiddled with his tools. How can she know about him? what had she heard?

In his confusion he started painting and soon found his paper covered with a rough sketch of the three pyramids of Giza.

After a while he looked up from his work. He had failed to notice that some people were standing behind him, watching him work. "That is so cool." "Where'd you get that idea?" said another. Gwydion felt his face turn hot as he bent down a little more to hide.

The teacher stepped over and asked, "Have you been there?" And Gwydion just nodded his head a little, then he flipped his hair back out of his eyes. He noticed a pair of combat boots step over and stop right near his easel. It was the girl in the purple dress. Now he could barely breathe. His hand jerked and he made a black smear on the page. But no one noticed but him and kids oohed and ahhed at his painting.

They soon went back to their own smudgy paintings for a while and then the bell rang. "I will let these dry and put them in back for next time. Be sure to put your name on them at the bottom, folks, so we know whose is whose!" said the teacher loudly as the noise level tripled in the room as the kids began to pack up their bags and shuffle out the door. Gwydion moved onto the rest of the day, but it was a blur after the intensity of art class. and soon he found himself on the bus going home. There was a writing assignment in his English class. He had never really written anything before. And Gwydion thought it was too advanced for anyone to do. It was too vague and everyone had groaned as the teacher gave it out. Write a short story of something scary that happened to you. Halloween was coming up and the teacher was trying to get everyone into the mood. He had read in front of the class The Tell-Tale Heart, by Edgar Allen Poe, and Gwydion, like the other student's had been entranced. So much so that he had gone into the student store and bought himself his own copy of the works of the writer. He read all the stories, but the "Tell Tale Heart" was the most vivid, the most scary. So when he wrote his short story for the class assignment, he was inspired, he thought he might do something scary like that.

"As I walked down the cold stone steps, the air around me turned to a bracing chill". The teacher told him to use lots of adjectives with each noun, at least one, anyway. so he tried hard.

"I could hear the tick tick tick of the water dripping from the damp stone ceiling, as the steps took me deeper into the cavern. I pulled my new yellow coat closer around my shoulders. I had left it on the stairs earlier and had come back to get it.

My mother would have been mad at me if I had lost it for good.

"So here I was being drawn into the dark depths of the stone temple deep in the jungle. Mysteries surrounded the history of the stone temple. And no one knew it's true purpose. There were no real rooms in there. Only a deep stair case and one small room at the bottom where it is told they held human sacrifice, and stored the hearts in the stone tomb."

And here on the paper, the teacher had written, "Gwydion, stick to the facts" in red ink. and Gwydion thought how unfair; these were facts, according to his professor grandfather. Just wait till I tell him about my dumb teacher.

"I continued down the steps, drawn by some unknown force, into it's black maw. Then a sound began to penetrate my consciousness. A deep thrumming sound I could not locate. It seemed to emanate..." he liked that big word, "...from the very rock surrounding me. Boom, boom, boom, it resonated until I felt it might be my very own heart banging on my chest. Or was it the sound of the many still-beating hearts stored in the stone tomb?"

And here the teacher had written, "Oh, I see, like "Tell Tale Heart" " Boy, was he slow", he thought.

"I stepped down into the dark and heard a rustling in the corner. A rat, perhaps? I listened and heard it again, only louder this time. Too big for a rat. What could it be?

I called into the dark, "Who goes there? Anyone there?" And suddenly out of the gloom materialized a face; a white moon of a boys face, with a grimace full of sharp teeth. And it was the face from my nightmares. For each night a ghoul haunted my dreams, a face jeering and grimacing, its foul breath bathing me in its horrid stench.

I jumped back and landed on my rear on the cold stone floor. "Who are you?" I screamed.

It just laughed a menacing laugh and said, "I'm your worst night mare!" And with that it began to stride towards me, bony fingers reaching out. I turned and began to bolt up the stairs, the menacing form scrabbling right behind.

My feet felt like lead weights as I tried to flee. The harder I tried, the heavier my feet. I could feel it's cold hands clutching at my coat. The thing caught the hem once with its steely fingers.

"I will get you. I will kill you! I will end your still- beating heart that echoes on these walls of terror!"

The monster from my nightmares screamed at me in its rage. And still I climbed the stone stairs, my terror ripping the air from my lungs, stripping the strength from my limbs. More that once his cold fingers grasped my new coat, and still I ripped it free.

Just as I reached the light at the top of the stairs, I felt his hand grip the back of my coat. I squirmed and let out a terrified groan as the specter behind me tripped, and yanked the coat from my shoulders and fell backwards with it. I heard him scream as he tumbled back down the cold stone stairs, his cry of agony fading as he fell, until it was quieted by a sickening thump as he hit bottom."

And what was written at the bottom in big red ink letters by his teacher changed the course of Gwydion's life, although he wouldn't realize that for many years to come. "That is very good short fiction, Gwydion!"

# Chapter 10.
# Stack of Scriptures

"It seems," answered Antony, "that those monks would later, years after the Christ was dead, issue edicts, warning devout people of heretics and the heresies they espoused as ancient truths. They decided that some of the Gnostic writings were not worthy of including in the big book because they were falsified as to the date they were written."

"It was just a way of denouncing things they didn't want," added Will.

"Right," said Antony. "But more, they were refuting the actual age of these ancient documents, saying the dates were falsified and not really good old ancient wisdom. And therefore not worthy of being included."

"Well, they were calling them not true wisdom because they really weren't old," said Will.

"Oh, I see," Said Mags. "So they were saying that if they actually were old, that then they would be "better" wisdom. So they refuted their age there by refuting their worth."

"Right," said Will. "That was their own implication."

"Which of course we know now that they *are* actually older than most of the new testament," said Antony.

"And now that our new dating machines are saying that they really are older than most of the New testament writings, and that they actually date from *before* the time contemporary with Christ, now that its been proven that they are older, now they say they are worthless *because* of it."

"So two-faced," said Mags.

Will snickered. He enjoyed Mags commentary. She always brought things down to earth in an everyday way of understanding these erudite things.

"Maybe. Definitely frustrating," said Antony. "But now I think we are finally between these two places, in the middle between this bigotry that has some ulterior motive. Between these two hard places and we have to work it out."

"As a society, you mean," added Will. " I agree. Our awareness has been forced open. We can no longer close our eyes to this reality of the existence of these ancient documents that the church has been suppressing for so long."

"I think we are asking questions we never could have before," said Bethany. "People are beginning to see from the outside that this is just another era, we have left the one, the one that believes that religions are the only way to see existence. We only believe it at the time that it is the only way. "

"Right," said Will. "We are gaining that eastern mystic perception of an outsider that can observe the phenomenon of what we can call religious belief."

"Well, looking at ourselves from the outside, and observing our behaviors," said Bethany. "Did you know Dr. Freud said that?"

"What?" asked Will.

"Dr. Freud said we do not know ourselves, and that results in oppressed thoughts and impulses, and that results in psychoses and hysteria."

Antony looked at his wife. "I did not know he said that. What have you been reading?"

Bethany just smiled and shrugged her shoulders.

The group gazed at the stack of copied manuscripts on the table before them. "So that's it, then?" asked Antony.

"We have gathered all of them together," answered Will.

"Even the Berolinische Gnostica?"

"Yup. They even agreed to have it translated by our people, any people for that matter. Any one who wants to take it on," said Will. "They seem to have completely lost the will to fight over who looks at it."

"They've had long enough to get over it, that's for sure," added Antony.

"Is that the one found by the Thule at the turn of the 20$^{th}$ century?" asked Mags.

"That's right," said Will. "They hid it for a while, then the curse of the Egyptian Zombies returned and brought them to a screeching halt."

"Ya, so they went to South America and wreaked havoc on our dig," said Bethany.

Antony chuckled, "Yup that's the one. But, from what I have read so far, I'm just not that interested in any of this so called library," said Antony.

"What?" said Will in a shrill voice.. "Seriously?"

"i am kind of sick of the holier than thou stuff this seems to be, what I have read so far," said Antony. His wife looked at him dumb struck. Not like him to not take a translations job.

Antony continued, "I mean really, and I quote 'They praise the second and so then the first; the way of ascent is the way of descent'. It is New Testament hog-wash re-write. I feel like I'm in catechism again."

"It's not all like that. Take the Gospel of Mary for instance," said Will.

"Sure, but we had that in the older stuff from Egypt, the Dead Sea documents. That gospel is really old. Predates the Christ birth. But this new find is almost all re-writings of that. Even the secret Book of John is all rewritten into patriarchal sexist hog wash. I can hardly read it. "When they learned of the expressions of the father, they knew, they were known, they were glorified, the gave glory." HUH? What silliness. Maybe sounds good from the pulpit, to sound menacing to an ignorant audience."

"Honey!" said Bethany.

"The really sad part," he continued, "is people feel uplifted by reading that tripe. They really feel they've learned something and have been up lifted toward saintliness by reading something that is essentially essential-less. Meaningless." Antony let out an exasperated breath at his diatribe.

"My, haven't we gotten spoiled over the existential finds of earlier," said Will sarcastically. "Maybe we can find you some things here that might interest you. I mean you are a valuable asset and we should like to keep you interested, keep you on."

Now that was starting to sound a little like a threat to Antony, and he put his hands on his hips. But in his mind he was thinking maybe it just wasn't worth it anymore. He had to be interested in it to do it. And most of this wasn't even catching is attention at all. Except to irritate him.

"We will find you something you want to work on, don't worry. There's plenty out there. You have this in your brief case, right?"

"Ya, its been sitting there for a while, yes," answered Antony. "Did you know?" he started in, and stopped himself.

Did he dare he tell Will this. Why not, the jerk. "Do you know that I used to read those Dead Sea stories to Gwydion at night?"

Will just looked at his older colleague and friend.

"Those stories were really kinda beautiful. But you know, not one of these, not one! would I read to him. With that Gothic language they were dreaming up and the sexist crap, no way. He used to sneak into my case and read them when we weren't around. Most boys grab a playboy. But no, not Gwydion. He grabs grand pop's old documents and goes for a 2000 year old spin in weird land. He actually like the Dante-esque apocalypse of Peter. He was fascinated." He shook his head vigorously. "But this stuff, no way; I'm locking it up."

"Now you are over-reacting," said Will.

Antony breathed deeply. "Ya, I know I am." He looked at his wife and daughter, who both looked uncomfortable and about ready to leave. "Don't worry about me. I'll find something productive to work on."

"Well, remember," added Will as they were all walking out the conference room door, "The conference in Italy is in a few months. We'll have to have something."

"Oh," said Antony. "I'll be ready."

# Chapter 11.
# Oh, Hallowed E'en

Gwydion wondered what he was going to do with this huge picture. He noticed that the girl in the purple dress was working on her painting already. But he didn't want to work on this one anymore. He was kinda embarrassed it was so big. And graphic. He hadn't even thought about it and the picture had just appeared. Then he was embarrassed it had caused so much attention. He never meant that. People in the class thought it was good. And they wondered where he got the image. But they didn't know that he was actually there last year. They knew almost nothing about him after all. The Jacobs family was very new to the area.

But does she always wear that purple dress? He wondered to himself. She had her black combat boots on too. Like a uniform.

And what was that she was painting. He stared at her paper up on her easel. It looked like a giant skull. With a dagger going through it. And a red rose. How strange.

He rolled up his now dry acrylic painting of the pyramids and laid it next to his back pack. Maybe my mom might want that. She probably hang it up and think it was wonderful. He smiled. So silly.

He slapped on a new big paper to his upright easel and stared at it for a minute. Then he looked over at the girl in the purple dress painting black into the background of her giant skull picture and an image flashed in his mind. Stone steps surrounded by deep green. He picked up a thick brush dabbed it in watered down acrylic paint and began to sketch shapes on the paper.

After a while he seemed to come out of a trance. He looked around and there was some activity in the room. The girl was still painting, finishing the very red rose in the skull's mouth. He got up and stood behind her. She had a book open on a stool next to her left knee. It looked like a medical manual.

She felt his presence standing behind him. "I like skulls," she said. "The bones are really beautiful, sculpted like art."

He grunted and shuffled his arms across his chest. "Do you like it?" she asked him.

"Oh, sure," he said defensively.

"Death fascinates me," she said turning toward him and looking into his face. Her irises were light colored tan, and her eyes he could see now were drawn in with black pencil with shadows painted under them to make her look sort of spooky. So she wasn't sick, after all, thought Gwydion, just painted to look that way. He wondered at this death child here, and noticed how the irises were lighter, like yellow almost.

She turned back to her painting and held the brush up and tilted her head. "All done, I think."

Just then the teacher said loudly, "OK, class is dismissed. Sign your art work and leave it there to dry. Remember, it's Halloween tonight so be careful and be safe! See you on Monday!," she called to the class as they began to make noise packing up to get out of there.

Gwydion packed up his things. And as the girl in the purple dress was walking by, she stopped and said to him, "Are you going to the Halloween dance tonight?" When he just looked at her, she said, "It should be fun.

Wear a costume, dress up in something. It starts at 8." When he didn't say anything, she just smiled, hoisted her backpack onto her shoulder and walked out of the art room. He had never been to a dance before. He kinda didn't know what it was. Dancing? He didn't dance. He had no idea what that was. The image of dumb boys gyrating stiffly to canned music from the LP was just a little nauseating. And girls were there too? Dancing with them, expecting them to dance and act casual. That sounded dumb, he told himself, but inside Gwydion was terrified.

But the girl in the purple dress had asked him to go, sort of. Implied he should be there anyway. He should go. She was interesting, in a weird kind of way. What would he wear? A costume? What would that be?

Well, he reasoned, I have to ask permission anyway, so I'll ask my mom about costumes. She will probably think I'm stupid for wanting to go, he thought to himself.

Mags tried really hard to control gigantic smile and a giggle when Gwydion asked her if he could go to the dance that night. She didn't care that it was a last minute thing; she was sure it had been planned for a while. But that he had just not known about it, or wasn't paying attention, seemed kind of a typical boy-thing to her.

Or had just simply never gone to a dance before; that much she was sure. Things like that did not happen back at the school in Egypt. Well, he really wasn't in regular school. He pretty much attended the audit's college courses at the University with the college students. But here, this was different. These were his peers, and Mags was really happy about it.

So when her son asked her if he could go to the dance that night, which meant him riding the bus alone at night both there and back, worry was pretty far from her mind. She was actually thrilled that he was interacting with the other kids, and wanting to go to an after school event, by himself no less.

And in a costume? Now that was encouraging. Maybe her little boy was starting to fit. Such a consideration was thrilling after all of the tumultuous years of this child, and Mags struggled to keep a somewhat straight face, and not squeal out in glee and reach out and grab and squeeze her son like she wanted to. Because she knew that would totally turn him off. She knew that he wouldn't want to please her too much.

"Well, let's see. A costume," she said scratching her chin. "We really don't have all that much stuff around here. Maybe some junk from Egypt I stashed away. Most of that got left behind. Then let's go get them box of clothes and see what we can find".

They dug through the box and found mostly clothes that his mother wore, things handmade in Egypt, with mirrors and stitching and jingles on them. Things no one in America would wear, at least not for another 10 years. But when they got to the bottom of the box, there was a pile of hair. And Gwydion grabbed that and pulled it out.

"Oh, that nasty old thing," said his mother. "It was a gag gift from one of your grandmother's bridge friends. Somehow it has stayed in the bottom of the box all this time. To Egypt and back again."

Gwydion pulled it out and shook it loose, for it was crushed and packed together in a wad. And as he shook it long green snakes shook free, their red tongues rattling in the air.

He screamed and dropped it to the floor. Then he realized the snakes were just rubber although very realistic, and both he and his mother burst into gagging laughter at the silliness of this black wig with green rubber snakes dangling from it.

"Oh dear God, that's perfect," she said to her son, as Gwydion wiped tears from his eyes from laughing so hard. He grabbed the wig, dragged it over his dark curls in front of the mirror. And stood looking at himself gaping as a parody of Medusa. Transformed into a demon.

"Really," she said, "you wouldn't have to wear anything else. That is so perfect."

And indeed it was, thought Gwydion. So perfect. He selected from the pile of clothes a bright colored cape with black and orange designs stitched in it with tiny reflective mirrors. "I'll wear this too. Can I wear this too, mom?"

"Oh, my cape," she said. "I guess. Be careful with it, I like that one. It's kind of, I don't know, magical. Just don't lose it like you did that yellow jacket in Honduras last year."

He frowned at her with her remonstrance. Why did she have to bring that up. What a scary day. And he lost that stupid yellow coat, too. Twice, actually. And he shuddered at the thought of the boy who had chased him down and dragged that coat off his arms as Gwydion had fled up those stone stairs into the light of day. Where had that boy gone? Was he still wearing that ugly yellow coat that belonged to him?

She saw has frown, and said, "Sorry. I know that was a hard day. But we will forget about all that soon, it will all be in the past."

How wrong she was.

# Chapter 12.
# New Translations for Antony

Will and Antony had gone through some of the stack of copies of the manuscripts they had managed to get a hold of from the Nag Hamadi Library. There were many varied stories and scriptures in this large stack of infra-red photo-stat copies. There was really no one place to start, as the so called "book" had been merely all kinds of folios stacked together, and sewn with gut into a pile of skins that would have to be called a book. The outer cover was a fully intact goat skin, crudely cured in the manner of two thousand years ago, with the front and back covers thickened and secured with stacks of what were news stories of the day. This was often how these ancient documents could be dated, was by the dates on these various pieces of paper that were sewn into the covers of these ancient books.

But when viewed together the book was very coarse and strangely shaped. So Antony was actually glad that they had before them the copies of said book, because the actual book, the stack of pages wrapped in the ancient goat skin, probably stunk. And it probably was dirty. And it was probably falling apart, and then that would be Antony's fault for handling it until it was ruined. Ancient documents just weren't handled by hand any more these days. Copies copies, a stack in his brief case.

So just the better that they had clean photo stat copies of the pages. Where they wouldn't be distracted by the quality of the pages themselves, the texture and the colors and hand written ink strokes were mesmerizing in their own way.

As if you could feel the person long dead bent over some wooden table that was now dust, with some ancient writing implement, writing those letters 2000 years ago. Those delicate pages were now packed away in some thermostatically controlled cold, light-less room somewhere, where very few people could get near them or ever touch them.

But the knowledge was here for them to review. Some of it had been translated by others. And some of those published papers were here in front of Antony and Will as they sat at the round table in the office at the Foundation.

But where to start. Antony had reviewed some of the already translated material and was dismayed at its verbiage. There was such a huge difference between the writings, if he sampled a tiny bit from each of the currently translated bits. So he simply started at a place where no one else seemed to have. His frustration seemed to evaporate as he got into the words themselves, and seemed to be drawn in and mesmerized by the ancientness of the languages.

> "I was given a great task by my fore bearers.
> They to me a garment of Yellow made fit.
> And they wrote a covenant in my mind,
> that in my journey I shall not forget.
> 'You shall to Egypt go,
> and the white pearl to find,
> it lay in the devouring serpent's lair,
> under a garment you shall don,
> your earthly appearance unbind.' "

He read another short verse:

"The leader of the authorities was blind.
In his arrogance he shouted,
' I am one and only god!'
His blasphemy echoed down to father Chaos,
and down to mother Abyss,
as he followed it down
at the suggestion of Pistis Sophia.
For the visible was born of the first invisible."

"How am I supposed to pick anything?" said Antony in an exasperated way. "There is so much stuff here. And it is all so different!"

Will just nodded his head. "I know. Its kinda nuts. There is simply so many different kinds of writings here. That's why they called it a library. There were many books, but each bound book contains lots of different kinds of things."

"I really had no idea," his said spreading his hands apart in the air, "last time I guess I had sampled such a small amount. And the Dead Sea group was so similar throughout. The stories had a certain flavor." Will just nodded his head at Antony's apology about his last rant.

"I don't think it matters which one. Just choose something that hasn't been started by anyone else and go with it. There's different languages too, so you are going to have to be comfortable with that dialect and the individual style. Just include all that you do translate with the folio if you do give up and switch. Then the next translator can start from there."

"No wonder they just gave up with their exclusive rights to translation. It'd never get done."

"I'm working on this one," and he handed Antony a page with his name and the single work he was translating. On the page was a long list of names and titles. "And the rest is the most current list of participants from the museum list. They are trying to keep track so there wont be too much overlap. Be nice to get this project done before the turn of the millennia." Will smirked as Antony looked up at him and smiled.

"That's 45 years away," laughed Antony.

"Ya, but you've seen this pile of stuff." Will put his hands in his pockets, and said, "and that is if all these scholars stay organized and work together."

"Hopefully," smirked Antony. "What a nice change from last time that would be."

# Chapter 13.
# Dead Dance

At 8 o'clock Gwydion stepped into the High School auditorium. He was right on time and there was almost no one there. How embarrassing. What a stupid party. No one was even there. And the music blared in the hollow auditorium dolefully.

So he walked over to the counter with refreshments and got a big cup of punch. It was bright red and thick and tasted really good. He drank down one cup of it and then had them fill him up again.

As he was sipping his second cup of blood red punch, he turned around and looked at the crowd. It was growing. People were flocking in the doors. And they had the wildest assortment of costumes on. He was glad then that he'd worn something for Halloween, even if he didn't feel weird wearing an Egyptian Cape, and a plastic wig with green rubber snakes.

The blaring music wasn't so bad now that the auditorium was filling up. And voices made a clangor against the auditorium walls and bounced off the ceiling to make a tumbled blurry sound.

It wasn't long before some people gathered around him people he knew from his art class mostly. People he barely knew, but who, like him, were somewhat outcast and not part of the cool athletic group. The girl with the purple dress was there, and so was her purple dress and combat boots, and he thought to himself, well she didn't have to dress up much. But her makeup was heavier and somehow she had a fixed too long fangs onto her eyeteeth and they hung out onto her lips when she closed her mouth and dangled menacingly when she laughed. And her tongue looked black when she opened her mouth. The others laughed and seemed to feel less strangely than Gwydion, and he figured that it was better to be in a group of strangers than to be alone. But they were loath to dance. Not many of the kids danced. Some couples that were established boyfriend and girlfriend couples spent the entire evening on the dance floor together. And were unaware of anyone else.

Not this group of artists and strangers. They sulked in the corner, and then they sulked by the punch table, and then slunk back to the corner and sulked some more. But it was a quiet friendly kind of consolation that they found in each other's presence. And they had never spent any time together other than in the art room classroom anyway. All freshmen, all slightly afraid of this new status as a high school student. And most of them were new to the area, so they had not brought friends with them from elementary school or Junior high.

After a while one of them said, "Do we want to go outside?" The air was getting stuffy and hot with of so many students panting and dancing and talking. So this small group of students friends now, straggled outside and gathered on the large cement covered porch of the auditorium. A couple of them lit up cigarettes, which surprised Gwydion, it seemed strangely adult occupation for high school students to be smoking cigarettes. But they seemed actually to be very comfortable doing it as if they had been doing it for years so he said nothing. It didn't seem to be fakery.

After a while one of the boys said, "Do you want to see something?" And this of course intrigued everyone. The dance was becoming very dull, and the music was very loud and they were not interested in going back inside. So there were a couple of voices that chirped in, "Sure." Another said, "What?" And the tall boy answered, "There's this house down the street."

And so this group of kids who barely knew each other from the art class, walked together as a group down the street. Several of them peeled off and went back, not wanting to leave the safety of the school auditorium and the dance where they were supposed to be, where they had told their parents they were going to be until 10 at night, when they were, then, supposed to walk home.

Halloween night. When most young children dress up in goofy costumes concealing their identities, and walk around town with a big shopping bag begging for treats from any door that seem to be lit with a pumpkin and a candle. But these children had grown beyond that now, and would've felt ridiculous doing trick or treat. So down the street they headed together in the dark the cold brisk on their bare fingers, making their breath into puffs in the night.

They walked down the street, and their leader turned the corner and headed into a dark area of town. There they found and stopped at the front of an old mansion with boarded up windows with broken glass.

"This looks a little scary," said one of the girls.

"Ya, well, it's Halloween," said the boy that had led them there.

The five of them stood and looked at the old house, mustering up courage. It was obviously abandoned and people were not supposed to be in there. But all the better to be spooky on Halloween Night.

So they walked around the back. And sure enough, the door on the back stoop was ajar. "Hey, Eric, what is this place?" So obviously one of the students knew their leaders name to be Eric. And Eric was leading them into trouble, Gwydion was sure. But he could not back out now. But all too fascinating and strange. A new adventure he'd never had before.

So the group slowly made their way up the creaky steps of the back stoop. And Eric their leader pushed open the creaky door. And went in.

The others followed. "This is a mistake. We should not be in here," said the girl of the purple dress and Gwydion stopped walking.

"What? Are you afraid?" Taunted Eric.

She didn't say anything in response. But the other girl did. "Ya. Just a little, Eric."

"Oh shut up Linda," said Eric with an edge to his voice.

"Oh, you shut up Eric," said the girl called Linda.

The other boy said quietly," Shshhh, what was that?" And he froze in his steps and looked up the staircase into the upstairs.

"Oh, knock it off John," said Linda.

He just laughed, then said, "What, are you afraid?"

Gwydion tried to memorize their names, realizing he'd been invited with the small group of friends. They knew each other but they really didn't know him. He thought they might not even know his name. But then John said, "Are you afraid, Gwydion? Do you want to go back?"

And Gwydion threw his head back and gave a snort chuckle. Afraid? This was kind of nothin'. If only they knew some of the things that he'd heard and seen.

The boy named Eric led the way up the stairs, and that little group followed, the stairs creaking under each step. Someone produced a small flashlight and helped light the way up the stairs, it's weak light showing an old worn carpet on dark wood of what was once a regal mansion, now having fallen into disintegration.

When they reached the top landing they turned and headed into what was once a master bedroom, but was now empty, looted, and littered with junk.

Eric found a place along the wall, kicked aside some junk and plopped down on the floor. The others did the same and formed a small circle in the gloom. Someone took out a cigarette and lit it, and passed it to the next person. Gwydion did not smoke so he passed it past himself.

"What is this place," asked Linda.

"Just the coolest place in town." said Eric.

"This is pretty cool, " said John, taking a drag off the cigarette. And then coughing.

"I think its creepy," offered Linda. Eric just chuckled. Gwydion said nothing.

"Speaking of spooky, what was that story you wrote in class," purple dress said in the general direction of Gwydion in the gloom.

"Hmmm?" he said noncommittally.

"Oh, come on. The teacher raved about it. And you got an A. Come on, what was it?"

"I just made some story up," Gwydion lied.

"But is it spooky?" Said John.

Gwydion just shrugged.

"Oh, some dumb spooky story you wrote. Who cares," said Eric.

"Shut up, Eric," said Linda sternly. "I wanna hear it. Come on, tell it."

Gwydion groaned a little. And started slowly, "last summer we went on a trip. It was to an ancient temple in Central America."

"Oh this sounds dumb," said Eric.

"Shut up, Eric," said Linda for the third time.

"Ya. I want to hear it," said purple dress.

"Ya, me too," said John. "So shut up Eric!" He said and then laughed.

Gwydion felt uncomfortable being put on the spot, but he didn't like being made fun of either. "No, it's true. It happened," he said to the group.

"Go ahead. Tell it. I want to hear a spooky story," said purple dress girl.

"Well, there's this creepy guy that was following me. Stringy haired and crossed eyes and he was tall and skinny. And he'd been following me since Egypt."

"Egypt! Now that's ridiculous," said Eric.

And the other three said in unison, "shut up, Eric!" So Eric lit another cigarette.

"Well anyway, we went to this ancient temple, and I climbed all the way as the top. It was really tall and steep."

"The temple? What kind of temple? That sounds spooky."

"It's an old Mayan temple where they used to do human sacrifices."

"That's not even true!" Said Eric. They just looked at him.

"It is true. My grandfather is an anthropologist. And this is what he studies." The two girls said wow in stereo. Gwydion was encouraged. "Ya, he travels all over the world and gives lectures. He's pretty smart. He speaks lots of languages."

"The Temple..." Said purple dress girl.

"Right, the temple. So I went up to the top and no one is watching. But there was this dark staircase made of stone down into it. And my grandfather talks about in his lectures that these people believed that they were created by a sun god that flew down from the sky. That he and his brother fought in the sky lobbing balls of fire at one another, until brimstone rained down upon the people on the ground. And that this was so frightening to them that they came to worship the hero twins from the sun. And these primitive people developed a religion where they honored their gods by sacrificing humans to them."

"What do you mean sacrifice?" Asked Linda.

"They killed people, stupid," said Eric.

"Shut up, Eric," said John. "I want to hear this."

"How did they do it?" Asked combat boot girl.

"They took the King's son down into this cavern of stone, and placed him on this magic altar. I saw it. It's a carved slab over a big tomb. They tie the boy down, do some ritual and chanting, and then they take knives and hack his heart out."

The girls gasped in unison. "No way!" said Eric, impressed for once.

John laughed and said, "cool."

Gwydion was on a roll. "Then they took the heart out. It was all bleeding and they took the heart and placed it in the ceremonial bowl they had.

I forget what it's called. My grandfather would know. And then they put it in the tomb where there's this magic, and the heart never dies. It beats, and it beats, and it beats forever in this tomb. And when I went down there, I heard it. I swear I heard it."

The other four kids were silent. They each were listening to their hearts beating loudly in their own chests.

Just then there was a loud boom, and the chandelier tinkled overhead. The girls gasped in shock and jumped to their feet. "What was that?"

The other boys just looked up, white with fear.

"Probably nothing," said Gwydion. "Just the still beating heart of the sacrificed boy knocking on the roof."

Linda screamed, and ran from the room, with two boys following her. Fang girl dove into Gwydion's lap. At that moment the chandelier began jangling, and there was loud thumping on the floor boards. "Get under my cape," yelled Gwydion. And he threw the edge of the cape over her and his legs, and buried his face underneath. A something went on, thump thump, thump thump, thump thump, for quite a while. Forever it seemed to these two kids. Until finally it grew quiet, and the two of them could hear their own breathing slow, and their hearts beat slow in their chest. And they relaxed and sat up.

They just looked at each other in the gloom. Not willing to say a word in the silence. Not willing to chance that it was their voices that had conjured up this spirit of Halloween night. The spirit conjured by Gwydion story of the still beating heart.

Slowly they stood and Gwydion led her ahead of him, both still wrapped in a cloak, out of the room and down the stairs.

As they left the disintegrating mansion, Gwydion noticed the mirrors on his magical Egyptian cape were reflecting a red glow, as if they were cooling off from repelling an evil spirit.

In a church far to the south, the young man sought refuge in the pews of the huge church. In fact many people did. It was Halloween and many feared the very air around them. Outside there were revelers, practicing the ancient religion of death, wearing bones, costumes and rattling and banging musical instruments, they sought to connect and commune with dead relatives. And this was the one day of the year when the veil between life and death was the thinnest. When the ghosts of dead relatives came to visit. And many people sought out these spirits to communicate with those long gone.

But the more devout of the people did not appreciate this view of the season at all. They thought it somehow extremely unchristian and avoided the revelry like the plague. And many sought the safety of the church on this night.

The young man hung his head in prayer. His prayers were strange and mixed up. But his mentor instructed him that in time his head would clear and he would become free of his demons. His mentor father Micheal told the young man that things would get better. His evil dreams would often with time and the spirits that haunted his dreams and even his wakeful hours would diminish, if the young man practiced his verses, repeated his prayers and followed his instruction in the church closely, and was obedient to his elders in the church.

And this all had a calming effect on the young man. He had never had things explained so clearly to him.

He had been beaten so many times by his father, and his uncles, brothers and cousins, that his mind had closed off. But he felt himself opening up, felt himself blooming in the warm bosom of this sacred place of learning. In fact when father Micheal had learned that this young man had lived in far away lands, he realized that he had a penchant for foreign languages. And father Micheal cursed his own vanity that he felt excitement at the shared interest that this young man held for scripture. For father Micheal secretly fascinated with the ancient scriptures of the church, and longed to travel and behold some of them from the father land himself. He longed to travel and see some of these ancient documents with his own eyes. And that his new student and disciple had once lived there and studied with some of the scriptural professors caused not just a little bit of envy for the priest. He did not tell these interests to the young man, but he held them inside himself and nursed this sensation with regards to this new acolyte from off the streets.

# Chapter 14.
# Late Night

The fog floated through the trees and coalesced onto the leaves like a million diamonds, and dripped on to the heads of the two young people as they made their way home after a terrifying evening of Halloween fun.

She stumbled on the corner of a cobblestone and swore to her self. Gwydion looked into the shadows of her smooth face and said, "I don't even know your name...What's wrong?" said Gwydion quietly.

"Sophie. Its Sophie. I don't want to go home," Sophie said.

"What?"

"I don't want to go home."

"Why not!' Its gonna be OK." Gwydion lifted her a little with his arm and she stood straighter and took a few tentative steps.

"It was just some old house," explained Gwydion. "I've seen that place by daylight and it is just an old house that no one has lived in a long time. Its falling apart and that was what we heard and saw, something falling out of the ceiling."

"No," said Sophie.

"What?" said Gwydion becoming exasperated. "An old house, ya."

"That place, its an old..."

She stumbled a few more steps. "an old..."

She let out an exasperated sigh as they tottered along like ancient people in the cold San Francisco fog, miasma swirling around inside and out of their young heads.

"...meeting place. Its dark, I can feel it."

"What are you talking about?"

"It has a history. You haven't lived in this city for very long. It has stories around it that every body tells. " They walked along in the half dark, what light there was was diffused by the swirls of fog.

"Those are just stories. Those are stories they tell to scare young people." Gwydion shook his head and let out a stream of steaming breath.

"Not just old stories. They are all true." She stopped and looked up at him. "All true. Everything you think you know is not true and everything they told you were fairy tales is absolutely true."

He held her by the shoulders and looked her in the eyes. "Now, Sophie, you're starting to sound like me. Listen to me starting to argue with you." He laughed out loud, raised his face to the sky and let out a belly laugh. "I must like you because I'm contradicting my self just to make you feel better."

"Nothing is going to make me feel better. I have to go home. That's scary enough."

"Now what are you talking about?" he asked her with a tired exasperation.

"My parents are creatures, " she said quietly. " Creatures from the black lagoon."

He laughed again. "oh, come on. They can't be that bad."

"Oh, yes they can," she said looking suddenly up into his eyes with something like terror in them. "Give me the ghouls in the old IOOf building any day."

"In the what?"

"The old IOOf building. Don't you know what that is?"

"I have no idea what you are talking about." said Gwydion shaking his head.

"That building. The IOOf building. The International Order of Odd Fellows?"

"I have no idea still, what you are talking about."

"Ugh," she let out an exasperated growl. "They built buildings all over the west during the gold rush. They all look exactly the same, same square brick nonsense, with exactly the same shape windows, two floors, a door and stairs in the front and in the back with windows on either side that look like eyes staring out watching everything everybody does. It was supposed to be a brother hood of longshoreman or some such. No wait, they were Masons. Like the free masons."

She stopped and looked at him again. He said," I've been in Egypt studying ancient middle eastern religions and language."

"You have?" she looked at him with total incredulity on her young face.

"I was over there for 5 years with my family. We came back here for my high school. Well, and because of some other stuff."

"Well, I tend to be a historian of Western American culture it seems, at least in comparison to you." She sniffled and wiped her nose on her sleeve. "I always thought they were some kind of friendship group. But boy was I naive. They were religious fanatics. Oh, I know, you know about the inquisition?"

Gwydion nodded his head, his wet curls sticking to his forehead and nose. He wiped his face with his sweatshirt sleeve, catching some of his hair in the mirrors of the cape. "You know the guys with the red crosses on their white capes. They were purportedly started looking for the holy grail."

"Oh sure. The inquisition and the holy purge in the middle east of heretics. "Gwydion looked over at his friend. "That's the connection?"

"They are the same group. And that was one of their buildings. They say its haunted and I think they are right. I have never been so freaked out in my life."

Gwydion shrugged his shoulders and began to walk along, pulling Sophie along by the arm. "I have. On numerous occasions." He rolled his shoulders and Sophie glanced over at him tentatively. "In fact," he continued. "I think I might take ghosts any day of over some of the junk I've seen." There was a silence between them that Sophie did not want to break right then. She wasn't sure if she wanted to know what he was talking about. His thoughts and memories hung between them like ghosts that would have to wait some time to show themselves to his new friend, if he could help it.

# Chapter 15.
# Late Nightmares

They came to the corner of two streets.

"This is where I turn," she said to him in the gloom. The street light barely cut through the thickening fog.

"Ya, I go that way," he indicated with his shrugging shoulder that he turned the other way. About to separate, they became suddenly afraid and pensive, wanting to hurry home to their respective warm beds, but unwilling to break the bond that had formed between them on this freaky night. Who knows what the light of day might bring. What change of perspective might occur with sunrise. How this magic would fade with the harshness of everyday life.

"Monday at school then," he offered.

"Ya," reality setting in colder than the fog itself. They let go of one another's arms and stepped away. That was the hardest one. Then the next ones became easier as they turned and walked down their streets in opposite directions.

His footsteps faded in Gwydion's ears as he scuffed along the damp pavement. When he couldn't hear her steps anymore, he turned and could barely make out her dark form against the fog lit by street light. Was she turned to look at him? He could not tell for sure and maybe only imagined it. He continued toward home as the cold penetrated his sleeve where her arm had been, and penetrated his heart where for a small moment in time there had been a kindred spirit. The house was dark when he approached.

He found the key under the fake rock and unlocked the front door. He stopped and listened. His awareness of empty dwellings was enhanced this night, after the experience at the old house. A house now suspected of being a once used place for ritual perhaps of an occult nature. That was tantalizing. He knew nothing of that sort of American myth. He wanted to talk to Sophie about it more sometime.

He locked the door behind him and slowly stepped up the cold cement steps of the foyer. The floor above him creaked and he froze. "Oh knock it off Gwydion," he admonished himself. "Its just this stupid old house." he walked a few more steps, and then thought, ya that's what you thought about that last place you found yourself in just a few hours ago. And just about got eaten by spirits.

He reached the upper door and began to ease it open. It creaked on its hinges. He was amazed at how all the sounds were amplified by the lack of awake humans.

Was that it? Lack of awake humans? It was so quiet, everything creaked and moaned. Or were his senses just heightened from that experience.

He gingerly stepped into the hallway and began to make his way down the hall. There was a faint light under the door at the top of the stairs. They were not allowed to go up the stairs. There was nothing up there but stored stuff.

So why was a light on?

Wasn't any of his business.

Ya you're just scared, he told himself.

I am not scared, I'm minding my own business. Besides I'm not supposed to go up there.

You're a chicken.

Am not!

Am too. Chicken.

Oh, shut up. I'll just go up there and turn the light off. No one must have noticed after going into one of the rooms when there was the light of day. And now everyone was asleep. I'll just go up and shut it off.

Slowly he stepped up the steep carpeted steps up to the upstairs level. Every other step squeaked with what seemed like a demons yowl that echoed through the house.

Or maybe he just imagined it. But he stepped on the side edges of the stairs anyway as it seemed to diminish the squeaking sounds.

When he reached the top of the stairs, he stopped and listened. He thought he heard something thump. He froze. Then the noise stopped. He took a step toward the room with the faint light under the door and he thought he heard another thump. He froze. And he stood there and listened. He thought he heard a thumping, a gentle thumping just barely stroking his ear drums. He held his breath. His heart beat seemed to become louder.

As he listened he heard the thump thump, thump thump become more pronounced as he listened. Then he realized he was listening to his own heart beat in his own ears and he sighed with disgust at himself for being so scared. He breathed easily and took the two steps toward the door and grasped the handle. It was cold. Very cold.

Brass is usually cold, but Gwydion felt like his hand had stuck to the metal. It was that cold .

Gwydion you are imagining things, the voice in his head said to him. He grasped the handle again and began to turn it very slowly. Then he heard it again. Another faint thump. And then another. The light under the door quivered slightly. Gwydion felt his ears fill with his own heart beat again, obscuring any sound that might or might not be coming through the thick old door from the room inside.

Oh stop it, he scolded himself again. Just go in and turn off the light. He turned the handle and cracked open the door. Faint light flickered across the walls and an eery red glow came from somewhere around the corner behind the door. He heard faint rustling rather clearly now as the throbbing entered his ears more directly from its source. Somewhere around the other side of the door. He looked up at the wall and noticed that there was furniture there. And an old bureau with a very large mirror on top, with a dark wood frame. It was tilted downward somewhat and he could see movement there reflected from around the other side of the room. From where the rustling noise came from.

Light flickered and there was a gasping . But not his own. But unmistakably human. The form in the mirror broke into two deeply shadowed forms as one of them turned at looked Gwydion full in the face, the old mirror reflecting it grotesquely in the candle light. But it was unmistakably the face of his mother.

The scream was his as he yanked the door closed and bolted down the stairs, ran into his room and slammed the door.

He dreamed that night. Some strange colorful dreams. The scent of baby powder permeated his senses as he struggled with the pastel images he saw in his mind.

He felt a warmth he had never known before and became aware of another presence beside him in the room. 'Shalom' it said to him. He felt happy and comforted by this presence. It lifted its hands before him and there just above its hands revolved some small objects that Gwydion could not identify. Shalom giggled and smiled as she swirled the objects around in the air.

Then she looked at Gwydion and said sweetly, 'hello brother'.

Gwydion bolted upright from his sleep. The sky was just beginning to clear and show the streaks of a new sun. He groaned and pulled the covers back over his head. Thank goodness it was Sunday today. He needed another day of sleep after the kind of night he had had the night before. Halloween was over.

# Chapter 16.
# Morning Church

"Gwydion!" Cried a voice from the hallway. "Gwydion, get up! It's time to go to church."

The door was closed tightly, and the voice was somewhat muffled. But Gwydion was sure he heard someone say they were going to church today.

He rolled over in the covers and buried his head under his pillow's. But that couldn't be. That's not possible, they just didn't ever go to church.

So he rolled over the other way and faced away from the racket in the hall. But again the voice of his mother persisted. "Gwydion!" The doorknob turned and the door cracked open. "Are you up?" She yelled into his room. "Are you even getting ready?" It was as if she expected him to be getting ready, as if this always happened every Sunday. As a matter of fact it never happened Sunday. Except for that day they went to the funeral for Professor Happenstance. And that was on a Sunday. But the stress in his mother's voice was enough to scare Gwydion out of bed and to begin scrambling for some clothes to wear.

The door cracked open again, and his mother cried, "Gwydion!" Then she stopped when she saw that he was out of bed and said to him, "What is wrong with you? I thought you were getting ready to go to church?"

"What is wrong with *you*? We never go to church!" He yelled back. He was not much for arguing with his mother but this was too much. He really did not understand her hostile behavior.

After a while he came out of his room a bit rumpled but fully dressed, and wandered into the kitchen where his mother was making coffee. His grandmother and grandfather were there too. Antony quickly cast in the furtive look. By the look on their faces Gwydion saw that they didn't understand what was going on either, but were going along with the commands.

"Maybe it's for the better," his grandmother commented offhand, seeming to understand the unusual nature of this early morning activity. "We haven't been in so long."

"For him and there was the service at Canterbury," commented his grandfather. "Now that was a beautiful church." And Gwydion was transported back just over a year ago, when they attended the funeral service for his father's friend. The church had been an ancient one, and Gwydion had been moved in ways he never expected. In fact he had a hard time tolerating sitting there in that huge expanse of Cathedral surrounded by memories and ghosts of the ancient past. His grandfather had told him that it was an ancient place, with more history than could ever be known. But Gwydion had not realized what exactly that meant. Egypt had always been a strong memory. But a child's memory, one involving things Gwydion could not understand in such a young inexperienced mind. But he was becoming a teenager now and the change from one ancient culture to another very distinct and different one was shock enough to awaken his mind in new ways. So the church at Glastonbury was quite a startling experience for him.

The ancient gray stones roughly hewn and piled atop one another, not anything like the construction that Luxor. But distinctly British. Cold and strange. And vibrating with stories, memories and ghosts from eons past. A very different violent and cold history, quite apart from the golden sands of Egypt.

And within the cold space of the Cathedral were held captive spirits all held within the ancient Catholic ritual and the gilded staring statues of Jesus and Mary and the gilded angels of wing. And in the midst of the chanting and singing within the swirls of the smoke of incense, those gilded wooden statues of Angels had vibrated and come alive in Gwydion's mind. As he spirited a glance at that gilded Angel, its head seemed to turn, and the whites of its eyes became bright with life, its dark pupils seemed to stare directly at him and bore into Gwydion's mind, speaking to him in whispers from centuries ago of deeds and misdeeds, potentials and dreams of the humans who came here and prayed, and of the expectations of the supernatural beings that were channeled through this Celestial portal.

And Gwydion had hardly been able to tolerate the long time sitting in the hard wooden pew between his mother and his grandmother, his grandfather holding onto the Bible and closing his eyes. But Gwydion imagined that he was not praying so much as tolerating this strange ritual experience. But afterward nothing was ever said about it to him. Only his grandfather explaining how they were on the Glastonbury plane which was a place of ancient beliefs, of ancient people living in the wild lands of Britain who were conquered and changed by invaders from the north and east. That the ancient peoples of Britain had built monuments to their gods and goddesses of ancient times. And that these monuments still stood in their austere simplicity, hand hewn erect stones towering over their human worshipers. He called them the rings stones of Stonehenge.

Gwydion didn't know what that meant. But after the service the family had driven in a taxi northward on the Glastonbury plain and had driven by the monument of tall gray stones with wide flat Stones on top 20 feet in the air. And Gwydion had realized what he was talking about. Similar ritual artifacts as he'd seen in Egypt. But on a much smaller seemingly more primitive scale. Nonetheless Gwydion had been moved and understood now the ancient nature of man's worship of gods he did not understand. He remembered the motion of the car and the faint car-sickness that he was experiencing in the pit of his stomach. And how when he knelt up on the seat and watched the towering stones pass by as they rounded the driving circle around the monument, his car sickness vanished. He pressed his warm face against the steaming glass of the taxi and stared in wonder. "Stop that!" his mother's sharp voice had jolted out of his reverie. "Don't act so strange. Now sit quiet like a good boy." His mother had admonished him and sharp tones and instantly his car sickness had returned with a sudden vengeance.

He stopped suddenly in the shoveling of his bowl of cereal at the breakfast table at the memory, as the others were getting ready to go to church. He was going to go into a church, for the second or third time in his life. He did not want to meet those angels again today, but he feared that his awareness of their living nature and his awareness of them might draw such an encounter towards him again. This cathedral was different. The stones were newer and the memories less ancient. He didn't feel the age of the planet so deep in his bones this time as he entered the tall metal doors of the church. Perhaps he could tolerate being in there for as long as his family would expect him to be.

It was cold, and he sat down on the wooden seats, but was afraid to look around for a long time. He did not want to invite the stares of any angel statues if he could help it. And he refused to look at his mother; feelings from the strange encounter late last night or actually early this morning, had left a cold spot on his heart.

His mother looked at him askance when they had seated and the rustling had continued for a few moments as the family got settled. She saw what she took to be a look of reprisal on his face. She turned and faced forward, picked up a hymnal and whispered defensively, "Will couldn't make it this morning." After a few moments she said under her breath but out of the side of her mouth nearest her son, "And anyway, that's none of your dam business."

Touche', he thought. So that's it, isn't it?

# Chapter 17.
# Monday Morning

School the next day was normal, No more costumes, no more excitement. Just back to normal boring school. Except some of them had stories from their Halloween adventures. Some of the kids were staring at Gwydion off and on during the day. He wondered if he still had weird makeup on from that night. Or they could tell what was going on inside him, the way his mother was treating him like a pariah.

But when they were in painting class, one of the other boys came up and said to him, "Seen any ghosts lately, Gwydion?" then he laughed and walked off. Somehow people had heard of the adventure they had had in the haunted house. Word had gotten around. He looked over at Sophie and she glanced at him then sheepishly looked away. I'll talk to her later, he thought.

But he never got the chance. The day went too swiftly, and night time dark came all too fast. He didn't get a chance to talk to her for a while. Yes, the burning light of day had withered the delicate connection they had formed with the terrifying experience they had shared that night.

In another part of the world, a young man entered a church, but not through its front doors. He had been initiated in to the church as a budding young priest. He had never expected that, but he felt maybe he had deserved it. After all of the unfairness in his life, finally someone was taking an interest in his talents.

They had met at a conference of professors and clergy interested in the old inscriptions of the middle America peoples. Archaeology, the scientists called it. But religious cleansing is what they referred to it in the back halls of this church. These old religions were great for understanding how peoples had gone astray. And studying them was a way to help understand their mistakes so they could be avoided in the future.

The old religions were certainly not to be studied to be understood for any information or value of understanding of the human condition. No, these were thoughts and traditions to be avoided. In fact this church used to have a policy of destroying old documents when they were found. But science had taken over and insisted that these things be taken as valuable simply for their antiquity. And some scientists had even deigned to suggest that they should be saved and studied because they might have some value for man-kind, that perhaps in these old ways there might be some valuable understanding. That these documents and artifacts could have any real information in them seemed ridiculous at best. There was only one book. And its words came directly from the big man himself. It was fact and gospel and everything else was temptations of one kind or another, to take mans mind off the beauty of God.

The young man had learned this in his religious studies in this church. But he had always felt these things in his bones. His early education., though extremely limited, had been of the same strict nature towards thought and the great book. It was a different religion, but now as he studied this ornate one that was new to him, he felt a kinship to it. It seemed to fit. The strictness was the true path to strength. The obedience and solitude were the only path to salvation. And if he followed it correctly he felt in his chest that he would be allowed into the kingdom of the righteous. If only he could follow it and be obedient. Sometimes his mind strayed. And he castigated himself for these transgressions. He made himself suffer. He told his new mentor of the awful things he thought, confessional they called it. And he reveled in exposing these things to this strong older man. It made him feel cleansed when he did that. Often the mentor then punished him. Punished him in ways that he was not entirely unfamiliar with. But never did this mentor stray so far as did his other two mentors had. And they had suffered. For they had crossed the line. The line where the young man felt was no longer for the kingdom of heaven but for some other place that these ideas often came from. He could not put his finger on where that place was. But in his studies he was searching. Searching for that dark place that dwelt deep in his mind and in the mind of other men that sought to torture him, for he wished to rub it out. He wanted it to go away. If only he could annihilate that part of himself and of these other men, the world would be a better place. And perhaps he could find peace within himself finally.

And as he entered the darkened church and saw the ornaments of the rituals and of the sacramental worship, he sensed that he was getting closer. Closer to a resolution of this dark conflict within himself. Study, pray, debase himself. Read the old scriptures and find the heresy there and destroy it. The heresies that the other had discovered in the jungle and in the desert where he had come from. Only if he had gotten a-hold of those manuscripts first, he could have done with them what his god demanded, and what his mentor was working toward, destroy them so the heresies could never be read by human eyes again, never be misunderstood and stand against the one and only true word of god.

His prayers were answered one day soon following. He was allowed into the brotherhood of the priest's secret circle.

Father Micheal smiled gently and laid an old gnarled hand on top of the initiate's head.

"You have entered the circle, my friend. Now you are one of us."

The boy took a deep breath and felt something infuse his whole body. A warm satisfaction perhaps. Or maybe the holy ghost. He hoped it was something more like that. He was not sure.

He only knew that he felt fulfilled and vindicated somewhat by his hard work, concentration and yearning.

But this was not the real initiation, the one that would take place in public. That, he was told, was some time in coming. When he earned it. When he had done enough for the brethren itself, in sacrifice and self-debasement, then he would be able to acknowledge his acceptance in front of the people of the church.

"And how long will that be?" he asked his mentor, and brother, Father Micheal.

"We shall see," was the oblique answer. "We will see how things go and at what levels of self-sacrifice you can manage. You are young and you are new here. There are others that have been at this a lot longer that you have, my son. And they deserve to move up in rank a little faster than yourself, even thought they might be younger than you are."

The thought of this older man spending this kind of time with the other boys brought a burning into his chest. He knew it was true, but hearing it made his chest constrict and his face burn. His hands clenched tighter and he grasped at the fabric hanging in front of him.

The older man saw this and interpreted this as jealousy. "Now, don't feel that way about it. You know it is the way of things." In a moment he continued, "And besides, someday after you are truly accepted in the churches fathers, you will have a group of your own to watch after and to help pass through the rack of initiation and acceptance."

He was always a part of some older man's ranks of young boys. Always., Back at home, always his older brothers and cousins had belittled and humiliated him. His uncles and even his father a couple times had debased him and locked him in the room of tears after ward. Why was it always that way? The younger man thought to himself. Why? Always? When it came time, he thought to himself, he would get his revenge on those younger boys. He would not treat them well but initiate them into the tortures that he had undergone as a child, and at the hands of these older men who were stronger than he.

The young man bowing in front of the older man sniffled and tried to stifle some angry tears as he suppressed these thoughts. And with a flood of pain he was suddenly filled with self-pity. He deserved better; he deserved more just by his devotion to the cause. The old man had noticed the welts and dried scabs on his back and his privates where the boy had been debasing himself in front of the alter each night in an effort to purge his dirty sins. Surely this old man could see that? But he held it in, again. He knew he would wait and he would get what he deserved. Each of them would. He would wait.

"I know that is hard for you to accept, even at this time of exaltation," said the older man as he began to rise. "We shall see with your dedication and vigor just how quickly you shall rise in the sight of your god." He stood and stepped away from the young man still kneeling against the skirt of the alter.

The young man waited with his face buried in the tear-stained fabric, as the older man walked out and closed the door behind him, leaving the young man behind once again to clean up the candles and the rumpled covers and wet towels, and rest of the mess in the bedroom.

# Chapter 18.
# A Story

"Do you want to read my story?" He was sitting on the green lawn in the Indian summer sun when the voice from behind him broke him out of his reverie.

He spun his head around to face his attacker, and saw to his delight it was Sophie. He sputtered, "You have a story?"

"Yes. I have been writing it for quite a while. But I cant seem to finish it. I just keep rewriting it and rewriting it." She sat down on the grass and stretched out her young straight legs in front of her and popped off her boots. They never seemed to be laced or actually buckled. They had buckles on them that slapped when she walked. But she never seemed to have them buckled closed. And her socks were pink striped. He tried not to stare.

He looked up at her face and smiled. "What is it about?"

"Well, its about this girl that gets lost in the forest. She was going for a walk and minding her own business, when this squirrel runs by and runs into the dark forest. And of course she follows it. But then she gets turned around and gets lost. "

"Maybe she needs a hero to help her find her way out," suggested Gwydion.

Sophie looked at him askance, "Is that a chauvinistic comment?"

"A what?"

"A chauvinistic comment. You know, male chauvinist pig and all that." They had been studying political science in civics class and this was one of the new modern terms that was being batted around in the newspapers.

"Oh, right. So you don' think that boys should rescue girls?" Gwydion asked her.

"I just think it is a knee jerk reaction to say that kind of thing. Maybe the little girl is going to help the little boy find his way out of the forest. Or maybe they cant get out and she saves his life because she knows all kinds of forest skills that he doesn't."

"Well, what does you story say?" he asked her trying to save the conversation from exploding.

"Well, they both are equally versed in forest living skills, and he wonders what she is doing there. But she starts arguing with him about the political situation in the kingdom and he realizes that she doesn't want to leave the forest. Things are getting too awful out there and she doesn't want to go home."

He looked at her for a moment. Until she said "What?"

He turned away. And said, "sounds like you."

"Well, I suppose all good fiction is a reflection of the authors wishes and dreams."

"And their denials about their own character."

"What?" she said again. Gwydion looked at her and smiled. And she punched him in the shoulder.

"So there is a kingdom. And I suppose it is ruled by a glorious King." said Gwydion after they quit laughing.

"No, actually. It is run by a queen. A good queen although she can be tough as nails sometimes. When she needs to be."

"So this is a feminist story?"

"What?" Sophie said for the third time.

"It just sounds like it is going to be a woman power story, that's all. I think boys might be bored with it."

"So you don't want to hear my story," she said flatly.

"Actually I would really like to hear your story. It sounds different than the usual tripe I hear all the time."

She looked at him for a long time. So long the bell rang and they had to part ways and go to their separate classes.

"Next time," she said as she walked away and smiled at him.

"OK," he said back as he stumbled on the sidewalk.

# Chapter 19.
# Trip

The trip was set. They were getting ready to go to Italy.

After the first year of high school and all of the strange events that had happened, and the tension between the members of the family and the Happenstance Consortium, Gwydion was looking forward to this trip. Looking forward to this sojourn away from all that had now become mundane and boring to him.

Everything had become boring. The people, the fighting, the school subjects. He supposed he was yearning for some travel to a new place because he had traveled so much when he was young. Well, heck he grew up in Costa Rica alone with his mother in the wilds of the jungle. His short trip through New York really counted as the side trip through the jungle, and that was interesting. But certainly did not rank as "normalcy" to him. Then those years in Egypt. That really changed him, he thought. He was there a long time and went from a boy to....well, what? He thought. A bigger boy, really. He had no confidence in his abilities to fit in and be a part of things. He still felt that he stood outside of some bubble that other people lived in. He was a stranger. But he was finding that really only he was the one that noticed it. No one else seemed to notice that he was really that different. Except certain bullies who seemed to zero in on it. But he was becoming aware that they treated everybody with disrespect, not just silly little Gwydion. So he was learning that if he just stood there with nothing on his face, and acted inert, people just walked around him.

So walk around him they did and what a swirling mass of boring people it was, it seemed to Gwydion. Just leave them be in their little swirling worlds and they usually left you alone, he thought to himself, as he saw his family packing for the trip. After all they weren't so different from the rest were they?

Except for that Will Smithershins. Sometimes when that guy looked into his eyes, it was as if he knew something. There was some link through the eyeballs to the mind thinking things and the two of them connected. And that was a strange feeling for Gwydion. All those years of not holding eye contact with people. And now that he was doing it, he was picking up on information. Picking up on the information people were hiding there. And some of them, yes some of them like this Will character, had something going on in there. And if Gwydion looked too long into eyes like that, he saw begin to burn something terrifying. What, hostility? The preparation for attack?

Once you saw that in someones eyes, you learned to move them quickly away, onto something inert.

Maybe that was why I always avoided peoples eyes all those years, he thought to himself. Of course he had been a tiny child, and could not have really known any of this. But maybe there was some animal part in his brain too that had known, had alerted him to the true nature of the hostility of people that had shied him away from eye contact. From any contact really. Always glancing and running, glancing and running.

Well he wasn't running anymore. He was trying to stand still and look. Maybe be a part. At least act as if he were a part of it. His girlfriend was a part of that. She was weird and was a part of it all. She didn't seem to care what anybody thought.

She did what she wanted and joined in with things whether people liked it or not. It gave him confidence. If he just acted like he was a part of things, then people would just let him be there.

In fact she had kinda done that with his family . She had showed up a couple times, and his family had hardly noticed. Then they just got used to her. Although Gwydion hadn't let her come around too much. He didn't want them getting too cozy. Keep her for himself . And when he announced that she was going to come with them, they had just glanced at him and smiled, so he thought perfect. She gets to come with us. She explained that it was fine with her family and that they would even make the arrangements for her if he just told her when and which flight.

The flight over was long and a bit dull for Gwydion. Since they had made separate arrangements, the two kids were unable to sit together, and Gwydion was tucked between his mom and his grandmother the whole flight. As the 12 hour flight settled in and people got up and wandered or went to the bathroom, Sophie came back and sat down with him for a while.

They talked quietly in confidence like teenager's do, not letting his mother or grandmother into the conversation at all. Will and his grand father had moved to an isle seat when a section was vacated and spoke practically forehead to forehead and great conspiratorial tones about important things, Gwydion supposed. Sophie leaned over and spoke into Gwydion's ear. "So we are finally on our way. Are you excited about going to Italy?" she asked him over the hum and rush of the airplane engines.

"Oh, ya, I'm so glad to get out of the states. So insulated from the world." answered Gwydion.

"I totally agree," said Sophie as she sat back down looking forward. There was a few moments of silence when the two kids just enjoyed their time together on this screaming jet. Then Gwydion spoke again, " Aren't you excited?"

"Of course. What an adventure. Italy is so old, so beautiful."

"You've been there before?" said Gwydion.

She turned and looked at him with a startled look, and then her flaming eyes simmered down. "Well, I've read a lot about it. Venice is so beautiful. The Doge's palace, the Bridge of Sighs, the place were so many people were executed for religious and political treachery."

Gwydion just looked at her smooth face. She was fascinating, this child of such strange tastes. That's one reason he liked her so much. She was just so different from the other kids he knew. It was as if she had some of the same experiences as he had. Maybe some of the same horrific ones as he had, although they had never talked about that kind of thing.

The food service was announced which meant that everyone would have to go back to their assigned seats, if they wanted to get a meal that is. Sophie stood to get up and go back to her seat where ever it was in the rest of the hundreds of seats on the plane.

"I could come up and sit with you, couldn't I?" he asked her.

"No, they put me in first class. My parents spoil me sometimes. And they don't allow anyone else to go up there, not even to use the bathroom!"

Gwydion twisted his young face into one of exasperation, and Sophie got up and squeezed her way forward, Will and his grandfather came back to their assigned seats on the other side of his grandmother, and the dinner service commenced.

# Chapter 20.
# A City of Ancient Angels

Venice is an ancient city, built on the marshes of central Eastern Italy, on the northern edge of the Adriatic. Over a thousand years or so, the city on stilts has sunk deeper and deeper into the marshes, where now the streets are under water. Cobblestone lay many feet under the surface of the water and are buried by layers of sand and garbage. So instead of streets, now, Venice has canals. Lots of canals. In fact more canals than streets or walkways.

It is a strange old convoluted city of winding ways and decayed brick and rock work. Beautiful archways hang over sparkling waters of the canals. And many houses now have no other way to get to them but by barca. Picillo barca. Small boats. They line the water ways and are tied in small spaces defined by upright logs buried in the mud and silt to make what they call in America 'driveways' or carports. Except these hold the family boat. And this boat is moored securely because it is the only way to get off the little island. But as in all quaint European towns, the boats are not locked. How dare someone even consider stealing someone else's boat, unless it were dire emergency. And then you would return it carefully to the rightful owner, with apologies and gifts, afterward.

Steps have been built down to the water level, because the water level has now risen above the foundation line. So really walking around you are really seeing the second floor. And under water, and only at low water tides do you see what was once the first floor. This has been happening to this beautiful historic city for hundreds maybe thousands of years, since it was first chosen to build this strategically located city on a swamp. The hotel where the Jacobs family stayed in Venice was, by virtue, old. There were choices of new lodgings, and not necessarily more expensive ones by reason of boring-ness to avoid. But by their fascination with things old, this place was chosen, right in central island Venice just off St. Mark's Square..

And what a delight for the family it was. All except maybe Mags. She complained of the old pipes that made noise when you turned the spigot. And the sometimes brown water came out.

"Just drink bottled water, Mags," her mother would say. It was a luxury in America that the water out of the pipes was generally clear and sweet. Sometimes straight from the ground from a well. But not so here in Venice where the ground water was brackish, part of the ancient marsh that was sweet only to the crabs and fish that dwelt within.

But the brick work was old, and each window was framed by an arch of interesting plaster and stonework. And the view out the window was onto the balcony of the neighbor just across the narrow canal 30 feet below the window, where often was hung the wash to dry. And for more enterprising Venetians, potted plants and small gardens hung from specially made racks, where edibles and flowers could be grown and enjoyed for the ground-challenged city of canal dwellers.

The rooms were small, and the floors were wood. And in no time Gwydion and Sophie found a hidden doorway at the back of a small closet that had been boarded up long ago. It was part of an old staircase that had led down into the lower rooms.

The first floor, the one that was now officially under water most times, was never used, as it was occasionally flooded. The air smelled dank and cold to the kids as they crept down the creaky stairs.

"I hope this wood doesn't give way, Gwydion," said Sophie in a shaky voice.

"You're light as a feather. It should be fine," said Gwydion. "Just don't stomp like a monster and you shouldn't break through I don't think." Just then he stomped and growled like he was going to get her, and she shrieked in a muffled way, realizing that there were others just above them and they didn't want to get caught on their adventure.

"Did you bring them?" she asked.

He put his hand on his pocket edge and shook it a little, with a big mischievous grin, said, "Right here. Pops will never notice they are gone." He took a tentative step on the moldering wood.

"Well, as long as I get them back before he gets back later today."

"OK, well, let's have a look." She stopped and turned and shook her hands in excitement.

Sophie opened up the comforter she had slid off the bed and carried with them down here. She folded it into a square that they could both sit on and laid it on the damp wooden steps. Gwydion sat down and folded his long legs on the step below. She sat next to him and looked expectantly as he pulled out the folded papers and spread them on his knees.

"This is some of the new stuff that he is translating. Let me see here." He shuffled a few pages around. There were the hand written pages of his grandfather's scribbling script. And there were dark smudgy printed pages that looked like the photostat copies of the originals of the ancient manuscripts.

Sophie gasped as one of those came to the top of the pile he was shuffling. "Look at that," she said, pointing.

"What?"

"Those look so old. They look moth eaten or something," she said.

"Ya, like 2 thousand years old," said Gwydion. "The originals are in some library museum somewhere. But these are the copies of them. They don't let you take the originals out anymore. But still, I bet these copies are worth something, too."

Sophie's eyes got misted over as she looked at these ancient hand-lettered manuscripts. "They must have been really meaningful back then, to someone." She looked at Gwydion. "Do you really think that those people that wrote these met Jesus? I think he really was a God or a visitor from another realm or something, don't you?"

"I really don't know," said Gwydion. "But the way everybody gets all wow oh wow over the guy, makes me wonder that there really wasn't something going on back then. Something supernatural or cosmic or something. Because the awe factor is still really strong for people. Even today. And that they found these ancient books seems to just drive everybody wild. "

"I've never really believed the bible or anything. My parents think it is a bunch of old poetry. " She put her hand on the copy of the 2000 year page of hand written words, and said, "But when I look at that, and I know how hard it was for them to write anything down, I mean they had to use skins and stuff, it must have been really important."

"And to think they went to such great lengths to hide it all, some priests put this stuff in jars and sealed it in the mud of the Nile river. And somehow it lasted just long enough and then it was found, nearly at the same instant that those were found at the Dead Sea caves.... so strange, it seems like it was planned to happen that way. That we were supposed to find these things right now for some reason."

"It's almost like people had to wait to get to a certain point of mental evolution before they could handle this discovery of these old ideas," suggested Sophie.

"Ya, the last ones they found, when my grandfather was translating them, they were all fighting and trying to kill each other over the rights to translate them, and over whose translation was right or not."

"What? Kill each other?"

"Yup. That's why we got the heck out of Egypt so fast, and left all our stuff there a few years ago. Someone tried to kill my grandfather."

"Did they catch they guy?"

Gwydion smiled and big Cheshire Cat's smile.

"What?" said Sophie, smiling now too.

"He got his own. Just by a different person and in a different way."

"What do you mean?" she asked.

"That guy I told you about? The one that attacked me?"

"You mean in the temple?"

"Ya. The same one." Her eyes widened. "Yup. He did it. He killed him."

She shook her head and laughed. "How do you know this stuff, Gwydion. You cant know that stuff."

He shrugged his shoulders and just said, "Well, I just do. That's all." He looked back down at the stack of papers and said, to change the subject, "Here. The Great Seth. He came down from the Majestic world of Yaltabaoth, and Jesus took possession of a human body, thus throwing out the previous tenant and using the body for his own purposes. It was a joke of course, and when the silly humans tried to kill him, he was somewhere else watching them and having a great laugh." read Gwydion from the hand written text he had borrowed out of his grandfather's leather case.

"No. It does not say that. You are reading that from some fiction that some crazy person wrote." objected Sophie.

"Nope. Its right there. This was found in this group of folios in what they call the Nag Hammadi papers."

"That's unbelievable. What else does it say? Keep reading!" cried Sophie.

" "Someone else, Simon, bore the cross on his back, someone else, not me, wore that crown of thorns. And I was up above watching, laughing at their errors of ignorance, at their conceit and the excesses of their arrogance." "

She just looked up at him when he paused to take a breath. "It was after all just a body that the holy spirit borrowed for the duration, and not his spirit that they crucified."

"Sounds to me like Simon was an angel doing God's dirty work, bearing the pain for one of the greater spirits."

Now it was his chance to look at her funny. "And how do you know that?'" asked Gwydion.

She gave a sheepish shrug and said, "I don't know. I just do.

Angels come down and can be mortal for a while, and take the place of the spirit who doesn't need to feel pain."

"But does the angel feel pain?" asked Gwydion.

"Oh, yes, Gwydion. Angels feel pain. It is their job."

# Chapter 21.
# Grande Canale

The two of them walked on the stone flags, the water lapping at their heels in the Grande Canale. The sun was setting and picked up the bits of blown glass hanging over the boats. Blown glass was one of Venice Italy's specialties. To Mags, the globes looked dark and foreboding. Primitive, like some piece of an ancient mariners boat. And she then thought that was probably true. This city had been here for centuries. Just like this, sitting in an ancient lagoon, stinking, slowing sinking.

But by god it was strange and beautiful. And she let out an audible sigh as she watched the sun set behind the crumbling red tiled roofs.

Will looked at her and wondered what was going on in there. "Don't say it," he laughed. She looked at him, then got the joke, and said loudly, dramatically, "Ahhh, Venice!"

He turned and laughed across the water, his deep voice vaguely echoing in the relative silence of the evening. A few boats came and went, pushing softly against the slight ocean current of the evening. The small flat boats hugged the center of the Canale, where they could speed along to the inner canals to begin making their night deliveries of produce from the mainland. Everything here was boated in. There were no huge bridges to drive trucks over in the vulgar fashion of more modern cities. Venice by Ancient Design.

They walked for some time in companionable silence. Finally Will broke the silence, a silence that had been going on longer than just then. Some subjects were very difficult to bring up.

"So, Gwydion has been pretty irritating of late," he started trying to be diplomatic. He had his own opinions but was trying to sound like he agreed with her point of view so she might be more amenable to the conversation.

"Irritating? That's putting it nicely," she answered.

He laughed a little. "He's at those awkward teenage years," Will said again diplomatically.

"I don't know know if it's any different."

"Ya, but you seem, I don't know, like its starting to get to you."

"Maybe I just need to cut the apron strings." He was glad she said this and not him. That usually pretty irritating thing to say to a gal. A mother.

"I've wanted to do that for so many years," she said with relief, like she'd wanted to say that for many years too.

"Oh," he said, not used to someone being so direct. And not sure where to go from there.

They were silent for a few minutes as they ambled in the most romantic city in the world, along one of the world's most arguably beautiful waterways, glowing gold and blue in the setting sun. Will knew to stay silent. He wanted to talk about this, but knew sometimes it was easier for people to pick their own route, filling up an unknown void than to be pushed with questions.

She started again quietly, "After Stan left, it was really hard. I thought it would be good, that I would feel relief. But it just wasn't like that."

"That was in Egypt?" asked Will. He knew but was trying to sound curious, but not too curious.

"Ya, he went off to work and just never came back." Will almost said that they had always been curious about that but stopped himself just in time. When she didn't say anything for a minute, he decided to ask, "How was that hard?"

"Oh, not just the money thing. My parents do fine and it was good to have Gwydion with his grandparents. He and his grandfather have such a great relationship. I think it was the only thing that brought him around. He was so inside himself. He wouldn't even look at people. He never spoke. And he shunned physical contact. What a hard thing." She hugged herself with her crossed arms, and there were tears in her eyes. No one had ever asked her these questions before. No one had been brave enough.

Will answered with his own observations. "Well, he still doesn't talk. He makes sounds and he answers in some simple body language, and you know he's listening. But if you didn't know him, you would think there was nothing in there. In high school we used to call that an air head. Not very nice, and I think probably really wrong."

"Ya, he's really smart. He just knows stuff, and remembers everything. He seems to know when things are going to happen. I don't think in an ESP way; I think he just processes the tiniest details and figures it all out, on some subatomic level and then reacts. Like an animal reacts to the slight changes in weather most people don't even perceive. And us big adults, we're so sure we know it all, talk and talk, and miss what's really happening." She was emoting now and Will smiled.

He had wondered what this mother thought of strange Gwydion. But she continued before he could respond. "Costa Rica was really tough. He was always getting into things. He was just a tiny guy. No one around us spoke English and he didn't talk but I didn't think anything of it. "She hugged her arms and shivered.

"And sometimes he would just take off. He would just disappear."

Will looked at her in question. "Huh?"

"At night, I'd go in and he would just be gone. Five years old and out in the forest at night. I'd go out and find him with the dog roaming around in the moonlight. "

"What?" asked Will, a little alarmed now.

"He was so weird, it freaked me sometimes," she cried out a little, kind of defensively that Will had reacted with alarm.

Will shut his mouth; he knew that mothers often had troubles with their little kids, especially if fathers weren't around to help and do things with them. So he tried to act detached from what she was saying. And he just kept quiet.

"And that time at the Temple, I'm just remembering this now, how strange. We went to that same Temple and he got lost there. Inside the Temple. And he came back later, after we searched and searched, and he came back later all dirty and rumpled. Like he'd fallen or something."

"Oh, you mean the Singing Temple on the Yucatan? The one we just went to?"

She looked at him in the eyes, a little spooked, both of them, "Ya, that one. I just remembered that. Weird huh?"

They walked along for a while, thinking about their experience at the Temple last year, the one called the Temple of Inscriptions, incorrectly so, because there are no inscriptions in it except the huge plaque of stone carved to depict what looks like an astronaut in a fiery vehicle of some kind. The Temple where they had all met 15 years before in the dig that went haywire when the war broke out.

"But I can't just lock him in his room and restrain him like I did then. He's too big for that. I guess I just have to learn to let go of him," she said in the glowing dark. She leaned a little closer to him and their shoulders touched lightly. He put his arm around her shoulders. And Will thought she probably hadn't half begun to do that, letting go of her son. But the word restraining lodged in his subconscious for later.

"He's a pretty fascinating little guy," Will said to put a little distance to suggest the conversation was about to be changed. "How about dinner somewhere?"

"He's not very little anymore," she said, her mind still far away. She laughed a little thinking of her son, now a young man. "He's taller than me now. But he still slinks around like a kid. It's kinda weird. Probably why I am kinda on edge about him. Looks like a man, but isn't yet. And he still doesn't talk. Still doesn't look at me." She sighed and crossed her arms. "Maybe I ask too much."

"Oh, I don't know. Maybe just let it go. He seems fine." Will answered diplomatically. And walked them down the Canale toward a well-lit eating establishment. And as they bent under the old sign painted with a cat over the low doorway into the warmth of the restaurant, it started gently to rain.

# Chapter 22.
# Damp Stones

The two children hung along the damp stones of the ancient stairway as it began to rain outside the higher window of the cairn.

"Wait, wait, I love this part," Sophie said as she crinkled the paper in the growing darkness. Gwydion leaned over her shoulder and looked at a new typed-out translation she held there.

Drip drip drip a small formation of drops fell onto the widow sill.

"It's a tragedy of the Aeon, Sophia, before the formation of our planet in the dark chaos, she chose to produce an offspring with out the participation of her consort. The result was a monster god who had the power to create, and destroy, and he was named, Yaltabaoth. Sophia saw her mistaken creation as a malformed being. He decided in his delusions he was the one and only true God, and he set about to prove it by the creation of the Prison War planet Earth, which did not exist yet. As this tragedy unfolded, the supreme beings who watched sent some of their own to instruct the imprisoned inhabitants of the violent blue and green planet with the knowledge necessary for their entrapped mortal souls to escape to the higher plane."

Gwydion's eyes were wide. "How old is this?"

"Pre-Bible. This is the stuff the bible stories were developed from. Or thrown away. This says Genesis 1-4."

"Where was that found?" he asked her.

She flipped the page but there was nothing written on the back. "The Nag Hammadi folders." She said with a certitude. "That's all that's here."

"I'll see if I can find more in my grandfather's case tomorrow," said Gwydion. "It's getting dark," he added. "I can hardly see."

"It's raining," Sophie said to Gwydion, smiling. "I love it when it rains, especially in ancient cities when I'm underground."

Her morbid humor was not lost on Gwydion. "Ya, we should get back. It's getting dark and I think I missed dinner."

They turned and began to walk up the ancient steps, warn smooth in the very center from a billion treadings of human feet. After eons even soft leather will wear rock down. Sophie had her hand placed against the side stone of the wall for balance when it struck the edge of something, and she stopped. "Look at this, Gwydion," she gasped. Upon closer inspection they realized it was some kind of doorway that had been boarded over.

"I bet this goes up to the other rooms. And by its placement I bet it goes to my room."

"No, let's just go back," Gwydion's fear of strange places in dungeons was beginning to take over, with the gloom developing in the evening and the drone of the rain outside on the canal and the rock walls making a humming in the air that was beginning to press on them.

"No, wait. Let me just look." She pulled at one of the boards and it popped off, and they were able to see that indeed it was a door. She pushed the handle and the ancient door began to creak away from them into a totally dark void. She wedged her skinny body through the crack and disappeared into the gloom just as Gwydion reached to stop her.

"No, wait," but she was gone in an instant. Just then Gwydion heard the front door of the apartment open and bang shut and running steps into the living area of the hotel overhead. He thought he'd better get back. Just then her head popped through the slit in the door and Sophie said, "It's fine. I found it. Go on!" And with that, he turned and fled up the stairs and pushed his way through the coat-stuffed closet.

# Chapter 23.
# Convocations

The door flung back with a jingle as 2 figures dashed into the foyer of the Hotel. They were laughing and shaking off the rain.

"Buona Serra!" cried the inn keeper to the two wet figures, recognizing them as the American professors. They just laughed and started running up the stairs. The Venetian just smiled and returned to some paper work on the desk. What a rainy night. A bolt of lightening lit the sky and the dark alleyway outside. 'A night for romance, or maybe one for nightmares,' he thought to himself, as a wave of thunder rode over the ancient city for the probably the millionth time in its lifespan.

Will and Mags hustled into the apartment, in a hurry to shed themselves of their drenched clothes.

"How was I supposed to know it was going to rain?" cried Will defensively. "Next time I bring a bumbershoot just for good measure, huh?" he said looking into her wet face.

Her face registered confusion. And he added, " An umbrella!" And laughed and she laughed remembering the funny British term. "You Americans!" he said with exaggerated false derision in his thick Liverpuddlian accent.

Antony and Bethany were in hearing distance and they came in and laughed at his joke, and at how unbelievably wet they both were.

"Boy, did you two get caught in it!" he said.

Will regarded his colleague and now sort-of dad- in law. "We sure did. A nice dinner at Pas de Chat and this happened."

"Where?" asked Bethany. "That sounds French."

"Ya, I know," said Megs. "Weird, huh?" She pulled off her drenched wool blazer and hung it on a chair. "But the best darn cabbage wrapped pork meat balls I've ever had."

"It was very strange," said Will. "It was American cafeteria style, with the plastic trays and the old wizened chef serving you from a buffet behind glass. But oh, my gosh, the food.... wow."

"OK, then you'll have to take us next time, Will," scolded Bethany.

"So, you two up for tomorrow night?" Asked Antony.

Will looked up through fogged glasses and said, "Oh, ya. The reception. Ya, sure. Why not?"

"Just wondering. It's not required. But you know how that goes. We really have to be there."

"Not me, though," said Mags. "I mean, mom, you can go. But I really don't have to."

"Well, technically, you are a teacher with the Institute now. And this trip is about them." Antony would be the one to say anything to her. She probably wouldn't listen to anyone else. Bethany turned her head and rolled her eyes so no one would see. She was pretty sure she knew where Gwydion got that part of his personality, autistic or not. Apples after all don't fall far from the tree. She retreated to the tiny kitchen to wipe dishes after their Provencal style dinner of some things she had picked up at the store. Bread, cheese, some fresh vegetables, biscuits. There was no refrigerator like back in America, but the simplicity of eating in Europe was refreshing. A clear white wine that was really from a vineyard, and not a metal factory, shone gold in the glass.

The discussion continued in the main room. "Well, I'll go. But do we have to take Gwydion?" complained Mags in a quiet voice.

"Yes, I think he should go," both Antony and Will said almost in unison. They were careful not to look at each other. Will crossed his arms.

Mags looked at her father but not at Will, but she felt him cross his arms next to her. "Fine." She stepped toward the washroom to get a towel. "What time?"

"4 PM-ish. Afternoon. I don't think it's supposed to be that fancy," said her father to her back. He looked at Will and gave the tiniest of shrugs. Antony turned to walk back to the kitchen.

"Where is Gwydion, anyway?" asked Will.

"He's out. As usual, prowling around," answered Antony. Will gave him a questioning brow. Antony dismissed it with a wave. "He's fine. He always does this when we travel. You know, back at home, too, really, with his tall dark looks, they'll just think he is a local, and he will rarely open his mouth to dispel that belief."

Will smiled and nodded his head slightly. "Ya, he's probably picked up the language by now."

"Ya, but he never talks. He seems to just avoid situations where he is required to speak. He's figured it out somehow." Antony shrugged.

"He doesn't say anything, does he?" said Will. "Its funny though, after living with him for a while, I seem to understand what he is doing and saying, almost like he is actually speaking to me." Antony looked at him funny. "No, not ESP or anything. But like a sub-verbal communication, like with an animal or pet. It's interesting. I think we could learn from that."

Antony looked at him like a stranger for a moment, then said, "No, I understand you. I've just been living with him for so long, I don't even see that that's how we communicate, he and I."

Will looked at him with interest. "I think, Professor Jacobs, that maybe your being an Anthropologist may have helped you having him as a grandson. Probably interested you in some professional way."

"Ya, you might be right. Although I've never thought of it that way before."

"Probably what's allowed you to be tolerant instead of irritated at his weird behavior, like other people mostly are," said Will. "It interested you, this weird, sometimes frightening behavior of his."

Antony looked at his colleague. "I guess it is frightening. I get so caught up in protecting him and teaching him I forget people are afraid of him. And now he's turning into a handsome young lad, and people expect certain things from him. Which he just cannot fulfill, and then I think they become angry and frightened. Each time I see that, it makes me just a little bit more sad."

"Ya, I feel sorry for him too, sometimes," answered Will.

"No, not for Gwydion," Antony answered just as that person burst into the main room from the closet.

# Chapter 23.
# Listening

Gwydion couldn't stand it any longer. He burst through the door and ran thru the main room into the hallway.

He'd been listening to them talk, his ear pressed against the old door at the back of the coat closet. Listening to his grandfather and that guy, Will, talk for some time now. He heard his mother leave the room and go into the washroom. But he had to go; he couldn't hold it anymore. So he burst through the door, unfortunately revealing his hiding place, which he considered to be a really a bad thing to do. But he had too. Maybe if he ran through there into the hall down to the public bathroom, maybe they wouldn't think anything of it.

Once relieved, his mind turned to what he had heard them talking about. Another one of those dinners tomorrow night. And he was expected to go. He used to look forward to those things, all spiffy and shiny like they wanted him to be, show him off. Smile and be quiet.

But that last time in Egypt, with that other kid following him. And he could tell some of those other professors were openly hostile to his grandfather. How could adults get away with that kind of thing. They were supposed to be adults. And they told him to be mature and not fidget and wiggle. He was always quiet because he just didn't think he had anything to say to them anyway. With their hidden motives and their body-tells shooting off in all directions. Like animals reacting to each other, and then getting mad at him when he rolled his eyes at them and didn't want to go.

And then that other boy. The one that was following him around. And no one even cared. No one even *believed* him. He tried to tell his grand father about that mean boy that was following him. But his grandfather had given him *that look*. That look that says he not only doesn't believe him but that he thinks that Gwydion is having some kind of mental break down. Which certainly is not true. Just because I see how fake all you old people are.

Gwydion sat down on the bench outside on the walkway along the canal in back of the the family's apartment with all of these thoughts rushing through his head.

But they are going to make my mom go tomorrow night too. He could just hear her complain about that too. On and on she'd go about those stuffy professors and their superior ways. And then he thought maybe they were superior to her; she didn't have all that education and stuff. But maybe he was starting to sound just like his mom. And his vision cleared a little thinking that.

He felt his stomach do a flip and make a noise and he remembered he had been down below in the wet basement stairs for a long time, and he had missed dinner. He knew his family just dismissed his being missing half the time and didn't even ask him where he was anymore. After all those years of his hiding and going off, they had gotten used to it and stopped trying to tie him down.

He walked back up to the apartment door and knocked on it because it locked behind him when he ran out. His grandfather opened the door and let him in. "Where'd you go?"

Gwydion looked up at him sheepishly which said it all. He just walked in and made his way over to the kitchen where his grandmother was stacking some dishes. "You missed dinner Gwydion. Where were you?" she asked fully not expecting and answer, but asking anyway in a nice tone to let him know she did care about where he was, even if she didn't need a verbal answer. She put together a plate of food and he sat at the tiny table and ate dinner by himself.

The two men in the main room took seats opposite each other near the window. Will looked at Antony. "What in the world was he doing in the closet?"

"Hiding," was Antony's oblique answer. And they laughed. Their conversation turned to the subjects of tomorrow night's talks. The families could go home after the introductions, but there would be some sort of discussions afterward that were compulsory for the professors and their aids.

Gwydion listen quietly for a while and realized they weren't even talking about him. And not the closet or anything. Then his secret hiding place downstairs in the forbidden basement would remain a secret. He would check later and make sure the door was completely shut and hidden like it was when he found it the first time. No one would be the wiser.

# Chapter 24.
# Dinner

The pre-convention dinner was the usual thing for Gwydion. He slunk away as soon as possible and went and stood over by the food table, where there was a buffet of strange little things on platters. He tasted every punch there was, and he really liked the thick red one. It was so strong he thought maybe there was alcohol it it. Or maybe not; it was just so thick, almost like bright colored blood. He fascinated with for a while as he sipped it and he became a little dizzy from the red additives in it. He wandered over and filled one of the little plates with strange little food parts that were arranged on the large silver platters.

There were all kinds of people here, some of them dressed in weird clothes, like people from all around the world wanted to be identified with the country they were from. Otherwise people wore regular clothes, the men in black suits and the women is dresses. Everyone stood around and laughed and held drinks. Soon people wandered to tables were they sat talking in groups and then someone got up on stage and started talking about stuff. The convention and what they were all there for. Gwydion scanned the room for anyone he knew. There were almost no faces he recognized besides his family and Will and Doctor Hillard from the Institute. And maybe a couple professors form their past trip to Egypt. His grandfather approached with one of these men from their past trip. They walked right up to him. Gwydion thought maybe they were just getting food and would pretend not to see him, but his grandfather was beaming at him and leading this older man straight for him. He tried to look away, but his grandfather said, "And this is my grandson who is now going to school in San Francisco. Gwydion, this is professor Martin, you remember?" Gwydion allowed his hand to be taken and squeezed by the very old professor, he smiled into his face. Gwydion knew he seemed weird to people and knew that when people smiled at him like that, they had been told all about him and his disease, and they were trying to be nice, but inadvertently showing pity for his 'condition' as his mother was now calling it to people behind his back. When he didn't answer, the professor looked at his grandfather and waited for him to pick up a conversational thread.

"We will be hearing some short reports from some of the linguists on the new discoveries from the Egyptian Nile find. You might actually find this interesting, Gwydion." He did not return his grandfather's gaze. So Antony looked at the Professor Shallot and said, "Gwydion is quite a fan of the things we are studying. He enjoys reading some of the stories we find and translate," he turned to Gwydion and added, "Don't you Gwydion?" His face flushed hot red and he looked even further away. He wasn't sure if he was in trouble for reading what was in his grandfather's suitcase. Maybe it was a test to see if he would admit that he dug around and read those forbidden pages. But he wasn't about to give any of it away. It was his, and now Sophie's, secret. It was his secret domain, with his grandfather and with his friend from school, Sophie. He thought about Sophie and that she had not wanted to come to this tonight. He had wished he could bring her like a little angel on his shoulder, so she could see all of these people forced into this charade, and the way they always put him on the spot. She would have rolled her eyes and said, "Oh, Gwydion. Just ignore them. They are just adults."

He felt better when he thought that, when he thought about having her as a friend, where she never judged him for what he was and seemed to not be able to help being.

"Well, it should be interesting," continued his grandfather, Professor Jacobs to this older man, Professor Martin, from Egypt. "We have a pretty big contingent from the Ecclesiastical community." He turned toward Shallot who had a big grin on his face. "And that promises to be quite a stir." And Antony's grin widened and the two men shared a look and a chuckle. Gwydion took it to mean that these other men from the church were insulted about something and would argue about a whole bunch of things just to get a rise from the professors that were more like his grandfather and professor Martin.

Some people came onto the stage and moved some chairs around. One of them stepped to the podium and the micro phone and tapped it to see if it was working. "Tap*Tap" was the microphone's loud response, and all heads turned toward the stage, and people began to wander to tables and sit down. Gwydion hurried over to a table and sat down near the back. Easier for escape, he thought.

"Good evening, ladies and Gentlemen, Madams et Messieurs. Welcome tonight to the special convention of minds, the International Archaeological and Anthropological Society of Study. Tonight we welcome the best minds in the fields of the study of ancient man, with guests from around the world." Gwydion listened with half an ear as he watched the colorful persons walk around and take chairs at tables, and set their drinks down and look up at the man on stage speaking into the microphone.

"I am professor Amin Teklat from the Museum of Antiquities of Luxor, Egypt, and I welcome all of you into the celebration tonight of the discoveries of the Ancient books of Jubal al Tariff, that special place on the Nile delta." He adjusted his bow tie and cleared his throat away from the mic, then turned back and said, "With no further ado, we shall commence with tonight's speakers in their short presentations of field notes and thoughts. First up for the introduction is our renowned professor from Prague, Poland, Dr. Rushlav Shitzlew...." Gwydion's mind turned off at the pronunciation of that name. The new speaker replaced the first one amid a round of applause, and began to speak with a deeply intoned voice, his accent so strong that Gwydion tried for the first few words to follow him, but could not, so he turned away and began looking at people again. He noticed the way some people fidgeted, and some people were smiling and enraptured with the talk of the Polish gentleman doctor. A small group dressed in church garb were all scowling at the stage, and visibly fidgeting at the professor's words. Gwydion noticed the gentleman professor had doffed his black bowler and placed it upon the podium in front of him and was staring at it as if it divined the words of his speech there in. He droned on in his hypnotic thick accent. Then Gwydion noticed he was understanding the thickly accented professor now, and he could follow the meaning of his words, if he didn't focus on them or try too hard. "...Latin and Greek also were found in this ancient collection of folios, as in the several works of the Greek,

Plato, most of them were pious in tone, not herseolgical in voice. This would seem to indicate that these texts were even older, and had been saved not to be read and studied, but to be held onto and preserved, valued for their already antiguitous status *then*, in the year 367 AD, when they were buried, which was the latest dates found on any document, of course no later date, no more recent date, would be found than the burial date."

Gwydion did quick math in his head and came up with about 1600 years; that long they had been buried in the Nile banks. About 350 years after the Christ was born. Time enough for his story to become popular.

"But why, we ask ourselves, were they buried and not simply destroyed? Why did someone go to the effort to seal them in jars and hide them in rocks in the sand of the Nile? Whoever "they" were, they were very careful and meticulous in hiding and preserving them, as if these documents would have certainly been destroyed if not been sealed and hidden and buried?" He let that hang for just a moment. Then continued.

"Perhaps an answer can be found in that significant date. In that year, 367 C.E., the Archbishop of Alexandria issued a canon, one that was to define the 27 books of the New Testament just being compiled and formalized. He decried that all other works were heretical, all Apocryphal works would be considered heresy. He cited these works were all written by heretics and had been falsely dated attributing them to an earlier time, falsely giving them more credence..."

And Gwydion wondered at this. Would that mean that if written before the birth of Christ meant they were true? Or only if they were really written between the birth and then this

Bishop's canon they were true? He felt that somewhere in this lay a trick played by both ancients and moderns, in twisting the meaning, casting dispersion's on the validity of these documents.

The foreign professor looked out upon the listening crowd and paused a moment, letting some of this sink in. Then he asked them all, "So how do we approach these newly discovered texts, once considered apocryphal, nay, heretical, by the then burgeoning new Sect of Christianity?"

The group of Ecclesiastics near Gwydion audibly groaned at the speaker's word choice.

"As we near the $21^{st}$ century, I feel it necessary that we maintain an historical outlook on these finds. That we begin to understand our religious traditions as historical development. They represent almost a thousand years of recorded intellectual workings of an ancient people. An ancient people that we have grown from, these, are our roots, all of us." Near Gwydion the men in church robes were becoming visibly agitated.

"This find near the tiny ancient town of Nag Hammadi is tremendously important in the fields of Anthropology and Archaeology and linguistics. That many of these works predate the Christian era is astonishing. That they tell of a savior long before His birth, does this discredit their words? Or does it verify it as prophecy? Does it matter? Do we no longer believe in prophecy, when once it was crucial to the validity of the story? Does their actual age of over 2000 years old discredit their validity? Or does it verify their actual value? Traditionally their scholastic value versus their biblical validity may be exactly the difficult debate, still, for many."

Lots of nods and shifting in seats as the foreign professor's thickly accented words swept across the room full of listening crowd. And the professor swept his hand out toward them all, including everyone in the conclusion of his speech.

"But I present to you that such a large gathering of intellectual minds such as yourselves, from all around the world, from all points of the globe, certainly would indicate the importance of this discovery, the sheer magnitude of this find, this latest Treasure of the Nile."

# Chapter 25.
# The Alley

The Polish Professor replaced his hat on his head and turned to walk off stage. The audience erupted into applause and Gwydion sat and absorbed the stir and excitement that his introductory speech had brought. As another man walked up to the mic, Gwydion thought it was time to escape. But the doors to the auditorium were over by the stage. So he turned and ran into the doors in the back, which led him straight into the kitchen.

The space had grown quiet as the talks had begun on the stage, hungers slaked by the groaning boards of hors d' oeuvres. There were a couple workers sitting at a table, eating from full plates of appetizers, talking in hushed tones. They hardly looked at Gwydion as he slunk by.

There must be an alleyway door out back. And hopefully it doesn't drop off into some canal, thought Gwydion to himself.

He hurried between the shining silver cooking counters and found the dark door at the back. He pushed it open a crack and looked out. Not much light, but at least not the surface of water he half expected.

The smell of smoke on a slight breeze and the shimmer of festoons of lights over the inky black waters of the canal. Slick black shapes glided by, the boatmen upright in the slim shaft of black lacquered barca, two lovers holding closely together, lit by a small swinging lantern on the prow.

Gwydion stepped out into the alleyway, and let the door slowly slip closed behind him. There was a little bowl laying on the door jam to keep the door from going all the way closed, and Gwydion thought maybe it was to give the small group of smokers huddled together in the almost dark a bit of light to take a cigarette break by. Then he thought just as he kicked the bowl and it slid out of the way of the closing door, maybe it was because the door would lock from the inside, thus locking everyone outside. Someone yelled an Italian invective at him from the smoking group. Then they mumbled among themselves and Gwydion slunk off to a darker corner. He didn't smoke, but that didn't mean he couldn't stand and enjoy the dark, warm breezes off the canal. He thought about Sophie back at the hotel alone, and wished she could be here right now and see the beauty of this place. Maybe she was out on the tiny balcony gazing up at the slender slice of moon setting between the two black towers of the apartment buildings on either side of the tiny narrow canal at the back of their hotel apartments.

I guess I better be getting back. He didn't even stop to think what his parents might think about him just disappearing like that. He always just showed up at home eventually. He heard a rustling down the alley just a ways, and turned to see a dark form coming slowly his way, a bright red cherry of a cigarette lit up as the smoker inhaled on it. Gwydion paid no attention and leaned back against the cool stones of the wall. Then he heard a low voice, just in his ear. He at first did not understand what it said, figuring it was Italian, which he had only just started to pick up. But his mind twisted around and he found himself understanding the speaker and was horrified to realize it was in Egyptian. In his years there, he had picked up the Coptic language almost as if he were a native speaker.

But how did this person know he understood Egyptian? This person must know me.

He leaned a little away from the dark figure next to him, and looked down to the side, to get a periphery view of the person in the dark. Perhaps this was someone from inside the hall, someone who knew him from convention group inside. Yes, that was it. One of his father's professor friends.

Then the voice spoke again, and Gwydion realized that the voice was younger than any of his grandfather's friends from the Institute. So he turned and looked into the face, and was mortified to see two dark eyes staring at him from the gloom, two eyes just slightly crossed.

He turned and ran.

# Chapter 26.
# Escape

"Where's Gwydion?" Mags turned and looked at Will sitting next to her talking to her father. He turned slightly and said, "Huh?" He turned away and began talking to Antony as she turned toward her mother who was actually looking at her, and asked the question again. Bethany shrugged and gave a look of helplessness to her daughter, and they both started hunting with their eyes for their wayward boy. Their eyes found nothing but mostly strangers milling around.

"I'm feeling a little nervous about that, why don't we head back home?" she said to her mother.

"I think we're done here, the boys are through with us, so, ya, let's head back. Maybe we will find him on the way or back at the apartment. I'm tired of all this smoozing anyway," laughed Bethany. The two women stood up and kissed their respective men on their cheek, barely rousing them from their engrossed conversation with some brightly dressed men from over seas. "Well, I think he's asking for trouble, being to bold as to suggest..." said one of the strangers. "Yes, we've been there, done that. But we cant let that deter us from doing the translations in the most sincere...." Antony continued, and the two women walked away toward the from entrance. They found their way through the lobby and out into the moist Venetian air.

So he ran. He ran down the dark alley past some people standing there smoking cigarettes. He kept running, the dark water on one side and tall apartment walls and locked doors on the other. He ran until he turned a corner and found himself in an even darker alleyway. He stopped and tried to catch his breath. He doubled over at the middle and rested his hands on his knees and breathed in and out, the black spots soon fading from his vision. He looked up and ventured a peep around the stone corner at the way he had just fled. Nothing. Just some dark figures silhouetted by the dimly lit canal.

He looked around and got his bearings and continued down the very dark alley toward a more populated place along one of the larger canals. He stepped over an arched bridge and entered a small courtyard ringed by some tiny restaurants and patrons talking laughing and sipping drinks and eating dinners by the late night lights strung between and on the trees. He breathed a sigh of relief. He would not be attacked in this area. The presence of these people comforted him somewhat.

He picked out an empty table and plopped himself down on the chair. His breath labored and his heart pounded in his ears. That boy again! He thought to himself. After these years of peace, that boy again!.

Why didn't I see him inside the hall? Was he hiding? I didn't see him at all. I felt like I had actually gotten some rest and maybe it was over. But Gwydion was so wrong. He couldn't know how wrong.

That boy! There he is, thought the older boy. After these few years apart, there he is again. He's come back to take this part of my life over again. I thought he was gone for good. I have been praying and keeping to myself and doing what the priests want me too. And see how I am rewarded? Sometimes I hate you, he glanced up. Then felt a shiver of guilt. Sorry, I didn't mean that.

Then he thought maybe there is a reason for this boy to come back into his life. Maybe there is unfinished business. He hated that man on the stage for the awful things he was saying about the work they were doing. How can those intellectuals get it all so twisted around? We are here to make sure these documents are translated correctly, not find a new truth in them to spread around like a plague. And at every turn, they thwart us. Like some new disease, these so called scientists tell us what is in these ancient books. As if we cannot know. As if we cannot read Latin and Greek ourselves. And they way they twist meanings? That cannot possibly mean those things. Our Lord would never write those things in books. The body's elimination processes, prostitutes. How dare they even talk about those filthy things.

His rage boiled up inside him from a festering wound deep inside him. He hadn't felt this boil break open in a long while Something about finding the younger boy at this meeting of minds brought back all the old pain.

So that was it. The boy was his sign that it was time to make a difference. Do something about the travesty brought on by all these so-called smart people being handed those precious documents. Documents that belonged only in the hands of who deserved to see them, even touch them. Not these heathens, but the Men of God. So that was it. Show them, make a difference. Sacrifice this boy and show them the power of God.

From the corner of his eye at the end of the first talk, he saw the boy slip out the back door through the kitchen. He got up and went out the front entrance and went around the building. And just as he turned the corner into the dark alley behind the place, he saw the boy emerge from the back kitchen door, stand, and look around. When he drew in deep on his fresh cigarette, he saw the boy look his way and freeze. And when I walk up and try to talk to him? He bolts. What a waste of a cigarette, he thought, as he enjoyed it for a few more moments. I know where he is now. I know that he is here for his final slaughter. I can wait. He will be around.

And with that he threw down his almost finished cigarette, and started to saunter down the dark alleyway toward where his prey had flown.

Gwydion sat at his table alone for a few minutes until the waiter saw him and came over. "Would you care for something to drink?" the waiter said in his late night Italian voice. Gwydion did not look up at him, but he knew he had to order something or he was not allowed to stay seated, using the chair and table that a paying customer might use. So he said one word, "Coke." and the waiter understood perfectly and whisked off to get him one. He was soon sailing back over and deposited a glass with no ice and a cracked open can of coke in front of Gwydion. "And will *sir* be dining tonight?" asked the waiter before he left. Gwydion shook his head in the negative without looking up at the waiter. So the waiter quoted him a price in Italian lire, which sounded like an awful lot to Gwydion, so Gwydion produced a pile of change from his pocket with the waiter sorted through and took what he needed. He also picked out a couple of the larger coins and tossed them on the table as a tip for himself to be left when the young boy left. Gwydion sipped his simple beverage after the waiter had taken his leave, not even bothering with the glass, even though he had paid for it's use.

He was realizing a few things as he sat there sipping, after seeing that boy, the one with the slightly crossed eyes. He realized he didn't even know his name. That kid that attacked him in Egypt and then again in the stone Temple. How can his luck be that bad? Thought Gwydion. How can he keep running into the creep time and time again?

And what is his problem? Why does he keep following me and showing up and scaring the crap out of me? What is with that guy? Why cant he just leave me alone?

But I have a table here in broad day light, well its night time which maybe makes me harder to see, Gwydion thought as he sat there for a while. He tried not to look around himself as he sat there listening to the sounds of people around him. Was he listening for that voice again in Egyptian? It sounded so strange to hear that here in Italy, isolated Venice. What a shock that was! He was getting used to hearing the Italian being spoken around him and then that voice! That voice sounding in his ear in that language he had hoped he'd forgot.

But he remembered it perfectly well it seemed. He hung his head and wished he could forget.

Now what do I do? Thought Gwydion to himself. He was almost done with his drink and he would have to leave.

I guess I have to get back anyway. They will be wondering where I am, as usual.

Just then a figure slunk around his chair and plunked down into the chair opposite him at his table.

Gwydion froze in place. He never suspected the guy to have the nerve to just plunk down in front of him like that.

He was trapped. Trapped and frozen in his chair, staring at his can of fizzing drink. He couldn't just get up and walk away. The guy had him.

"What are you doing here, young boy?" asked the older boy across from Gwydion. "I didn't expect an idiot like you to be here with all these smart people."

Gwydion studied his sweating can still in his hand and he wondered what he was going to do. I cant toss this can at him; that's a crime. I cant just get up and walk away; that's rude.

He sat there and stewed in his fear and confusion, trying not to look up.

His tormentor saw his torment. "What are you going to do now, boy?"

Gwydion squirmed a little in his chair and he made a small animal sound and the young man smiled and made a derisive sound in his throat.

This boy had him trapped just by his boldness. A boldness that was new when Gwydion had remembered him being kinda clumsy and rash. And Gwydion wondered what this boy had been through since the last time he saw him about a year ago. He had grown. He seemed more of a man than back at the college in Egypt. He smelled like a man too. Like a predator, Gwydion noticed.

What am I going to do.

The unexpected, he decided.

He cant just keep me here just by sitting over there. I haven't even looked at him and yet he is talking to me like we are having a conversation. I haven't acknowledged him so he doesn't exist for me. I will simply stand up and leave.

Stand up and leave.

Let go of the can, slide the chair back, and stand up and leave.

He sat there and felt the sweat start to grow around his neck. He felt his face getting red, his finger tips were getting numb. He began to hear the roaring in his ears. He stood up. Knocked the wooden chair back onto the flag stones, and his can of almost finished drink flipped off the table and onto the ground bubbling.

He kept his eyes down as he walked past the other boy and quickly walked out of the lighted restaurant area as several waiters came hustling over and surrounded the table to clean up the mess and right the chair. And the other boy was momentarily held back sitting in his chair with concerned people milling around him.

Gwydion knew he had only a few seconds lead. And as soon as he was free of the lighted barricaded area of the restaurant, he sprinted. He knew the other boy would be right behind him as usual. But he didn't look back to check. He ran.

Ahead was a dark hole of another alley between three story apartment buildings so classic for Venice. He bolted for the dark.

He ran. And he ran some more until his lungs were screaming at him, so he stopped and leaned against a damp wall to catch his breath.

When his breathing calmed down and the roaring in his ears began to subside, he began to hear the soft sounds around him. He could hear the soft rustling of the wind in the laundry drying over head on wires between the two buildings. He could hear the gentle lapping of the water in the narrow canal that ran along side the narrow walkway he was on. And he was relieved to hear that there were no other footsteps on the stones of the walkway. He had gotten away.

"That little creep!" thought the older boy as Gwydion simply stood up and ran. "He just ran away from me. I was talking to him and he just got up and ran off!" He struggled to stand up with all of the people standing around him trying to clean up the mess and pick up the chair and ask questions and apologize. Someone there said the word police, so the young man thought he'd better get out of there.

He apologized several times and made his way out of the crowd, out of the restaurant and in the direction of which the young boy ran.

"I cant believe he just got up and ran. And when we were having such a nice conversation. I was just going to try to explain to him why I disagreed with what they all are doing at this conference." He walked strongly toward the next alley opening, although he did not really know where the boy went, only his general direction.

"If only he would let me explain, I could make him understand how important it is," he thought to himself as he left the lit area where the restaurants were. "I'm never going to find him now," he lamented to himself as he began down a darker alleyway.

"He always seems to run away. He never talks, he never looks at me, is there something wrong with me? Maybe he thinks there is something wrong with me? I just try to do what is right, and do what I'm told. It's him that there's something wrong with.

I am not the one that is weird and following around in the dark, and running away when someone tries to have a conversation." He stomped his way down the half lit alley, where there was no one and nothing. Just the tall black apartment walls, and those silly canals everywhere.

"If I could just get him to sit down and hold still, I could explain to him what this is all about. If I could just explain it to him he would understand. He is not that much younger than me. He's grown too. In just a year, he is getting tall." The older boy thought to himself as he strode through the semi darkness in the late night breeze.

"If I could just get him to look at me and talk to me, but he must think I am awful or something. How dare he think that? When I am just trying to be friendly. And he just wont hold still! I'll show him some day.. I will make him sit down and hold still and listen to me. I will. Someday."

Gwydion felt exhausted with exertion and fear. He slumped down and leaned against the damp wall. There were few sounds around him and he felt his body relax from sheer exhaustion.

If I just sit here a moment, then I can find my way back.

He was so strung out that he really had no idea where he was in this labyrinth of canals and alleyways. He figured he could follow the light and get back to a courtyard where there were some people, and then ask somebody directions back to the hotel. Venice was small; people knew where things were. If you could speak the language correctly, comprehensibly to them. Although it seemed many of the locals wanted you to speak English. But Gwydion was not sure he could speak anything right now, his mind was such a jumble.

So, I'll just sit and be quiet for a minute.

He knew not how long, but he was awoken by a noise. Grogginess filled his head and sand paper had covered his eyes, so he figured he must have fallen asleep for a moment. Or two. Some people were walking down the alley way, talking and giggling. They came up to him, and quieted, their pace slowed. Then one of the girls giggled and pointed at him slouched on the ground and called him a silly old drunk. The boys giggled in amusement, and the group ambled on it's way.

Gwydion shook his head and rubbed his face. One of the group broke off and stepped back to Gwydion, leaned down into his face, and grabbed him by the collar.

"There you are," the voice hissed at him. And Gwydion was horrified to realize it was spoken in the Egyptian language.

"You asshole!" it hissed again spraying Gwydion's face with spit. "Who do you think you are? Can just walk away from me!" The eyes of a demon started into Gwydion's face as the older boy yanked on his collar, lifting Gwydion of his feet. Gwydion was too shocked and exhausted to struggle. "Oh, God save me," Gwydion's mind said inside himself. "Help me, please, someone," he thought quietly, unable to move his lips for exhaustion and terror. Then he thought of Sophie, home safe and quiet resting with a slight head cold. "Oh Sophie, I wish you were here," then he thought, "No, maybe I don't. This guy is crazy and I don't want him hurting you too."

"What are you saying, Freak?" the bigger boy snarled into Gwydion's face. He must have been mumbling. "Speak up! You never say anything, you freak!"

Gwydion blew a puff of air into the older boy's face, and the boy jerked back. "You are nothing, you don't even fight.

Why do I even bother." Gwydion tried to swing up and hit the older boy in the face. It was rather ineffectual except to piss the older boy off, and he shook Gwydion harder by the neck. "You listen to me, you freak. You stay away from my people. All of you, stay away from us. In fact you should all die!" The older boy lost himself in his rage while he spoke incomprehensibly to Gwydion there in the late dark of the alleyway. He was ranting now in a language that Gwydion did not comprehend, but he understood it's intent if only by its violence. His native tongue, from the country where he was born, Gwydion thought. Some where else where his hatred and violence was born when this young man was a child. Deep in the darkness of his mind, before there was even real memory available to him as a child, vague sensations of abuse and pain had buried themselves and festered.

And now this festered wrath was breaking over Gwydion, anonymously in the dark of a foreign alleyway.

He was shaking the younger boy so hard and with such fury that Gwydion's legs spasmed and shot out and caught the other boy in the groin, and a shriek of rage erupted from the older boy's gaping mouth. "You foul demon!" he raged at his captured prey. "I will kill you! Kill you!" All of his rage poured out over poor silent Gwydion struggling to maintain consciousness from exhaustion and stark raving fear.

"Oh, god save me," escaped Gwydion's lips.

"How dare you speak of God, you heathen filth!" the older boy frothed. But Gwydion was thrashing now, mumbling incomprehensibly. "God." "Sophie".

"Call for help, but no one will save you now. I have you," threatened the spent older boy, his face hot and wet with exhaustion and spent rage.

There was a commotion behind them, and suddenly they both fell to the cold stones at their feet. The sound of the water lapping at the sidewalk was heard and some rustling of clothes as a dark form leaned over Gwydion. "Are you alright?" a soft voice asked. "Gwydion? Are you alive?" it asked again, gently putting a hand on his shoulder. She looked at her white hand in the darkness and there was a dark stain on it. He was bleeding somehow. She didn't see a knife or gun, but she looked around just in case. No, just the slumped black form of his assailant and the stone she had slugged him with. She shoved him over and he rolled out of the way toward the canal. "Gwydion? Wake up," she said into his face.

His eyes opened slightly and he peered through the swollen slits, "Sophie," he said. "You came for me." Behind them they heard his attacker struggle to get up, let out a gasp, and run down the alleyway grunting and groaning. "Coward!" said Sophie, as the other boy bolted away into the darkness. She turned her attention to Gwydion laying prone on the cold flagstones.

"Yes," she cradled his head in her hand and her lap. "We were worried. So I found you."

He breathed a sigh of relief and slumped into her arms. They breathed together for a moment. "OK, lets get you going. Do you need a hospital?"

"No. I'm just banged up."

"But you are bleeding."

"Just from where he split my lip. He didn't shoot me or anything."

"Then let's get you back to the hotel. Your family must be worried sick."

Suddenly there was another commotion at the end of the dark alleyway. Sophie jumped up with fear, trying to drag Gwydion along with her. "Get going!" she hissed. "OK, OK," he said as he was struggling to his feet. He was having a hard time coordinating his movements he was so groggy. She sped off down the alleyway, expecting Gwydion, who was usually so agile and quick to come racing after her. He could not quite manage it and she disappeared around a corner as he turned to look at the small group of people coming down the alley. One of them in front broke into a jog and came running up to Gwydion. He looked at the scene, a boy on the pavement, bloody and struggling, and the large stone with a bloody mark on it and said in surprised Italian, "What happened? Are you alright?"

"Oh, my head," was all he could get out.

"Oh, English," answered the stranger in heavily accented Italian. "It looks like you were clocked pretty good," pointing the rock with a blood mark on it. "Did you see who it was?"

Gwydion could only shake his head at the boy's misunderstanding of the situation. He held his head and shook it some more.

"Do you need to go hospital?" Gwydion continued to shake his head.

'The rest of the crew came up to him and one of the girls looked at him and cooed like a mamma bird. "You poor baby," she said in Italian. "Let's get you some cognac!" They laughed and said it sounded like a good idea. They hoisted him to his feet and led him down the darkened alleyway into an area where there were people quietly having drinks and talking at a couple small restaurants still open this late at night.

They hosted a small party for him as they sat around a small table, bought a few drinks and tried to make Gwydion drink a bit of some sweet liquor while one of the girls cleaned up the blood on his face and neck.

As she leaned into his space to wipe his nose off, she said, "I'm Nikka. What's your name?"

Gwydion hummed his name as she wiped his nose and lip, which had just stopped bleeding.

"There!" she said sitting back and admiring her work, Gwydion's face now somewhat free of blood. "Here." She moved the snifter of cognac right in front of him. " Now drink some more of 'dis and you will be zhust fine."

Gwydion smiled as a thank you and pretended to sip the drink. It stung his lip too much. Then he wrinkled his brow as he turned and listened to what the others were heatedly discussing. Most of it was in Italian, but he recognized the words doctor and sanitarium and electric drill and he wondered what they could be talking about. Nikka noticed Gwydion's questioning look and said loudly, "Oh, they are talking about the haunted island again."

Gwydion pulled an even more questioning look. And one of the boys said, "Out in the lagoon, just out there," and he pointed south over St marks Square. "Poveglio, the haunted Island. You can see it right from the edge of St. Mark's Square, about a quarter mile out. Although no one is allowed to go there. No tourists. Too haunted, too dangerous." He wagged his finger in the air in front of Gwydion.

The oldest boy, the one who seemed in charge said, "We are

selling it to help clear up some of our national debt, no thanks to......" He said some words that must have been some current events political stuff here in Venice that were completely incomprehensible to Gwydion.

"Ya, but it's haunted. They will never get people to buy that retched place." This boy looked at Gwydion and said, "Dead Plague victims from the dark ages. They were burned alive there!"

"Not alive! Edvard. They were dead."

"But they say the ground there is 50 % human remains ashes. Brrr!" Edvard added as he looked at Gwydion. Gwydion smiled.

"Ya, but the real thing is," added the first boy, who seemed to be a little older and more in charge, "Just until recently it was a sanatorium, you know, insane asylum. And the doctor was crazed. He used to give illegal lobotomies to his patients..."

"Victims!" interjected one of the girls quickly.

"... with an electric power drill."

"Madre de Deus," said one of the younger boys.

"But," added Edvard, "he got *his*. He fell off the highest tower to his death. But they say, no. He did not fall. He was chased by the ghosts of the people he tortured to death, and *they* threw him off the tower."

Gwydion thought, that's just great. Middle of the night and I have to walk home with that on my mind. My family is going to just love the fact I'm bleeding and being walked home by a band of drunk Italian kids.

Nikka looked in his face, and saw what was going on in his mind, and smiled. "Don't worry, my young friend. I will walk you home."

"Say, where are you staying?" asked the boy in charge.

Gwydion stated the name of the apartment hotel they were at and the kids knew right where it was. "Finish up and we shall deliver you." There was clapping from the small group as they began to stand up from their tiny table.

They lifted him up out of his chair, and the small group of guardian angels escorted Gwydion back to his hotel, much to the celebrating relief of his family.

# Chapter 27.
# Guardian Angels

His mother was yelling. He was trying not to look.

"I'm sure it's not his fault," Will was saying to her. "Do you think he went out looking for a fight? Gwydion?" He was exasperated at Mag's reaction to Gwydion coming home in the middle of the night, early morning really, looking literally like the cat had dragged him in.

"And those kids he chose to take up with!" she yelled some more. "Drunk local Venetians. I've heard stories about this city and now I see they're all true." She threw her hands in the air and dropped them with a flap at her sides. Will rolled his eyes at Antony, who was standing spectating the playoffs between Mags his daughter, and Will his associate.

"They said they saved him," Will continued to try to explain, "but from what, we may never know." He looked at Gwydion huddled in the corner. "He's never going to give us the story. Look at him . He's terrified."

"YA, terrified I might smack him and knock some sense into him!" Mags said with a red face turned toward Gwydion, who huddled tighter. "I am soooo done! I am so done raising kids. He's 16, he's on his own now."

"Why are you acting like this?" Will said to her.

"I am so tired of caring. And worrying. And wondering where the hell he is all the time."

"I thought we agreed it was pretty harmless, when he went and did stuff on his own," Will said.

Antony interjected wisdom, "Well, not now. Seems like someone beat him up this time. And we may not know who or why." He turned and glanced at the shaken and battered boy. "I think we should discuss this another time when we've all calmed down."

There was no way Gwydion could explain. This darkness that surrounded him and being followed by someone who by all accounts could not be here overseas from the last trip in Central America. And then the attack and chase, and then Sophie showing up? Oh, his mother would go into a rage about her. Probably tell her to go home now, fun and games were over. Sophie was already hiding as if her life depended on it. Hadn't seen her since she fled when the strangers came running up to help Gwydion. Didn't seem like she was adapting very well to foreign people and places.

And those nice kids that found him and nursed him back to consciousness. That was pretty darn friendly really. He wondered if he could go find them again and hang out later. Then he thought he was probably was going to be grounded for the rest of his life anyway. They were going to be here for another six days of conferences and lectures and stuff, which at this point he had absolutely no wish to attend. I wish they hadn't made me go last night, he said to himself.

"He's not going anywhere," stated Mags to the family. "He is not allowed out at all, not till we leave this island."

"That's a little harsh," said grandma Bethany, knowing the little scoundrel would probably find a way around it anyway. "Maybe he could just stay here and not go to anymore meetings. And not go out at night." She looked at Gwydion who glanced quickly up and then away.

They had a secret bond, his grandmother and him, and he liked her as an honest friend. He used to think that of his mother. But not since that Will Smithershins had come around. It had all changed then.

"Right!' said Mags. "Like he would really agree to it."

"Of course he will," said Bethany. "He's a good boy who got caught in some one else's trouble last night, that's all." She looked at Gwydion, who was still too withdrawn to say anything. "Right, honey?" She spoke to him even though she knew he would be unable to answer right now. Maybe they would have a little talk later, when people cooled off and they could be alone for a few minutes. But it was hard to be alone in this tiny cramped apartment hotel room in this tiny cramped miniature city. Not like that huge old mansion in San Francisco where they could go hide and study in other rooms all over the house when they wanted privacy. Sometimes Bethany thought that huge old place had actually divided the family a little, because everyone could withdraw to his own space. She had noticed her daughter drawing away from her grandson since they had lived there. But maybe that was something else, she pondered. Gwydion's father had been gone for many years, and maybe it was time for her daughter Mags to have some male company her own age. And funny Will had shown up just at the right time. But then again, Gwydion was in his teens, and typically time for a youngster to start cutting those old apron strings, even if the boy seemed immature from anybody else his age. Strangely infantile really. Sometimes his withdrawn silence bothered Bethany. But she had grown accustomed to it. And in fact she understood his moods and thoughts maybe better because he didn't communicate by yelling and screaming like she had seen other teenagers do. He was introspective, and she suspected smarter than your average bear, which made her love him all the more. And she thought, against her will, that maybe all this fighting might actually get him moving in his own direction.

But looking at him now, slinking in the corner, she wasn't so sure. And she feared that he might have just gone further into his burrow. And looking at his swollen eyes, busted lip and tear streaks on his cheeks, she feared maybe for good.

# Chapter 28.
# Capture

He wasn't all that broken up about not being allowed to go to anymore of the meetings or seminars. He felt he'd had enough of that stuff anyway. He could read the translations and papers here with his grand father anyway. And study things on his own time, with the tedious lectures and talks and hand shaking that went on at those things anyway.

He was going to miss going out on his own and doing stuff. Especially at night. He seemed to relish the night, hiding in the shadows, watching the lights play on the waters of the canals, the quiet swish of the piccilo barca sliding among the waves and the inky waters.

But he would find things to do. He learned the back way out of the hotel and would sit at the water's edge and read. Sometimes Sophie would join him in his quiet time, and they would speak infrequently. His family said it was for his safety. And he felt safe. Maybe a little insulated.

But the memory of that boy coming after him that night lay hidden away and he never talked about it with them. It sat in a dark place in there where he healed like a scab over it.

He didn't let them see him go outside. So when they were home he would slip into the closet with its hidden doorway into the cellar. And there Sophie would join him, and they would read to each other quietly, or talk about home.

"I don't really want to go back," he said to her one afternoon in the dank dark. "All those kids just hate me anyway."

"They don't hate you Gwydion," she would say in comfort. "They are a little afraid of you. You are just a little different." And he would curl a half smile and look at his hands, his big hands he was yet to grow into. "I like you though."

And he would look for just a second into her golden eyes and wonder at how she was here with him now. He would get embarrassed and look down. Today he pulled out a folded piece of paper from his back pocket.

"Look at this."

She bent around and looked at the typed page he was unfolding on his lap.

"You will like this one. Its about a woman. It kinda goes on and on. Its beautiful. "

"Thunder," she read out loud. "The Perfect Mind. How strange."

"I was sent from the Grand Place above,

to be among those who contemplate me.

Do not turn away, do not be ignorant of me.

Am Alpha and Omega, I am wife and daughter,

I am whore and I'm holy.

I am the incomprehensible silence, I am insight, whose depths are dark.

I am found in the utterance of my own name.

You who speak of me in truth, tell lies of me instead.

You who know me, can not know me,

and those who don't, then know me well."

She looked up into Gwydion's eyes. "How strange."

"I like it."

"Strange." She continued reading over Gwydion's shoulder, him drinking in the soft sound of her words, the soft air of her warm breath on his ear.

"See the words of this verse;
study the texts of old.
Pay attention you people;
listen well, too, of angels told.
All who have been sent,
and spirits risen from the dead.
I alone exist with none to judge me,
you should feel no dread, while,
seductive sins abound, and deeds without restraint,
disgraceful desires and fleeting pleasures,
followed and embraced.
Until sated and rejected,
all can become sober and rise up to their resting place,
there they will me find, and enter into grace.
And live and not die again."

He quietly folded the piece of copy paper and slipped it back into his back pocket. And the two of them sat in quiet silence for some time. Until they heard noise overhead and Gwydion knew he would make waves if he wasn't there in time to have dinner with the rest of them.

"What do you do in that closet, anyway?" asked his mother. He just shrugged his shoulders and sat quietly at the table. His mother and grandmother shared a look but said nothing and began serving some dinner.

After some time, Antony said, "We are going out for a while.

There is a reception for one of the dignitaries that just showed up. Late contingent from Buenes Aires." He looked at Gwydion, somehow thinking he would want to go. But got no reaction."Well, OK, then we get ready in a few minutes. Take care of yourself. We wont be gone long. It's already late."

Which left Gwydion alone for the evening to find something to do. Out back by the canal was his usual haunt these evenings if he could sneak away. It was quiet and dark, and perfect for him to get away and be outside. And besides he was not really breaking the rules, was he?

He took a book and a tiny torch with him, blocked the door open with a tiny rock and sat out in the gloom against the stones of the ancient apartment wall and read his novel with the soft shushing of the water and the thumping of the small boat as background music.

Once he was deep into concentration of his book, he did not notice the dark form rise slowly out of the boat. The shadow jumped to the sidewalk edging the canal and begin to walk toward Gwydion. He looked up just in time to see the dark shape jump at him. And then all went dark.

# Chapter 29.
# the Island

Stop moving!", said the quiet voice in Egyptian.

Gwydion felt muffled by something over his face and he felt the rocking of the small craft under him. He felt dizzy and disoriented. But he knew he was not on land anymore.

He must have moaned because the other voice said, "Shut up, complainer!" and a foot kicked him in the side. "We will get to where we are going soon enough, little man."

Gwydion relaxed a little, and tried to not draw attention to himself. What was that smell? And that horrid taste in his mouth? Maybe he threw up. Or the other boy had drugged him with something. And the back of his head hurt. And when he tried to touch it, he realized his hands were bound.

Then he realized with terror that if they were to capsize, he would be unable to swim. And would drown with out a chance.

The boat clunked against something hard and jolted Gwydion awake. He must have been sleeping for a while and crust had formed on his face inside the stinky burlap bag. His hands were raw from the rough ropes and his feet. Well, he couldn't feel his feet. And the air had gotten cold. He could feel it on his wrists and his neck and his back where his coat and shirt and coat had ridden up. There was a little water at the bottom of the small boat and it had soaked into his clothes and he was shivering.

His captor let out a sigh of relief as the reached the shores of what ever destination this was. He grunted as he secured some ropes and bent over to hoist his prisoner up off the bottom of the boat.

"Come on sleepy bastard. We go meet your maker now." he said gruffly. He pulled off the tape around Gwydion's ankles and hoisted him to his feet in the rocking boat. Being moored by a rope only helped a little to keep it steady and Gwydion lost his footing several times before his captor was able to maneuver him off the boat onto shore. Gwydion fell flat on his face when his feet touched the tarmac, his cheek landed in some gravel and dirt there and he could feel his skin peel away.

"Get up," was the rejoinder to this move, and a swift kick to his kidneys. He scrambled to his feet, and wobbled to stay upright.

"This way," and a yank on his tethered arms, sending jolts of fresh pain into his wrists and up his arms.

The two of them scrambled up a slight incline of gravel with hard tarmac underneath, and Gwydion got the impression of a place out of use, of untidiness and disarray. Weeds clutched at his bare ankles and the cuffs of his wet pants. *Good god, where are we*, he thought to himself. He could hear soft toots of ships out on the water and the sound of the lapping of waves against what ever they had disembarked upon, which grew softer and more quiet as they ventured further up the incline.

There was a grunt and a slight decrease in speed of his captor and the sound changed, echoed off a hard surface in front of them, and Gwydion knew they had reached some sort of building. He's taking me in there. It is silent; there are no people here. Not sure if that was a good or a bad thing. Alone with this creature, this hunter. This sick man who had been hunting me for years now. God, he's finally captured me, all that I was running away from for years. It has finally visited me with ropes and sticky plaster. And a really rotten attitude. What did I ever do to deserve this? I dotn even talk to people. I don't even look at people. And yet somehow I have drawn his wrath.

He was shuffled through a doorway with no door and into the interior of some kind of building that echoed mightily every tiny sound. No furniture or upholstery, Gwydion thought. In fact this floor doesn't feel like a floor at all. It feels the same as outside. Like the floor of a barn or dirt yard. And yet I'm inside a hard dwelling. What is this place?

"Right over here, creep," said his captor, "and have a seat right here."

He was spun around and forced into a sitting position and pushed down. And Gwydion felt himself for just a moment flinging backward into space. And jarringly Gwydion's bottom landed on a chair. Quickly more sticky plaster was applied around his wrists and the chair arms. And before he could react, Gwydion's ankles were re-attached with a sticky around the legs of the chair.

"That should hold you, brat."

Gwydion tried his ankles and wrists but they were tight, very tight and they were already hurting and going numb.

I suppose you are wondering why I haven't just killed you yet. As I've been wondering the same thing to myself for a while now."

He rustled with some things that Gwydion could not see for the blindfold over his head. Then all went quiet and footsteps were heard retreating form the room, shoe soles crunching and scuffing on gravel and weeds.

For an eternity Gwydion sat re-breathing his old air inside the hood on his head, and his mind raced with crazy plans for escape. But he was bound too tight, and each time he moved, it seemed the tape dug further into his already bleeding ankles and wrists.

He could hear the footsteps approaching again. Crunch crunch crunch. Then some shuffling and a thud on the ground. Then a zipping noise and some more shuffling. Then a short shuffling and the sharp sound of a match being struck. Then the acrid smell of a match head alight.

Oh God! He thought. He is going to burn me! The animal part of his brain flamed to life. And he began his struggles anew.

"Quit your mewling like some wild animal, you freak. I am not burning you. At least not yet!" and there was a snicker that chilled Gwydion's blood.

There was some shuffling around him, beside behind, beside than in front, and the light had changed, what little of it he could see through the burlap bag. A flickering, like candles. Yes, he had lit candles. In a circle around him.

"Now, I want you to pay attention, freak." His captor squatted in front of him, and breathed in and out noisily a couple times. "I am going to teach you some things. You need to learn to appreciate us. The Word. These ancients of the righteous. You have no respect, you pip squeak."

And Gwydion heard the other boy start to rustle around, kicking off his shoes, then a zipping noise and the sound of a heavy garment dropping to the floor. Then the unbuttoning of his shirt as his captor began to take his clothes off. Gwydion held his breath and prayed it wasn't going to have to be this way.

Then there was more rustling and it sounded to Gwydion like the other boy was wrapping a blanket around himself. Robes. Gwydion visualized black robes of a priest going on this boy in front of him in the candle lit dark. A clinking of chain as he put some type of necklace around his neck.

"Well, now I am ready," he said to the shaking Gwydion. "How about you?" And he laughed at his captive quaking in the chair.

Gwydion felt the other boy's hand on top of his head. And with a yank of the burlap sack and a good chunk of his hair, he whipped the stinking thing off the boy's head.

Gwydion was blinded for a moment, his eyes accustomed to the very dark of the blind fold and now watering in the cold of the night air.

Without preamble the older foreign boy in front of him shot his hands in the air and began to call into the night sky looking down on them from the broken through ceiling of what looked like an old cellar room.

"HEY VAH, HEY YODD!!" he screamed into the night sky above.

Gwydion looked around at the room, and noticed old rusted equipment. Not like a work station, but like old medical equipment, glass shattered, a few wires hanging frayed. This must be the old island village for the insane. There they burned plague victims 400 years ago and made a soil of human ash.

Then his captor began screaming again.

"I request from the original! The virginal spirits of Barbelos. Give me Fore-Knowledge!"

What was he blathering in Latin about? Thought Gwydion to himself. What nonsense was he saying? It sounds kinda like the stuff he had been reading from his grandfather's brief case. But it was just sort of off, not quite right. Like the boy had read it wrong or just made up parts.

The enraptured robed boy swung his gaze down at Gwydion tethered in the chair, and regarded him with is outstretched arms, his hands open to his captive. "Free this heathen from his chains of ignorance!" His spit was praying out in front of him, some of it hitting Gwydion who was disgusted and tried to struggle or tip his chair away from the barrage..

The wild priest's arms shot to the heavens again. "By Christ!! and the Divine Autogenies. I call thee!!"

Gwydion hung his head to keep free of the frothing spit of the impassioned young priest lost in his fantasy of his own religion.

"Relieve this pagan of his wrongful mind. Remove his deamon of ignorance. By the First Archon who used your flame of Luminous Fire to create this ignorous seed." He shouted to the starry sky.

The priest frothed at the corners of his mouth and Gwydion tried not to look. He didn't want to catch whatever this freaked-out person had. Look away; don't be a part of his nightmare.

The young priest in the wrinkled black robes shouted into the candle lit night air, rising motes of old dust into swirls in the candle light. He thrust his robed arms into the air again and shouted, "Hey Yod, Vey Hodd! Remove this deamon and unveil his eyes! Great Yaltobaoth! COME! "

And with that, both boys screamed in agony.

A blood curdling scream that filled the chamber and echoed in the dirty crumbling halls of the old asylum for the deranged. The screams echoed and found comfort in these old halls, where prisoners had lain and rotted in their own filth and personal nightmares. The priest in robes slumped to the dirty floor and continued to scream, his torture mingling with the pain of the ranks of tortured ghosts still haunting these broken halls with their ignominious deaths.

Gwydion slumped in his chair and tried to keep his eyes shut tight and his face away from the sight in front of him: his captor writhed in pain and screamed his bloody screams into the silent night, for none could save him.

And Gwydion heard above him the sound of a thousand wings fluttering in the rafters, as gray doves chose the cool night sky to this chamber of horrors below.

And the wind shook his jacket even after the birds had departed, and the wind came down and surrounded him in a cooling embrace, showering his with dirt and feathers and bird droppings, and dousing the candle flames that surrounded him. The soft flapping continued around them as the air settled and they heard the wing beats and the thump of two feet landing onto the floor, a different kind of bird of prey altogether.

The boy priest twisted and squirmed on the filthy floor in his smoking robes, moaning in pain and bewilderment, as the light of the Deamon's fury poured out of his eyes like liquid amber.

Gwydion fought the urge to look up. He would not regard the torture that was taking place. No, and risk it seeing his innocent gaze and entering his soul. He squinted as tight as he could and dug his chin into his chest to hide his face from the amber fury of the demon torturing his prey; captor now captive. The boy on the floor was moaning in agony and Gwydion heard, no he felt a clarion bell peacefully chime in his mind. And then light hands rested on his shoulders, and a soft cooling sensation moved down his arms to his bloody bonds. And a sweet sound spoke into his ears, a voice he had maybe heard before but he wasn't sure.

"I have come in my Cherubim of Fire of four corners, with each of the eight shapes of stars within. We are only part of the Ekklasia of Angels of the 8th heaven. You call us here to your plane in your foolishness and your impotent rage."

The cool touch moved to his wrists and touched the bonds away.

"I take you now. For our dotage as you have desired it so. And as you age, the seven angels will join and create suffering, lamentation, and bitter weeping, so as your mind will flay from its moors until you are ripe for our harvest at your meager life's end. "

The boy priest on the floor spasmed and flipped flat on his back, ridged with terror and pain. His mouth and eyes unnaturally open to the sky pouring out an amber force of liquid fear and horror, an unearthly roar emitting now from his tormented chest.

Gwydion wrenched his gaze from that horror and hid his face against his shoulder. A cool hand caressed each side of his smooth cheeks. "And you, young chosen boy. You have chosen the unenvious Androgyne, and follow a path in dappled sunlight to the hallows of truth, love and the face of Pistis Sophia. And you will not know it is so, that is was a blessed journey, until the end of your days, in the volition of the arena of testing in this world."

And with a mighty clap of great hands. And the fierce gust of winds from it's mighty dark wings, it was gone.

Gwydion's face hung down to his chest, and sweat dripped from his nose. He knew not for how long he had sat there, in a daze, not asleep, not awake.

The boy priest in his soiled and tattered robes lay in the dirt on the floor in front of him, not moving at all.

He heard a rustling behind him and tried to turn to look, but the pain from his dug-in bonds kept him from moving. The pain was everywhere in his body.

The robes in front of him seemed barely enough to cover a body underneath. But surely his captor must still be there, exhausted by his tormented wake performed on Gwydion, a ritual that seemed to have turned instead on himself.

There was another rustling behind him, and Gwydion thought he surely he was not just imagining it. The rustling came closer and then a soft step. Then another.

"Gwydion?" the soft voice he knew he recognized. From where he couldn't recall right now in his exhausted mind.

"Gwydion?" it repeated softly.

He grunted in response.

A soft hand lit on his shoulder, and he winced from pain and terror of his experience at the hands of this mad man on the floor in front of him.

"I think he might me dead," suggested Gwydion.

"No," said the voice thoughtfully. "Not quite. But deathly, for sure. A very sick boy, for now and forever, I should think."

Gwydion moved away from the touch on his shoulder. "Are you hurt, dear?" she asked.

Her hands moved softly down to his hands and lifted them up. She came around in front of him and moved his feet and pulled the sticky plaster tape off them and threw it to the side.

"We've got to go," said Sophie urgently but quietly. "They are coming!" she whispered harshly.

"Who?" he asked. "Who is coming now?"

"Well, I suppose the police." She paused. "And the others," she added cryptically.

She found his shoes that had come off some how during the ritual and she pushed them back on his feet. "We have to go. Now."

Slowly, and with support from his friend, he rose from the chair and stood up, wobbling just a little. He breathed in hard a couple times to anchor himself back in his body on this earth. Then avoiding the prone bleeding form at their feet, the two of them made their way outside and back down to the shore to the little boat he had been kidnapped and brought here in.

They could see lights and hear a siren coming from the direction of town, of Saint Mark's Square. They quickly embarked the tiny water craft and Sophie started its tiny motor. The motored away just as the other craft were coming around the jetty of rocks that was the circular 'driveway' of this little island of horror.

# Chapter 30.
# Rescue

After they had cleared the small harbor of the tiny prison island, had left the lights and the siren of the police boat hitting the island shore, she found a dark quiet spot in the canal where there were no other boats. Sophie cut the engines and let the boat drift to a shifting halt. She was deathly concerned for Gwydion's injuries. He was just laying there at the bottom of the boat, in a small dark pool of water not moving or making a sound.

Sophie found the small on-board red cross knapsack that was attached under the rail, and dug around and found a small battery torch. She flicked it on and thanked the stars the owner of the boat kept the batteries recharged. She held the beam of light up so she could see Gwydion laying there in the water. She reached out her hand and touched his shoulder, on a part that didn't have any blood on it.

"Gwydion?" she said quietly. He did not stir.

She spoke his name softly again, "Gwydion, are you alright?"

He awoke and moaned a little, and his body stirred just a bit. Inwardly she sighed a bit of relief that he was not dead laying there in the wet.

"Are you OK?" she asked.

He moaned and turned his messed up face toward her. He was a mess, she thought. One eye was closed again, and scrapes and dirt and some blood everywhere. She might not have recognized him if she hadn't known who he was.

"Are you gonna be alright?"

He nodded his head slightly and groaned, "I think so."

"I am going to take you home now. Just sit tight." And with that she started up the motor and began their slow thread through the chop and other lit up boats towards the shore and the canal where his family was staying. It would take some time and the sun was coming. She needed to get out of the shipping channel as fast as this little boat would let her.

Gwydion only felt himself be dragged on his feet and out of that dank building, the gravel crumbling and popping under their feet. When they were clear of the walls, he could hear the clear sound of the water in the deep canal and a couple big boats hoot in the shipping canal.

Then he felt himself be lifted into the air a bit and he felt the bottom of a boat on his side, a little bit of cold water lapping at him. But it was cooling and refreshing after the candles and the wild incantations and the blows to his face and the kicks to his shins. He swore to himself that he was alive and felt a bit of gladness and relief that someone had come and gotten him.

The boat roared to life and sped forward. He heard another boat or two close by and even a siren of some sort. The police? What was happening?

The small boat rocked and bucked rhythmically as it fought the chop in the broad channel. The motion settled Gwydion into the bottom of the boat and he felt the cooling puddle of water start to soak into his clothes. It soothed his bruises and Gwydion felt the terror and fear fade away as he dropped into a slumber.

The motor noise lessened and the speed broke off and Gwydion was shifted so his face was facing the cool sky. He thought he saw some light but his eyes were partly swollen shut, so he was not sure. His vision was far too hazy to focus on anything. Everything, his whole body hurt and he could only half focus on what was going around him. A gentle hand pushed at his shoulder and he faced the light for just a moment. His rescuer. Another guardian angel. He knew he should recognize the voice, but his mind was a jumble. But it was a gentle girl's voice soothing and asking him gentle questions. He knew that voice, didn't he? He smiled and moaned in delirium.

The soft voice called him by his name, told him he was going to be fine. That she would take him home to be with his family now.

"Oh, no, my child," it said quietly. "Do not fight me. I am here to help, but only for a moment."

He struggled to understand the comforting voice. He was reliving the violence of the black robed boy priest of an hour ago and struggled in his delirium against these voices tormenting him over and over.

"No, you will not accept me yet. I know that," the sweet voice said into his delirious mind. "But I will be there to help you pass, when many years to come, it is time for you to join us."

He struggled against these words in his mind. "Nooo," he said quietly, squeezing his eyes tight.

"You have some work to do however. We struggle against forces that would change and destroy what is truth and sacred to all. This is the force we saw tonight. They struggle still, for 2 thousand years they struggle against what was once known, in your innocent entry into this world, as truth from the gods." He was comforted for a moment, then he mind went back to his torture at the hands of the black robed fiend. "Who is that crazy man?" he said to his rescuer.

"He is just a man. A boy. But in his ignorance and desire, he has led these forces into himself. And dragged you into his horror."

Gwydion moaned. She held his head up and said into his face, "The God called to himself is even older than your world. "

Gwydion thought in his mind about the incantation the boy priest had said, "And what was the thing he called down? Black wings and a stench. He used some weird words, not just the Latin and Greek bits."

The soft voice made a small laughing sound and Gwydion felt a sweet breeze lightly scented with a perfume of flowers.

"Oh, yes. In his ignorance he used the word incorrectly, and in reciting it backwards, drew down upon himself an evil demon. An all-pain-giving angel.

And Gwydion realized what she was saying, and the word letters he had used. Yod Heh Vod Yey, he had said it backwards. Hebrew is read right to left! The realization made him smile and it hurt his face.

"These scriptures from long ago are finally ready to be found by your race of mortals. But they must be understood. For 2 thousand years I lay in that bottle with the dreams and wishes of the old carriers of truth. And when it was broken I was released."

Gwydion thought, Scriptures? Broken bottle? The poems in his grandfather's suitcase?

"Who are you?" he thought inside his head, and he tried to open his eyes. But the light was too bright, and there began a humming increasing inside his skull.

"I am the arch Angel SophieL, and I have knowledge of the vining things in the rocks of the hills, and the wind that breathes life into it. And I've come to ask you to help us."

"You must be strong, and not worry yourself of your pursuer. For I say unto your pursuer, let him be confounded who persecute you, Gwydion. And be you not confounded, for he follows his false ideas. Let him fear, and not you. For I am here to take your pain, and register it to he who is more worthy. And he now carries the memory of the torturing angel within ."

She held his head up and her light shone into his face. "And that ignorant fool used our truths unwisely, twisting them into a plan of his own torment. And in doing so rightly pulled into himself a thing that will bring him only pain."

And with that, the light left, the engines roared back to life and the little boat sped quickly through the waning night, into the morning in the ancient city just awakening from a close call with evil.

# Chapter 31.
# Homeward

The heavy drone of the airplane engines rumbled around inside Gwydion's head. He slumped over in his seat and tried to sleep, keeping his eyes closed.

He didn't need anymore guff from anyone about that night. As if it was his fault.

His mother had blamed him for going out into the night and getting beat up. That accusation had shut him up completely. He wasn't about to explain what happened. Not with that kind of accusation.

Will had actually stood up for him. Trying to explain to his mother that it might not be his fault he got beat up. He has a right to walk around and have people leave him alone.

But his mom would have none of it. Too many things have happened and he should just know better.

So, no way was he going to try to explain what happened that night.

Sophie had navigated their way back to the hotel ramp behind the building, unloaded herself and Gwydion onto the walkway and then set the boat adrift to find its way back to its rightful owners. Someone would find it and figure out if it had registration and get it back to the right place. She wasn't about to report it or try to figure out where it was supposed to go, by herself. She did not want to get blamed for any of it. She had got them home, she explained to Gwydion. And that was good enough.

Then Will had argued that they should report the incident to the police. Gwydion fortunately didn't need medical help, but he looked pretty bad; this was obviously assault.

But Antony had argued, against his good judgment, that they needed to let it drop, and just get home. Their plane left the next day, as it was the end of the convention. And if they reported it to the police, they would have to stick around longer and file reports and give statements, and on and on.

They all opted to just go home and call it an experience. And everyone ignored that it was Gwydion was bearing more than a little bit of pain silently. But inside Gwydion knew that his guardian angel that had taken away most of it with her rescue that night. And he felt perversely strong in his silence among his family.

They had scanned the newspapers the next day to see if there was anything there about a fight or accident that Gwydion might have been involved in. But the only thing they saw was a small piece about a police raid on what was thought to be a Satanic group performing a ritual on the abandoned Island of Poveglia. But there were no arrests mentioned.

"I've heard of that place," said Will Smithershins to the Jacobs family. "Its an old insane asylum on the 7 acre island way out in the lagoon. Hasn't been used in like 20 years. And its said the dirt there is made up of 50% ash from the bubonic plague victims that were burned there 4, 500 years ago. And the Doctor of the asylum was said to have been killed in revenge by the ghosts of the inmates that died there, tortured by his illegal use of a power drill for lobotomies. Its all hear-say. But that's the story.

And they want to keep it hush because they are trying to sell the island for a resort site."

"Perfect," quipped Mags. "If it weren't for the ghosts."

"Oh, no," said Bethany. "That sounds perfect for some American interest. The fact it's haunted will be a public draw."

"*The Haunted Hotel*," said Mags in a foolish spooky voice. And Antony and Will laughed.

But Bethany just folded her arms across her chest. She was thinking about the haunted Island, and the Satanic Rite, and Gwydion coming home early the next morning looking worse than being dragged in by the cat.

But all through their day of packing up, his mother still simmered. And Gwydion found himself avoiding interaction with anyone.

So when they boarded the plane the next morning, they were happy to be going home, but they acted somber at their mixed experiences abroad. Once on the plane, when they were finally aloft, he had gone and found a quiet seat somewhere else on the plane alone. He was embarrassed and didn't want to talk to anyone.

So he plugged in his ear buds, got out a book, and shut everything else out for the duration of the flight.

Somewhere in the middle of the Atlantic, "Where's Gwydion?" asked Mags of her mother.

"He's parked himself somewhere else on the plane," his grandmother answered.

"I guess that's just as well. I don't even want to talk to him. He is so resistant," Mags shifted with discomfort in her seat. "

And all that stuff he was saying the other night? When he came in all beat up. What kinda nonsense lies was all that?"

"You know he has a great imagination," answered Bethany. "Maybe he thought he was the hero of some story.

But those cuts and bruises weren't make-believe. They're undeniably real."

"What do you think happened?" asked Mags.

"He obviously got beat up. But I don't know. Maybe that wrong crowd of drinking kids like the other night before," speculated Bethany. She was not going to discuss her irrational fears about a haunted island and that silly report of a Satanic cult ritual. There couldn't be any possible connection to her grandson's brutal attack. Could there? He'd obviously just gotten in a fight.

"He's always avoided trouble before," Mags groaned. Then added, "But what was that stuff about a girl? Somebody rescued him?"

"He called those kids that night his 'guardian angels'," answered Bethany.

"No, last night. He said something about a girl named Sophia? You didn't catch that?" asked Gwydion's mother.

As far as Bethany was concerned, that stuff about a guardian angel and a girl named Sophie was just a made-up story. *That* was not going to be discussed. Her little grandson was going to safe and sound once they got him back to the states.

"There's no girl named Sophia that I know of," she answered. "Back home or here in Italy." She patted her daughter's knee and added, "He'll be fine. It's just a story. You know what a great imagination he has."

# Chapter 32.
# Imprisoned

They had not been able to return by aeroplane from Europe; they had had to take a slow cargo ship back to Buenes Aires. This trip had not been comfortable for any of them. Slow and cold. But was worst for him for sure, nailed up in that crate and labeled as exotic animal so people would keep a safe distance.

But he was alive. And with time they would dig into the old texts the boy had been translating to try to find the ceremony to reverse what had been done. To try to free his tortured soul from what ever deamon had been summoned from the depths of some flaming hell.

Father Micheal hated coming down here, but someone had to feed and clean the poor wretch.

Deep in the dank crypts of an old church, an old stone church built 500 years before, on the bloody backs of enslaved natives, in the sepulchral darkness grown thick with time and imprisoned pain, a twisted figure screamed in the dark, his eyes crossed, tortured, burning from within, the fires from hell.

Book 6

# The Abduction

NM Reed

# Prologue

On his death bed....

Antony was satisfied with the life he had led. There had been many adventures. And, he chuckled, some close calls, as he recalled the rage and violence he had received from some of his colleagues when they were faced with the new and perhaps terrifying concepts found in those ancient texts.

And suddenly the memory of a long ago dream popped into his head. One of his grandchild before he was born, the baby boy calling for him from within the smoke and fire of a long ago nightmare. And Antony instantly saw now the meaning of that dream here in his last days of his life.

He leaned over and reached the pen and paper pad from the small bedside table and began a note for his wife of many years, Bethany, giving her some final instructions about some boxes he had been keeping for his grandson, his voice now gone from the cancer that had invaded his throat, the doctors said, from too many years of smoking that infernal pipe.

But what a convoluted trip it had been, he pondered. He had started his post graduate studies believing himself a firm Atheist, poopooing the Bible and its adherents. But in the course of studying its origins he had come, not to a greater affiliation with Christianity and its god, but to a greater understanding of the scholars and holy people who had created them with their written works. As the advent of Christian thought had caused an apocalypse of mind, which then buried the classical Roman world of government, science and philosophy, so was his new understanding an apocalypse of thought in his own life and perhaps to the world around him, which now seemed so bereft of any deep understanding of the basic principles of life.

And he realized that the small plaintive voice in his long ago dream was that of his future grandson, Gwydion, egging his grandfather to follow, to keep up on a path that Antony was afraid to follow, but that Gwydion, in his innocent wonderment of the mysteries of life, plunged gleefully headlong into.

# Chapter 1.
# Wild Lands

The sun was high and burned in the sky like a rogue star. The soft sounds of the horses hooves crunching on the rocks underfoot had lulled the boy to sleep. And he awoke to the sound of Sheridan's voice riding next to him.

"Are you even awake, Rocky?" She asked.

"Hmmm..." He mumbled as he lifted his chin off his chest from the sleeping position and looked ahead at the trail. He looked ahead at the red rocks poking out of the ground, like the only thing that could grow there. And in most places around here it was. This landscape looked most definitely like the surface of the moon. But he thought it was beautiful, desolate, lonely, and pretty much devoid of people. Which suited him just fine. And Sheridan here riding beside him thrown into the mix wasn't such a bad deal either.

But the sun beat down and the top of his hat must've been 200 degrees. Thankfully he kept it firmly strapped onto his head whenever he went outside. The sun was brutal, the sky mostly cloudless on most days. And he felt that living out here in the wild lands, your hat could become your best friend.

"Do you think will find them?" She asked him.

"Hmmm..." He just said again, his shoulders and hips swaying to the movement of the horse picking his way across the rocks.

"They said they was out here," she said dubiously. "But I don't see nothing but rocks and sagebrush."

He chuckled under his breath.

They rode some time in quiet, birds flitting from underfoot in the rocks. Soon she said, "We have a few hours before sunset. So let's ride a little further around past the outside watering hole, and will still have enough time to circle back around the ranch."

Again, he just said, "Hmmm..."

And they continued on down the trail side-by-side riding in the old worn jeep tracks that could possibly have been hundred and 50 years old. Still visible in the rocks from the time when the first settlers ventured westward from Utah and Colorado towards the promise of the gold and silver mines in California. And took a chance to cross the wasteland of Nevada, where many of them lost their lives, their dreams floating away in a burst of hot Nevada wind and moon dust.

As they approached a climb up a black hill, the shale dirt sliding downhill behind each step of the horse's hooves, Rocky lifted his arm slightly and pointed with his index finger and a tilt of his chin, and Sheridan saw it too. Just a hint of dust rising up from just beyond the hilltop.

"Wonder what that could be? Might be them."

"Maybe," was all he said.

The horses' ears flicked forward, maybe they knew something more than the riders did. Perhaps it was their sixth sense, knowing where others of their kind were hiding. They were herd animals after all. Or maybe their ears were better and sharper than their riders' kind, and could pick up the sounds they were so familiar with.

But as the two riders crested the black hill they could see the small band of horses stomp at flies and kick up dust and dipping their muzzles in a big tank of shimmering blue water.

Rocky pulled up his horse with a quiet 'whoa', and Sheridan's horse did the same without her asking. "Well, look'ee that!" She said dryly. Rocky grunted in agreement.

"I just hope Cinnamon is there with them."

They stood and watched a small band of feral horses kicking up dust in the canyon below. They hadn't seen the riders yet and hadn't smelled them yet either because fortunately the humans had been approaching from downwind. Otherwise the wild animals would flee from just the smell'a humans. They needed to get down among them and try to cut free from the herd their domestic mare that had gotten loose the day before. She was missing, probably coming into season, and smelled the wild horses and broke free of her corral. Nothing new for living out here. Just another of the many chores, the occasional problem that cropped up.

"Well, let's do it," was all he said. They loosened their lariat's from the saddle, untying the latigo straps on the right side in front of the pommel, and nudged their horses forward on down the black hill, towards the small band. Far down below, the lead mare picked up the sound, raised her head, pricked her ears and spotted the moving objects up on the black hillside. And she let out a whistle to chill the bones any man, and set that band to running. The two mounted horses immediately set chase. They knew what their job was, they had done this before and they were soon eating the dust of a band wild horses as they fled across the Silver Range.

In the noise and dust Sheridan pointed, and Rocky saw Cinnamon galloping with the rest. And they edged their horses over closer to where she was. Cinnamon must've known ; she saw them in hot pursuit behind her and her pace slowed. She knew personally the horses Jet and Tommy, and nickered softly and slowed her pace down to join the other two domestic houses. Perhaps she'd had her fun, and perhaps she needed a good night's sleep in a barn and domestic hay and grain fed her. And so Cinnamon turned with the other two horses as the three horses and two riders turned towards home. They slowed to a walk as the feral horses fled in a cloud of dust over the further rise of the rocky hills.

"Now Cinnamon," said Sheridan to her mare. "Where have you been, girl?"

They heard a shrill cry behind them and they turned in their saddles to see where the wild horses had fled. And as the dust was settling they could see the silhouette at the top of the rise of one horse that hadn't followed the others. Mane and tail streaming in the wind, this black silhouette let out a shrill scream that Cinnamon answered with her own knicker. Rocky smiled and chuckled and gave Cinnamon the little swap on the rump with his coiled riata, and Sheridan said, laughing, "yeah, he's handsome, but let's get on home old girl."

They rode in companionable silence for quite some time, heading into the setting sun west towards the ranch. "Mark your calendar," said Rocky.

Sheridan laughed. "You gonna give us little Mustang colt next year, huh Cinnamon?" Cinnamon shook her mane and snorted a half-whinny and started cantering down the hill towards home.

# Chapter 2.
# Morning

Big chunks of fur were coming out in the comb. "I guess it must be spring time, Cinnamon," said Sheridan softly to her horse, and the mare nickered softly. She stroked the multi-colored fur that up close looked like lots of different colors of hair, but far away the mare looked pink, hence her name Cinnamon. She stroked her slick neck and the mare turned her head and nuzzled Sheridan's arm, wiping some dirt and horse snot on it. It seemed to Sheridan that Cinnamon always knew what she was talking about. Almost like the horse knew English.

"What do you want to do today, 'ol girl?" she asked her. Cinnamon flipped her mane back and looked Sheridan in the eye. What was the old mare trying to tell her. Her adventures over the last few days? Who was that handsome stallion they had seen on the ridge? Obviously a wild horse, but I haven't seen him around before, she thought to herself. The feral horses roamed far and wide, always on the look out for patches of edible grass here and there. It grew sparsely so they were always on the move. And the bands were usually small, and the stallions seemed to change frequently, with the younger ones that survived the battles among themselves, going and fighting the older stallions to the death, stealing the bands of mares and foals from them.

But Sheridan was glad to have her mare back. It was an awful feeling to come and find an empty paddock. The horses were often allowed to roam during the day, but they always came back in the evenings for some hay and grain and a safe place to sleep, away from the rattlesnakes and coyotes at night. Cinnamon must have smelled or heard the other horses out there.

Just then she heard a knock near her on the barn wall, and Sheridan looked up from combing her mare's mane. And just then Rocky rounded the corner with a smile.

"My girls," he said sweetly. "Cinnamon has had her grain, but I wonder if my other girl would like some coffee?" He held up a plastic and aluminum can-like glass with a plastic lid on it. The only way to bring coffee out to the barn. Otherwise it got cold in a minute. And coffee had to be hot.

They sat down on the plastic chairs in the shade against the wall that faced out into the desert canyon. As usual it was already getting hot out here. This was a desert, and the temperatures would swing wildly from morning to night, as much as 50 or 60 degrees sometimes. There simply was not enough moisture in the air to hold the warmth of the day when the sun finally went down.

"I trust you slept well," he said.

"Ya, I'd been so worried about Cinnamon that I had to come out and see her. Her fur is shedding like crazy."

"Well, that's to be expected," answered Rocky. They sipped coffee in silence for a few minutes, listening to the dusty bird song in the morning air.

"I had this dream last night, maybe that woke me up this morning, thinking about that," said Sheridan. They often talked about dreams in the morning, even though neither of them were really morning people. But on a ranch, early was usually the name of the day.

Sleeping in was just sometimes impossible with the ducks and the birds and often the horses going off just before sunrise.

He turned and looked at her. "Really? What about?"

"The skeleton of a friend. Why do I have to dream about an old friend being a skeleton?"

'Someone you know?"

"Used to know. Haven't seen in a while."

"Maybe you should call. See if she's OK." he suggested.

"Naw. No interest. Really don't care. Which is why its weird I dreamed about him."

"Hostile feelings?"

"Ya, maybe that's it. He was always trying to make something that wasnt there. And then this other guy, sort of an ex-boyfriend, told me I should just go have this man's love-child, he called it."

"Oh, so you were an item?' he asked.

"Not as far as I was concerned. But this guy has fantasies I guess. And I told him I didn't even want children. It felt like some kind of slave scam." She tuned and looked at Rocky. "I just don't get the presumptions of people. I mean, why push this having a child thing on me? But I know that's not it. They were just in their own weird head space, which had nothing to do with me."

"They both wanted you and neither of them could, so they made up stories between themselves to entertain themselves and try to confound you," Rocky said, turning toward her again and smiling.

It was a compliment, and yet probably just perfect. Untangling her from other people's nonsense. She smiled at him and said, "Probably that."

"Then there was this other thing, this sheep thing." she said after a minute. "I've worked here for Mr. Mac Gruder for all my life, my dad used to live here. But for a couple summers, I went away to live with friends. Up to Oregon on a small sheep ranch. I lived in a camper out in the barn which was just fine with me. But the lady had lots of animals and this little flock of sheep, beautiful sheep with colored fur, I mean fleece, that she sheered from the animals and sold for good money."

He just looked at her and sipped his coffee. "I was working on making some furniture pieces in the barn, and one day I decided to go for a hike and check out the sheep pasture. It was rather neglected, I could tell, and the thistles were growing deep and thick. The pasture you could tell had been hacked out of the wilderness of the forest, and when I hiked to the far side of the paddock, it ended in a fenced off forest so thick I couldn't have climbed through it anyway. There was a nice little old barn in the middle, and I went inside. It was sectioned off in areas of pens I could tell for holding the sheep, sheering them and what not, like cattle. But the fences were so short, and I realized how small sheep were in comparison to cows. I walked around in there and one pen had a big pile of fleeces. They wrap and tie them, each one in a bundle." She stopped and sipped her coffee. "Now I remember this because it was vivid and maybe because I've thought about it a lot later, because of what the lady said to me later. I went into a little paddock, and turned and shut the tiny gate behind me. Then I left and went back to work. A couple days later the lady confronted me and asked me if I had gone out into the barn. Sure I had, but I felt guilty, like maybe I wasn't supposed to be doing that. I was a good kid and the youngest in my family, and I think I always got blamed for stuff. Maybe I did stuff wrong, but every kid does. But its that my older brother and sister tattled on me all the time. But this lady said the sheep got out and into all the fleece and kicked it around and made a mess. I swear I shut that gate, but I was too afraid at the time to defend myself so I think I got blamed for it."

"Oh well," said Rocky. "If all that expensive fleece was just sitting out there, maybe she wasn't taking very good care of her business."

Sheridan just looked at him. "You know you are right. She said later that she should get out of the business. Her sheep had gotten eaten by predators, and she said, if she cant take care of her flock, maybe she shouldn't have one. Some biblical reference I think." Rocky smiled at that.

" But, you know, after all these years, I think I figured something out. She had 3 daughters. And now I see that they were jealous of me, of the attention their mother gave to me while I was there. And I wonder, I just wonder, is it possible one of the girls saw me go out there and then she went out later and opened the gate and put some food in to get the sheep to go in a stomp the fleece around, and then blame it on me. Like I am a ranch girl; always always shut the gates. Those girls never had anything to do with the sheep, hated them. Is it possible that someone could think that way, be destructive enough to set that up, willfully destroy their mother's property to get me in trouble, because of their jealousy? "

Rocky looked over into her eyes and saw her pain there.

"Is it even possible, how can people think that way?"

"I don't know," he said and sat back and sipped his coffee from his travel mug.

"The last time I tried to call her, they never answered or called me back. I was actually thinking of getting sheep. But it just kinda cooled my jets thinking about that. The 3 girls are all fancy people now, a lawyer, a doctor and a teacher. That timeline shows the psychosis of the family: the eldest became a lawyer to get revenge and justice; the next became a doctor, still very important but more on a healthy help-people campaign; the youngest just a lowly teacher: the family has lost their extreme drive to excel and prove themselves." She sat back and sipped her coffee and listened to her mare stomp some flies just waking up in the morning warmth, soon to be relegated to the deep shade during the heat of the day. "Thing is, the father was kicked out of the house soon after I was there. The mom said that I told her to get rid of him. He went a lived with a mistress whom he soon married up in the fancy city. He was a doctor. I don't remember ever saying a thing. I was just a kid. How can she blame her choices on me? But I can imagine the daughters did." Rocky just shook his head a little and gazed out at the barren pasture of sage grass.

"Some things are happening up at the other house today." He turned to her and added, putting his hand on her knee, "Feel like taking another ride today?"

She smiled and said, "We ride almost everyday, silly."

"Just thought I'd make it feel like a choice."

"What's happening up there?"

"Some calves and stuff."

"Sounds like fun."

# Chapter 3.
# Branding

The acrid smell of burning hair hung in the smoke as the small group working in the sun. Not even the tiniest breeze stirred the air this morning on this desert land of rock and lizards.

They had gotten up early, saddled the horses and ridden over to Eldred's ranch. Doc Branson was there, and work had already commenced by the time the young couple had reached the holding pen. Black shadows reached across the sand westward as the sun struggled over the tops of the black peaks. There was no hollering or yelling, just a few grunts from the men and the animals alike as the lowly work took place in a crowded area inside the holding pen. A couple of people were on their horses, saddled with the big saddle, with the ropes stretching out in front of them connected to their quarry between. The calf mewled plaintively, and the hissing of the branding iron could be heard and the plaintive cry turned into a bellow of terror and pain.

Rocky hated this part. He had been helping on the ranches for a few years now. But never would he get used to this part of processing these animals in order for them to be allowed to graze the wild range lands. They had to be branded and ear tagged; it's just what had to happen in order for them to be safe from rustlers. It had been done this way for 150 years out here on this desert graze land, and probably for thousands of years previous in order to mark these animals with their rightful ownership.

But Rocky would never get used to this process of working cattle. He would help; but he was never going to like it.

Sheridan was an old hand. Her father had owned the ranch they were now living on and she had inherited it when he had finally succumbed to cancer, just a few years after his wife, Sheridan's mother, had died in a car accident, when the drunk had broadsided her downtown after he'd left the saloon midday with too many drinks on his tab. And her father didn't last much longer after that. So Sheridan had inherited the place and supported herself as a helping hand with the neighboring ranches, earning some badly needed cash to pay for modern expenses of living in the wilderness. There was no line electricity out to the house, and the water was pumped when the generator was started, and held in a large holding tank on the rise. Eldred's ranch, and Dr. Branson's too, were closer into town than the main highway, and both sported the fine new conveniences of local electricity wiring, and well pump that ran on the same, and it was rumored that Dr. Branson's house even had cable from the city. But that may have been just a myth.

Sheridan took the coiled rope off the side of her saddle, stepped her horse up to the gate, pulled the lever and cantilevered her horse's body through the opening. He did have to spin on a fore-hoof, shut the gate and pushed the lever back in place, never getting off her horse, and locked the gate. Rocky watched with admiration and said to himself, "Yup, old hand, she is." He admired her ease with handling that big bay quarter horse Mustang gelding of hers. She seemed more comfortable in the saddle than she did on foot.

As he watched, she walked old Jimmy around the perimeter of that old black corral, and joined another leather clad Caballero on the other side.

They walked their horses to a cluster of doggies, pointed and picked one out, she threw her lariat at the hind end of the calf, and he threw his at the other end and they secured him between the two horses. It always amazed Rocky how the two horses faced each other, and gently backed up until the ropes were taught. The calf then loses his balance and drops to the ground, bellowing something terrible. The riders would then dismount their horses, and one of them, the heeler usually, would walk towards the calf and hogtie 3 feet together, the ones that didn't have a rope around it, and secured with a clove hitch with a loop that could be untied quickly when the job was done. One of the hands would walk over with an ear tag, bend down and snap it through the calf's flap of an ear, and turn to the secretary keeping notes, who would enter the number and the calf description, male or female, bull calf or heifer. The branding hand would then race over with red-hot branding iron with the ranches logo in cast-iron on one end and a handle on the other, and press this instrument of torture against the calf in the proper position on his flank or ribs. And the calf would scream, and Rocky hated it.

But for that little calf, if it was a male, the worst was yet to come. Yet another ranch hand would come with his pocket knife, sharpened ultra sharp just for that day, reach between them poor little critters back legs, pinch the scrotum between forefinger and thumb, and slice through clean about an inch. Then with that same hand he would squeeze out the two small underdeveloped testicles and slice them off with a clean slice and jerk. And toss them over the fence to the dogs happily waiting.

Rocky had seen it all before. But never was he going to get used to that. He preferred to spend his time with the horses. His life here was about the horses. He knew he had a gift for that. It was why he stayed on these years. He had not grown up in the mountains, working animals in the dust. But since his time in that program, the one where they sent young boys who had gotten in trouble, to work hard, and learn some skills, and perhaps be tempered through injury and hardship, he had decided civilization was no longer for him. So he stayed on.

And when he met Sheridan, that time at the grocery store, when he was trusted to run errands, it was instant, that they liked each other. Instant. And he decided when he got out from his term of service, he would find her and see if they could make something of it. She was in complete agreement and they fell in together into an easy partnership. Two young people, alone, following a hardship in each of their lives. And they fell into a fairly quiet companionship out in the mountains, where Rocky could continue to practice the skills that he'd been learning in the program, where he had found that he had an aptitude for the handling of wild horses.

The calf screamed and he was jerked back to the moment and watched as Sheridan pulled the loop and the two lariats loose, and the calf laid there in daze for a moment, till she patted it on it's belly and it jumped up and wobbled off. She shot him a glance, and she could see that he was pale and disapproving, but holding it in. She knew he would help with Roundup and run back, but never with this messy part. She smiled at him the tiniest of smiles, she knew what he was feeling, and appreciated his distaste for this process, but she couldn't know that there was more to it than just that.

She walked back her rope, coiling it with the dust falling off it, back to Jimmy and mounted on the wrong side, and undallied the lariat from the big horn of her saddle. She smiled at him again, wheeled her big gelding. Then her and the other big cowboy rode over to select another calf. This went on for quite some time, there were 27 little calves, all about three or four weeks old, for them to do and finish. Rocky helped walk a small batch of the finished calves out the big gate into a smaller holding pen while the hand shut the gate behind him and his horse. Then another hand opened the outer gate and Rocky walked the handful of calves out into the open where their mothers were waiting, and crying, for their babies. The Calves quickly found their mothers and began whacking their fore heads on the milk bags for attention and a snack of reassurance.

# Chapter 4.
# Wakeful

Later that night she found him in the barn quietly stroking his mare's neck. This was a wild animal he had caught off the range and was taming for his own. Not many people could do that, and Sheridan stood and watched in wonder at his quiet movements that were being accepted by the wild horse standing in the stall.

He seemed to sense her and looked up at her down the lane of the dark barn. "I think I can probably ride her soon," he said to her, even though she hadn't asked.

She watched him as he stroked her fur, his hands running smoothly down the direction of the hair laying against the mares smooth flanks. He spoke quietly and even hummed a little bit of a tune now and then. She said nothing, just backed up a step and took in his methods.

He seemed to pause in his progress, and he turned and untied the rope around the metal loop attached to the barn pole. He began to lead the horse out of the barn in the back, to the first catch pen. Sheridan followed after a few moments.

When they entered the sunshine out the back of the barn, she had to pause for a moment to get her bearings and let her eyes adjust. Rocky shut the gate behind him and the mare and Sheridan stopped at it and leaned on the rails of the gate, and watched him unsnap the lead. He coiled the rope and held it up in the air, which startled the young mare just a little and she trotted to the rails of the round pen. Rocky walked to the middle and held the rope in the air, all the time facing the young mare, who was trotting at the rails and looking back and forth around her. When the mare was not looking at him, Rocky would step a step closer to her. When she looked over at him, he slowed and stepped back. Every few minutes he would close the space and the horse would look at him and stop, and then change directions.

Finally after about 20 minutes of this dance, the horse looked at Rocky and turned her shoulder, and Rocky stepped back and the mare slid to a stop and turned toward him to face him directly on. They both paused for a second, then Rocky murmured under his breath and stepped back one step, and the young mare walked up to him, her ears pricked and her eyes bright.

Sheridan watched in wonder at this non-verbal communication, as she stepped back out of the way and let them come through the gate again.

After Rocky had brushed the horse again, and put her back in her cool stall, finally Sheridan ventured to ask a question. She had been unwilling to break the magical silence before, while he was working with the wild animal. But now she asked, "How did you learn to do that?"

Rocky turned to her and asked, "What?"

"That with the wild horse. Like it was eating out of your hand."

"I don't know. It just comes naturally."

"No way that is all natural. You must have learned that somewhere."

"At the boy's ranch. You know that. I was there a year and a half."

"Well, ya. But did they teach that there?"

"We rounded up the wild horses for the BLM. We did tons of ranch work, and some of us even got to break horses. Some of the boys loved bucking out the wildest ones. They liked getting thrown in the dirt. It was some kind of macho thing." They walked for a moment down the dark alley way of the pole barn. "But I hated that part. It felt like violence to me. They used to make fun of me how I could go and catch the wildest of them. I would talk to the babies and they would come up and sniff me. And those guys used to make fun of me. Call me Rock Head and stuff. But I learned from those colts. They taught me something everyday. I cant really describe it, but every day working with those wild animals, I learned something about myself that I would never have learned in the society of men. I stayed away from those guys. And the teachers gave me things to do sometimes. We got a few of the wild horses and we trained them up and sold them to people. Not ranches; they broke their own wild horses. They just come in and get caught sometimes. But sometimes I think those aren't wild horses at all. But somebody's escaped horses gone feral, and they decide to go back to civilization."

Sheridan just nodded her head and hummed assent, and watched her dusty boots on the hard packed ground of the barn. He continued, "I got this one horse I named Sugar Pop. Such a sweet little mare, colored like sugar on toast, brown and white. She was a wild little baby that came in and I tamed her. She even smelled like sugar." His voice caught and she looked into her face. "She had an accident. She didn't make it." His face closed down and she wondered at that, what the story must be behind there

"What happened?" she looked him in the face.

"The other boys got jealous and they tired her up out in the pasture on a hot day. She fell on the rope and strangled. I wanted to...I wanted to...kill those guys. That was it for me."

"That's awful, Rocky. People can be so cruel."

"Ya, well, they got theirs too."

"Huh?"

"There were accidents among the boys too. The place got shut down because of it. Sad really, because it did a lot of good, both wild horses and the boys. I think they were helped by such a hardship program. But the state thought that boys dying was not good public relations. Although those 2 guys did deserve to die, the way they treated horses. I think some people are just created mean and cruel."

"Ya, Maybe," she said. "But you aren't. You are amazing sweet to that mare. "

"Ya, well, I don't know about that."

# Chapter 5.

# Convicted

They were making dinner later that night, and the steam was building up in the kitchen.

Ah, the weekend. There was always things to do on the weekend. But it seemed to Rocky that the weekends were just mellower for some reason. Maybe the rest of humanity was not so stressed out, and he could simply feel it in the air waves. He bent over the stove and looked at the water in the kettle. Almost boiling. Make some mint tea, cool off after a hot day and read a book. Sheridan was in the living room fluffing some pillows, making herself comfortable on the couch. He came in with two steaming mugs of homegrown mint tea and set them on the knee-breaker coffee table.

As he bent down and set the mugs on the short table, he clipped his little toe on the short curved leg of it. "I hate that coffee table," he said.

"I know you do, honey," Sheridan said. "That's why we keep it around. No really, it is nice to have in front of the couch, isn't it?"

"Ya, right, until I crack my knee on it again, then it goes in the wood pile."

"Or attack it with a hammer again." She laughed.

"I did not!"

"Yes, you did! Right there!" she pointed to a perfect hammer-head shaped hole in the frame.

"Ya, well it shouldn't have jumped out and bruised my knee!" he said in defense.

"Stupid coffee table, getting in your way!"

He sat down with a moan next to her on the couch.

"Watcha' readin'?" he asked.

"Just some crappy murder mystery. It's fun."

"Ya, me too. This one is a supernatural thriller."

"Oh, really? Maybe we could switch when we're done?"

"OK," he said. "No biggie. I just picked it up at the library last time. They have the free books outside."

"They aren't free," she said. "You have to put money in the drop box."

"Oh, I do," he said. "It's like 50 cents for paper backs, and a dollar for a hard back. Almost free. Pretty good deal."

"Ya, it is. I think it's cool that they just have the books sitting out there all the time and no one does anything to them. Not like people are going to steal books, though."

"Well, and its like, if they want to steal a book, well, maybe we should let them, if they are hard up enough. Not the worse thing you could be stealing."

Rocky laughed. "That's for sure."

"So you never have told me why you were in that boys camp anyway. I am curious, but you've never told me."

"Its hard to talk about. It was a long time ago. I still don't understand what happened myself."

"Maybe talking it out might help."

"You're not going to criticize me?"

"What? Criticize you? I live with you here don't I? Let you into my house? I think you are wonderful. And after watching you work with that poor little terrified filly today, I think you are the most kind person I know. Such a beautiful heart, you have."

"Well, that's comforting. Because I killed a man."

Sheridan let that hang there. And just looked at him while his face contorted and went through a set of emotions before settling on fear when he finally looked into her face.

And they just looked at each other for a few moments until she said, "why don't you just tell me about it.."

# Chapter 6.
# My Enemy

"I was at school back in California. That was a few years ago. I was in high school and things had settled down and seemed to kind of be going normally for once." He looked at her sitting on the couch next to him. "You know how it is. You went to high school, didn't you?"

She looked away from his face for a moment. "Yeah," she paused and swallowed heavily, "I hated it too."

"Ya, I pretty much hated it, every minute of it. Except for this one friend I had..." He didn't finish the sentence. But continued, "but after we came back from a trip abroad, people kind of left me alone. My mom said that I had grown a couple inches that summer, and I did gain about 30 pounds. So maybe people were kind of afraid of me. Or maybe they didn't recognize me from the year before. I don't know, All I know is things were kind of calm, and then this thing happened."

She looked at him with a concerned look on her face. "What happened to you, Rocky?"

"He found me. I thought it was over, but no. After all that time, somehow he found me. Again."

The boy was waiting outside at the edge of the track and field yard. He felt like he had been waiting forever. He had been waiting for his final opportunity to take back what was his. To take back his dignity and his strength from this little creep that had stolen it from him years before. He couldn't recall exactly what it was, but he could feel the pain burning in his heart, in his mind and in his groin, the centers where all passions originated.

Chains clanged in the dark dank air. A hinge squeaked as a heavy iron door swung just slightly open. "I've come to give you your evening ablutions, my boy. I know you don't understand what is happening. This daemon has possession of your soul and I feel that with the cleansing from God you can be restored, and it can be driven from your body."

The priest bent over the prone figure on the wet floor and touched his shoulder. "Josiah?" he said giving the clamming shoulder a slight shake. "Are you alright?"

An arm swung up and just missed smacking the priest in the face. And the pale body dressed in ripped rags twisted as if in agony and pushed itself into the corner and sat up against the dripping wall. From a pale face tormented with demons peered a young man with dark brown eyes, bearing the mark of Satan, slightly crossed eyes, now blood shot through with red. These wild eyes regarded father Michael with first hatred, then suspicion. And slowly this was replaced with the more civilized emotions of curiosity and understanding

The Father stood watching as his charge changed just slightly into a somewhat human being. He had been watching this gradual transformation grow ever so slightly more pronounced with each session with his prisoner he now called Josiah for lack of a better name. This ragged boy had shown up at the door of the monastery several years ago with just the clothes on his back and a new map of the town clutched in his hand. He had seemed disoriented but harmless and this kind father Micheal had taken him into the monastery and had given him tasks around the place. With time this young man had proven his intelligence and had learned the language that had once been totally foreign to him. Very quickly too, in father Micheal's opinion.

So he had begun tutoring him in religious studies. This was after all a monastery and the boy seemed to have no training in that regard at all. Father Micheal had no idea if the boy had been raised a Catholic or a Christian or what not. But the young man had never offered any information in that regard. So father Micheal did what he does best, and gently brought this young man into the fold.

Rocky continued with his story.

It was after school and I was just hanging out on the track and field. I didn't do sports or band or anything. I just liked being up there and watching all my friends playing ball and stuff. Well, they weren't really my friends, but at least I kinda felt like I belonged. But then *he* was there again. He was always just showing up when I totally did not expect it. Like the year before in Italy."

"You were in Italy?"

"Ya, with my family. They do archaeology and teach and stuff."

"Go on," she said.

"So anyway, he was there. Just standing on the field and this time I saw him right away. I could tell by how he was standing, it was him. Smoking his cigarette. And when he turned and looked right at me, I ran. I ran for the buildings, I figured I could find some people and be protected."

He looked away and breathed audibly for a moment, and Sheridan said nothing. "It was like he had been waiting for me and watching me for a long time. It always seemed that way. Just watching me, with the hair on my neck prickling, and I just couldn't believe it was happening again."

He took a sip of old cola and set it down with a slop in the pool of condensation of the table top. "I ran into the math building and there was no one there. So I ran down into the science building and there was no one there. So I kept going and went into the main building, the new one with the second story and ran down the long hall way and there was absolutely no one there. I couldn't find anyone. Maybe they were all up at the field. It was getting dark and the game was hanging over time. So I stopped in the foyer and listened. I couldn't hear anything but the distant noise of the crowd cheering. And my heart beating in my ears."

His eyes were bloodshot when he looked into hers for just a moment. "Then I heard him in the hall. He was right behind me, he must have flown. He knew right where I was. I hate him."

The tea pot let out a shrill whistle from the kitchen stove and they both jumped. Sheridan hustled to go turn it off and make them some tea. But by the time she got back, the terrified boy was curled in a fetal position on the couch, clutching pillows, sound asleep.

"OH, I really hate that kid. He is the worst," thought the older boy about his nemesis. "I thought for sure I had finished him last time. But he had help! Where did that come from? Out from the sky flew help for this punk kid that just needs to end.

So cute and pretty with his curls and the love of his nauseating family. Well, we'll see about them too. Those kind of lies can only last so long in this rotten world anyway. He'll see that all fall away and then where will he be? In a grave because I'm putting him there! His smug looks and his comfort with those kids in Italy, them helping him get away from me and get back to his family, disgusting. How can he be so lucky?"

He stormed and fumed in his black heart, the boiling rage that had been festering for years, and had landed on this one young boy. It was a rage from somewhere else, from long ago, from abuse and isolation suffered at the hands and filthy ingrown minds of his family in the outback of northern Greater Persia, a place where the new age of technology and internet had not even been imagined yet. A place where hardship and disease would destroy a young man's heart before it even had the chance to know love.

The priest captor had finally let him out of his cell. He had lost the moorings of his last vestiges of sanity after the attack on the island. He had felt his body become inhabited by a dark spirit from somewhere else, someplace infernal and dark, glowing with the red hot flames of hatred. He felt them burning in his chest now, but he had to control them; he had to keep them down. Just for a while just long enough. Enough to get out of here and finish his mission. That boy cannot be allowed to complete his translations. He held the key, and he could not be allowed to continue.

But he was out now. He had fooled this silly old priest. He had actually convinced him that he was going to be OK, going to be a normal boy again. Let me out and I'll show you just how good a boy I can be.

And the lowly priest had believed him. With practice and concentration he had buried his torment deep into his soul, where it smothered and writhed. But he had soothed it with promises of revenge and of fulfilling his mission of snuffing out the boy. But he had to get out of these chains. He had to get away from this simpering priest and get back to where the boy was now languishing in his comfortable American home, with its air conditioning and refrigerators, and television sets and headphones. He knew right where to go too. The dumb kid's wallet had fallen out of his pocket when he escaped the island, and in it had been his student card. His high school library card. So easy to track him down and find him And show him. Oh! He would show him. He would teach them all just how strong he was and just how dedicated he was to the cause. That boy could not be allowed to finish his translations and send his blasphemous ideas back out into the world. The scriptures that had been safely buried for two thousand years, that had been safely locked away with the memories and their own guardian angel for two thousand safe quiet years, while the real religion held sway, with its successful controlling of the minds of these rotten animal aboriginals through the fear and persecutions they deserved.

And now there he was. Just standing there across the field looking at me. He's spotted me. Of course he knows. All victims know they deserve what they get. Why else would they stand there and take it?

The priest had just stood there and taken it too. He thought in his hubris that he was fixing me. He was going to fix his little boy all better, because he was the big strong smart priest who thought he had god behind him. What did he know of god? Silly simpering human. With his vestments, and his pomp and his chants and smoking incense. And that smug loving look on his face. What a fool. I fooled him. And when I stood up over him, after all the humiliations he had subjected my body to, his huffing and puffing and grunting and sweating on me, telling me those sick simpering love poems of god and little boys, when I pressed my thumbs into the soft flesh of his flabby neck, what did he do? He reached out and asked for forgiveness? He said Please? Please what, Old man? Am I your deliverer of your grace? Finally you get to go meet your maker? After all these years of wishing to but not having the strength to do it your self? Just starve yourself or shoot yourself, and end your body's tyranny over your immortal soul. Finally I am the one to release this from the earthly bounds for you. And yes, you say please to me because I am doing it for you. And you think because you call it murder that you will go to heaven and me to hell. Like a last minute's recanting and confessing changes anything. They read from the entire book of your life, weak mortal, the entire book of your choices and misdeeds and you think the minions of judging angels will give you rest because of a moments recanting and regretting your sins?. I know not! I know now for sure you do not get off that easily, old man. So here you are your deliverance.

And I had pressed and held him, while he struggled against me and what he surely wanted, release from these mortal bounds but was too afraid to do for himself. And he struggled against my strength, and he fouled himself in the most vile and animal kinds of ways, even the the way he spilled his seed, as he had done to my mortal body during times of corporeal ecstasy, he fouled himself that way too, and disgusted all the angels and their minions of justice and revenge in the divine firmament.

# Chapter 7.
# Damages

The next morning Rocky had to go into town for supplies. It was a hot morning, promising to be a hot day. A very hot day.

So he left as early as he could, to catch as much of the early morning coolness that was left after the sun actually rose above the mountain.

Which wasn't much. It was probably already almost 90 degrees at 8 in the morning and the steering wheel of the old truck was hot to the touch. He loaded the dogs in the back and started up the old jalopy. It coughed and sputtered to life and Rocky pushed in the clutch, shook the stick into gear, and eased on the gas, and the old truck started to move forward.

He liked this old truck. Simple technology. Hand-crank windows for air-conditioning. And he didn't have to worry about the dogs ruining the interior. The seat could always just be duct taped again. And the gray back window? Well, the windows came pre-slobbered on. He wasn't even sure if they would even clean off at this point.

So they clattered and chuffed on down the road. And really that old dodge ran pretty good once it got warmed up.

He felt he was in no hurry. He rarely was. It was mid-summer, and early in the morning, so that meant animals in the road, and Rocky went along slowly. Why hurry, was his motto anyway. Enjoy the sun coming over the rocks and pines, and listen to the air whistle around the wind wing of the old truck door. They just don't make them like that anymore.

The dogs hung out each side of the pickup bed, one on each side like ornaments, drooling like gargoyles over the side and onto the metal walls of the truck bed. Their tongues hung down and their ears and lips flapped in the wind as he drove. Some said it was a smorgasbord of smells for a dog to drive along in the wind like that.

Whatever. But to Rocky, it sure looked like they were smiling.

Just as he came out of the sun and around a shaded corner he caught movement just off the side of the road, just as a deer jumped the fence to get out of his way. He slowed almost to a stop. Because where there was one deer, there was usually another to follow. And right now at this time of year, the mommas were having their babies. Some mommas were heavy and sluggish with carrying their loads of a soon-to-be-born babes, and some others of them were going slow, waiting for their babies to catch up and figure it all out. They had to all learn about the road, and to stay away or hurry off.

So Rocky sped up after he passed what seemed to be the game trail, the area where the female deer had just crossed. And the dogs ran around the bed of the truck looking for some game quarry to bark at. Mostly they found and ran into one another and then resumed their slobber positions just behind the windows of the cab.

In town he parked in front of the small store and slapped the dogs on the sides of their wet jowls and told them to "Stay Here!". They usually did. They weren't that protective of the truck. But woe to anyone who got too close to them. For they would be treated to a face full of slobbery dog kisses.

When Rocky came back out, those old fool dogs were waiting for him in the back of the truck, just a-slobbering and a panting away. But it was getting hot and it was time to get back with out further ado. The hardware store downstairs below the country grocery store was enough to supply the fence nails Rocky had needed to put back up the wire that the mustangs had pulled off the last time they visited and went through the gate.

Rocky popped a can top and settled in the drive home. It sure was heating up fast today. He was glad he had gotten some work done earlier this morning but maybe wasn't going to feel like it later today, not till later that night.

He turned the corner just as a truck sped past the other way going way too fast, and Rocky cursed fast drivers. As he entered the shade, he saw something up ahead on the road. Some kind of road kill.

"I guess I should stop and drag it off the road." He usually did this, and today alone he had already seen a dead wild turkey and a flattened skunk in the road. He usually stopped and dragged them off the road onto the shoulder or out into the grass. He didn't always stop. Not if they were too hamburgered or dry and flat. But a fresh carcass was bait for the carrion birds and the thing he hated most was when there would be a carcass and a dead bird there too, a big bird who had landed for lunch and then gotten hit by a car for his efforts. Just nature doing its thing. But people didn't care. They just kept on driving. And hoped their car didn't get any blood on it.

Kind of made Rocky sick. So he usually pulled over got out and quick-like pulled the dead animal off the road.

There wasn't much traffic this early, so he drove carefully over the dead thing, not letting his tire run on it again, and stopped just off the road. He quickly got out and walked back to the animal in the road. It wasn't very big and he wasn't sure what it was. A light brown jackrabbit with those big ears.?

But as he approached, to his horror he saw one long leg reach up into the air as if it was trying to get up. But the back end of it he could see was mangled. And then he saw its white spots. As he looked into its tiny face with the huge soft ears, its one eye rolled a little and looked at him, through the just-forming milky veil of death, and it seemed to breathe its last breath and go slack.

He cursed out loud and grabbed the little fawn by the back legs and pulled it off the road onto the gravel. Just as he turned to get back in the truck, a car drove by with some kids in it, going way too fast, and they shouted at him, "Slow down asshole, for killing animals!" Rocky just shook his head sickened by the irony, and made a split second decision. He hoisted the young fawn up into the truck bed with the dogs and clambered back in the drivers side and sped home.

Others might not have understood. But to him it seemed it was an honor to the useless, careless death of the week old baby fawn, to not let it go to waste, rotting on the side of the road, when it could feed his working cattle dogs.

# Chapter 8.
# Revelation

"I just don't know," he shouted at her. "I cant remember so stop trying to get me to talk about it."

"I just want to help you," she answered, sounding just a little too plaintive. She turned away and swore to herself she wouldn't sound whining to him. But she continued quietly, something was lurking in his mind sometimes, like a black shadow would pass over him and he wouldn't speak for hours, days sometimes. "What is it?" She sat down with a thump and a puff of dust onto the couch, folded her arms over her cotton button up shirt. Something to do with those dang calves. That's been eating you for months now, and just wont let go."

He turned his body facing away from her, and looked out at the sun setting behind the Sierra range. The sky was a flame red with the fires that had burned around the state today, now that summer was in full swing, there were always a handful of fires burning somewhere.

"I cant shake this feeling that it had something to do with my time in South America."

"But you were just a baby, weren't you?"

"I was a baby there, but we stayed for a while, until I was in like $4^{th}$ grade, when we went back for a time to Kansas."

"So like 9 years old...?"

He was silent and sat down on the barcalounger across from her. It squeaked in protest and launched a little cloud of dust all its own. Summer on a ranch.

"Why don't you just start and see where it goes," she said quietly.

He sat back and closed his eyes. "My mom was really young. I don't want to blame it on her but sometimes I just really hate her guts for what she did. She and my dad ran away from home during high school. My grandfather warned them, they didn't listen. They ran away to Mexico and I was born a few months later. And we lived near the ocean beach just a short walk from the cabin we lived in. It wasn't much of the cabin but I remember it pretty well. I had my own room.

"But sometimes at night I heard things. There were sounds that came from the jungle that didn't sound like wild animals. It sounded like drums and yelling, and I was often very afraid. Dogs would howl and screeching sounds I'm not sure where birds. And I would shut myself in the room and hide under my covers."

"Where were your mom and dad?"

"Thing as, I don't know. They just weren't there. And then when my dad left for good, my mom was there even less."

"What do you mean," she asked. "She just left you there alone?"

"Ya, pretty much," he answered ruefully. "So then I learned to escape. I remember being really afraid, like I was going to get in trouble, but then I realized that she wouldn't, well, no one was around to know if I went off." He stood up and moved away from the window, feeling like someone was watching him make this confession. "I guess I learned how to take care of myself that way. And I would just wander off into the jungle."

She just chuckled and shook her head. "But then they found me missing one time, and that freaked her out. She must'a yelled at me for days. She was worried. She left me there alone and she was worried."

"Oh, she was feeling guilt and trans placing it off onto you," said Sheridan with a laugh.

"Ya, you are probably right. But she was really mad. She started by locking the doors and the windows. But I managed to get through those anyway. Figured out the latches, and just climbed out into the night." He looked at her during his pause for breath. "Then when she found out I could still get out, she tied me down. At first it was a joke, but then she kept doing it. Tied me to the bed so she could go out catting around. No way was that going to stop me. I learned to chew through one. And once you have a hand free, I discovered you can untie yourself.'

"I cant believe she did that!" she said to him.

"Its true!"

"No, I mean its just wrong. I think its illegal to do that."

"Well, welcome to my weird world and my weird mom." He said shaking his head.

"So where did you go? What did you do once you got free?"

"I think I thought that once I was free, why stick around. I really left and went off to play. But then one time, I followed them. I got out fast and followed the noises. I figured they were having a bash-out party and wanted to see what it was all about."

"You went to the party, and you were how old?"

"I was seven. The first time I followed her, I was seven. It was the last time too."

"Why? What happened?"

"I don't know. It was just adults doing weird things."

"Like what weird things?"

"I don't know. Just weird adult things. I don't want to talk about it." He got up and went into the kitchen and got a glass of tea. She followed him in there, and got something to drink too.

"You aren't getting off that easy, Rocky. My interest is all piqued now."

"I don't even remember. Maybe I have blocked it."

"Why don't you just start describing what they were doing and see if we get anything?"she said encouraging him, sitting him down at the table.

He took a big drink of tea and then started. "At first they were all sitting around a big table and I was watching through the window. Remember these are not much more than huts down there. Nothing really like the houses we live here in the states. Most of those places don't even have windows. Never snows or anything. So I could see. They were bending over the table and sniffing at stuff. There was a pile of white stuff in the middle of the table. And bottles of beer. Just a party."

"Drugs," she said.

"Huh? My mom doesn't do drugs!"

"Really. Well, maybe she wasn't partaking in the white stuff. Or maybe she was."

"What are you talking about, Sheridan?"

"Cocaine, ding-dong. That would have been the late 50's right? They were just starting to make that stuff down there, that's where it comes from, right? You said Central America? Right?"

He let out a loud exhale and did not acknowledge her theories. But just continued in a monotone. "Then they all got up and went outside. They were carrying things, musical instruments and drums, and they walked off down the trail into the jungle, and that was it."

"Oh, bull. You followed them."

His face started to get red and his breathing was speeding up. "No, I don't remember anything else."

"By the looks of your face, you are remembering, or starting to remember. You need to let this out. This is bothering you."

"There's nothing more !"He shouted top of his lungs. "Leave me alone!" He stood up and his chair flew out, and he stomped back into the living room and sat down on the couch. She felt he was just willing her to come out and join him, that the subject was not really closed. So she stood up from the kitchen chair and went and joined him out there. She turned sideways and looked at him on the couch. "And then what happened?"

"They walked way into the forest, and I was totally freaked out. I mean I was just a little kid so I had to follow now. I would have gotten lost if I had tried to go back. So they walked and walked. Middle of the night, a little moon, and they came to a temple. You know one of those pyramid things they show in science magazines."

"Oh, ya, you mean the ones with the steep steps up one side. The south American pyramids thingies."

"Ya it was one of those. And they all walked up the steps, and there was light coming from inside the door at the top. So they all hiked up there and I watched them go up and inside. They disappeared inside the thing. So I wasn't about to stand there watching so I had to go up too. I went up the steps and went inside the door. There was a set of steps back down and there was music and voices and light and smoke coming from down there. I was freaky curious now. Like the cat whose curiosity gets the better of him. I climbed down to the bottom and saw what they were doing. I fucking saw what they were doing." He said as tears squeezed out of his eyes. Sheridan was too shocked to even say anything. She just stared at him, until he continued.

"There was this boy, a dark boy, one of the local kids, and they had him tied up onto the rock slab that was there. He was screaming and moaning, but I think they must have drugged him because it wasn't normal screaming, like he was only half awake." Sheridan just stared at him. "Tied and there with ropes. And he was...he was..."

"Yes?"

"He was naked. I mean totally. And there was a guy at his feet, reaching between the kids legs, you know, his, you know, privates?" He looked into her eyes beseeching that he didn't have to tell this story, knowing that he had to, he needed to.

"And the kid let out a terrible scream, like what the priest was doing down there woke him up in an instant. The priest held up a shining knife, and then reached in and swiped with it, and his hands came up red, holding something, dripping, and the screaming stopped, like the boy had passed out."

There was silence for a few moments. "That's all I remember until I woke up back at home. I don't remember anything more." He looked at her with tears in his eyes. There were tears in hers too. She simply reached forward and held him in her arms.

# Chapter 9.
# Mother on the Couch

"Well, doc, I was really hoping to get a little help with my son."

"Oh, well, what has he done?"

"Well, nothing really. He just wont visit us anymore."

"Oh, I see. And how long has this been going on?"

She shrugged and moved around in the deep chair facing the doctor's desk. "He moved out a few years ago. He had some trouble in school, and he went somewhere for a while."

"So, he didn't come back to live with you after that?"

"Right. He just stayed away. It's like he found another life or something. We were so close before. But then we started to grow apart and there seemed like there was nothing I could do. I tried to be friendly, you know, get to know my own son. He was going through that awful teen age period and just grew away. He had trouble. He always had trouble."

She sniffled and looked up at the doc. "And I was hoping you could help him."

"Well, let's just start with you since you are here," he said as he looked up from his notes to look at this mother estranged from her teenage son.

"I want to help him, but he wont listen anymore." She sniffled, "Well, he never really listened. He was such a strange boy . Right from the start."

The Doctor said, "Hmmm..."

This was an appointment paid by the institute, along with her working wages there, teaching in the large classroom with all ages, she might not have gone to a psychologist if it hadn't have been paid for by her work.

No, really quite frankly she definitely would never had taken this kind of an appointment if it hadn't been paid for by her work. Her boyfriend was kinda out of the picture, and since her father's death, she was really having a hard time with any of it. Slog to work in the morning, slog back to the house in the evenings and have a meal with her mother. But the boys were gone.

All the men were gone. What was it about her that she always drove her men off. She had often wondered that, and of course had never found an answer, but vaguely slipped a little further into a sinking feeling in her heart with each time.

If I could just have one of them back, she would tell herself.

No, I cant have any of them back. I am just going to have to learn to accept it.

"You can never accept these things if you don't talk about them. The human mind doesn't just stuff things to the back and they are gone. "Accepting" takes a kind of inner dialog with ones self, to talk about your life story to yourself and learn about what changes are taking place. Sometimes talking about things that have happened to you bring to light new things that are bothering you and then you might be able to let them go finally. So why don't we start there."

"Start where?" she asked.

"Start anywhere." I ran away from my home when I was barely in high school I couldn't stand my parents, they were so...so... smart. They knew everything. They always knew everything and always made me feel stupid. So I showed them and moved out on my own and left the country with a guy.

"Oh, you moved away from your family young, kind of like your son?"

Huh?" She looked at him stunned. With anyone else she would have yelled at him. But you cant do that with a doctor, can you?

"No, actually I was younger than him when I left. And I went further. I went to central America.

The doctor just looked at her. "Alone? No, with your boyfriend. And how long did that last?"

"Last? Right up until the baby was born. Then he was outta there."

"And he was American?"

"Ya, he left and went back stateside. We sort of picked up again after I came back to the states, and then the whole family traveled abroad." She twisted a handkerchief. "Then he left again. Haven't seen him in years."

"The father of your boy?"

"Yeah. A real dead beat. Doesn't give us support. Well, didn't. I've lived with my parents since then. Until my father died last year. Now it's just mom and me. Broke his heart you know. His grandson getting arrested and all."

"Arrested? Sounds serious."

"It was. Very scary. But they let him go to a boy's school instead of jail. He was too young to go to real jail."

"So, tell me about Central America, where the boy grew up."

"Not much to tell. We lived simply, I worked during the day doing fruit and shipping.

And the landlord watched over my boy. I think it was a nice life. So simple and clean. The ocean was right there, and we used to go for walks on the sand. And he would pick up shells and crabs and fill his pockets, and I would make him put back the live things."

The doctor watched as tears grew in her eyes as she wistfully recalled her first years with her baby boy.

"No sign of trouble yet for him?"

She looked at him with haunted eyes and shook her head almost imperceptibly. "He was strange. I loved him. But he was strange."

"Strange in what way?"

She looked away and wrung her hands. This doctor was new to the institute, brought in just recently. So he didn't know anything about his patient here, before him nor her son. She couldn't know that he was brought in specifically to help this woman and perhaps help her win back her son.

But the doctor couldn't know, not just yet anyway, what strange alley of human consciousness he had just wandered into.

# Chapter 10.

# haunted past

Oh, ya, your mom called."

"What did she want?"

"She said she had some stuff from your grandfather she wanted to give you."

"Did she say what it was?"

"Nope," she answered. "She just said it was wrapped up for you from him."

"Huh," was his cryptic answer. "Did you give her our address?"

"Yup. Again." she looked at her young boyfriend. "I don't think she likes me."

"Oh, you know, don't take it to heart. She is kind of a looper. Really don't worry about it," he said. "Besides its none of her business."

"She said that your sister misses you." She looked straight at him and put her hands on her hips. He avoided her stare. "You did not tell me you had a little sister. How old is she?"

"She is just two."

"She's, two and she misses you?"

"She's uh, different."

"What does that mean?"

"Precocious. That might be the word. Like I was, weird, but she has the gift of gab. She talks all the time, since before she could walk."

"Well, so what's her name?"

"They call her Cindy. But I call her Shalome."

"Well, I hope I get to meet her."

"Maybe some day."

"Your mom also said there is a thing coming up that you should go to."

He let out an animal groan from deep in his chest.

"Something in New Mexico. I think we should go."

"WE?" he said looking up at her.

"You are not going without me."

"What about the animals?"

"Doc Branson always has young students that need a place to stay and practice running a ranch. Easy-peasy."

He exhaled sharply. "And when is this thing we have to go to in New Mexico?"

"Later this summer. Whoohoo, a trip!" and she began dancing around the room. "Oh ya. And they want you to work on some of this stuff your grandfather left unfinished, whatever that means."

His eyes lit up just a little, "Is she sending some stuff?"

"Ya, with the box of the other stuff from your grandfather." She stopped and looked at him, and asked, "Do you think she will bring the baby? I mean your sister?"

He just shrugged like it was inevitable, and he was uninterested, and Sheridan started dancing again.

He just looked at her and said under his breath, "Ya, you're happy now. Just wait till you meet these creatures!"

## Chapter 11.
## Old Stuff

He had been so bold as to make copies and take them with him when he went off to the school for boys. He had them in his books and they allowed him some freedom with these things. There were two boys to a room and his room mate even had taken an interest in them. Simon had been fascinated by the pages of ancient letters, and had once commented on how it looked like what his grandfather had often read during Passover.

From the original Hebrew of some ancient scroll, he had told Rocky one night. And from then on the two of them had a secret friendship and bond like no other.

But they were teased, two nerdy boys doing weird non-boy kinds of things. But the wardens had encouraged reading and studying, after all they were skipping out on high school and he figured if the boys took to studying on their own, then great, encourage it and keep them safe from some of the more bullying of older boys.

But Rocky had started telling some of his ghost stories when he had the chance, especially at night, they seemed to be effective, and the other boys granted him a bit of respect and showed him some deference. His friend Simon had suggested that it might also be because it had been spread around really quickly that Rocky was in here because he had killed a man.

So what are you in here for, Simon?" he had asked his roommate finally after some of the newness had worn off and little mutual respect had been shown.

"I got in a fight," was the reply.

"Must have been quite a fight, to land you in this place."

"My family was livid. They didn't exactly stand up for me. Some things just didn't get said and so I get persecuted."

"Oh, religious persecution. I get it. So you stood up for your religion."

"Well, actually no. I stood up for my friend's. He was catholic. And they were taunting him about going to church every Sunday. So I stood up for him and the boys attacked me. I smashed some heads, that's all."

Rocky smiled at his friend. A bar room brawl was one kind of thing. But this was another, and he smiled and nodded his head at his new friend.

"So, what is that stuff you are reading?" Simon asked him one night.

"Some stuff my grandfather gave me. Well, I stole it from his briefcase and copied it. But I don't think he would mind. He used to read this stuff to me at night when everyone else was in bed. Old stuff from his work. He translated ancient manuscripts from Egypt."

"And you can read this stuff?"

"I cut my teeth on it when I was 5. We were traveling and I didn't really go to school, and just picked this stuff up looking over my grandfather's shoulder. "

"Let me see that." Simon grabbed the sheets and looked at the letters on it. "This is Greek."

"Some of it is Greek. You read Greek letters?"

"I know some of it," said Simon. "Some of our books are in Greek. The old Torah and some of the things we read at holiday. I cant really read it, but I recognize it. Will you teach me?"

"Well, you can follow along and maybe you will catch on."

Simon got a pencil and some paper from the office the next time he was there with the warden and used those to write and copy down the letters to learn them. Next was translating the lettered out words into English meanings. They had a dictionary, but of course the art of translating was not an exact thing.

"What is it that you are working on now?" Simon asked his room mate about the folded up papers he had under the small light at their shared desk. He pulled up beside him and read along with what he had been translating.

"It's called the Origin of the World, kinda like the Genesis in the bible."

"That's old testament, actually from the ancient Jewish bible." Obviously this boy knew exactly what he was talking about. How could he? It must be something about his religion. How many secrets could they have, If only I could pick his brain, thought Rocky.

"It's called the "Origin of the world" from the Nag Hammadi scriptures," said Rocky.

"Oh, ya. Its one of the apocryphal gospels."

"The what?" said Rocky looking at his diminutive friend in the upper bunk. You know about that?"

"Sure. The apocrypha are the stories left out of the bible when it was finally formed in the year 362 adi Domini, something like that. which was when the Christian church was formed."

"You know about this stuff?"

"Sure. Normal stuff we learned at Shule for boys. I know. Not regular reading."

Rocky was astonished. What a friend he had found.

So he read out loud for Simon what he had translated so far. It wasn't that much.

In the beginning, in chaos actually comes from shadow, and the shadow is sometimes called darkness. But a shadow comes from something that had existed before, so chaos came after what was in the beginning..

Sofia or knowledge flowed from Pistis, or wisdom and faith. Sofia served as the veil separating humans from those beyond.

When this shadow sensed that The Sophia was stronger than it, it became jealous, and became pregnant from this powerful thought. And it swiftly gave birth to envy. But this envy was an aborted fetus and therefore had no spirit in it and it came into being and existed as a shadow on the surface of a watery substance. Bitter wrath formed from the shadow and was sent to exist in the region of chaos.

When Sophia saw this darkness and deep water she wanted it made into a define image, and an arch on appeared like a lion in face androgynous with great authority but ignorance of his own origin. She named him Yaltobaoth, or Ariel, because he looked like a lion. And here the faculty of speech came, and it pertains to the gods, angels, and people. Things come to be made by the power of words.

But here it left off, and there was no more translations of this particular document. He really hoped he could find the rest of it. he knew there had to be more, and it was probably in the latest translations of his grandfather, the ones he made right before he died. But where would they be? Most likely, hopefully, locked up in those boxes his mother had for him at the old house in San Francisco.

"Oh, I like that. where did you get it?" asked Simon of his friend.

"This is part of a translation my grandfather was working on. And I stole this and copied it from his briefcase. But that's all there was. I know there is more somewhere."

"Ya, there is much more. I recognize that as the old beginning of Genesis. And it gets to the part about the fall from Eden. Paradise."

"I hope I can find the rest. Maybe when I get outta here I can look for either the originals or more of what my grandfather had translated."

"Then you come find me and we'll read it together. Now let's get some sleep." And the two boys tucked in their bunks for sleep.

# Chapter 12.

So what kind of stuff is coming from your mom?"

"I really don't know. Could be some books and stuff. I'm hoping its some of the old stories we used to read together."

"Your grandfather used to read to you a lot?'

"He was an anthropologist-turned-linguistic scholar. He could translate old documents." He got up and left the room, and she just looked at him, like what the heck was he up to now? She could hear him banging around and then some rustlings and some exasperated exhaling on his part.

And then he reentered the room carrying a small pile of papers, old, worn and heavily dogeared and annotated with scribblings.

"See here's one of my favorites. The Gospel According to Mary."

"What? Mary had a gospel? I didn't think people could ever read or write back then."

"That's what people think. But these stories were printed in books that people carried around and read. The society at the time was Greek and they published novels. I mean paperbacks that people read. In fact Plato was widely read at the time. Maybe they didn't have machines and air planes and stuff, but I think they might have even had a higher literacy rate back then than now. Like we are now in the dark ages in comparison."

"So strange," she said. "And Mary? Wasn't she a prostitute?"

"There is no evidence she was a prostitute. Or his wife. None of it anywhere. In fact, in this gospel it is understood by the other disciples that she is another disciple and probably closer to the savior than any of them. And in this story in fact, he reveals himself to her in a vision after his resurrection, something the other guys cant brag about."

"So what is this Gospel of Mary about?"

"She says some really strange things about the laws of heaven and earth. And the meaning of death."

"Like what?"

"Well let me read this."

""As the soul of a body was leaving the body for its journey upward to the kingdom of heaven, it encountered the first authority on the road to heaven and freedom, Darkness, and it was not afraid. She knew all of matter and spirit dissolved and found its way eventually to its roots, a cool stable place in the void.

And as the soul ascended, the Body of Desire, the second gate keeper toward the heavens, asked the soul, "I didn't see you come down into me, but now I see you going up. Why are you deceiving me? You belong to me."

"And the soul answered its body it was vacating, "You did not see me and you did not recognize me when I was there, inside, inhabiting you. You possessed me as you would a garment, and wore me as you wished, but never did you try to get to know me." And the soul felt joy at having revealed this to the body she once inhabited, and happily and unencumbered lifted toward heaven."

The ascending soul encountered the third authority, Ignorance, and it didn't know what was happening. But the soul could not now enlighten it, it accused the soul of wickedness. And the ascending soul replied, "How can you judge me when I have not judged. I was rules with ruling.

I was not known by my possessors, but I myself have come to know that all will be dissolved, all in heaven and earth."

There she encountered the fourth authority of ascent, Wrath. And it took the seven forms of Power: Darkness; Desire; Ignorance; Envy of Death (Divine knowledge); Kingdom of Flesh; Foolish Wisdom of the Flesh (pursuit of pleasure); and the seventh, Wrathful Wisdom. These are the 7 powers of Wrath, the fourth authority of ascendance.

And these powers all confronted the ascending soul, with questions. "Where do you think you are going? You kill humans and you destroy their worlds?"

And the soul replied to all, "What has been my prison and keeper has been slain. The earthly bonds of ignorance was temporary and I have remembered, and am now going home. And may I rest now in Quietude."

Rocky folded the papers back over and looked up at Sheridan. She was just staring at him, then she slightly shook her head. "Weird. Really weird. I sort of understand it though. It sounds Eastern. Like Mysticism."

"It is, really. It's Gnostic, which was around before the birth of Christ. And I think it migrated there as a philosophy from the east, Tibet and India, which I think have even older religions than anything in the west. "

"Except for maybe the Celts."

"Well, I think the Celts came from the East too. They were all over Europe before Romans took over. And the Romans pushed them Westward from Italy."

"Really? I never heard that before."

"There are religious similarities."

"Well, I really like that Mary has a gospel. I like that. Maybe Jesus was the first feminist," she said.

I think He didn't really care that she was male or female.

Just that she was smart and listened to him and remembered what he said to her. And then she preached it. The other disciples got all afraid and had to be reminded that they were supposed to, were told to by Jesus, to go preach and spread the word. And Mary had to remind them, and this Gospel tells us that."

# Chapter 13.

They decided instead of having the box shipped, the two of them would simply drive to San Francisco and visit his family.

But as they arrived, he was startled to find that his little sister was no where to be seen.

"Mom, where is Shalome?"

"She's down in the basement."

"What?"

"She is downstairs. She likes it down there."

So he found the door to the basement was locked with a small hook up high on the upstairs side. He unlatched it and went down the 14 stairs into the gloom of the basement. It had a cement floor and one tiny window looking out at the feet of people passing by. But it was covered with a thick layer of grime.

"Why are you down here?" he asked his baby sister.

"I like it down here. And *she's* not down here."

"But this is the basement." he said

"Now, don't worry about me. I like it down here, Rocky."

He just looked at her for a moment. "I like that you call me that."

"Its your name."

"Not really. I think it makes mom mad."

She smiled and said, "Ya, I think it does. Just like when you call me Shalome. She hates it I think. Shalome Shalome hello hello," she sang in her baby voice .

He looked around and saw that she had the dank place decorated just so. There were shelves on all the walls filled with books. And on the shelf over the desk there were rows of small pots with plants on them. And feeding them from above was a narrow row of florescent grow lights beaming the strange black light color onto the leaves. And they seemed to be flourishing. She saw him staring at her plants and said, "There are now 32 of them. And you know I didn't buy a single one. I picked and plucked baby plants off of big plants where no one would notice. I pulled a tiny spider plant baby from one in the administration office. And a tiny strawberry plant baby off of a plant on the library desk. And I even got the tiny nub from the huge schephlera from inside the mall. It didn't have roots or anything. And it is growing. I wonder how huge that thing is going to get, tho?"

He smiled at his baby sister and said, "You are amazing."

"Thanks big brother."

"Why don't we go upstairs and get some lunch. You can meet my friend Sheridan."

"Is she your girl friend?"

"I think it qualifies as that. We live together on her ranch. It was her parents ranch and they just passed away a few years ago. "He smiled and said, "We have horses."

And baby Shalome lit up at that. "I have to come see them sometime."

"Yes, you really should. Now some lunch."

She set down what she was working on and the two of them went back upstairs to find the others and have some lunch.

After a few days it was time for the two of them to head home. He had picked up a couple of boxes that his grand papa has sealed just for him.

He was glad they had driven down there, not just because they got to see everybody for a while, and that they all got to meet Sheridan. But that these boxes were bulky and he had a feeling that his mother would not have sent all of it. And chances are she would have gone through it and thrown out most of it. Towards the end of his living there, he had gotten the distinct feeling that she did not approve of him having all of these old documents from his grand father. She didn't approve of someone so young and without a proper degree being able to translate this stuff by himself. The institute had told him they wanted him to continue to translate and work on the things his grandfather had been delving into, even though he had had the run -in with the law. They didn't seem to blame him for that. In fact they continued to respect what he had written, what little he had written, on the documents that his grandfather had been studying. They kept telling him that his time at the boys school was really just a mistake of the law, and that it probably actually did him some good to get him away from his family. His mother was getting a little smothering.

But he couldn't wait to get home and dig through some of this stuff. He had to hold himself back from opening boxes while Sheridan drove. But he controlled himself and provided small talk all the way home so she could stay awake for the 10 hour drive.

But when they got home he dug through and found the fresh copy of what he had been remembering as one of the last things he had been reading. One that he thought Sheridan would find especially interesting.

"Here it is. I thought you would enjoy this one. I didn't have a copy of it, but its here.

"Well, here it is. This story was found in two of the great recent finds in Egypt, Dead Sea Commune and at the cliff of Jubal al Tarif."

"I've heard of those. Big stir up. But I didn't know that was in there."

"Wait," he said as he looked at the translations. "What is this thing? Looks like something my grandfather translated after I left home.

"Well, it just hasn't all been translated yet. Here listen to this." And he read from his translations.:

from The Pearl

"I was given a great task by my fore bearers.
They to me a garment of Yellow made fit.
And they wrote a covenant in my mind,
that in my journey I shall not forget.
'You shall to Egypt go,
and the white pearl to find,
it lay in the devouring serpent's lair,
under a garment you shall don,
your earthly appearance unbind.' "

"That's really beautiful, Rocky," Sheridan said. "I hope you will translate the rest of it and then read it to me. What a beautiful poem. "

He folded up the papers and began to put them away. When Sheridan asked, "What do you suppose it means?"

He again looked down at the poem fragment. "Well, yellow is the color of illumination, of wisdom to be gained. Egypt was then the land of sophistication and riches. The serpent means some sort of degradation of human character, in this case I think greed, earthly choices of value. And the pearl would be the greatest of riches, probably not money but wisdom and inner peace. And the garment? I think it is speaking of our body, our earthly bonds here as physical beings."

She just looked at him with something on her face, when he walked away and stowed the papers in a safe place in the bedroom. The look was something he did not see, and she was a little glad that he did not know just exactly how much she admired his amazing insight things most people don't get in a lifetime, let alone in just 20 years.

# Chapter 14.

Responsibilities reigned and it was several days before Rocky found himself alone and able to dig into the boxes left for him by his grandfather.

There was a lot of stuff there. Pictures from their time in Egypt, and other places they had traveled. There was a folder entitled Palanque 1944. But rocky didn't remember anything about that; he thought if he remembered correctly they were there in Yucatan in1965. And when he was a child in 1955, there abouts. He remembered hearing that they had all been there once before, when his grandfather was a student at the university. But not much more did he recall from that era before he was born. He held the old golden envelope, sealed with yellowed crackling old tape, and gold paper worn soft through the years, and he thought he would keep that little secret for later. He wondered what things he would find in that envelope containing memorabilia from that time that was wrapped in secrecy and trepidation by his family.

He kept digging into the box and stacking the sheaves of paper to the side. All kinds of copied documents, most of it in ancient foreign languages. When he came to the bottom of the box, he found another golden envelope, this one looking not as old as the first one with the old Palanque files in it. This one was taped and then sealed on the back with a dab of melted wax stamped with a seal from the institute. And it said on it in Greek letters: My grandson. And Rocky sat there with it in his hands until the sun set and the room got dark and he began to get cold.

He set that aside and as if in a trance he stacked it down below some other folders and decided to head off to sleep.

But as he was shuffling folders one popped out and caught his attention. On the front was written: "The Origin of the World: NHL 97, 24-98, 11".

No way! There it was. But his eyes were tearing up and he couldn't see for his big yawns, so it would have to wait for some sleep.

And he went to sleep with anticipation on his mind. And his dreams danced of pack-laden camels, swaying girls on worn carpets, moving to quiet strange drums, with the smells of the caravansary wafting around his thoughts.

# Chapter 15.
# The Couch

So how many times were you there?"

She turned to the doctor with haunted, tired eyes and said, "What?"

"How many times . You said the second time. So you have been there two times."

"The Temple? Ya, just two times."

"Do you think you would be open to hypnosis?" the doctor asked the woman on the couch.

"What's that?" she asked.

"Hypnosis is a new form of therapy that allows the patient to relax and recall his or her memories and recall experiences more clearly," began the doctor slowly. "It's a technique that's been around for a while, but came into greater use and practice by Dr. Freud. It's perfectly safe, I assure you. I think you might even find it relaxing and comforting."

"Okay," said the woman on the couch quietly. She was just beginning to relax and had begun to find the doctor's voice soothing, after a dozen or so meetings here in his office.

"So let's begin. Close your eyes and feel the fingers of your hands against the cool surface of the couch. Then imagine your hands growing light like a balloon and floating just above the surface of the couch. Now as you begin to relax you can feel yourself growing drowsy, and by the time I count five you will be in a deep sleep."

And after a few moments she wasn't aware of anything.

"Now let's go back to what you were saying about the Stone Temple that you visited when you were younger. So now you have visited there to that particular place, the Stone Temple on the Yucatan, and that was the second time."

"Yes," she said drowsily, "that was the second time, when my boy was very small."

"But I thought you said that the second time was later when he was a teenager, just recently when he was in high school. So when was the first time?" He asked putting it together now that the story was longer than she had recalled, with way more history, substantiating his suspicions that there was far more to the story and she was letting on, then her memories would allow her to expose.

"Ya, yeah the very first time I was there, I was just a child myself. I had gone there with my parents, my father was a just graduated anthropologist, and mom and I went there with him on a school dig. Do you know what a dig is, Dr.?"

"And what happened there on this school dig, as you call it?" He ignored her question.

"There were lots of other people there. It was very busy. And I was a little overwhelmed as a little child. And I really didn't know what was going on, except that I loved the forest and the trees, and the wild birds screaming overhead. And I enjoyed climbing on the monuments, the ancient stone monuments there, in the jungle, that all these people seem to be so excited about. But there was something about this monument in particular that everyone was very interested in. They were clustered around the front of it with machinery and lights and he wrote barricade to keep people away.

And there were people watching at first. And then their work on this and they ran the locals off. They scared them with their guns in their attitudes and their uniforms. Military uniforms. They were gray and green, and they had metals and bars and things on them and I recall one symbol now that still evokes fear in me: it was a four spoke wheel gray and red. And at the time I didn't know what it meant, other than fear and control." Here she stopped and the doctor noticed that her breathing had become heavy and more quick.

The doctor noticed this and he said to her, "it's going to be just fine. Everything is just fine, and you are safe. And how did you feel about these people there controlling things? Did they harm your family?"

"At first, when we first got there those people weren't there. And my father and my mother were allowed to climb the monument and we went inside and there was a photographer with a tripod taking pictures. And my mother and my father worked making drawings of what they were seeing. And as a child I didn't see anything interesting at all. It was just a long stone hallway with stairs in a small room with kind of a stone table on it and not much else. Now that I think about it there weren't any inscriptions or drawings or carvings on the wall, like were so common in Egypt, all over inside monuments and outside on the pillars and everywhere in the Egyptian monuments. But not here, it was very plain and I thought it rather boring and I ran out and played elsewhere. But then those men came with their machines and their guns and eventually everyone had to leave."

"Did you make any friends there, as a child? And how did that make you feel when these men came and made all of those people leave?"

"I remember a couple of children there, they were younger than me, and they were foreign. I didn't know at the time, but I think they were Middle Eastern. And they were the children of an anthropologist that worked with my father. But something happened. They did something to the little boy. He was a lot younger than me I was maybe 12, and he was more of a toddler. But the men with the guns did something to the little boy in the Temple, I don't know, but there was yelling and there was blood and the little boy was taken away wrapped up in white sheets."

"And how did that make you feel?" The doctor seemed clinical, uninterested, as if this was a curious fiction she was making up in her mind.

"I was afraid. I was fascinated as a child, by the blood in the excitement, and I didn't understand, but it made me afraid. Stefanos. Stefanos. That was their name."

"Who is that now? Whose name is that?" The doctor asked, the information coming in disjointed chunks now

"The family. Their name was Stephanos. I remember because my father was very very upset. And my mother was crying. And we left for home in the states as soon as possible. I think those people quit anthropology and we never saw them again. Even though we've done lots of activities with the world anthropology scene. I've never seen them again. They hurt their son Christos. His name was Chris, the little boy. They were from Afghanistan, Pakistan?."

The woman on the couch began to make animal noises,

starting with a groan, the fidgeting in the hands, and she started to sob. And the doctor quickly interjected his safe word to bring her out of her trance. The woman stopped her feral behaviors, and quieted and stretched out on the couch comfortably. And the doctor began his backwards count to bring her out of hypnosis.

"Why is my face wet?", she said after a few moments.

"Oh, you're fine. Sometimes people's eyes leak when they go into hypnosis. It means nothing. How do you feel?"

" I feel fine," she said. "Except that my face is wet and my hands hurt a little. What did I say? "

"Oh", said the doctor nonchalantly. "Not much you just described what you told me before about your experiences at the stone temple in the Yucatan."

"Oh, well I was only there twice", she said confidently.

"Okay then that's fine", said the doctor. "Let me know if you have any trouble sleeping or any other discomforts. And will meet again as usual next week.

# Chapter 16.

The next morning was hectic and he couldn't get away to read his treasures. A foal was born next door and there were a few complications and they needed his help. A couple more strong arms were needed for carrying and pulling, and fetching this or that. After a rough 24 hours of doctoring, the foal was fine and nursing happily on its contented mother. The humans were dead tired.

So it wasn't until the second day he was able to dig out and contemplate even opening the two files he, in his heart, so desperately wanted to read. In fact he had a hard time deciding which one to open first.

After some time of sitting there in a trance with the two sealed brown envelopes in his hands, he leaned over and switched on a light. He got up and sat in the easy chair, turned one of the envelopes over and popped open the wax seal. He pulled out a small stack of papers and began to read the letter written in his grandfather's hand, in the Greek letters, but written in the English words:

My dear grandson,

If you are reading this then I am gone. I have traveled to another world, like in one our pages we have so often read together explored in the ancient traditions of Gnosticism and other forms of philosophy. I do not know what it will be like. But I hope it to be an adventure to continue the ones we had together studying and reading and traveling. I would like to say I have gone to a better place, and will see you soon. But not too soon. I hope this letter and this folder find you safe and well.

I had hoped to help you avoid the problems of going away to the boys school. I know that the world of justice knows no gray. And that you have suffered for forces that none of us are able to control. Or even understand for that matter. I simply hope that it will serve you to be away from the ladies, your mother and your grandmother, my faithful wife of all these years, so that you can begin to become the young man that you are destined to be. See it as a time of growth and I am sorry to leave before you are free to join us here again.

I know that I am going; they say it was that blasted pipe I smoked all those years. It will be quick they say and I will not be able to talk to you and tell you the things you need to know. So many things I should have said but was afraid to drag you into it.

There are things I need to tell you. There are things happening in this world that will make great changes soon to come. Have you not wondered why those ancient documents were just so recently discovered, all within a few years of each other? And why the forces to conceal and obfuscate them were eventually thwarted? Though they still try and you need to be aware and careful out there. There are still ignorant men who wish to quell understanding and research. And I think that person who attacked you and dragged you down was one such force. I believe I know who that young man was. And possibly what force it was that possessed him to become so hateful. Perhaps it is too complicated, but I must try to explain. That boy was the son of one of my fellow archaeologists in Palanque. We all got swept up in that time and fervor of the 40's and the war effort, and some of us got swept away. We left that ancient cursed place in Mexico, your mother and us grandparents. Just in time. Others were not so lucky. This other family were not so lucky. Their son apparently, very young at the time, was nabbed and used to test one of their hypothesis in the chamber. It should have gone innocently enough. But I think there were some of the, we'll say Europeans, who knew very well what was going to happen. It destroyed that little boy. And his family. And when they returned to the middle East, Afghanistan, I think it was, they were never heard from again. Then the boy surfaces several times in the melliue he knows best: archaeology, his mind warped and out of control. Was he the one who attacked you in Italy? I suspect it is so. And what he did to you was part of what the officials thought was a pagan death ritual. But it wasn't quite that was it? I think you know precisely what happened. The Gnostic gospels warn of dabbling where we are not welcome. The realm of angels and demons is not easily understood by mortal man. And so it shouldn't be. It is the stuff of the gods and not ours to know.

But I am rambling. I am writing to you, well, because I miss you here. And I love you so much, my grandson. Gwydion. I know you are using a different name now and I understand. Your sister is a strange one and I hope the two of you strange cookies can find each other and help each other in the near future. For a storm is coming. I have seen just glimpses, though I think your sister is a weather vane. Or a telegraph. Or a time machine, so strange she is and such strange adult prognostications she has whispered to me in the late night when we read together. That a child of 11 months can talk and read along is beyond my understanding. But it is not for me to know what, just to accept and wonder.

Inside this envelope are stories. Stories from the greater list of stories that have been found in the last few years, the great Nag Hammadi Library, Berlinishe Gnostica, and the

Dead Sea library of scrolls. These, these few here have been suppressed. These were hard to get and I had to do some sleuthing, and felt I was in danger all the time. I copied them and began to translate them and received such a shock that I put them away. I hope that you are more prepared than my feeble self to take a look. To translate them honestly and know what to do with that knowledge.

For there are forces out there that do not want this known.

Back in Egypt, I was attacked. I didn't say anything, but it was why we left in such a hurry. You were just a young silent boy then. I was attacked in the basement by the man that later got his deserved end. And it seemed to point to me. But it was not me. And I suspect you know who it was. But "why" was always a question that was never answered. No one ever hinted at why the professor was killed. But I had a sense at the time. When I published my first translations, I was reviled and castigated for the truth of what I wrote. And there were some things in there that the ecclesiastics did not care for one bit, and they wished them suppressed. But I persevered, except for one facet I skipped. There was a passage at the end of one of the quatrains of the Gnostic rituals written in Greek that described a religious rite involving man -on -man. That part of the ancient scroll has since disappeared. Along with the passages about using mushrooms in their ritual ceremonies. These concepts are very uncomfortable for most people, not just religious people. And I felt uncomfortable publishing those particular bits.

And I feared for my life and my livelihood. I did have a family to support, after-all.

So I thought when I was attacked that this was what it was about: suppressing an undercurrent of homosexual society to the church, the Christian church. And I think perhaps partially this is so, and it hints at what kind of thing was going on when Professor H was killed in his bed.

But now I am not so sure. What you are about to read has not been widely published, and is usually taken with a grain of salt as an old interpretation of a story that accompanied the original resurrection story. But the references are undeniable. With the recent announcement of the finding of a celestial craft in the desert of Roswell, New Mexico, it brings these ancient texts to light. If you find when you translate them, with the illumination I found, and if you publish them as they are, in the context of this discovery in the desert, be careful. This may be the most dangerous knowledge and proof that there is.

My dear grandson, I hope you find life as interesting as I have. And that you find a way to fit and affect life in a way that pleases you and helps theirs. And I hope you write. And I hope you continue to translate what we have just found in the desert of the middle East and seemingly in our own continent of the US. The ancient texts hint that god was not what we think, and ghosts may be closer to angels and demons and fit into the same category. Now, do all of these experiences of other being fit into the same realm? And what of the spirits of the ancient Natives of north and south America? Do they fit somewhere in the scheme? I am thinking of Palanque. And you see that it is a great wheel, and we have come full circle as the Mayans predicted to occur later in this century. And perhaps you, Gwydion, are the one to bring it to light.

Be well, my grandson. Take care of your sister. Or maybe she will be taking care of all of you. And try to be patient with your mother. She's the only one you got.

Your loving grandfather,

Professor Antony Jacobs.

# Chapter 17.

Their trip had been long and exhausting. And they were lounging on the couch with the radio on with some sports game playing innocuously on the boob tube. He hadn't told her about any of the things he had found and read in the box yet. It was just too much to even explain.

But he was tired and in a kind of a trance when she started talking to him. Some doors had been opened by his letter from his grandfather, may he rest in peace. Which was maybe why he was able to recall the rest of the story to her. A kind of hypnosis on the highway.

"You never told me the rest of the story about the accident in the high school," she said the evening lounging around the living room, papers and envelopes scattered around, and Rocky looking off into the distance like a caged animal imagining other freedoms not afforded here. "You spaced out and I couldn't make myself shake you from what seemed like a comfortable eye of a terrifying storm of a memory."

He looked at her, somewhat dazed and just getting what she had said a minute ago. "Huh? Oh, the high school mirror. It shattered and broke around me like shards of some hot sun." He looked around himself at the golden envelopes strewn across the living room floor around him on the rugs.

That boy. He seemed to appear out of nothing. He was just there, waiting for me. Staring at me again..."

The story he was telling himself stretched and nagged in his mind, "That priest died so smoothly and easily.

And so too will this boy," he said to himself as he stood breathing in smoke as he watched the boy turn and run.

Run, run little rabbit. Soon for the slaughter and stew pot for you little weakling.

So his feet were light as feathers as he pursued the boy across the fields and into the hallowed hall of learning. And there the hunter found his prey crouched in the dark corner of the huge marble hallway.

"Stay away from me! What do you want from me!" said the young form in the corner.

He smiled smugly and said quietly into the silent air of the falling dusk. "Oh, nothing much, just your immortal soul, you fool!"

The younger boy made a feral sound from deep in his chest and he shoved himself off the marble floor and began jumping up steps. His pursuer leapt after him. He grabbed his coat by the back edge and the two of them fell on the stairs in a heap, the older boy gaining the upper hand by sheer size and strength. But not by much. The younger boy had grown, gained some pounds and strength in the last couple years at high school. A growing boy for sure, and his adversary was a little taken back by that change. He had known him first off years ago in Egypt and he was a skinny little kid, and the old boy much bigger stronger and wiser too.

But not now. The scales were actually pretty much even with them. Except that the pursuer had pure hatred on his side. And the boy, well, simple survival in the face of annihilation.

So they struggled against the cold stone of the marble steps. And just then the doves let loose from the ceiling rafters and flew down the stairwell at the two boys and burst against the windows, breaking one of them, where their dark gray forms all spilled through out into the gathering night.

The older boy looked up at the crashing sound, and the younger boy fled from him up the stairs. Up and up to the top floor he ran with the hot breath of his tormentor right behind him. He stopped and pushed the older boy right in the chest which stunned him for a moment and he stumbled back a couple steps and let out a roar of hatred. At the top of the stairs was hung a huge mirror, so that students running in the hall could see that there were students on the stairwell and wouldn't turn the corner and stumble on them as they began their descent. But tonight the two boys only saw themselves in it as they topped the stairs, the older boy hanging onto the younger boy's coat in the back.

"I got you, you whelp."

He turned to dislodge his attacker from his coat and in doing so tangled his legs and they fell in a heap below the mirror, their faces reflected in agony, each with their own objective: the pursuer, murder, and the younger, a riktus of fear to escape, once again, this crazed captor. He had him by the throat, the slightly larger boy had gained the upper hand, fueled on by rage and hatred. "You may not finish your work," a voice boiled up from inside the belly of hate. "You cannot be allowed to finish your work, I forbid you."

The younger boy just stared at the hatred in his face, drool dripping down from the foamy corners of his wild animal mouth. His teeth protruded like fangs of an animal, and the strangest of sensations took over the youngest boy.

He felt a warmth and strength permeate his body and a determination over take his mind. He was no longer afraid, but he simply needed to finish this, to win and to survive. There was a fluttering and dark flapping over his head and the black coat of the older boy on top of him seemed to swing and lift in the wind and his weight was lifted for a moment, then the hunter crashed to the ground and he let out a shriek of frustration and pain. The younger boy piled on top of him and held him down. "I don't know who you are but you will stop. Stop tormenting me. You will be damned to hell if you do not stop, your life forfeit to all that is good and real here. I read that boys like you will fester for a life time and then be taken away by darkened angels to a place where for an eternity you will hang by your neck over a river of molten fire which burns but never consumes, your body as your immortal soul has another lifetime of eternities to think over and consider your life of evil deeds. You can change this now with the choice of always doing good and being humble to your fellow man. Or you can go with your dark angel into the pit forever, evil boy. What's it going to be?" the words spilled from him, from a boy who rarely spoke, he was filled with the things he had learned from all of the scriptures he had read, and a few he had even translated himself from the ancient Aramaic, and he for once found the words to describe what he was feeling about this mean evil boy that had tormented him for the last 10 years. He had been following him and torturing him and even tried to kill him, which now was obvious was his evil intent. And for why? He could not fathom why. He thought of himself as a kind person who did nothing much to anyone. And yet this evil kid pursued him and followed him and tried to kill him. So be it, it was time for him to go.

And the older boy twisted in pain and rage and the younger boy saw his face reflected in the mirror on the wall. And the edges of the mirror turned red and began to warp around the form of the older boy twisting in rage and fury. Then came a whistling sound from the boy's throat and he jerked into a straight position on the floor as the archeon of some angel daemon took possession of his soul and wrenched it free right in front of the boy's eyes. He let go of him and slid away, blood seeping from his hands and smearing on the floor. And just as the devil's howl reached a crescendo, the mirror shattered and showered the two of them with shards of hot glass, the older boy in the bloody black coat inert on the floor. And the younger boy crouched in a pile sobbing.

It was a little while before anyone found them. The night watchman came around and discovered the two prone figures and the mess of glass and blood. He surmised that the two boys had fought and broken the glass, and that the boy who was alive probably strangled the dead boy laying on the floor. And in his terror the younger boy had once again lost his powers of speech and was unable to tell the real story.

"So you really didn't kill him," she said after a few moments of silence.

He turned and looked at her with haunted eyes. "What?"

"You didn't really kill him. Someone else did. Someone else was there. Why did you get blamed?"

"I didn't get blamed for it. They just didn't know. They showed up and there I was laying on the floor with this dead guy. They didn't know what to do."

"Why didn't you just tell them?"

"I couldn't talk."

"Why couldn't you talk?"

"I just couldn't talk."

"What does that mean?"

He was uncomfortably quiet for a few moments, then he said, "you don't know me that well."

She said, "What is that supposed to mean?"

"You just don't. Don't get mad at me. If you want to understand, stop yelling at me."

She grumbled a moment and then said, "Sorry, I just don't get it. You'll have to explain it to me."

"I was never good at talking. I could never explain anything to anybody. They called me names and stuff. But really I always felt that no one was really hearing what I was saying, so I just didn't talk. I stopped talking. They said I was autistic."

"What?" This startled her. What a strange thing to say about this person she was sharing her home and her bed with. "What does that mean?"

"I don't know. I was weird. And I was an only child living with my grandparents, and it just didn't matter. We traveled the world and I learned stuff on the move and it just didn't seem to make that much difference."

"But you are so smart. You translate stuff, like ancient Egyptian and stuff."

"Coptic and Aramaic. But ya." She laughed at him and he glared at her.

"I am laughing next to you not AT you. You are so funny and underestimate yourself."

He smiled and said, "Thanks."

"OK," she started again. "So they sent you to this home for boys because you ended up besides a dead person in the school hall."

"That's kinda it," he said and laughed a little. "Kinda stupid but maybe I was glad to get out of that school. All those perfect people who act perfectly. And no one was listening to me again. My mother had gone off the deep end and my grand parents were kinda getting old."

"And you got to learn how to train horses."

"Ya. I loved the ranch work. The hard work, I think it turned a lot of those violent boys around. Then someone got killed riding a wild horse. They closed the school down after that. I was only in there for 6 months. But when I went home I couldn't tolerate my mother. She had flipped. That guy had left her, and she just flipped. And grand pop was sick. I think he was sad."

"That's really a lot, Rocky," she said as she put her arm around his shoulder. "That's too much for anyone, especially a teenager. "

"I just needed to get outta there."

"But you found me and here we are." She smiled at him. "Good thing I walked into that bar that night. I would never had found you."

"Hey, what were you doing in that bar anyway? You were still a teenager?"

"This is Nevada. They don't care, as long as you aren't drinking. I can't drink. Makes my head swimmy."

"Oh, ya. I am just a couple years older than you. But that's OK. Everybody needs somebody. She grabbed him around the shoulders and dragged him down onto the couch, and kissed him solidly on the lips.

And he smiled a contented smile, one fraught with a few demons and worries still hidden from this best friend.

# Chapter 18

He was happy he had told Sheridan the story of his torment. It relieved some of the congestion in his chest after enduring all that with no real friend to tell it to. He felt so relieved that he got out the brown envelope and decided to reward himself with the story he had waited a long time to read. He thought of Simon and how he would never be able to hear this story, as told from the original texts. and Rocky wondered how the story was told in the original versions of the Talmud, which is where Simon would have read it, being a young Jewish boy studying in Schule, and wishing to be a Rabbi some day. But if Rocky had learned anything from his studies, that Simon was probably in a better place.

And this was the story that his grandfather had hidden away. The one he felt so radical and threatening that it could not be a story told in this age. He had had part of it before. But the rest of it lay sealed up in this old golden folder with a wax seal from the institute on the back.

His grandfather's writing came into focus on the page, after he had ripped open the wax seal on the back of the large flat brown envelope. And it started back at the beginning, the part the Rocky had read to Simon.

"In the beginning, in chaos actually comes from shadow, and the shadow is sometimes called darkness. But a shadow comes from something that had existed before, so chaos came after what was in the beginning. Sofia or Knowledge flowed from Pistis, or Wisdom and Faith. Sofia served as the veil separating humans from Those beyond.

When this Shadow sensed that the Sophia was stronger than it, it became jealous, and became pregnant from this powerful thought. And it swiftly gave birth to envy. But this envy was an aborted fetus and therefore had no spirit in it and it came into being and existed as a shadow on the surface of a watery substance. Bitter wrath formed from the shadow and was sent to exist in the region of chaos.

When Sophia saw this darkness and deep water she wanted it made into a definite image, and an Archon appeared like a lion in face, androgynous with great authority but ignorance of his own origin. She named him Yaltobaoth, or Ariel, because he looked like a lion. And here the faculty of speech came, and it pertains to the gods, angels, and people. Things come to be made by the power of words."

And here is where it began to be new for Rocky. His grandfather had translated this in the interim, between Rocky last seeing him, his release from the boy's school, and when his grand father, Professor Antony Jacobs had died.
And Rocky began reading it aloud to himself.

"Then seven androgynous beings appeared in the chaos, and each has a masculine name and a feminine name. You may find the masculine names and their powers in the arch angelic book of Moses the profit. And the feminine names can be found in the first book of Noraia.

And Yaltobaoth believed he was the only God, and in saying this he sinned against all the immortals who watched him carefully.

And Pistis called him Samael, meaning Blind God. Yaldobaoth had a son, Sabaoth, and Pistis Sophia gave him her daughter, Zoe, and he made himself a mansion with a large golden throne on a chariot with four faces called the Cherubim. And next to them were created the serpent-like angels called Seraphim. Sabaoth created another being, Israel, meaning one who sees god, and another, Jesus Christ, who is like the savior in the 8th heaven, to sit on one side of his throne, and another, the virgin of the holy spirit, on his left.

Yaltobaoth saw his son Sabaoth and his glory and became jealous and generated death from his own death and became the sixth of the Authorities of Chaos. Since Death was androgynous, he had sex with himself and produced seven more androgynous children. The males were named: envy, wrath, tears, sighs, grief, lament, and tearful groans. And the females: anger, pain, lust, sighs, curses, bitterness, and strife. These seven double-sided characters interbred and produced each seven children, so that there were 49 androgynous demons. You will find these names characteristics in the book of Solomon.

Zoe, who lives with Sabaoth, then created seven good androgynous powers. The male names are: the one not jealous, the Blessed, the joyful, the true, the one not envious, the beloved, and the faithful. And the female names are: peace, gladness, joyfulness, blessedness, truth, love, and faith. And you will find their characteristics in the book "Configurations of the fate of heaven beneath the 12."

Forethought fell in love with this messenger of light that passed out of the eighth heaven above and through all of the heavens of this earth, and he was called Adam of light or the enlightened person of blood, or holy water; (Adonis is another word for Adonais, Hebrew name for god, and he begot earthly love with his beauty.). Hence some androgynous arrows appeared, and all the Gods and their

Angels fell in love with him. And thus the first sexual desire sprouted on earth. Trees sprouted from this earth, that came from the semen of the Authorities and their Angels in their love for Adam the first.

Justice created beautiful Paradise, and desire dwells in the middle of its trees. The Tree of Life is eternal, and north of Paradise, to give immortality to the souls of people. The Tree of Knowledge stands next to it, and is there to awaken our souls from our demonic stupor.

Psyche, who loved Eros, was the first soul born on earth. She poured her blood onto him and there bloomed a rose within a bramble, to bring beauty with the thorn.

Sophia created the heavenly lights, the stars and planets, that there would be seasons,,chronological signs, years, months, days, etc. Adam of the Light had returned after just 2 days on earth, to his realm of light and there was darkness on the earth.

The authorities in high heaven saw Adam up there and asked themselves, "Is this not the one who will ruin our works?" The answer was 'yes' so they decided to make slaves in his form to work for them. But Zoe saw what they were doing, and laughed at them, because they created humanity in ignorance, born to work against their own interests, So she created one for herself, so he could instruct humanity how to escape the authorities. The Greeks called it Hermaphrodite, the Hebrews,

Eve of life, or female teacher of life, and the child who is born to her is Lord. But later the authorities called this child The Beast, to lead humanity astray, when really he was the wisest of all, this female-form androgyny born from Zoe, the first of Humanity. This Eve gave birth to the first blood human, without the help of a man.

The souls that were going to enter the bodies shaped by the Authorities were told to "flourish and multiply,..." And these souls were then taken captive by the Authorities and enslaved and locked up in the prisons of the molded bodies made by these Authorities, to stay until the end of an age."

"Wait. Stop." said Sheridan, startling Gwydion out of his reading out loud.. "What did you just say? Eve was on the earth first and she gave birth to the first humans?"

"How long have you been standing there?"

"Almost all of it, I think. I love listening to your voice. "

But he showed no embarrassment at all. He was so engrossed in what he was reading. "I think she was the first born there, and she gives birth to one guy, the Lord who is the teacher, the emancipator of mankind."

"OK, go on," she said.

"Then it seems the authorities get on with making their slave humanity from their semen, and this first one they call Adam, it is shaped after Adam of Light. But it is empty and has no soul like an aborted fetus. "

"That sounds like some kind of cloning to me," said Sheridan.

"It says in a note "seed" so maybe not 'semen' but more

modern interpretation would be DNA." He continued, "Then Zoe, Daughter of Sophia felt sorry for this dead thing and blew life into him and he began to crawl around but could not walk. (Note: Symbology: ignorance). The Authorities asked him, this breath, this soul within the body, "Who are you?" And it answered, "Through the power of humanity I've come to destroy your work." But they reveled in his answer, because now they knew their foe, it gave them rest from their fear and concern and called this day, the 'day of rest'."

"I guess it was a Sunday," said Sheridan. Rocky just shook his head and laughed. Then said, "No wonder they took this stuff out. Its all upside down on its head."

He continued reading: "The Authorities were happy with this thing (human/Adam-of-Light simulacrum) and they took him up to paradise where nothing much happens, and they left him there and retired to their heavens."

"So they created this ghastly empty thing for a human and left him, wow," she said shaking her head and getting up for some hot tea.

"No, wait! Wait! Listen to this!" he read from the text, "Eve Gives Adam Life."

"What?" She stopped in mid step and just stared at him from the kitchen doorway.

"Right here. It says it right here. Listen." He began reading some more.

"Zoe, who had given birth to Eve as an instructor to Adam, saw him struggling on the ground with no soul. She said to him, "How can our children be vessels of light if you insist on laying there on the ground?"

"It does NOT say that!" she yelled from the kitchen.

"Ya, you are right, it doesn't quite say that. But close. So she actually commands him to stand up and come alive, and just because she says it, it happens, her word became a real occurrence. Weird, just like Jesus did in the old stories where he kills people with a word and then with another word brings them back to life. And he is not ungrateful and realizes what she has done and says to her, "You will be called the Mother of Life for what you have done for me today."

Sheridan was carrying some cups in to set them on the table for tea. "So, on Monday, Eve creates life by simply stating it. I like that. I really like that."

"That's what it says right here in Greek." He smiles up at her and she smiles back. Then she turns to the sound of the tea kettle whistling., and disappears into the kitchen. With her gone, Rock reads quietly ahead the next paragraph and is looking ashen by the time she comes back in, and sets the tea kettle of water on the Unicorn-shaped copper heat doily.

"What? What's wrong?" she says looking into his face.

"I can't believe it says this. I cant believe it. Listen," and he reads.

"The Authorities got word from the gossiping Angels that their creation had stood up and was talking, and they were greatly distressed. So they sent seven archangels down to see what had gone wrong. Then they saw Eve talking with Adam, and said she looked familiar but who is this enlightened woman? Quick! Let's grab her and inseminate her so that she is unclean and she wont be able to go Into Her Light anymore, and so that her children will serve us.

But let's not tell Adam, in fact let's put him into a stupor so that he doesn't recall any of this, and we can convince him she actually was made from his rib so that he can control her and that she may serve him."

"But Eve is smarter than the Authorities and creates a simulacrum that looks like her, and she disappears into the Tree of Knowledge." He looked up from the papers. And looked at the startled Sheridan.

"It does NOT say that!"

"It says that, right there. It's a translation."

"This is some joke of your grandfather's right?"

"I seriously don't think he would think this a joke at all.

He died protecting it. He packed it away and sealed it here in this envelope. It may in fact be why he died. Imagine being a believer all your life, even denying that you really were but in your heart, you know, its there from childhood. And you translate this from two thousand year old texts. And like, a thunderclap. Its all been a joke. A ruse. A deception." They stare at each other.

"Unbelievable," she said as if coming up from a trance.

He set the papers down on the coffee table. "I cant read that to the convention. I'm supposed to read something at the meeting of minds, archaeological thingy. Oh, I certainly cant read that."

# Chapter 19.
# Indian Rocks

From the journal of Gwydion:

"When we arrived in the south west, the lands seemed so strange. We visited nearby the Zuni Indian reservation. They are reported to be very quiet and secretive. But in the rocks of the desert lay many drawings and diagrams of all sorts. I've seen pictures, but I was curious about it. That night before I had a very vivid dream about it.

"We stopped on the way to the convention to meet my mother and grandmother, and when I walked into the local country store, it seemed to take on an inflated feeling and my ears began to ring and my fingers went numb. I shook my head to try to clear it, and when I looked up I saw a big tall dark man looking at me. He beckoned me with one finger. So I followed him through the store and out the back. Where we walked for some time out through the sage brush and the lizards and red rocks. He began to speak to me in a voice from deep in a well.

"The sky people came to us from the stars, and they tried to teach us how to live. You can see the pictures here carved in the rocks. This one here has a dome over its head and a square kind of coat. We can't see them. But they are here." He paused and pushed some sand from around his boots. "We cant see them because they are just out of phase from us. We call them Kachina. They brought humans through a birth hole in the sky, and they were brought forth into the world of light from out of the underworld. The world of dark. Up there. The world is on it's head."

"I have heard of the Kachina. But I never thought about why they look so strange."

"Yes. They have helmets and that looks like a space suit. These are our star people, who came to this planet and seeded our planet. And they flew away in shining objects."

"This is not written down, is it?"

"No. The Zuni and the Hopi do not have written language."

They walked a while there in the sun, a shining that didn't feel like the sun. But felt like an electrical vibration of light. After a time they came to a dark wall of rock. And there was the dark entrance to a cave. The tall dark man stepped aside and motioned with his hand for the young man to enter the cave. Rocky could see within it a dim yellow light throbbing, throbbing, seeming to pulse with the beat of his heart. And as he stepped into the golden darkness, a hum penetrated him and shook him to his core. The pressure in his ears increased until he couldn't think or see anymore. And with a burst of light, he felt pain, the release and then thought no more.

Thanks for coming to me, Gwydion." said a disconnected voice above him. He realized he was now lying down on a surface that was neither sand nor rock floor of the cave. He struggled to open his eyes, but the light seemed to penetrate his eyelids and make him shy to try. A cold silver light it was and seemed to reflect off of hard surfaces around him an a room that was no longer a cave of rock on the Earth. He reached up and felt nothing but air.

"I recognize your voice," he said quietly.

"I knew you would not be afraid, I am relieved. We lose a sense of human limitations sometimes when we become so wrapped up in our work. But you are different, so different, we are so happy we found you."

"Oh, ya. Thanks. Have you been watching me?"

"Why, of course. We try not to meddle. But your species is so fascinating it has become a millennial obsession with us." The disconnected face above him turned a little, and a huff of warm comfort blew gently over his face, as if an angel had just laughed at him.

"Ezra. What exactly are you, anyway?" he asked.

"Hmmmm," said the disembodied voice. "We are just like you. We are trapped spirits, angels if you will."

"I am no angel. I killed a man."

Another warm chuckle. "No, that was not you, my dear. That was your guardian, Sophia. That one would do anything to protect you, I think."

"But why? Why me?"

"Have you still not realized the meaning of the ancient words you translate? They are of very special importance. They are our words. Our gifts to you, long ago. And there are forces all around us that would wish to cover these words up, and destroy them so curious others will not read them and learn the truth. Become enlightened. And you are bringing them back to life.""

"Those are your words?" he asked, keeping his eyes closed still for the glare that seemed to pulse and flare.

"Well, not mine exactly. But our kind. We have visited here many times. Have you not noticed that in your kind's history there have been several, no, numerous periods of miracles? And then long periods of disbelief?"

He tried to open his eyes and look at his interrogator. "Miracles?"

"Yes. Impossible things that your species cannot do?" another puff of warm air of angel laughter. "Miracles like you have now: computers, space flight, TV? Imagine how those things would have looked a hundred years ago. Your own great great grand father would have thought you a god. Or worse."

"My grandfather was a great man."

"Yes. He was a visionary. Very open. We never met him exactly. But here you are."

"Miracles? Those magic things that happened in those old scriptures? Moses and the Pharaohs, and those obelisks."

"Now you are getting it. That first time, when we made too many changes, it was really by accident, we're sorry and we've been involved ever since. Their story is that their craft crashed many years ago and without their aubule to re-phase the memory of them, they cannot escape."

"What? Who? Those ancients who wrote these things?"

"Yes. They were here for a long time. They were prisoners of this skin you call the human body. You see, the mind is a spirit possession of a wet-ware brain that thinks it is something from this planet. An animal. You think you are from this planet, because, your wet ware over-comes your "knowledge" you possess as spirits when you are born. Actually the first few years of a humans life is actually the forgetting of that knowledge that the spirit possesses from life in its higher plane. Although "life" isn't quite right either. Because there is no time up there. Time is created by the confines of the wet ware brain, the limitations of corporeality. There is only memory of the past, and memory of the future is burned out of the child very young. That's why we liked you so much Gwydion. Something about your brain refused to burn all that old stuff out. You chose to be quiet because the world is so different than you perceive it to be, what you perceive to be reality. You still see the past present and the future. You see the shadows of the angels that are not corporeal. You see where it all goes and are fine with it all and you never really grew up; you have a bit of that multi-dimensionality of the higher spheres, that which the human mind is blocked out of seeing. Usually. You see the dimensions are not limited to 3, or really, you humans have four, and you see three passing through the fourth, that's time. But there are more. And there is a place were it can be all experienced simultaneously, higher up there. But here, its like a blind man experiencing the elephant, remember that Zen joke from grammar school? One blind man sees the tail and thinks the elephant is like a rope; the 2nd blind man feels his ears and thinks he's like paper; and the third blind man feels his leg and thinks the elephant is like a tree. Just as people see you as a child and think of you that way; and another person will know you only as an adult, and will see you only that way. But you are all those things. But your human mind can only comprehend just one bit of it at a time: your total self being dipped through the one dimensional screen of time, and you are you right at this instant.

"The higher planes are where all spirit lives. It is simultaneous, all things and possibilities at once. Our spirits come into this limited experiential sphere for a reason. This plane is not a mistake: It is for the education, and punishment, of the spirit.

When a spirit is discontent or needs to learn some things, we send it here and trap him inside on of your bodies that you generate with your reproductive practices. Other animals have spirit, or animus, also, but their brains aren't as complex and so their spirit beings are less complex. But the real interesting ones are the rogue spirits. And we send them here to experience once again the pain and anguish of corporeal life; life in a body. They forget, you all forget, you're spirits when you enter this body, but these rogue spirits are especially mean, and they flaunt the rules and are cruel, and inevitably they learn the feelings of pain, again. And as they are passing through the painful frightening veil of death again, if they do remember and they always repent, but not until they are on that threshold again. Something about your human wet ware and bodies seduces the spirit into forgetting right and wrong of the universe, and they think they can outsmart it again. Think of your stories of the erroneous pacts with the devil that are always a scam, and he has you in the end, every time. Because where they go and what they go through then, after the shedding of the corporeal body, is even worse than death. It is the punishment that you all down here call hell. It is of your own doing and of your own free will. Ah, yes, free will. That's what you call it when you hominids use your brains to make a decision. You are changing your path when you do that. All paths exist, but you can choose, by free will, to change the path you are on. And it changes the paths of others too. That's why working for good will make good for others, too.

And that is our hope. You body-beings make good, and you can go home. Make the good choices and you can go home.

Haven't you ever noticed that the truly sweet and innocent beings die first? They go home. And the terrible ones, the ones that wreak havoc, stay around and continue to punish each other for a long time. That's why we wonder at your medical practices, keeping people alive for so long, and in so much pain. We often wonder at why you don't want to leave. I think it is your fear of the pain of death. I don't think its that painful. Just frightening since you don't understand."

"So, what are demons?" he asked her.

"Demons come down with out permission. You can call them angels too if you want; not much difference. They inhabit a body sometimes with out the permission of its born owner, and often can run that one out, if they are strong enough and stay in long enough. They cant stand mirrors because their energy gets reflected back and causes a feed back that dis attaches them from the mind wet ware. Then you break the mirror and they are released back to where they need to go to be punished again before they are given permission to inhabit a body. There are rules Gwydion, rules, lots of rules that I cant get into now. Things your philosophy and your physics are only beginning to describe.

"But why would they want to come down here to this prison planet of hard knocks?" he asked her.

"One word, pleasure. Pleasure of the flesh. The wet ware of your mind's bodies have this intensity that exists no where else. You never wondered why the young go on rampages for sex, violence and drugs? Pleasure, pure pleasure of the corporeal kind, something we don't have in the higher spheres of existence.

Very low on the experiential scale, but new and refreshing after being with the one-mind for eternity. A demon breaks the rules and slides through just when someone is vulnerable or even asks for it, I've seen it, and then he's in. And it will destroy its host while it sucks all it can from this world and its new body's pleasures. Even human with a new spirit rightfully born into a body can do this too. That's a sliding scale. Each born being has a certain intensity of experience and strength and can chose to not indulge the destructive urges it feels so fresh just after its born. Some can resist; some destroy themselves with the first chance at free choice from his training procedures of the parents. Which is what some of these spirits actually want: to reunite with the great spirit above, the great void where they just were, where there was peace and not pain. No animal games. Lately during your time, parents are spending less time with their offspring and the offspring are learning less and set free sooner, to indulge. Hence the destruction of your current society. It will come around again, and after a session of serious privation your kind will lapse again into superstitious mumbo jumbo to try to appease the 'gods' and deserve to not have all that pain. Instead of learning. We are amazed at how your kind are unable to learn and better themselves so there is less pain in your world. Its a choice, one you aren't making. But we've seen it come and go; it happens in waves. Your societies happen in waves. You cant help it; you are weak and not in full control of your consciousness.

# Chapter 20

But we are very glad you are here, Gwydion. You heard your calling a long time ago. We came here long ago. Not when your kind finally were able to travel by light speed; you have not even reached that ability yet. But we became interested in you when your kind became aware. More than aware, you, as your book says, ate from the tree of the knowledge of good and evil. Your brains acquired so much self-awareness that you became afraid and self destructive. You knew evil now, which the animals do not know, and you have the honor now of choosing between good and evil. And in your youth you are choosing evil, most of the time, your kind choose evil. It is more fun. You do not yet know why you should be choosing good. You do not know how. We came to help. You did not then and still do not want our help. Like children, you want to do it your self. You are destroying yourselves and you wont let us help. We suppose that you must hit rock bottom before you will grow out of that phase. But we can hardly help not wanting to help you change your path of self destruction. But when we hit your planets atmosphere, we crashed. We hit your Psyonisphere. Psyonisphere, the level which our craft could start to feel the aggressions and carelessness that your brains are now giving off. Your dissonance that you are thinking in your youthful exuberance and confusion, base desires and aggression."

"There are changes coming, changes to your world that you are not yet aware of. Things that will happen in the next 50 to 75 years, and want to be ready for them. I will try to explain.

"Already they are calling this era "Anthropocene" meaning the age of humans. When humans have single-handedly changed the planet to the tipping point. Very soon there will begin to be seen very great changes. Changes even in the weather. The gases on this planet are in a very delicate balance. And this balance between oxygen making and the oxygen breathing will be tipped by your carbon dioxide breathing machines. And the pride of the human will not be able to see these changes nor make changes soon enough to make a difference.

Then the planet will begin to warm and the seas will boil, that is, the ice will melt and become part of the great seas, and the oceans will rise and inundate your coastal cities, that will be most of the population Gwydion, because that is where most of your cities will be centered. But as this ice melts, it will uncover things buried deep in the ice, deep in the layers of frozen waters and gases. Animals and microscopic flora that they harbor will become warm enough for them to once again escape, after a hundred thousand years or a million years of being safely stored in your great warehouses of ice and carbon gases and microbes, these remnants of your planets beginnings of life, the ancient RNA microbes will invade your planet ecosystems. And great plagues will reign. Millions upon millions will be wiped out as your weak and prideful medical systems in the huge mega cities that will form upon your free-wheeling use of petroleum energies are slow to respond. At first it is just your poor third world nations that are effected and your prideful leaders will ignore it for too long.

Ironically as your oceans rise some three hundred feet in just 100 years and overcome your great coastal cities, your inland water sources will dry up. Great weather cataclysms will occur and turn rivers backwards, and silt in lakes and pollute underground natural cisterns. And in some areas the storms will be dry, and fire will rage and clear out mountains of ancient forests in swift sweeping conflagrations. And many of your kind will flee underground.

You see Gwydion, we need to get off of your planet. We have been stuck here for many many generations but now will come the time, in about 75 years, your own home- made cataclysm will come and with one fell swoop of a shower of thermo - nuclear instruments of destruction, after the natural cataclysms have brought civilization to its knees, then those humans that remain, a few who have the keys to these destructive weapons in their ignorance and hate, will take care of the rest of your planet turning it into a glass covered orb, completely uninhabited nor ever again uninhabitable."

Azreal looked into Gwydion's soft brown eyes, which were now wide with wonder at all she was saying. And we need you to guide us out of here. Only you can do this for us. We have been watching you for so long. We have seen you in our future, riding over this time of total destruction and bringing us back to our rightful place among the stars. For we have lost the ability, being here on this alien planet for so long, we have lost the ability to navigate. We cannot visualize our way out of this gravity well, back into among the stars. And we are sure that you can. We have seen in our aubule that you can do it. And will do it. We have seen it; it is in our memories"

He just looked at her and a fear began to grow. "And my family? What of them?"

"They may not come. They are born here and will stay for the duration. "

"Why cant my sister help? She is special too. I have seen her float things that cannot be lifted in the air by nothing. She has the power of speech over the animals only more so than me. Why cannot she come? She would be better help than stupid old me."

"No, Shalome is too young. We were hoping but she is not yet grown and her abilities are firmly rooted here on this planet. She is a female and she will have children and grow and die here on this planet. You must forget her, and remember your destiny . You are destined to save us Gwydion. Save us from the ruination of your planet by its own aborigines."

Gwydion looked down at his hands and stared at them for quite a while. All became quiet inside the ship and there were just a few of their kind milling around him doing import ship things he knew not what.

He looked up at the strange eyes regarding him. "I will not do it. I will not leave my family."

# Chapter 21

Gwydion awoke again but in a different place. Still within the sterile ship walls and that hum. That weird mechanical hum just below consciousness. He hated that sound. It was the sound of all that man, and these weird guys too, and all of their inventions of metal and science. The inventions that all of them were so caught up in they couldn't even see the birds outside. Couldn't hear the hum of all life, and the uneven, gentle beating of natural hearts.

Only this hum. This steady cold hum of electrical energy on metal.

The door opened a crack and one of them looked in. It saw that he was awake and it said, "So, are you ready to resume your responsibilities?"

"I'm going home."

"Hmmmm...." it said without inflection.

"Let me see Azrazeal."

It turned and shut the door. In a few minutes, the one he knew and recognized as Azra entered the small room.

"So you are ready?"

"When did I say that?"

She hmmmed like the other, without inflection or meaning, as if what he said meant nothing to her, only a distraction.

"I understand, Gwydion. You are a kind person. You have a good heart and a beautiful kind soul. But it wont do any good. We simply need to save our selves and by taking you with us, because of your special mind, your more active and complicated brain connections, you will be helping us save a part of your kind with us. We just need your help to pilot this broken ship."

He shook his head, closed his eyes, and sat down on the hard floor with both his hands tucked under his bottom and began rocking and humming one of his secret tunes from childhood..

He awoke with a start to find himself laying on the sand in that cave again. Light was just dimming from the rock walls as if a great energy had just been extinguished by their cool surfaces.

He got up and walked out of the cave and followed his tracks back to the general store when he had first seen that Indian guy.

"Why in the world did I follow him anyway," he was thinking to himself, as he pushed open the screen door at the back of the store. He strode through and stepped through the front door.

And there was Sheridan, standing there with her hands on her hips.

"Where the hell have you been?"

He was thunder struck that she was just standing there, like he had never left. It had been hours, maybe a day, since he had gone out back. And he wasn't even going to try to explain where he went. But like he'd never left?

He opened his mouth to speak, and she said, "I don't even want to hear it. Its been like 20, 30 minutes. Where the hell have you been? No! I don't want to hear it!" and she turned toward the car and just said, "let's go, they will be waiting for us."

"20 minutes!" thought Gwydion. So it all was a hallucination.

They drove in frozen silence for quite a while until they

arrived at their hotel, where they unpacked and got some good hot showers and a good night's rest. Tomorrow, Gwydion was supposed to speak. What was he going to say?

The next morning he was awoken by a shock of bright light and a boom that rattled the very bones of the building he was in and the bed he was on. And he wasn't so sure this was a dream anymore. He woke up in a tangle of damp sheets, with Sheridan no where in sight. His vision was blurry and he looked around at the room, and hoped it was made of real stuff, and not of hopes and dreams, nor of the intentions and constructs of others. As his vision screwed and adjusted, the phone rang, assuring him that he was awake and in a hotel room.

"Are you ready?" his mother's stern voice spoke over the phone line.

He grumbled something nonsensical but his mother understood completely. "I will be over in a moment. Go get in the shower," she said over the line.

Again he mumbled something incoherent. "But Shalome?"

"Now", says his mother with no hesitation.

He knew he would soon be in front of the huge audience at the convention, and had not decided what to speak about. He had promised to read from some of his grandfather's works, from some of the most recent translations he had been working on. Everyone was expecting that. More of Professors Antony Jacob's work.

But the latest translations from his grandfather, from the ancient Nag Hammadi, he just couldn't do it. He couldn't read it out loud.

He had read one of them last night. And maybe it was the source of those weird ass dreams he had had all night long. The story was still in his mind.

# Chapter 22.
# Light Beings

"Pontius Pilot gave the soldiers orders to guard the cave where his body was stored. They slid a huge rock to the front of the entrance, and sealed it with seven layers of incantations and spells to keep it safe and closed. And there they pitched a tent for the night.

And when the sun rose in the morning, it was the Sabbath, a crowd came from the surrounding area and Jerusalem, to see the crypt. But during the night before this dawn as the soldiers stood two by two to guard the crypt, there came a voice from the sky. And then in the dark the sky opened and great light came and two figures descended to the surface. They went to the rock in front of the cave, and the huge rock was seen to roll away from the opening all by its self. And these two bright beings entered the cave."

This was the story he had considered speaking for the group. But after his illuminating dream the night before, it felt like he had traveled miles and miles, he could not be sure, but this story cut a little too close to home.

It was a small stack of papers, two sheets really, with the Greek lettering of the original gospel of Peter, who wrote about the events that occurred around the death of the savior. It was just a portion of the gospel of Peter, and his death. But this passage was short and was about the resurrection of the Savior.

He had never read such a thing and it had obviously been taken out of the finished bible stories. He had always questioned the idea of the savior being resurrected, who can do that? A god that is strong enough over life and death? Or something else that had been misunderstood at the time?

"When the soldiers saw these things, they woke up the elders and Roman Centurions. As they were explaining what they had just seen, three figures emerged from the cave, the two bright ones supporting the third between them, and a bright cross followed behind them. The two bright ones were so tall their heads went up to the skies. But the third between them was even higher, far above the skies. And a voice came from the skies and asked, "Have you preached and taught the ones that are asleep?" And the cross, the one once holding the Christ, said in answer, "Yes."

While the guards were making their plans to go tell Pilate what they had just witnessed, the skies opened up again and a figure was seen to descend, and he too went into the cave. So the guards hurried to Pilate on this night, in the middle of the night to explain, and they told him, "'He truly is the son of God.", as he had come directly from the sky and had gone back up again with Shining Beings.

And Pilate replies, "I have nothing to do with this. You did this and left the tomb unguarded." And so he ordered them to be quiet and not say a thing, because this was an impossible thing that they described and would only incur the wrath of the people and get them stoned for allowing their savior to escape and be taken away by Impossible Beings.

Now Mary Of Magdalena came with some mourners and

wished to mourn now, as they hadn't before, as they should have, as law and decency required. But they wondered who could roll the stone away, it was so large. But when they arrived there, the stone was already rolled aside. So they peered into the crypt and saw a shining bright man sitting peacefully in the middle of the cave. And he said to them. "If you have come for the one who was crucified, he has already left and been taken back to the place from which he was sent." And the women fled in fear of this strangeness. "

No, he could not read that to them either. Maybe it was too weird for them. Or maybe it was too near his heart right now, he wasn't sure. But either way he could not read that to them. No way.

Instead, he set aside the small stack of papers that he brought with them, and placed them on the shining podium there in front of him. He put out of his mind that there were a thousand eyes watching him, waiting with baited breath for the words he was about to say.

And he began to recite one of the poems that he'd been translating from the ancient texts. But as he began, the story itself changed and became a story of his own.

"When I was young, I ran away from home, from the shining comfortable home my parents had provided for me. They were as a king and Queen to me.

But I needed to learn many things and find my own way. So I left the comfort and love in the jeweled tower of my parents, and ran into the deep jungle.

But I knew in my heart, from the wisdom that my parents had given me, that I was setting on a journey to my heart. To the heart of the world, to gain access to the core of its meaning. And I would find in the center of the deep dark cave, that Pearl which lay in the grip of the shining cruel Dragon hiding in its lair. And as I neared the land where the serpent dwelt, it became apparent that I was different, and I stood out among the crowd of locals. And for that my parents had sent me a garment from the skies. It covered my true self and helped me to fit within this society new.

And as I dwelt there for more than a year, I became alike the others that surrounded me in this new place. And I had slowly forgotten my original toil, my original quest set about for me by my parents, in their tower of glittering wisdom, where once I dwelt.

I dressed as they did, I spoke as they did, so they would not recognize me as something different and turn their Dragon loose on me. I never once let anyone know of my true quest of heart, for that pearl that lay deep in me, in the cairn that they had hiding.

I ate of their new foods, I played new games, I had new pleasures, formerly unknown and un-experienced by me. And soon I no longer remembered that I was the son of the king and queen of great wisdom in a high tower.

I fell into a deep sleep and slumbered in my soul from the heaviness of what they provided me, they, here in this new land.

And my parents in their tower saw that I had strayed from my past. And they lamented it so.

So they sent me a message, a vision from high, in the form of a brother that I seemed to know although he was a stranger, and that spoke to my soul and reawakened me to my original purpose.

Awake and arise from your sleep, Simon had said. Remember who you are, and your once worn Golden raiment. Re -claim your star -like garment, and remember your quest for the Pearl at the heart, that lay wrapped within the coil of the serpent.

I found this Dragon, for I had always known where it lay. And with my father's voice I subdued its strength, snatched the Pearl from its loose claws, and turned to go back to my parents home.

I took off my old dirty clothes and found my clean self beneath. And there on the road east, I met a woman who would become my friend, my Oracle, who, with her gentle voice, would guide me into the light.

It had been so long before that I'd left my parents home, and I had forgotten my original beauty. But on this road my Oracle became the mirror, in which I saw myself and my golden raiment once again. And I saw the two selves, my old self and my new self, join and become one again.

And I am speaking here today, of the words of wisdom given us, so many centuries ago, by the parents of us, who we are. For it is they who are stronger than all of us; it was him, my grandfather, that was so much stronger than I, and my friend-brother Simon, both who attend now in spirit only, and for whose sake I am here today and will continue to study the knowledge and words of the ancient worlds.

I bow my head now, as the young son did in the old story of the Hymn of the Pearl from the third century acts of Thomas, which is thought to originate from a much older text before even the time of the Christ, to my grandfather and Simon's grandfather's that set me on this path of wisdom and light, so that I might with this Pearl and star-light raiment, appear before my king and queen once again."

With that, Gwydion picked up his thin stack of papers. And with un-shed tears in his eyes turned away from the podium. In dead silence he walked across the stage and made his way to the stairs that led down to floor level. As he did so a few claps were heard from the audience which started other claps, which crescendoed into a wall of applause.

And Gwydion realized in the dark of the side wings of the stage, that they were clapping for him. He found Sheridan and his mother in the wings and they pulled him out of the auditorium into the hall and they each gave him a hug.

"That was amazing, Gwydion" Sheridan said, with tears in her eyes.

"Come on, let's go," said his mother briskly and clasped them both by their hands and pulled them away from the wall of sound.

As they got to the auditorium door, they opened it and let themselves out into the brighter light of the atrium entrance way. Where people were standing around and clapping and pouring out of the auditorium to meet him there. There were claps on his shoulders and on his back and many people asking him questions and shoving their face at his to try to get his attention.

And he heard such things as "when are you speaking next?" "Where you going now?" "Who wrote that?" "Will you come to our event? We're having an event we'd like you to speak!"

And so it happened that his speaking career was launched in such a humble beginning, to a boy who once could not speak. From a talk he did not want to give, and a paper that he did not write. But a story he had made up as he was reciting it from memory of an old poem from the Nag Hammadi library from writings more than 2000 years old.

# Chapter 23.

They headed home as quickly as possible. His mother returned to the old house that had been bequeathed to the family when Antony died and the Happenstance foundation was disbanded. Grandmother Bethany and little grandchild Shalome were there waiting for their return.

But Gwydion and Sheridan returned to the desert of Nevada. And they couldn't wait to get home back to normal life.

When the unlocked the front door and walked into the living room, they had a shock. There on the couch sat little Shalome reading a book.

"What are you doing here? You are supposed to be in San Francisco with mom and grandma?"

"Oh, I am," she smiled. "Oh, no, they wont miss me."

"How did you even get here?" She simply pointed at the ceiling. The sky. And then shrugged her shoulders.

"And what do you mean they wont miss you? Oh, wait. I don't even want to know." Rocky turned to go to the bathroom after the long journey.

"That's 'cause I'm there too," said Shalome.

He just shook his head and went and did his business. When he returned, he was less agitated and sat down next to her. "They couldn't get the timing right after I visited them. I went on my own you know. So they deposited me here, just in case. I cant run into my other self now can I.?" She sat for a moment and wrung her hands. "I suppose when that one goes up to visit them I will just dissolve and then be in San Francisco again. It kind of tickles."

He reached over and grabbed his tiny little sister by the shoulders and pulled her into is lap and started tickling her. She erupted in peels of laughter and they squirmed a while laughing on the couch.

Rocky sat up a moment, caught his breath and said, "I think you should arrange it to come stay for a while if you can. Maybe you all should come live up here. Pretty peaceful, you know."

Rocky stepped into the kitchen to make some food. He heard a knock at the front door and looked out to see Shalome walk over to the door and open it. He heard her say, "We don't want your religion! We don't want your alien program! Take your angel Maroni from the Plaides and go away!" Rocky walked up in time to see two young men dressed in black suit and tie run back to their bicycles and pedal on down the highway.

She turned quickly away to slam the door, and said, "Or, is it the arch alien ruler Xenon and his Thetans?"

"Geez, Shalome. You sure know how to handle them!" They both had a laugh and some sandwiches. "Where is Sheridan, anyway?" he asked her.

Just then Sheridan burst through the back door, red in the face, "Quick Come quick! In the barn." and she grabbed a sandwich and peeled back out the door for the barn.

When Shalome and Rocky reached the barn, and rolled open the big wood barn doors, a warm soft sense wafted out toward them. They found Sheridan in the back stall, the one with the most light and air coming from the outside sunlight. And she was kneeling next to the big squirrel-colored mare, Cinnamon, and there across Sheridan's lap was the soft face and neck of a baby foal, snorting and shaking her head from the flies.

Shalome was just kneeling there in wonder, petting the young foal. She got up and had a strange staring look in her eyes. She backed up to the stall wall, and there, her form and image began to disintegrate before the eyes of her brother and her brother's girl friend.

"What's wrong, Shalome? You look strange?"

"I lied Gwydion. I lied to you. I am actually going away with them. I can show them how. I can make them leave. And maybe they will leave us alone."

And with that, Gwydion reached out and just felt his sister's baby hand disintegrate against the touch of his fingers. And Sheridan began to sniffle and cry softly. "Good bye Shalome!"

And through the thin air, although they could not longer see her, they heard her thin child's voice say, "Gwydion, be careful. They are not what they seem."

# About the Author

N M Reed is the author of other books, including:

- *Horse, My Heart Wind in My Mane: Endurance Ride Stories*
- *Home is Where the Horse Is: Surviving the Jackson Butte Fire Evacuation*
- *The Littlest Coyote*
- *Romancing the Scroll*
- *The Glass Planet Series*
- *"What's It Gonna Be, Captain?"* SciFi series
- *Adventures of Elf and Troll Series* and Editor of *Worrisome War of the Whimsical Wizards* by Whitney Lee Preston

# Bibliography for the Glass Planet Series

My curiosity started with the Holy Bible; I was not raised religious, which is maybe why I've been able to look with such a different view point. My sheer curiosity for those old strange stories was as old as speech for me. I don't watch TV so I had no knowledge of the new wave of alien beliefs and study. I had no way of knowing that I was not alone in my questioning the origins of the god myths around the world, and that the answer may lay in ancient experiences with extra-terrestrials, however this cannot be proven, as strange as some of these passages are. As a child, I had been gathering little bits here and there, and it was time for me to delve into them, as on some level I think I knew I was dying of cancer and I needed to make it good and deep, no matter how embarrassing. I didn't care what people thought; I needed to find out.

I have struggled with the concept of putting down a bibliography and have poopooooed it many times. I thought maybe the authors of those books would not want me using them as proofs for my thesis, the subject matter being what it was. And at first I thought it would be only a few really obvious books. But with each addition to the Glass Planet list of stories, the book stack became rather large. And with 2 stacks on either side of me, this is daunting; I should have done it earlier. 28 books in this direct bibliography for the stories of the Glass Planet; and ironically, I will start with a movie.

The very first book of GP, The Clear Beings, was most

definitely inspired by the movie, Planet of the Apes. I watched that movie one exhausted day, and with that image of the Statue of Liberty half buried in centuries of sand on the ancient coast of Manhattan, I stood up and wrote the first story, The Clear Beings, about beings stranded on another planet, ours, but way in the past. And they weren't humans, but as you would come to find out, they were proto-humans: our ancestors. It was a short story with a twist at the end. But after I wrote it, I had found that my human characters in the near past had come alive, and had a lot more to say.

And I had found that the Holy bible was still speaking to me. But it was running out of strange things and clues to tell me. And it occurred to me to look at its sources, at the sources in ancient scrolls that were now being translated, the actual origins of the passages in the bible so I could find the things that they had taken out over the years. I bet there were a lot of strange secrets there.

And I was right. And that led to this stack of books. Amazon is a wonderful thing for finding all kinds of books, some of them long out of print are listed in private stores; most are a few dollars, but one was a hundred something upon my first search, but their algorithm must have found it in another store and listed it for a couple dollars. (A note on my translations: I did my own paraphrasing; no where did I copy text. I read from several sources and then paraphrased in my own words, telling my own story's as I saw them.)

But as this story developed, I have come to realize that there is a huge story simply about the discovery and translations of these old stories, Alien weirdness aside.

And now that I've taken out the fantasy elements here in "Romancing the Scroll" I find that I have a historical fiction novel of quality. With the fictional characters I invented 10 years ago, and some murder mystery elements thrown in, its makes for a riveting thriller, with some **gasp** educational history along with it.

Here is my bibliography listed in order of importance, rather than alphabetical. The obvious and the oblique are listed last, for I would like to introduce a couple of these books that with the new translations are no longer so hard to read. And I think every body should read these. The great religions have been so pivotal in human survival over millennia, but we need to see their original words that describe some long-ago experience with fresh, objective, eyes. And realize how those words are twisted and changed with translations; and how some of the pre-biblical forms of these old stories are really very beautiful and fascinating. And if we say they are God's words, we can just as easily say they are alien influenced. Otherwise they are just the words of Ancient Humankind.

"Eyewitness to Jesus": by Carsten Peter Thiede and Mathew D'Ancona c. 1952. The first book to scientifically discuss the possibility that people who wrote these old texts were actually contemporaries of Jesus. It demystified the bible phenomena and made us realize that we could *know* what happened then by studying these newly found ancient scrolls which were accounts contemporary to the living person, Jesus of Nazareth.

"The Apocryphal Gospels Tests and Translations" by Bart D. Ehrman and Zlatko Plese; Oxford University Press; ISBN 978-0-19-973210-4 Greek and Aramaic on the left and translations and text on the right.

The Gospel of Mary can be found here. She was The Christ's best disciple. Also the birth of Jesus is found here in the Infancy Gospel of Thomas. The
Gospel of Peter tells of the resurrection of Jesus, obviously extraterrestrials.

"The Nag Hammadi Scriptures; The Revised ans Updated Translation of Sacred Gnostic Texts"; Edited by Marvin Mayer. "The Nature of Rulers" is fascinating. "On the Origin of the World" is astounding, the early Origin story; obviously extraterrestrial in origin. "Thunder, Perfect Mind" is a feminist poem, which might be a bit surprising for more than 2000 years ago.

"The Dead Sea Scroll Deception": Michael Biagent & Richardi Leigh. Inspiration for The Broken Scroll. The story of how they tried to persecute to hide the truth. (There is another work and I cant find it, it has a camel train on the front.)

"The Sacred Mushroom and the Cross"; 1970 John M Allegro, although it was written far earlier than this, he dared years later to publish it.. The man whose life they ruined because he dared to translate the texts honestly. So he wrote this book about a small passage in the scriptures about sacred rights and native plants. This original passage in the scriptures has since been lost, although there are other hints hidden, and this book became famous after he wrote in in the 60's, which shows you how pivotal the things are that they are trying to hide from us. The publisher actually issued an apology for publishing this book, and the book has numerous defensive postures, indicating the severity of their attack on him.

"Lost Scriptures: books that did not make it into the New Testament"; Bart D. Ehrman. Adam: The book of John. "The Hymn of the Pearl".

"The Divine Comedy" by Dante Alighieri. The classical work of death and punishments, as written in the ancient texts of Revelations. Where all these words cross: Armageddon, Apocalypse, apocrypha, Revelation in the vivid story in the Apocryphal Gospels. I cant say which story it is in right now; you're going to have to read "Stone Temple Nightmare".

Those are the main influences.

Secondary influences:

"Waterless Mountain": Laura Adams Armer. A sweet story about Native American life in the mysterious desert.

"Song of Heyoehkah": Hyemeyohsts Storm. Classic work of Native American spiritualism and symbolic writings. These stories are a very advanced form of subconscious symbolism that pervades the Native American cultures. That they know and acknowledge that their religion is based on subconscious and symbolic belief systems is something Christians and other one-god religions could learn from.

"The Mists of Avalon": Marion Zimmer Bradley. The great modern de-mystifyer and mystify-er at the same time. The book that illustrates how to rewrite historical works so they easily fit a different religious paradigm.

"Communion: A True Story" by Whitley Strieber. This story shows how a physical encounter with a terrifying and awe-inspiring extra-terrestrial reality would manifest as a spiritual experience.

"The Key of Solomon the King; by King Solomon: Translated from Ancient Manuscripts in the British Museum" by Samuel Liddell and MacGregor Mathers. This book is mentioned in the Origin story from the Nag Hammadi, along with 2 other key books of secrets, which seem to be lost for good. This work is so strange and symbolic, that we cant help but feel inferior and mystified by the depth and complexity of our ancestors thousands of years ago, that appear to have had a much deeper and satisfying relationship with mystical secrets of the natural world. So much so that it begs that they must have had contacts with entities much greater and more advanced than we foolishly fancy ourselves to be today.

"Alcoholics Anonymous": c 1939 on up. A great a mystical under-rated book of healing, with many mystical secrets to life. The surrendering to a greater power, whatever that may be which may be written into our genes from our original experiences with entities not from this sphere.

More related texts and discussions of ancient texts:

"The Gnostic Gospels": Elaine Pagels 1979

"Dead Sea Scrolls: The Untold Story". Kenneth Hanson, Ph.D.1997 Some great pictures.

"The Dead Sea Scrolls and the Christian Myth"; John M. Allegro. Great pictures and discussion of the Dead Sea find.

"Lost Christianities: The Battle for Scriptures and Faiths we Never Knew" Bart D. Ehrman Time-line of ancient Pre-Christian religions, some pictures.

"The Lost Gospel of Judas Iscariot: A new Look at the Betrayer and the Betrayed". In the ancient paintings, Judas is made to look like a dark hairy brute, and Jesus is painted to look like a clear being with light coming from his head. It appears from the ancient gospel that Judas came to deliver Jesus from this sphere, and was not the enemy, but His savior. I never really got into this theme but there are a lot of books on the subject.

"The Lost Gospel: The Quest for the Gospel of Judas Iscariot" by Herbert Krosney. Beautifully done with color pictures.

"The Gnostics" by Tobias Churton. Gnosis means knowledge. The writers of much of the ancient scrolls of the Nag Hammadi and the Dead Sea. Black and white diagrams and illustrations, discussions.

Printed by Libri Plureos GmbH in Hamburg, Germany